THE RULES OF PERSPECTIVE

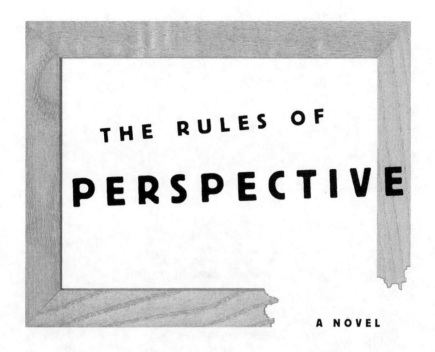

THE RULES OF
PERSPECTIVE

A NOVEL

ADAM THORPE

A JOHN MACRAE BOOK

HENRY HOLT AND COMPANY ■ NEW YORK

Henry Holt and Company, LLC
Publishers since 1866
175 Fifth Avenue
New York, New York 10010
www.henryholt.com

Henry Holt® and Ⓗ® are registered trademarks of
Henry Holt and Company, LLC.

Originally published in Great Britain in 2005 by Jonathan Cape.

Library of Congress Cataloging-in-Publication Data

Thorpe, Adam, [date]
 The rules of perspective : a novel / Adam Thorpe.—1st ed.
  p.   cm.
 "Originally published in Great Britain in 2005 by Jonathan Cape"—T.p. verso.
 ISBN-13: 978-0-8050-8042-1
 ISBN-10: 0-8050-8042-2
 1. World War, 1939–1945—Germany—Fiction. 2. Americans—Germany—Fiction.
 3. Landscape painting—Fiction. 4. Museum directors—Fiction. 5. Art students—Fiction.
 6. Art and war—Fiction. 7. Soldiers—Fiction. 8. Germany—Fiction. I. Title.
 PR6070.H696R85   2006
 823'.914—dc22   2005052544

Henry Holt books are available for special promotions and
premiums. For details contact: Director, Special Markets.

First U.S. Edition 2006

Printed in the United States of America

1   3   5   7   9   10   8   6   4   2

In memory of my mother,
Sheila Thorpe,

and my father-in-law,
George Wistreich,

who both knew the cost of war

. . . no one who confines himself to the limits of duty ever goes so far as to venture, on his sole responsibility, to act in the only way that makes it possible to score a direct hit on evil and defeat it. The man of duty will in the end have to do his duty by the devil too.

Dietrich Bonhoeffer, *After Ten Years*, Christmas 1942

No harm must be done, not even the very slightest, which is not dictated by military consideration; every kind of harm may be done, even the very utmost, which the conduct of war requires or which comes in the natural course of it.

The German War Book ("The Usages of War on Land" issued by the Great General Staff of the German Army), trans. J. H. Morgan, London, 1915— from a copy in the possession of the author, inscribed "Sept. 17th, 1943"

World War II is estimated, rather uncertainly, to have cost between 35,000,000 and 60,000,000 lives. The U.S.S.R. has been reckoned to have lost 11,000,000 combatants and 7,000,000 civilians; Poland, 5,800,000 lives altogether, including, however, some 3,200,000 of the 5,700,000 Jews put to death by the Nazis in the course of the war; Germany, 3,500,000 combatants dead and 780,000 civilians; China, 1,310,224 combatants . . . with civilian losses dubiously estimated at 22,000,000; Japan, 1,300,000 combatants and 672,000 civilians; Yugoslavia, 305,000 and 1,200,000; the United Kingdom, 264,443 and 92,673; the United States, 292,131 and 6,000.

Encyclopaedia Britannica (fifteenth edition, 1974)

THE RULES OF PERSPECTIVE

Do I know myself? Am I who I am? What is this shadow that passes for me? I am wood, I am dust, I am darkness. I am a single point in the universe but the universe does not know me. I am the creak of a floorboard and must extinguish myself. Yet I must live, or the universe will die.

1

Just before eleven o'clock, during the daylight bombardment that preceded the final armored assault on Lohenfelde by units of the 346th Infantry Regiment on April 3, 1945, the city's art museum received a direct hit from a phosphorus shell and caught fire. The solid walls of the Kaiser Wilhelm Museum now encased flame. Gallery after gallery was filled with smoke that flashed and spat into flame. Flames crawled up the walls and writhed across the ceilings. Great balls of twisting flame burst through the double doors that Herr Wolmer the limping janitor would close carefully behind him each evening and whose round brass handles the head cleaner, Frau Blumen, would polish with enjoyment to a shine every Monday morning. Now, like a small color television thirty years before its time, each brass knob mirrored the glare of flame in perfect focus. The rooms, happily emptied of their last precious artworks over a year before, waited in turn for the flames to enter them. The dull thudding of the bombardment outside was obscured by the roaring and crashing within the walls of the museum itself, though in the gallery wings not yet touched this internal business seemed as far away and faint as the sea. The odd large sculpture, too heavy to remove—mostly modern works by (or in the style of) Arno Breker, Wackerle, Klimsch— grim, heroic figures with wrestlers' chests, their abdominal muscles chiseled squarely in crude imitation of Hellenic models, leaning their weight on the left leg, relaxing the right, holding vast Teutonic swords or Olympian torches, dumb and brutal rather than Hellenically lithe (almost pornographic in the case of the one female nude, *Dawn*, her nipples like bullets, her back arched . . . a piece the youngish sculptor had hoped might bring him to the attention of the Führer)—these large works waited like the remnants of a greedy god's praetorian guard for the flames to arrive. When the flames did step over the threshold, they seemed to occupy each room swiftly, almost hastily, the stone or bronze figures vanishing and then reappearing in gouts of gold streaked with black (smoke, or the shadows the fire made upon itself as it twisted and spun), their faces in the cube-shaped heads taking on a dazed, cretinous look rather than one of heroic defiance. Perhaps if they had been genuine works of the Hellenic school, or fine Roman copies of the Greek, their expressions would have yielded an infinite sadness as the holocaust did its work around them; but they were not. They were, in fact, vulgar imitations that muddled the plastic ideal of abstraction with surface realism; the nude *Dawn* showed swollen veins in the crook of her elbow and on her ankles, but this labored detailing wriggled about on a crudely realized geometry of perfection. The result was something cheaply pretending to be flesh, but flesh unanimated by the breath of humanity and vulnerability—as, say, the Aphrodite of Cyrene breathes, for all its idealization of a certain form of beauty. Yet how many visitors had greatly admired the Kaiser Wilhelm *Dawn*, set at the top of the sweeping staircase as if on the landing of a brothel, their hearts swelling with pride at the manifold achievements of the Reich? Now, as the blaze mounted the staircase like a lithe athlete, three steps at a time, *Dawn* looked like a common bawd waiting for a client. The flames licked her cold body, hugged her in their spiraling vortex, enfolded her so completely that it was as if she had never been. Then the ceiling above collapsed, weakened by the initial impact of the shell. A beam struck her head and, broken at the neck, the head rolled down the stone stairs until the staircase gave way in a jet of sparks, the supporting girders buckling in the heat; part of the iron balustrade, however, remaining suspended in its usual position. A fine porcelain milkmaid from the Allach factory in Dachau, set in an oyster-shaped depression halfway up the stairs, remained untouched—the kind of freak marvel that often happens in fires. Similarly, the janitor's folded newspaper on his table was still there when the American soldiers arrived, picking their way over the smoking rubble while an old woman in black with a cane watched from the road, hand to her mouth, crying softly. The table stood in a sea of destruction, quite intact, with the newspaper folded on top and unmarked under its coat of ash and soot; while plump, chain-smoking Herr Wolmer, janitor for thirty-one years, friendly once you got to know him, the position of every painting in the museum fixed in his head, who had a secret passion for the reclining *Dawn* and had once pledged himself stickily to her in the silence of the night hours, lay like a charred log beside the table, indistinguishable from the blackened sculptures scattered in the rubble beyond.

Listen: voices. Voices below. When you have no voice, you are a book without words or pictures. I have no voice. Those voices belong to others, and are come to tear me to shreds.

2

Most of the paintings, the sculptures, the elaborate church carvings in worm-eaten wood and the precious old books lavishly bound in pigskin and vellum, as well as a small but important collection of

Renaissance globes that showed Iceland but not America, were deep down in a salt mine some thirty kilometers from Lohenfelde. They had been placed there some months after the firebombing of Hamburg, which disaster had persuaded the curators (encouraged by an order from the Propagandaministerium) that the contents of the museum were in danger, despite the relative unimportance of Lohenfelde as an industrial or strategic center. An inventory was made and, as soon as the salt mine was sufficiently prepared, the works were transported to safety through the Thuringian woods on a foggy March day in 1944.

Few of these works were ever recovered. Of the 480 paintings in the picture galleries, for instance, 431 were lost—some of them no doubt looted before the salt-mine depot was destroyed during fierce fighting between American troops and a contingent of the Waffen-SS on April 5, 1945.

A certain number of works had been discreetly concealed in the vaults of the museum itself. These hundred or so paintings—not necessarily the most valuable—had remained hidden in the vaults throughout the last years of the war, a fact known to very few.

I must keep the shape of time. But time does not exist outside myself. My blood is time. I can hear it, beating. Blood is not a shape, it is sound. Maybe I must keep the sound of time.

3

A photograph taken in 1901, on the occasion of the unveiling of an illustrious burgher's memorial, shows a fence behind the gathered crowd—the uneven planks covered in torn posters—and a few thin trees peeping over. This was the site of the museum, which had previously been "a castle, a tanner's shed, a wine store, a potash factory, a wasteground on which Gypsies' tents had been pulled down in

1799, and a pine-walled school for orphans that was burned to the ground in 1863" (Werner Oberst, *A History of the Kaiser Wilhelm Museum*, Lohenfelde, 1935).

Through all this movement the castle's ancient vaults ("like two giant communal bread ovens set at right angles to each other," in Oberst's description) survived, reached by worn steps and serving at one time as the local temporary lockup.

Two years later, planning permission was granted for a museum (in the words of the local paper) "worthy of Lohenfelde's fine culture and rich history, in which the artworks now on display in three cramped rooms behind the Rathaus might be gathered together with the renowned Schmeling fossil collection as well as the older books and manuscripts of the public library in a spacious and clean environment representative of the new century."

Having been built in record time, the museum was opened by the Kaiser himself with great ceremony, to the stirring tones of the town's excellent military band, and showed an exhibition of Dürer prints which received 13,191 visitors in three months. According to one report, the visitors had to walk on planks around the laying of a mosaic by Hans Thoma (his design consisting of wide-throated flowers and naked infants) in the central hall where the main stairs rose in a magnificent sweep of marble.

The museum's most successful exhibition was "Entartete Kunst," which came to Lohenfelde as part of its German tour in March 1938. "Degenerate Art" received an astonishing total of 149,568 visitors, five times that of any previous exhibition. They filed through the cramped spaces created by the false walls of trelliswork and burlap, talking loudly and laughing a great deal, as if at a cabaret, and frequently knocking the modernist works askew with their shoulders, elbows, and bottoms. Unknown to them, the deep vaults beneath their feet had already begun to receive a certain number of the museum's permanent paintings.

I am very lucky. I can watch the light move. I hear things no one else hears.

4

The vaults burned.

The Americans found charred canvases, blackened frames with traces of gilt, and the bodies (though the Americans did not know this) of four of the staff. The heat overhead had been too great. Perhaps the four had been cooked to death, as in a bread oven; perhaps they died quickly when part of the roof caved in; perhaps (the most likely) they had been gassed by carbon dioxide as a result of the flames above—an effect noted in Hamburg. The soldiers couldn't tell and weren't interested anyway.

They were looking for liquor, not paintings. There were five of them in there, out of the eight on patrol. They were house-clearing, flushing snipers, checking out booby traps. There weren't any snipers or booby traps, not so far. It was crazy, anyway, this patrolling order—the town was crawling with their own men and with German civilians wandering around like refugees among the refugees. Otherwise they could've fired at anything that moved, like in the other places.

All of the men climbed out again, but one.

The one who hung back in there was supposed to be in charge of the patrol, but Corporal Neal Parry had taken art classes in his home state of West Virginia to help him get along in advertising and then he was surprised to find how well he was doing; he had even got the Kensitas girl in front of a waterfall. He fingered the remains of the burnt paintings, stooping in the gloom. He could see patches of oil paint on the canvases, burnt sienna and umber, the surface bubbled and split like the grease on the bottom of a pan. He found a label with the writing mostly scorched away, bar a couple of words.

MIT KANAL

He put the label in his breast pocket. His mackinaw tunic, its pouches and belts and straps, felt to him like a lunatic's straitjacket and was too thick for the first warm days of spring. When he got home he would put the label in a frame, under glass, and call it *The Pity of War*.

The label of the label.

The four deads were seated against the wall in their last position like the plaster deads of Pompeii; he couldn't think of them as human, despite the spectacles. They were more like rough casts, ready for smoothing off. The light was poor, but he knew their darkness was a dark purple or mauve. One had its arm around the other beside it; the happiness of the heart had burned as things do burn that are inflammable.

He sat on his heels, not wanting to join the world above, where he was never alone, where orders were given or received and somehow you were in the eye of everything. A big beam had saved this part of the vaults from the collapse of the building above, and daylight filtered through in rays picked out by the cloudy air. He wasn't even sure if it was safe to be down here. Somebody shouted for him, one of the new kids, but he ignored it. He was extremely tired. He was being a bad patrol leader, he knew that, but he was at the bottom of a curve of tiredness. Anyway, this patrol was a waste of time. So many orders were a waste of time.

He pushed back his helmet and squeezed his eyes, which were full of smoke. They'd waited outside in the plain rolling fields while the artillery worked and the town burned; the tanks waited on the giant concrete highway in a long column, with the infantry behind, watching the black smoke rise beyond the gentle slope, and where the shells were hitting there were tints of red flushing into the smoke.

Hell, they couldn't even see the roofs of the town—only a church spire was tall enough to show over the crest of the slope—but they knew what it would be like when they got to take a walk in there.

They had done all these minor and major places, places with

bridges and market squares and their very own major and minor streets, piling in the artillery when Heinie wouldn't give over, then shooting them up some until all the streets were major and entering and walking through the streets like it was a Sunday except that now and again a sniper picked off a man when you were least ready for any of that.

They had crossed the Rhine like the goddamn Romans—over two weeks ago, at Wesel. Wesel was left with only its radiators intact. And a stink of damp soot. And rubble you couldn't touch, like you couldn't touch a searchlight just extinguished. Strange, how rubble always looked the same wherever. The Germans who gave themselves up had panda eyes and were mostly too old or too young, but it made the men mad when some out there among them wanted to play rough, despite the game's being over.

He kicked at the debris, at the burnt frames and scorched canvases, and turned to climb out. Color down there caught his eye, like a patch of clear sky in storm cloud along a flooded rut.

He rooted carefully in the mess and pulled out a small painting.

Sure. He knew more about paintings than he knew about science or monkeys or riding goddamn horses.

Or poetry, although he had written poetry for a year when he was sad and fifteen or maybe sixteen.

This painting had three and a half sides left of a gilded frame that was very loose, the work no longer sat snug in the outer frame and it nearly dropped back to the floor so he had to hold the canvas from behind. He blew off flakes of something like burnt paper and took the painting to the light filtering down between the shattered beams and the picture kind of rose up to it like a shoal of colored fish.

It was landscape. He wanted to sob a little.

Trees and pools and rocks.

This is a helluva painting. He wanted to go screaming about it. This is first of all old and second worth more than I can know and it is nice as a girl is nice when you aren't being too specific.

His heart was beating a great deal, and up in his throat.

He squeezed his eyes, which had grit in them always, and looked again. The flames had closed their teeth on one side of the frame and loosened the nails that had kept the picture in place but had got no farther. Maybe if he looked too hard at it he would see blisters but right now he didn't see blisters or even pimples, although he knew that paint and heat did things chemically together that were surprising. He would've taken out his flashlight but it needed new goddamn batteries. There were snowy mountains and a golden village way back. Now he was happy after a long time.

The light was good enough to make out some letters on the scorched label of the frame—a *ch* and an *o* and maybe two *nn*s and then *Christian Vollerdt (1708–1769), Landschaft mit Ruinen*. The name of the artist sounded German. It was unknown to him, but then he knew very little about German art. For the moment, he couldn't recall the name of a single German artist. OK, Dürer. It was a shame the label didn't say Dürer. Or Rembrandt or Titian or Michelangelo or Vincent van Gogh.

He held the picture in both hands, ignoring the shouts and laughter from above.

A tiny guy with a wide hat and some fallen columns in the foreground. Sheep, not bushes. It wouldn't look like this if it was van Gogh, stupid.

He knew what they thought he was doing; they thought he was answering a call of nature. In actual fact, he'd found some black bread in a pillbox outside Offenbach three days back and nothing at all was moving inside him now. Waiting in reserve for the big assault.

There was a scuffle and a cough and a cloud of dust and he turned and saw Morrison, cradling his M-1 as if nervous of what he might find down here, his face smeared with smoke out of which the eyes peered too white.

"I'll have an iced Campari, Neal. To go."

"With lemon or without?"

Morrison was special only on account of Parry being with Morrison and Morrison being with Parry right from the beginning—from autumn in Normandy, to be specific—from this side of hell and its sweet mash of soft windfalls and burnt hedgerows and the goddamn

Ardennes and thinking of good breakfasts in snow inside mined woods and feeling hungry and cold and getting shot up or ducking shells right up to here. The last two sleepyheads of the original platoon. They weren't buddies. At least, Corporal Morrison wasn't a man Parry'd ever choose for a buddy—in fact, the guy got on his nerves—but there was some kind of feeling that the air was safer around Morrison. They were a team. The nearest the enemy had got to either of them was a single piece of shrapnel that burst Morrison's canteen and nicked Parry's ear somewhere in the Saarland. They'd started as privates first class and picked up their lowly stripes only because others had lost them; it wasn't through talent or heroism, it was just through staying alive. For about half a day, on a difficult run into someplace a few days before the Rhine was tucked safely behind them, Parry had commanded a whole platoon when all the officers had been hit. He'd been acting captain for five hours, but they didn't keep it that way after, so he must have done it pretty badly. He didn't even know all the officers had been hit and that he was technically in charge until right at the end, when it was too late to shine. Neal Parry could never believe he was any kind of rank, anyway, and he seldom had reason to pull it. It was not that kind of war. But he did what he had to do; he was an average soldier, neither good nor lousy. And he'd survived right out in the front for six months. With Morrison.

"Hey, Neal, seriously, you know why I'm looking good?"

"You wanna bet?"

Morrison laughed and explained why he was looking good. He'd just heard how they'd be stopping over in this town, maybe for a couple of days, to get dried out and fed and into a bath, and then he'd have himself a girl because he'd got so much sex stowed away in him he couldn't walk anymore. They'd been moving too fast and the whole line was getting confused. Outfits were taking the same town from different sides and shooting each other up. That was secret. Parry nodded, only half listening. Morrison always talked too loud and the vaults made it worse, bouncing it back. Now he was picking his way over.

"I'm gonna scrub good," said Morrison, "and eat and have me a first and then a second girl. What the hell is that?"

"It's a painting," said Parry.

"Yup, I can see it's a painting. I'm gonna scrub good and hit the sack some and eat and drink and then get me a girl to adjust my center of gravity and then a second at the same time, maybe. Are you stealing that?"

"It showed up."

"I never painted in my life," said Morrison. "I could never get my circle right in math."

"You mean it never closed?"

"Yup. Even with a compass."

"Then it wasn't a circle. Like a canal is not a river."

"Hell, my mom said it was a sign of genius. We could steal that together and go halves. What do we do with these sandbags?"

Morrison was brandishing his gun at the deads.

"They're guys, Morriboy."

"These two are not guys—although, hell, they could be," said Morrison, twisting his head to look at the two deads who were linked by an arm.

"Never believe any of that," said Parry, not thinking what he was saying.

He was too tired. He wanted Morrison to go away. He wanted to be left alone with the painting, with the lost landscape that reminded him of something far back in his childhood.

Mr. Christian Vollerdt. Great painter. The greatest. Maybe. You don't always know.

Morrison slung his gun back on his shoulder and walked around over the debris, raising clouds of ash that caught in the throat. His boot struck the foot of one of the corpses and the foot fell sideways as though detached, but he didn't notice. His stocky neck had gingery stubble on its folds between the rim of the helmet and the stained tunic collar, like a pig's bristles. If only on account of the neck, Parry would never have chosen Morrison for, say, a day's excursion up the creeks, not even half a day.

"You know what the guys are doing, Neal? They're screwing this really beautiful girl, only the problem is she ain't got a head."

"What?"

"Yup." The soldier burst out laughing, coming in too quickly. "She's made of marble. She's a statue."

And he laughed again, almost crazily, while the four burnt corpses sat there openmouthed and safe as stone.

Please, God, think of me. There are so many demons in the forest. So many eyes. There is light, and there is shadow. But I am somewhere where there is no light and no [shadow?]. Yet I don't believe I am dead.

5

The one with the spectacles still balanced on his nose was Herr Hoffer, the museum's Acting Acting Director.

The sirens had started at six in the morning, and they had continued—which was very unusual—for an hour. He had left his paltry breakfast on the table, seen his wife and two daughters into the apartment's shelter along with their three emergency suitcases, donned his Volkssturm armband, and headed immediately for the museum on his bicycle.

It was approaching half past seven. The foolish people like himself who were still aboveground were scuttling everywhere, and he fancied quite erroneously that they were all scuttling in the opposite direction. The shells were dropping haphazardly and not very near. He crossed the main square, his teeth juddering from the cobbles, and passed the heap of rubble that had been his favorite building in Lohenfelde until a heavy raid in January. No one had cleared the rubble. That was the Ortsgruppenleiter's job, of course, but he was a soak. Perhaps this not touching the rubble was out of respect for the loveliest and oldest house in Lohenfelde, blush pink between the beams and exquisite in its natural proportions. No date had been carved into it, and the archives had no record of its construction, but it must have been one of the very first buildings put up after the Swedish sack of 1631 and had remained, until a few years ago, a very popular and respectable inn.

Herr Hoffer would muse on such local features as he pedaled past them each workday. It had always tickled him, for instance, to think that one of the first new buildings after the Destruction of Lohenfelde was an inn, which he thought fitting. (He enjoyed his clean white beer; its absence in the last few years had been intolerable.) Then, he supposed, the authorities had set to on constructing the cathedral. No doubt the inn was also a hostel at that time, with available girls. The population of Lohenfelde had been wiped out in the Destruction of 1631—twenty thousand of them—so the only folk present would have been builders and stonemasons and carpenters: thirsty types.

He would often run through this particular little history, bicycling to work in normal times, the bells of the clock on the Rathaus chiming harmoniously as he passed at the same hour each morning, increasing his satisfaction with the order of the world—especially when the sun shone down, or when the spring light was mother-of-pearl just after dawn, bringing the hint of a freshness from the gardens and fields that only the great painters could convey: Corot, for instance. Or Claude Lorraine.

An orange flash lit the sky, followed by a crashing noise. It was said that the American troops were close enough to shell the city. Perhaps these were shells from artillery pieces. He had seen no bombers in the clear morning sky, heard no crackling of antiaircraft batteries. It might all be empty rumor.

He thought of his wife and daughters. He slowed, wondered whether to turn back, wobbled a little, then pulled himself together and pedaled on. He had his duty to perform. As a member of the Volkssturm since October, Herr Hoffer ought to have been in the field facing the enemy, but since his unit had almost no weapons, no standard uniform, and a gray-haired Kompanieführer last seen pedaling out of town on his grocery bicycle, his duty was clear: to defend the museum and the remnants of its collection from any sort of harm.

He pedaled on, on through a sudden mist of smoke in which people were impressions of people, shadows in panic. He was afraid suddenly of what he would find when he arrived. A vivid mental picture came to him of the Kaiser Wilhelm Museum in ruins, touched with ivy and rather romantic, with nothing around it but rubble-strewn fields and a lone shepherd. The sky in this picture was swept with rain clouds, interspersed with a pinkish clarity. A wind. Lohenfelde become as the Forum Romanum: a subject for artists. Would there be artists, after the rubble?

He bumped across a sunken tram rail and his bell rang.

The museum stood on the corner of Fritz Todt Strasse (formerly Lindenstrasse) and Otto von Guericke Strasse, occupying several blocks' worth on each side; built in 1904, it showed all the playful extravagances of the period, with a tall round-topped tower, a long roof set mostly to glass, and attached steep-roofed structures whose façades and gable ends were inspired by various German cathedrals. The broad pavement in front, with its stocky memorial to an illustrious burgher standing like a sentinel at the corner, lent the rather muddled building an air of importance.

Herr Hoffer would always alight from his bicycle and walk the last few yards; the pavement's generous breadth relaxed him. Even today, with shells dropping on the city and the city probably about to fall to the Americans, he alighted and walked his bicycle the last few yards, its tires bumping on the steps that rose in shallow stone curves to the porch in which Herr Wolmer stood like a memorial statue, watching him arrive.

The janitor was smoking, looking anxious. He too was wearing the Volkssturm armband, but his uniform was an old Imperial German greatcoat and a battered helmet with a spike on top, from his days in the trenches. The bombs were not too close; it seemed they were mostly concentrated again on the perimeter. As if to correct this notion, there was a crash from beyond the large villas and trees along the avenue and a black cloud puffed up.

The two men conferred very briefly and went inside, Herr Hoffer coughing in a cloud of the janitor's cheap, bitter tobacco. Alas, it never seemed to run out!

The staff was gathered in the general office at the base of the tower, beyond which was a glass door leading to Herr Hoffer's own den. Frau Schenkel and Werner Oberst were present, as was Hilde Winkel, the pretty young research student who spent hours sketching the museum's sculptures. The one attendant not dismissed (there had been almost nothing to show in the museum for the last year) had not come. Neither had Frau Blumen, the last of the cleaners, who usually worked each morning from six to eight. It was, Herr Hoffer was fond of saying, a phantom museum.

Frau Schenkel, the museum's secretary, looked very solemn behind her old-fashioned typewriter, smoking one of her hoarded cigarettes, while Werner Oberst, the blotchy-faced archivist, had turned white about the eyes. He too was wearing his Volkssturm armband on his civilian jacket: With Herr Wolmer they were a battalion of three (Herr Hoffer would joke), dedicated to the defense of art.

Herr Hoffer wheeled in his bicycle between the desks, smiling encouragingly.

"The Americans are shelling us," said Werner quietly. "These are not bombs from the sky."

"I've come to the same conclusion, Werner," said Herr Hoffer.

"They will reduce us to rubble first, and then the tanks and the infantry will enter to mop up."

"I'm going back to Berlin," said Frau Schenkel, not meaning it, "if you carry on like that."

"I didn't know you were a Berliner," said Werner Oberst, not meaning it either.

"Better the Americans than the Russians," said Hilde Winkel, fingering the top button of her blouse.

"Not that it's us choosing," said Frau Schenkel.

"I think Fräulein Winkel is right, however," said Herr Hoffer.

"Soldiers are soldiers"—Frau Schenkel sighed—"especially when they aren't German. My dear late husband was given a basket of black mushrooms by grateful villagers outside somewhere in Russia."

"Fräulein Winkel is young and pretty," said Werner, almost gleefully. "The American infantrymen are hardly likely to reserve their attentions to kissing her hand."

Hilde Winkel held her throat as if strangling herself.

"Fräulein Winkel, no American soldier will lay a finger on you without dealing with me first," said Herr Hoffer.

Werner snorted.

"While in this building," Herr Hoffer went on, encouraged by his own rhetoric, "you are under my official protection. As is everyone. Even Herr Oberst," he added, determined to keep everything light.

"I am unlikely to be the object of even the most desperate or depraved of sexual attentions," said Werner Oberst, "but thank you for the thought, Heinrich. I can now relax."

"Herr Hoffer," whispered Hilde Winkel, "I am genuinely grateful to you."

Herr Hoffer nodded (very pleased), took off his gloves, and bade the others sit around the table.

Now he was here, he had no clear idea what to do.

Most of the artworks were deep in Shaft IV of the salt mine at Grimmenburg, thirty-three kilometers north of the town; the American troops would stomp over it unwittingly and when this wretched war was finished with, Herr Hoffer would retrieve everything. He had nightmares, of course, in which the salt mine was flooded by criminals as he was bicycling towards it, the wave roaring over the 440 square meters of the mine's floor and sweeping everything before it. He was always somehow above and below at the same time, and he would wake up spluttering and gasping for air, Frau Hoffer having to calm him by stroking his damp forehead with her cool hand.

"I think," said Herr Hoffer, after a brief discussion during which they distinctly felt the floor tremble and heard the panes rattle in the windows, "we must go down immediately to the vaults. This is not an ordinary raid, as Werner pointed out. They are shelling from quite near. I appreciate your reporting for work on this day of all days, but if you wish to return home I will not stop you. Though obviously it would be very dangerous."

Werner snorted. "What do you think I am, Heinrich? A deserter? I am once again in the armed forces," he went on, not altogether seriously, tapping his yellow armband, on which the words DEUTSCHE VOLKSSTURM—WEHRMACHT were even more unevenly stitched than on Herr Hoffer's.

"I too am in the Wehrmacht," said Herr Hoffer, "and my duty is clear: to stay with the paintings in the vaults."

He was staring at the table; he disliked speaking to more than two people at once. He forced himself to look up and caught Hilde Winkel's admiring gaze, which was always directed at a point just below the eyes. He blushed. He wondered if she had lost her father at an early age. Perhaps he was still, in fact, young enough. Men stayed young much longer, if they didn't—

"But you've got family, Herr Hoffer," said Frau Schenkel.

"So has everyone," said Werner Oberst.

"Some more than others," said Frau Schenkel, her bottom lip giving a little quiver.

Herr Hoffer felt terrible, thinking those thoughts about Hilde Winkel with Sabine crouched in a shelter with the girls.

"I know what is expected of me," he said, his voice rather too high. "If my eyes prevented me from serving on the front in previous years, they do not prevent me from defending my country at home. I would be of little use in a pillbox, and my own dear wife urged me to do my duty here. So here I am—and here will I stay to the bitter end!"

He had countered his nervousness with a forceful note, going so far as to strike the table lightly with his fist. Sabine had, in fact, urged him to stay put. But that detail, and the fact that he had no intention of killing a single American, was neither here nor there. He had not yet sounded out the others on this business of defense; he could not even be sure that Werner was unarmed—that he hadn't brought along his famous pistol.

"I'll come with you," said Frau Schenkel. "You know I've nothing to go home for now."

"Me too," breathed Hilde Winkel. "This is my second home."

"And me," Werner sighed, raising his hand as if at a meeting.

"Not me," said Herr Wolmer.

They looked, astonished, at the janitor in his spiked helmet and Imperial greatcoat.

"My job is to stay up here," he growled. "I got through two years in the trenches before my leg wound. They're not going to finish me. I'm untouchable."

Everyone laughed at this bold display of defiance. It reassured them.

"I don't think," said Frau Schenkel, "that the Americans will bomb too much. They know we are lost. Our boys are finished."

"Frau Schenkel, be careful what you say," murmured Werner, hardly moving his thin lips. "Defeatism. A capital offense against the Fatherland."

One was never sure with Werner Oberst if his dryness was dangerous sarcasm or plain speaking.

"I was not talking of the Eastern Front, where we are definitely winning, Herr Oberst," snapped Frau Schenkel, her blue eyes fierce.

"I didn't say you were," Werner replied.

"Good."

Even now, thought Herr Hoffer, even in extremity these two quarrel.

He went briefly into his office to collect the most important files. The others did likewise next door, while Herr Wolmer locked up and fetched the paraffin lamp.

Herr Hoffer loved his office. He loved his glass-topped desk and the way in which the window behind it seemed to continue on down into the glass—an optical effect he would paint, one day, when he had time. The room smelled pleasantly of paper and wax polish and the sweet, lingering suggestion of pipe smoke from Herr Acting Director Streicher's days.

Herr Acting Acting Director Hoffer pulled out of the top drawer of his desk a single sheet of thin-lined pinkish octavo paper. He looked at its four typewritten columns before tucking it into his pocket.

Cleaning his spectacles on his handkerchief, noting the far-off thumps, crashes, and crackles, he felt very weary. He thought he could smell fireworks on the air, then realized, replacing his spectacles, that the mistiness he had taken for dirty lenses was smoke. The telephone sat on the desk as in normal times, its ugly black flex coiling straight up to the ceiling as it always had done. Yet there hadn't even been a buzz on the line for over a week. Nevertheless, he tried it, pressing the piece to his ear.

Silence.

There was something unforgiving in that silence, as if the whole of the Reich had folded up or been buried under snow; it was the silence of the mountains after an avalanche.

He wondered about taking down with him the bottle of vintage cognac secreted in his desk. It had been given to him by the present SS Sturmbannführer, who had one of the jewels of the museum's collection in his office: Jean Marc Nattier's *Mademoiselle de Guilleroy au Bain*. The SS Sturmbannführer's predecessor had simply helped himself to it. He was legally entitled to do this; a week before the SS Sturmbannführer's black Maybach had scrunched to a halt outside the main door, Herr Acting Director Streicher had been ordered to cross out every item in the museum's official inventory and cancel the insurance. He had called Herr Hoffer into the office and said, "This is a museum without walls." Then Herr Streicher had lit his pipe, put Schubert's Heine songs on the gramophone, picked up his paper knife, and started to draw it firmly across his left wrist. Fortunately, the paper knife was blunt. This was Herr Acting Director Streicher's second nervous collapse.

Frau Blumen had scrubbed the spots of blood off the leather chair and Herr Hoffer had taken his seat there, behind the director's desk—not without a certain satisfaction. It had always been the director's desk: since 1904! So it was that, when the SS Sturmbannführer's predecessor walked in with three of his men and took the Jean Marc Nattier without asking, Herr Hoffer was behind the desk and technically in charge. But there was nothing to be done. There wasn't even a loan contract to sign, because it wasn't a loan. From now on, all cultural property belonged to the Reich. Herr Streicher was quite right: The walls of the museum did not exist. The Reich had broken them down. The walls were now the outermost frontiers of the Reich. The SS Sturmbannführer's men trotted in and strode carefully out on either end of the huge Nattier, and not a word was spoken beyond the usual civilities. They carried the painting all the way to the Sturmbannführer's office, covering it only with a tarpaulin, while the Maybach crawled elegantly beside them. It reminded Herr Hoffer of a funeral.

That was nearly seven years ago, in 1938. The present SS Sturmbannführer had been stationed in Troyes. He had returned with many cases of the vintage cognac. The cases had been stacked in the Sturmbannführer's office, opposite the window—whose glass Herr Hoffer now imagined embedding itself in Mademoiselle de Guilleroy's ample thighs.

"Here," the new incumbent had said to Herr Hoffer, handing him the 1921 cognac, "please don't think of me as unappreciative."

Herr Hoffer decided not to take the cognac to the vaults.

Instead (mainly to please Werner), he took the battered gramophone, which closed up into a portable box like a briefcase, and several records in their brown paper sleeves that Herr Streicher had also left behind.

Herr Hoffer was quite convinced that the building was somehow protected, perhaps supernaturally, simply because the Americans and the British deliberately avoided dropping things on its distinctive tower. There had been five or six serious bombing raids over the past year, and it (and he, obviously) had survived all of them. He was not a deeply religious man, but he did attend church most Sundays in deference to the general tenor of the townsfolk. He found more spiritual conviction, however, in the contemplation of the many sacred works in his care—most especially the wood carvings in the pre-Renaissance gallery. These had all been stored in the salt mine, apart from one glorious piece: a life-size cedarwood figure of Mary Magda-

lene in sorrow, from the thirteenth century, that he and Herr Wolmer
had carried between them to the vaults.

It was his own decision to do this, yet again; he had not referred to
Herr Streicher. As it was his decision, and his alone, to build a cupboard behind the double door in the Prints Room—the door that led
to the stairs down to the vaults. A hidden handle opened another
door in the cupboard's back wall; he and Herr Wolmer had constructed it themselves. Thus the only access to the vaults was skill-
fully disguised. Not even a surprise search by the Gestapo, looking
for hidden Jews, had found it.

He was hoping that, after the war, he would be rewarded officially
with the post of director and any decision would be his automatically.
As it was, he always felt a little nervous and small behind the desk
with its plate glass and bronze paperweights, as if he were a pre-
tender. But Herr Acting Director Streicher was aging, depressed, and
ill—unlikely, after his third nervous collapse, ever to shoulder his old
responsibilities.

The Reich had broken him. It had not broken Herr Hoffer.

Herr Hoffer thought of Herr Streicher as the four of them walked
now through the empty galleries on their way to the vaults, Werner
slightly ahead as usual, carrying the gramophone records under his
arm. There were discolored rectangles below the empty hooks, as if
each work had left its phantom presence. Herr Hoffer suddenly
wished very much to return home, to sit in the apartment block's
shelter with Sabine, Erika, and Elisabeth and their three suitcases.
But he could not return, of course; he had his duty, his position. And
anyway, the shelters were smelly, dark, and full of spying Party block
leaders. Also, there was the man from the ground floor who sniffed
waterily every two minutes. And the screaming baby, called Ulrike. It
was sheer torture, to be honest.

The thuds and crashes seemed to have intensified, sounding not
quite so muffled by the thick walls as before. He gripped the paraffin
lamp in one hand and the gramophone player in the other and tried
to calm his breathing. Above all, he must not start to think that the
shells and bombs were aimed at him personally.

As they were passing through the pre-Renaissance gallery he heard Frau Schenkel mutter, "Good God!" next to him. At that precise moment (although it must have been a little before), the glass in the great window to their right quivered and then carried on coming into the room.

I am so lonely. Fear is my closest playmate, but he is a bad companion. He plays tricks on me. He makes me see him where there was nothing before. His favorite game is hide-and-seek, but he never lets me hide. Why should I always have to seek him out, when I don't care if he never comes back?

6

Corporal Parry did not know what to do with the painting he had salvaged.

Or rather, he knew what he *wanted* to do with it, but there were two elements that constrained him.

First, the army rules concerning loot (who are you kidding?).

Second, the object was too large to be buttoned down somewhere on his tunic and he wanted to have himself some fun in this town and not be burdened.

He could hear small-arms fire bouncing off the ruins of the town, and every now and again some artillery that whistled in such a way that they were definitely 88s. Some jerk was always willing to play it rough. In not much more than an hour, however, his patrol would be back to base and dispersed and having some fun. A long time, an hour. Three seconds was a long time.

Quite a long time can be any amount. It depended on your mind and how your spine felt and your muscles and your innards.

The unit had found a smashed-up grocery store with a yard and straw and beds a few streets away and established their CP there; he guessed they would be staying here now for a couple of days to allow the line to make sense, if Morrison's latest dope was correct. They'd been driving so hard they might jump right over the Germans and finish in Minsk, at this rate. Things had to slow up, shake down into some kind of order, like the order General Omar Bradley must be staring at on his neat strategy table, all those little flags moving gently forward like a goddamn flotilla in Chesapeake.

Morrison and he were checking out the remaining area of the museum vaults, dreaming of finding beer butts. They had found beer butts or even brandy butts in other similar places. The remaining boys in the patrol were doing likewise aboveground, under the pretense of rooting out Heinie nuts who thought they could turn the war alone with a single Mauser.

The vaults spread farther around the corner than they'd thought. It wasn't burnt there and it was looking like a schlock shop; Morrison flashed his light over broken frames, church-type benches, plaster things, big old chairs, and bolts of green cloth. There were no beer butts, but Morrison did give it in spades to a painted wood statue whose shadow seemed to leap out at them with its hands out, the head blown off by the shots that temporarily deafened Parry and made him think of consequence and ricochet.

He felt jumpy now; this was just the kind of place the nuts could be making their last stand inside. The fire had hardly touched the far end, though it smelled nasty, and everything had this greasy film on it. Morrison reckoned anybody down there would have been suffocated by carbon dioxide, saying it in his soft Wisconsin drawl as if reassuring himself. Parry wondered why the four they'd found back there hadn't tried to make a break for it, gone deeper into the vaults. Maybe the blast of heat was instantaneous. Maybe it was the heat's gas the medic had told him about, which maybe *was* carbon dioxide and Morrison had surprised him again. The consequence. The ricochet.

There was nothing left of the museum above but a gable end and part of a wall; he wouldn't even have known it was an art museum if the girl in the long coat hadn't told him. She was part of a crowd of about thirty people, staring at the ruins as if they couldn't believe it.

He'd thought it was a big church, from the look of the gable end. There was a tiny white statue in an oyster-shell niche that must have been the Virgin and it had survived like a miracle, too high to bring down.

Then the girl, who was about eighteen and very thin and wore spectacles and spoke some English, told him it was the town's art museum, the Kaiser Wilhelm.

"It's not the church? Kirk? Hey, you reckon I read German at Harvard? *Ein Kirk, das there?*"

"No," she said, ignoring his German as if he had tried to kiss her with it or something. "It is the museum. Art. *Kunst*. And books. It is the library and the museum of art."

Maybe she'd used the present tense because her English was not advanced, or because she hadn't gotten used to the idea that the museum was a thing of the past, now. The others were nodding and saying, "Museum, museum," which he had a hunch might be the same word in German. These people must have been the town's art lovers, except they were the usual down-at-heel and half-starved and miserable fucking crowd. There were deads with newspapers over their faces, the pages lifting and falling in the breeze as though the mouths were breathing. The footwear of deads, if they had any, always looked too big. He wasn't quite sure what had seen him through so far with barely a scratch; he didn't pray to God too much, and when he did it was more like a badass insurance policy.

Maybe it was Morrison. Maybe Morrison was his guardian angel!

Morrison could have passed for a stocky kind of tough-boy angel. He had a rosebud mouth that curved at the corners and dark lashes that didn't go with his gingery head, shaved close all over and very square. His nose was small and flat; Parry wondered if the guy also had Indian in him, like himself, and maybe Irish, and the two hadn't quite blended properly, like water and oil.

"Well," said the guardian angel, "there ain't nothing in here by way of liquor."

"It'll show up someplace."

"Not here. We'll go halves on that old painting that was always our true objective."

"Maybe," said Parry.

"For sure," said Morrison. He flashed his light in Parry's face. "Neal, it's never hard to say yes to a buddy."

As if, Parry thought, they'd both found it.

Like they found the fifth corpse by both nearly falling over it; it was lying in the corner by the far end of the vaults. It changed the subject, as deads always should do or you're finished inside.

"Well, here's another one," said Morrison, moving his head in his usual way, like he was a rooster pecking corn.

He pointed his light at the face and the open eyes flashed back and so did the moisture on the teeth. It was not burnt at all, but the rats had been at the right cheek and the nose. As far as they could make out, it was a young guy dressed in peasant clothes, but he didn't look like a peasant. What was left of his face was kind of sensitive.

This term *sensitive* flashed like the light through Parry's mind, straight out of the dime novel he'd been reading for the last four months, his nerves only allowing him very slow progress through *Deadline at Dawn* even in the times of waiting and waiting. He'd pick it up and have to check back a couple of pages and then only read one page and so mathematically, like the universe running down, he was heading backwards and would soon arrive at the beginning.

The dead with the sensitive face had been shot, not suffocated. The bullets had hit below the neck and those holes in the weave were not goddamn moths.

Morrison pointed this out, playing the light over the body like a cop, his lips pouting and yet curling up at the corners in that weird way he had: rosebud lips for sure, the lips of a film star, maybe Clark Gable or someone. Not Tony Martin. He was wondering if it hadn't been one of his own chance bullets, but the face was too pale and the blood too dry. The dead was definitely dressed in the kind of baggy corduroys and shabby cardigan that the old peasants here wore, which didn't go with his face.

"Maybe he had ambition," said Parry. "Maybe he wanted to canter instead of trot. Or maybe he was a crazy Red."

"Maybe he's starting up on a whole new life," said Morrison, and hawked up another gobbet of spit.

They searched the pockets and found a picture of home, maybe, and a woman in a creased photo who was no doubt the mom and a notebook that was red with the name of the museum on the front: Kaiser-fucking-Wilhelm. Maybe he was still alive. The one that was growing tulips. The red notebook had a lot of close writing in pencil that Parry kept because it might just point in Heinie to where Adolf H. was hiding out, and the pages were purple-brown with blood. One page had a shaky drawing of some trees on a hill. Maybe it was the wood where Adolf H. was lighting his last cigarette, suggested Parry.

"The cocksucking bastard never smokes," said Morrison.

"So he's crazy."

"We know that, Neal."

They went back to where the four charred corpses lay, two on each side, beyond the burnt heap of paintings. There was a living woman on the edge of the hole where the sky showed; she was peering down between the fallen beams and her face seemed fair in all senses. She was flax-haired and distraught and saying something in German. It was as if she was calling someone. She *was* calling someone.

"Heinrich? Heinrich?" she cried.

Parry reckoned she couldn't see the deads. She had tousled flaxen hair covered in ash, and red-rimmed eyes, and she was fair. One of the deads was bound to be Heinrich. The problem with death was that it didn't end there.

"You might as well go up, see what she wants."

"Would you mind if I take a little time to think that over?" Morrison grinned.

Parry was too tired to tell him to go easy with her. Instead he shrugged, not smiling.

"Check she's not Mrs Himmler. That dead over here with the glasses could be Heinrich Himmler. He's got the right style of glasses."

Morrison laughed. "About time we had some luck."

"He has to show up some time," said Parry, looking at the dead with the round glasses still on, like a clever trick.

"I'll cut it with you, say, thirty-seventy. I get the seventy—"

"Morriboy, what the hell."

He felt imprisoned in the tiredness of his physical body, tired enough to stay down here for good like a fish in the gloom of a pond.

"That's the Injun blood in you, Neal. Mean as fuck."

"Come on, get moving."

He turned around to deal with the salvage that was a beautiful and valuable painting.

Morrison, however, clambered back up to the surface and the woman. He has some kind of trouble with the blood-Indian part of me, thought Parry. It was only my goddamn grandmother. And my ass is very uncomfortable.

I am at the bottom of a deep lake, without a head. My headless body floats among weed, attached to the surface by a rope. One day someone will come and pull on the rope. There is always something to live for, if you choose to. I might have turned by the pear tree to look back but I didn't, I ran out of the garden without looking back. The one with the thin face brought me bread today.

7

The shattering glass billowed in front of them like a gray sail.

Herr Hoffer was not aware of any noise except a low whistle that went on and on. Blood was dripping from Hilde Winkel's mouth, splattering down from her chin onto her chest. Werner Oberst seemed to be studying his shoulder, his scrawny neck twisted like a cockerel's. His right ear was cut. Blood welled from the lobe and was dripping onto his shoulder, splashing the paper sleeves of the gramophone records under his arm. Herr Hoffer did not know quite how to act behind his whistling wall of deafness. The noise of the explosion seemed to be trying to push through into his mind.

Then he felt warm liquid on his fingers and saw that he too had been caught by the glass. His left hand was red with blood; the lamp with its precious paraffin was broken on the floor. He felt, for some reason, embarrassed. He had been sure the glass had missed them. But no; they were standing in glass, on the edge of the sea of glass. It had cheated, he thought. That is very unfair. He even felt dusty glass fragments on his lips. Frau Schenkel had not been touched, though she had glittery bits in her graying hair and on her long coat. She was telling Werner that his ear was cut—Herr Hoffer could just hear her shouts as if through a thick mattress. She had given Werner a handkerchief, which he was holding rather hopelessly over the wrong ear; it comforted Herr Hoffer to see poor Werner, who was always so precise, coping so badly. Hilde was holding her sleeve to her mouth. Her generous upper lip had been hit in the middle and Herr Hoffer could see the flap of the gash.

They were smearing the blood on the floor with their shoes. There were spots of blood on the bare white walls as well as on their faces. If only they had gone immediately to the vaults, as they would have done in the early raids!

He felt a terrible sense of dread, holding his hand, not daring to examine the extent of the wound. The cut had started to sting only now, as if thinking about it before leaping into action. They might have been blinded, he thought. Frau Schenkel's arm was on Werner's back, astonishingly. They stumbled on, and as they went through the cupboard in the Prints Room they tripped on the brooms and one struck Herr Hoffer on the nose. He fumbled for the hidden handle in the back wall, his vision blurring; the strike on the nose had produced tears. Halfway down the stone stairs to the vaults, there was a bright orange flash and the lights went out.

Herr Hoffer heard Hilde Winkel give a little scream; his hearing was back. He could not believe that the shells were hitting so near, though down here they sounded more like the thumping and booming one gets on a wildly windy day in the city.

They felt in the gloom for the steel door to the vaults, unlocked its heavy lock, stumbled in, and caught their feet on the paintings stacked in rows on their wooden trestles. There was only a stretch of wall left free on each side, with threadbare cushions, and a narrow line of floor down the middle.

The four of them made themselves as comfortable as possible.

Frau Schenkel briefly examined the wounds in the light filtering down the stairwell and found them to be superficial, mere scratches. Herr Hoffer wasn't sure whether to believe her. Hilde's looked deep and ugly, at least, and her lip was already swelling. It hurt her to smile, she said, holding a handkerchief to the wound. Don't tell any jokes. At any rate, seeking medical help now would be a folly.

It was very dark without the paraffin lamp, and with the door closed it was pitch-black. Werner knocked the resident bedpan with a clatter.

"Thank God it was emptied," he said.

"Ow," said Hilde. "Please, no jokes."

Such blind darkness gave Herr Hoffer the sensation of being suffocated. He asked if the door could be kept open, despite the added danger this entailed, and the others agreed. With the door open a little, life came back. Death is pure darkness. But then, so is pure whiteness. Three coats of size to stiffen the canvas. He glanced nervously over at the ranged paintings. He was nervous because he had a secret, and he was not someone who dealt with secrets very well. Why had he bothered with three coats? One would have done. Or none at all. And what is white when there is no light? Or, for that matter, what is red, ultramarine, yellow, burnt sienna, carmine, black? These from which all colors can be made. All the miracles he had devoted his life to!

Without light, nothing exists. Death, perhaps.

There was a cupboard in the corridor upstairs, with emergency candles and matches. Herr Hoffer mentioned this, but no one volunteered.

"Well, well," said Frau Shenkel, "we must count our blessings."

"Start counting then," muttered Werner, as if angered by the pain.

They sat leaning against the wall, two on each side: Hilde Winkel next to Herr Hoffer, Frau Schenkel next to Werner, who had his elbow on the gramophone.

The Acting Acting Director felt he had already failed, especially with the loss of the lamp. He wished once more that he was with his family in the apartment cellar. All he had wanted was a quiet, industrious, contented life, and it had started so well. He had been lucky to get the job of Assistant Director so young, before the war, fifteen years ago now, in Herr Director Kirschenbaum's day; he had been blessed with this opportunity, living among beautiful pictures, building up the collection, working somewhere civilized and quiet, a priest of the sacred temple of culture. He had been blessed with his lovely plump wife and his two little beautiful girls, Erika and Elisabeth. So very blessed.

He wrapped his handkerchief around his hand, thinking to himself (between empty words of comfort for the others, through his own stinging pain) how stupid and unnecessary all this was, and how perhaps such suffering and pain was the reality and everything else was camouflage thrown over it like a blotched canvas sheet. Even his nose still stung.

"We should have covered the windows," said Frau Schenkel out of the gloom, as if telling him off.

"There are about a hundred windows in the museum, not counting the glassed roof," Herr Hoffer replied. He and the Acting Director had costed it as far back as 1938; it was quite impractical.

"They should have thought of that when they built it," said Frau Schenkel.

"Everything was peaceful in 1904."

"Who wants to live in a giant pillbox?" muttered Werner.

"I didn't say that," snapped Frau Schenkel. "I said they should have protected the windows. They've covered them in the Rathaus and the SS headquarters."

"That's a privilege," Werner murmured, "reserved for the elite."

They all had little wounds on the face, with unseen fragments of glass that made them sting. Herr Hoffer's hand was stinging more than his face; a bloom of red was appearing on the handkerchief. He wondered if it would stand him in good stead when the Americans came. They wouldn't shoot an injured man, would they?

"We should hang out a white sheet of surrender, anyway," Frau Schenkel went on, as if picking up his thoughts. "Or they might shoot us when we come out."

"The Party will shoot you first, if you do that," said Werner flatly. "That's what happened in Hannover a few weeks ago. Gauleiter Lauterbacher personally supervised the executions. My sister told me."

Herr Hoffer was surprised at the strength in Werner's voice; perhaps the cut on the ear was, after all, superficial. The handkerchief lay neatly on the archivist's shoulder to catch the blood—though Werner didn't have much blood, it seemed; it had stopped dripping. That certainly wasn't surprising.

"So?" said Frau Schenkel. "That's Hannover. What they do in Hannover is not our business."

"I'm from Hannover," said Werner. "And I am in the Wehrmacht."

"Please, don't quarrel now," said Herr Hoffer.

"Anyway, I tell you what I'm afraid of," Frau Schenkel said.

Herr Hoffer's heart sank. At least once a week the same discussion took place as if it had never taken place before.

"That little problem was all dealt with, I was led to believe," interjected Werner, as usual, word for word always the same.

"They won't stay where they were put," said Frau Schenkel. "Jews never do. They're always wandering here and there. They'll be on their way back soon. They won't be in a good mood, either. That train I saw full of them, stopped off at the station—they looked terrible. They really did."

There was a silence. Frau Schenkel must have told them about this train a hundred times over the last couple of years.

"Don't worry, Frau Schenkel," said Werner, as he always did, "the Russians will finish them off first. You can sleep soundly in your bed, like all decent Germans."

"Who's going to sleep soundly in this racket?" she scoffed, lighting another sour cigarette. Like Herr Wolmer, she had hoarded them for years and was now cashing in.

Hilde Winkel said, not very clearly with her gashed and swelling lip, "Some of them never left. What about Herr and Frau Pischek?"

"They're not Jews," said Frau Schenkel, with a snort that implied they were something just as bad. Herr Hoffer wondered how she knew the Pischeks, who were his neighbors.

"No, but Frau Pischek's brother in Berlin was hiding a whole family in his cellar," said Hilde.

"I never knew that," said Frau Schenkel, perhaps sarcastically, perhaps not; as with Werner Oberst, one could never be quite sure.

Werner Oberst shrugged.

"They'll creep out of hiding and denounce everyone," he said, "as long as they're given a good price."

"Not everyone," Herr Hoffer said. "There's no point in denouncing everyone."

"Of course not everyone," said Werner. "Of course they won't denounce those who had the foresight to keep a little Jew handy, just in case."

"How disgusting," said Frau Schenkel. "Some people have no morals."

"At any rate," said Werner, with a peculiar smile, "don't expect the returning packs to show any mercy. It's an eye for an eye and a tooth for a tooth, for the Hebrews. Isn't that what we all learned?"

"*Burning for burning, wound for wound, stripe for stripe,*" Herr Hoffer quoted, in the dramatic tones of the pulpit.

"Ten out of ten, Heinrich," Werner muttered.

"I thought you said they'd be finished off by the Russians," said Frau Schenkel.

"Oh, some will get through. They always have."

"They haven't had much practice, like the rest of us," Herr Hoffer pointed out. "I mean, at shooting people and bombing and all that nonsense. Not recently. Maybe they've lost the habit. It's been a couple of thousand years now, if you think about it."

He hadn't ever thought about it before, in fact.

"I don't know what you're talking about," said Frau Schenkel.

"They belong to no nation," explained Hilde Winkel, holding her hand over her lip. "They're internationalists."

"They've been doing it behind the scenes," Frau Schenkel said. "Like the Communists. Anyway, half of them *were* Communists, on the quiet. They invented it, didn't they? They're sneaks and they're clever. They'll use their bare hands, as they did on Christian infants to get the blood."

"And that's why," Hilde went on, ignoring her, "international capitalism has been so successful at infecting the world."

Herr Hoffer pictured the dark polished wood of banks behind vast doors on broad avenues.

The walls shook suddenly as if a huge train were passing, and what felt like plaster or mouse droppings pitter-pattered about them. The air made them cough, but it wasn't shell smoke.

Suddenly, and without meaning to, Herr Hoffer felt very afraid. The vaults were like a tomb. It would be extremely easy for the inanimate matter of stones and mortar to shift and become a tomb. This was not good. He would have to feel just as inanimate or be sick. There was not a flicker of conscience in stones and mortar. Nor in paintings, for that matter. If he thought about his humanness too much, his desire to be alive, he would throw up from fear.

And then, as if understanding his dilemma, there was a plaintive mewing outside and Caspar Friedrich, the museum's tabby cat, slipped in to join them.

"Good morning, Caspar Friedrich," they all chanted, as if hiding the truth from a child.

Caspar Friedrich made straight for Hilde's lap, kneading her thighs like dough before curling up and purring loudly. There was plaster dust on his fur.

"The Destruction of Lohenfelde, 1945," said Werner quietly, folding his hands together on his chest as he would always do when discussing a historical fact.

"It never gets anywhere, does it?" said Frau Schenkel.

Werner cleared his throat. "Did you know that, according to the

archives of certain districts, the rural population of Thuringia was reduced by some eighty percent between 1631 and the Peace of Westphalia in 1648? Then—listen to this—it increased by up to one
hundred twenty-five percent in the following decade."

"Good gracious." Herr Hoffer smiled. "Folk must have been very
active."

"Redistribution, Heinrich. We mustn't get excited and jump to
wrong conclusions. Refugees fleeing open country for the walled
town, then returning to their fields when peace came. Like the Jews.
Lots of coming and going, Frau Schenkel."

"Probably," said Frau Schenkel, who hadn't been listening.

"Even the famous Destruction might have been exaggerated,"
Werner went on (as he usually did). "The great Lohenfelde Fair, for
instance, was held in 1631. It wasn't canceled. Only three months
after the laying to waste. We have—or, rather, had—the original doc-
uments. Fascinating, isn't it? One day I will write a popular history of
Lohenfelde based on the dry truth. If they leave me my archives. The
problem is, no one wants the dry truth, which is full of holes. They
lock it up in boxes and call it dull."

"History," said Herr Hoffer, "thrives on color."

"That's to hide the holes," said Werner. "No one likes a threadbare
rag."

"They didn't exaggerate the cold in Russia," Frau Schenkel remarked quietly. "None of them had the right socks."

"*Let Truth, when hostile times exile, / To Fable for her refuge fly,*"
Herr Hoffer intoned, with his finger in the air.

"Keep Schiller out of it, if you please," said Werner.

Herr Hoffer smiled, feeling he had won.

"The Peace of Westphalia," announced Hilde Winkel, rather in-
distinctly on account of her lip. "The destruction of the Peace of
Westphalia was the Führer's chief war aim."

"That's good to know," murmured Werner. "I had been wondering."

Nobody said anything.

Werner had suddenly withdrawn into himself, like an ascetic. His
philosophy of life had an ascetic's simplicity: facts before beauty.

He had watched his precious archives being taken out of the building by clumsy SS functionaries and driven off in diesel-fuming trucks as another man might watch his daughter being ravished. Werner's specialism was Luther, and most particularly the original Luther manuscript in the possession of the museum since its foundation: *Vom Bekenntnis Christi*, dating from 1527. He would study the manuscript as if it were a treasure map, working hours into the night and producing solemn exegeses for obscure journals in old-fashioned German. Werner had never married, but he was married to the museum library. There were great books attached to the desks with chains, and this had always been an image for Herr Hoffer of Werner Oberst's attachment to his job; since last year's removal of everything but a core of reference books, Werner had crumpled into himself, his cheeks sinking and his eyes retreating into their bruised sockets. Even his bad arm (from a bullet in the last war, he claimed) seemed shorter and more twisted. He reminded Herr Hoffer of a bulb left in a cellar, drying up almost to a fossil and yet somehow retaining life. He was only fifty-three.

Now they were all dried bulbs in the cellar, Herr Hoffer thought.

Characteristically, Werner had worried about damp in the salt mine, but it was in fact too deep to be damp. Herr Hoffer had first visited the mine with a member of the SS-controlled Amtsgruppe Kulturbauten a month before the removal, and ascertained this straightaway. The Kulturbauten official said that salt mines were excellent depositories, as the salt absorbed any excess moisture; he showed Herr Hoffer very ancient salt layers in which groundwater had not circulated. The great caverns were very dry, perfect for the needs of preservation. The official, while showing a knowledge of salt mines, was quite ignorant of anything to do with art, being an architect specializing in the upkeep of stone castles; quite why he'd been sent was a mystery. In fact, Herr Hoffer decided the man was touched; he babbled on about a feudal Reich, with his restored castles overlooking thatched villages and towns as in the nursery tales of childhood, silver-armored knights galloping about with death's-heads on their helmets, and ancient cultic ceremonies—which even the Führer had dismissed as superstitious rot.

Herr Hoffer was glad that Werner, with his dry wit and absolute precision of thought, had not been there to get them into trouble.

"How is your hand, Herr Hoffer?" asked Frau Schenkel, leaning forward and tickling Caspar Friedrich between the ears.

"Mere flesh, mere flesh, Frau Schenkel," he replied.

His hand hurt, in fact. He was not very good with wounds; after the first raid, at the sight of the terrible injuries sustained by his fellow citizens, he'd had a good vomit behind a heap of rubble from which an infant's hand stuck out, white with dust. He had thought it was a porcelain doll's.

"Mind it doesn't get infected," Frau Schenkel said.

Werner put a record on the gramophone and wound it up: Mendelssohn's "Auf Flügeln des Gesanges" filled the vaults with its unearthly beauty.

"Ah, Mendelssohn," Herr Hoffer sighed.

It was a most suitable song for their position, the poet transporting his beloved to a paradisal garden beside the Ganges, where gazelles were skipping and violets whispering and looking upward to the stars. Even through the hiss and clicks of the old record, the song made Herr Hoffer's spirit sway and soar as he closed his eyes. They would play records almost every time they had to take shelter in the vaults; not only did it distract them, it filled the embarrassing silences. The poor light and the anxiety made it hard to read, and neither Werner nor Frau Schenkel liked to play cards—the only point they agreed on.

The song faded into the violent knocking that spelled the end of the record. Werner slipped it back into its brown paper and there was a general sigh of appreciation, a pride in German artistic achievement that was, they all knew, supreme in the world.

"Both Jewish," said Werner suddenly.

It was such an odd comment, like a raspberry instead of applause. And Werner was smiling one of his thin, sardonic smiles.

"Only his grandfather," Herr Hoffer pointed out.

"And Heine?"

"That was Herr Streicher for you," said Frau Schenkel. "He did like his music, no matter where it came from."

"What a pity we didn't bring the chess," said Herr Hoffer.

"I always beat you," said Werner. "You got upset last time. That's why I didn't bring it."

"He was an internationalist," said Hilde Winkel.

"Who?"

"Mendelssohn. Down with national music! That's what he said, once," Hilde explained, looking intense, her head on one side. "He was a true Jew, in fact. He was no good after about the age of seventeen. There was no inner conflict. That Jewish impurity in his blood, it sapped his romantic part, you see. His striving part. He never reached the heroic heights."

"Ah," said Werner, "I'm so glad you reminded me, Fräulein Winkel. I was just thinking of playing the other side."

And then, incredibly, he took out the record and snapped it in two over his knee.

Supposing time does not exist at all, or only as a surface made of ice on which we can slip from here to there, so that I might slide backwards one day and all this will be a possibility in the future, but not a certainty? And supposing the ice was so thin that we could fall through it? Where would we be, then? . . . The thin one came up again and comforted me and I cried. I should have looked back from the pear tree, I said.

8

Parry placed the antique painting by Mr. Christian Vollerdt in a slit in the stone wall, where maybe they had a rush light once. Its height just fitted, so he pushed it until it was hidden in darkness. Swell, he thought to himself. He kicked at the heap of burnt paintings, but they weren't paintings anymore. It was really too bad.

He noticed suddenly that the dead with the Himmler spectacles had one lying on his chest. In fact, the dead's arms were crossed over it, which was why it had not been noticed before, and the dead's knees were drawn up and the bottom edge of the frame was resting on his pelvis and the top came to his throat. The canvas was black but that was only the back; the front might have been shielded by the dead's chest and belly and groin.

Parry started pulling at the picture from the top, his hands next to the dead's face. This face was not the way it looked when it started. Because the arms were crossed over the burnt picture and the hands clenched the frame on each side, and not wanting the charred frame to break and not wanting to touch the dead either, he had made it into a struggle that must finish one way or the other. He had to ease the burnt picture forward but the arms were holding; they were like iron. That is like a man with only one arm, he thought; you reckon he's weak but he turns out to be stronger than when he had two.

Then he yanked hard and the arms shelled off largely to the bone and the picture came clear. He almost fell over. He was breathing hard. The knuckles of the hands were the color of new-sawn beech; they hung there in their stiffness and all they needed was someone to put their flesh back and they would serve just fine. There was a scorched watch on the wrist, its cogs visible. Maybe it had been a beautiful piece.

"Thank you," he said to the dead, smiling. "My, you look hungrier than ever. I'm sorry about that."

He tried to work out what the wrecked picture had been, in the dim light, knowing he would never work it out but only that it must have been special, held on to right up to the end like that, like a bag of gold. The frame at the bottom had been tucked into the dead's pelvis so it was only scorched, and the label was almost legible. The canvas under the crossed-over arms made a kind of **X**, while the rest flaked off into soot. The canvas **X** had blistered into black, however;

there were patterns in the black—shinier black on black—but that was all. This black reminded him of kicking the floor of the pine forest back home. When he was a boy he had seen one time how black and moist it was under the coating of needles and he had understood, all of a sudden, that this moist blackness gave sustenance to the trees and that it was the same as the mushroom compost on Joe Saville's mushroom farm. That this fine black soil was the falling of pine needles over years and years and that everything grew out of its own death.

He was amazed now by how vivid the memory was—of a certain day in the pine woods when he was staying with his grown-up sister in the mountains, the sadness still in him from his mother's going away like that, without warning, and then his father not coping too well, getting drunker and drunker back home; and the walk under the pines alone, the kicking of the soft floor, this realization (in the sweet, rich smell of what he now knew was called humus) that everything grew out of its own death and how that's what Jesus was doing with the Resurrection. And he pulled out his mountain knife under the pines and with this knife he etched, he dug and he etched with much labor a big black cross on the forest floor. Which was no doubt why, in turn (he thought), the remains of the picture took him over to that time some fifteen years back in the mountain pines.

Nothing happened, however, in the outer world as a result of that cross. His father drank more and more and then he died.

There were shouts from above, happy drunken shouts: some German, some English, some Russian. That wouldn't be the Russkie army, though; it'd be the Russkie prisoners of war. Most men were off duty and getting themselves some fun for a day.

The first town they liberated, back in France, had given Parry the greatest experience of his life. He threw bars of chocolate to the kids; he was buried under girls and flowers in the back of the troop carrier. The German towns were the same, strangely enough, but by then he'd got sick of it—in a matter of days, especially since the run had got easier, he'd got awfully sick of it. There were too many deads of all types and sizes, too many hurt and frightened and grieving people, too much of plenty of nothing but noise and thrown-up stuff and blown houses and this and that operation that crawled off the paper and messed itself.

He took the black picture into the shaft of light so he could read the label better. The gilt had bubbled but he could make out letters, parts of words: *au* and *Bur* and *Waldesraus* and a date that could have been anything. He tore off the label and placed it in his breast pocket, along with the label that said *mit Kanal*. He chucked the remains of the picture on the floor of the vaults, creating a cloud of ash.

Then he shot a glance at the bespectacled dead, because he thought it had moved.

Morrison was calling down, cupping his mouth with one hand; the woman was not Frau Himmler but something like Haffer. He reckoned the woman was looking for her husband or brother or boyfriend in the ruins; now she was wandering around in a bad way. Maybe one of the dead guys down there was him, maybe the guy with the Himmler goggles, even. What's *husband* in German? He'd lost his phrase book. He wanted Parry to get his Heinie phrase book out of his satchel and look up *husband*. Was it something like *Man*?

Parry heard all this with half an ear, wondering why Morrison was so concerned about the woman. Everyone was in a bad way, every motherfucker here was in a bad way, and in the whole goddamn world they were in a bad way.

He couldn't recall, just at the moment, what *husband* was in German. He was more interested in what *Waldesraus* meant in English— if *Waldesraus* was even a complete word. He had no idea why he was so interested in the label; maybe it took his mind off ruins and deads and burp guns and his chafed ass. He reached into his satchel and found the phrase book, but it had gotten wet from rain and snow and a lot of the pages were stuck together. *Husband* was somewhere in the stuck pages. *Wald*, however, meant a wood or a forest. Maybe *Waldesraus* had something to do with a forest. The guy with the spectacles had been holding a picture of a forest. That would figure. The dead's mouth was open and lipless and it was imploring him not to whatever. Or maybe it was just a large yawn because that's when the heat had hit them.

He told Morrison to do whatever he thought best, but not to let the woman know there were deads down here. Say *nein* or *nicht* or *take me to Berlin*. Another of the guys, one of the young kids who looked like he was in the Boy Scouts, had put his face next to Morrison's and was beaming down at him. Parry couldn't stand it, he couldn't stand being in charge anymore. There was no point to flushing snipers or checking out booby traps with civilians breathing down your neck. The order was crazy.

Parry squinted at his watch.

There was an hour to go. Another sixty minutes pretending they were doing their duty.

He saw it sharp and clear, now: He needed to be on his own. He was an awfully bad patrol leader. His guts had begun mounting the assault.

The kid called down, "D'you want us to cover you, sir?"

Which meant, What the fuck are you pissing at down there?

Parry shouted back at him, surprising himself. "What's that *sir*? Don't ever call me *sir*. OK? We told you that, man. Or corporal. D'you want me picked off and dead? Didn't we tell you that? I'm Parry. Or better still, I'm Neal. You know that, Carter."

"Cowley. Yes, sir. I mean—"

"You're a fuckwit, Cowley. I don't want to be dead on account of a fuckwit, do I?"

"No, Parry."

"Call me Neal. Yeah, even better, definitely call me Neal."

"OK. Neal."

"Hey, you're learning! You're only half a fuckwit now."

"Sir. Neal. Parry."

"I'm an English knight now, am I? Where's my fucking horse? My kingdom for a fucking horse!"

His shouts were echoing in the vaults. He had once been a soldier in *Richard III* in junior high but that was another day and now he was a soldier again. His face came over in a sweat. A great Russian sweep was happening inside his bowels.

Morrison's grin appeared again beside Cowley's, those lips curled like some goddamn film star's.

"Everything OK, Neal?"

"Listen. Patrol temporarily disbanded. Report back to the platoon CP in the grocer's yard with the others in an hour to get counted off, meanwhile you can do what the fuck you like. No, regroup back here in forty-five minutes. If you're late, I'll assume you're a casualty. That way you might get a posthumous medal and still appreciate it. Forty-five minutes, back here. Just fuck off and have yourself some fun."

"Are you serious, Neal?"

"Yeah, I am. I am figuring hard. Objective accomplished." His head was spinning. The Russians were advancing towards his knees. "A little early, that's all. What the hell's a few minutes? It won't lose us the war. Now scram, Morriboy. Go fuck off for forty-five minutes and just watch out. Watch out for company commanders and the last crazy sniper of whatever this goddamn place is called."

"Hicksville. Hicksville-on-the-something. What fucking river is it, anyway, Neal?"

"Just don't let Georgie Patton know, OK?"

The Boy Scout squealed his laughter and Morrison shouted down, parroting General Patton's drawl so they understood it quite clearly, *"Yeah, we're gonna get to murder those lousy hun cocksuckers by the bushel-fucking-basket!"*

"Morriboy, you know the whole fucking speech."

"Yup, and every fucking line, Big Chief."

Morrison was going over the top, now. This was his tendency.

"Someday," he drawled, the boy next to him whooping his appreciation, *"I want to see them goddamned Germans rise up on their piss-soaked hind legs—"*

"Hey, Morrison, quit—"

"And howl, 'Jesus Christ, it's the goddamned Third Army again and that son-of-a-fucking-bitch Patton!'"

The dim space echoed with Morrison's crazed voice: *bitch Patton . . . bitch Patton. . . .* Yeah, what a bitch. Parry remembered how quiet it was when the general paused, not a man in the thousands of massed ranks sitting there in the English field stirring a muscle, so you could hear the breeze rustling in the leaves.

"We are not interested in holding on to anything except the enemy's balls!" the fresh meat called down in a pathetic sophomore's voice, breaking the memory, trying to join in.

Morrison pushed him over with a shove of his hand.

Parry was already off, farther down the vaults, unstrapping his canteen belt as fast as he could.

The shadows on the beams move very slowly. It's like watching the minute hand on a clock. They move, but you don't see them move more than you see the moon move unless you let yourself [move] with it. The silence moves, too. One day I'll miss that.

9

The walls kept trembling very slightly, but the noise of the shells or bombs exploding remained faint and far away. They might not have been far away, of course. Underground, everything felt far away. Shots were always louder than you remembered. Herr Hoffer very much wanted to be aboveground, despite the shelling and the possibility of shots. Inspired by the Mendelssohn song, he was picturing himself walking in the meadows or the woods with his two darling little girls and his dearest Sabine. He should have stayed at home. But the idea of the museum being hit and the Acting Acting Director crouched shivering in his apartment cellar, his staff coping on their own, leaderless . . . !

Such things go down in history, in local history—and what other history matters as much to a man?

He could not stand the gloom any longer. After Werner broke the record, nobody had spoken and it was really very gloomy, both literally and inwardly.

"I'm going to fetch candles," he said. "Herr Wolmer will have one or two, if there are none in the cupboard. And I will bring some first aid."

Despite their protestations, he went, closing the door firmly behind him. He was not made to sit underground. He was a lover of light.

There were no candles in the cupboard he had built at the top of the stairs: string, a few precious matches, a roll of oilcloth, some magazines—but no candles.

He hurried through the galleries on the first floor like a hunted man, stepping carefully over the broken glass in the pre-Renaissance room, the spots of blood already dry on the floor and walls. Several of the high windows in the farther galleries had also been shattered; he smelled the spring air tinged with smoke, as if a heavenly stovepipe were in operation, and saw how smeared the sky was.

The huge rooms had never seemed so empty, so friendless. The paintings *were* his friends, when it came to it. He could visualize their every face, still, after a year or more of separation. He had come to love even those works he had wrinkled his nose at in the early days: the stagey historical erotica by the likes of Holmberg or Steinbruck, for instance. Why else had he placed even those in the vaults, along with Beck, Moscher, Flinck, Salomon van Ruysdael, Johannes Hals, and all the other wonders—Poussin, Corot, Cézanne? Van Gogh? Ah, but the van Gogh was a secret. His little secret!

He did not like to think of his friends huddled deep underground, in the lightless silence, as if suspended between life and death. They would turn in his sleep like the pages of a book, every work clear in his memory. Almost a quarter of the collection! Concealed without permission!

He had, of course, descended into the vaults via the broom cupboard in the Prints Room at least once a week—and into the salt mine at least once a month to view the rest. His poor dear friends had the same enfeebled look as real prisoners. The stagnant dryness in the salt mine, its primitive electric lighting; the anxiety he felt in the vaults, the fear of discovery: These made it harder to marvel and adore.

Herr Wolmer was in his glorified cubicle off the main lobby, gripping his spiked helmet between his knees and polishing its leather shell with a boot brush. He shared his space with a sink, a broom cupboard, and a crooked stove on which a small copper pot steamed gently, heated by the burning of wood filched from the rubble of bombed-out houses. Herr Hoffer admired Herr Wolmer's ability to remain impervious to disaster, although his taciturn manner—the expression that rang only tiny changes on what would, in other men, be a scowl—had very often depressed him in the mornings.

"We need candles," Herr Hoffer said. "And first aid. Fräulein Winkel and Herr Oberst were struck by glass." He lifted his cloth-bound hand, the coils of blue cigarette smoke writhing around it. "And so was I. Nothing serious."

Herr Wolmer looked up at him through bushy eyebrows, twitched his thick Kaiser mustache, laid boot brush and helmet on the table, and rose to unlock the cupboard. The clock on the wall ticked loudly over the rumbles and coughs of the bombing and shelling. The janitor produced a box on which a large red cross had been painted. Herr Hoffer, wishing the fellow would say something, searched for the little key on his key ring. At that moment the room slid to one side and back again, leaving Herr Hoffer doubled up over the table. The side of the table had struck his stomach, winding him. Herr Wolmer had kept his balance; he had slept through a bombardment many a time, thirty years back, in his dugout.

They had both heard the hiss of the glass, like the sea withdrawing after the crash of a breaker. And then silence.

They went out into the lobby. The colored glass in the front doors and the double oval of glass above—painted by Jacob Kluge, no less—were scattered in glittery shards across the tiles. The windows were unharmed.

"And I'd always fancied a quiet life," Herr Wolmer joked.

"What a pity," said Herr Hoffer, feeling his heart beat in a jittery, uneven manner. "They've got the Kluge."

The two men unlocked the main door and peered out.

A fog of smoke and dust, through which they could see that something had changed: The illustrious burgher was no longer on his marble plinth. Black smoke billowed over the roofs beyond the blossoming trees; every other second it seemed to flash orange, like Morse code.

The dust entered Herr Hoffer's open mouth and made him cough. He'd knocked his injured hand, and the blood was oozing again.

The two men stepped out to inspect the damage. The front wall was peppered with holes, as if sprayed by a machine gun. They looked up. High in the sky, through the whirls of black smoke and dust, they saw a formation of bombers: Americans. A dull throbbing roar followed after. A huge flame shot up in the direction of the Rathaus, then another next to it, spewing a mushroom of smoke and debris and shaking the ground under their feet.

Werner was right: The Americans wanted it rubble.

At that moment, a crowd of about thirty or forty people appeared on the avenue, with a horse and cart in its midst full of bundles and boxes and cases. The people—women and children and old codgers, mostly—were haggard and miserable. Some of the old codgers were wearing their Sunday best, now dirty and torn: old-fashioned country costumes, knee breeches and broad hats and quaint jackets.

Herr Hoffer, from his studies of peasant genre pictures, was quite an expert on regional wear.

"They are from the Oder region," he said.

"Where's that?"

"The Polish border."

"The Polish border? That's a—that's a long way off, Herr Hoffer."

"They are fleeing the Reds, at any rate."

"Who wouldn't?"

One of the refugees spied the two men at the door and shouted. The crowd seemed to swerve as one, like a giant insect moving towards them in the smoke and dust.

They hurried back in and locked the door, bolting it at the top and bottom. The slam of the door seemed to echo forever through the caverns of empty rooms. For the first time, Herr Hoffer believed the museum might not survive. He shifted the fragments of the glass painting with his foot, waiting for the door to be beaten down. The Kluge glass was so familiar to him! He would glance up at it each day, on leaving the building; it had become pleasantly embedded in his life, as if they were mutually dependent. Apollo the blond Visigothic warrior, Diana the Rhinemaiden in her transparent shift: Anything could happen now. The mob might surge into the vaults and destroy the paintings.

Herr Wolmer locked the shutters in his little room—but the refugees had vanished.

"Are we wrong?" said Herr Hoffer.

"Wrong?"

"To be slamming the door in their faces?"

"Better to be done in by a shell than raped and crucified by the Reds," muttered Herr Wolmer. Which didn't help at all.

"We must always put the paintings first," Herr Hoffer declared, on Herr Wolmer's behalf.

"I'll stick to my post," said the janitor, taking out a broom from the cupboard. "No one gets in except it's over my dead body."

"Unless you know them," said Herr Hoffer. "Not all the staff have reported yet, and there are our families. The last thing I said to my wife was, If you're in trouble, come to the museum."

"Stick together in trouble, that's what I say."

"I did try to get her to come along with the children, but she pre-ferred to stay at home."

"There's no place like home, Herr Hoffer."

"No, but there's also one's duty. I'll do a very quick check over the building, Herr Wolmer. You never know. Bombs are funny things. I do feel worried about you being up here while we're sheltering below."

"You just said it," said Herr Wolmer, holding his broom like a sen-try with his rifle. "It's called my duty. Your duty's to the pictures."

He started sweeping up the colored shards in the lobby as Herr Hoffer hurried away with the first-aid box, three candles, and a spare box of matches. He had once declared, in an obscure arts journal, when curator of the nineteenth- and twentieth-century galleries, that the Kluge glass was sentimental and even old-fashioned. This had come to the attention of the local press; furious letters, calls for a sacking. Oh, what it was to be young and naïve! Now the Kluge was being swept up, and there would be no furious letters. Herr Wolmer, for all his faults, was a marvel.

He inspected the upper galleries. The skylights in the Long Gallery were intact; given that the roof was mostly skylight, this was just as well. Birds would knock their heads upon the roof, thinking they could fly straight through. He mounted the stairs to the little-used third floor, following the janitor's usual routine, and walked briskly along the corridor. He had many projects for expansion, but at present these rooms were empty. At least a third of the museum building was redundant. After the war, Herr Hoffer planned to devote himself to those projects for expansion, including the establishment of an art school. One must never stand still.

There was a scraping noise above his head, near the ladderlike wooden stairs up to the attics.

He stopped and listened. He was terrified of rats, and this sounded like a very heavy rat. Caspar Friedrich had killed one the other week, which had surprised them all, for the corpse was very large and fierce-looking. The noise stopped abruptly, as such noises always did. Herr Hoffer disliked entering the attics, owing to his rat phobia. He didn't even like being up here alone, so close to the rat kingdom. The vaults had been cleared of rats by poison, over the years, but not the attics. The attics were too vast to clear, too like huge Swabian barns. He hurried away.

The bombardment thundered distantly, pretending to move off like a storm.

Clutching the candles and the matches at the top of the stairs down to the vaults, he thought of the lines in Virgil where Orpheus enters the high portals of Dis, "the jaws of Taenarus," and felt that he too was bringing life to the spirits of the dead.

I am not at all certain I am alive. What is being alive? Occasionally I see birds. The birds are alive, but that is no proof of my own existence; just as words in a book can bring pictures, but the words are not alive, they are an illusion of life. I hear someone just below, but then I might still be a ghost. Or a god in my heaven, all alone.

10

Parry found some cognac in a big mahogany desk aboveground. There was a hillock of rubble and the desk was poking out near the top, covered in broken glass, and he'd pulled on its drawers. The cognac was a fine vintage one, he could tell from the label. He considered burrowing down somewhere and getting drunk on his own. They'd be meeting up in twenty-five minutes and then it was back to the CP in the grocer's yard, packs bulging with liquor, and no one would know that for forty-five minutes the patrol led by Corporal Parry had gone AWOL. It made Parry feel good.

Then they'd split up to hit town, the bombed-out town, but he would go off on his own. He started to feel lonely at the very thought of going off on his own. He didn't really want to be alone anymore; that was too sad, to get drunk on your own. He was superstitious, these days; it was fatal to be greedy and selfish. He would drink to and with his guardian angel, Abel Morrison of Whitehall, Wisconsin, the kind of guy he'd never have known without the war. He would play pinochle with Morrison and lose as usual, his pack of Uncle Sam cards so greased and stained it was hard to read them sometimes.

He scrambled up to the top of the hillock of rubble, as if he were hiking back home, and looked down on the two shell-cratered avenues that met in front of him, crisscrossed by broken trees and debris and corpses, and then out to where blackened, ruined streets traversed the long perspectives. Lying on the hillock of rubble was a thin metal shaft, like a spire. The girl had told him this had been a tower of some kind.

Thirty minutes to go.

He lit a cigarette and felt a thrill of awe at his own state of disobedience. Obedience is a sin; look at the Heinies. But his scattered patrol hung about him in gray shadowy shapes of bad conscience. He had to believe in himself more, in his right to assert his own individuality against the machinery of war. It was a moral gesture. They had flattened this town, then they went around kicking down doors in this flattened town. So he had broken up the ice, the pointlessness of the ice. The men would regroup in thirty minutes and turn back into a patrol but something would have been declared, even created.

He shook his head free of too many thoughts and calculations that stopped him seeing. He looked instead; he let the moment open itself to him. There was a very nasty burnt-out smell, chemical and bitter, already faded by familiarity. You couldn't paint or photograph smells, only the light and the shade and the color. Dusk was figuring whether to come in.

It was April.

He had to remember that. For a moment he thought it was November.

You could see a whole lot farther in a bombed-out town. It looked like King Kong had torn with his teeth at the buildings, leaving shreds, upright portions as thin as chimneys, pipes coiled like licorice, radiators clutching the one wall left of a home. Already there were paths established down the streets between the rubble, like the paths animals make in underbrush. The men in their green uniforms flitted into view here and there, with slower-moving civilians and prisoners. He could tell the prisoners from way off because they were in columns and had their hands behind their heads: youths and old guys in ill-fitting military jackets, mainly. Dark clumps lying in the debris: deads. What looked like the remains of an antitank gun, with a severed arm next to it, just below. He must've walked straight past it, not even noticing.

All the sounds felt distant; he could almost orchestrate the shouts and cries and far-off explosions and crackles with his hands. Was that really small-arms fire over there?

He kept still for a moment, and then he unhitched his rifle and cradled it in his lap. Now he'd given himself a role. He could stay up here till nightfall and no one would know, and then he would deal with the painting of the snowy mountains and the golden light in the valley. For the moment it was sitting pretty in a niche in the vaults. Mr. Christian Vollerdt. Nice item of salvage. He, however, was exposed. Snipers smile before they bust you.

He relaxed, chucking chunks of plaster between his boots so the chunks rolled down, trying to forget his tender ass on the unyielding masonry. He rolled some Old Gold and lit up from the half-smoked Chesterfield, his tongue already sore. Hitler hated smoking; he reckoned it was bad for you. The man was not sane. How do you fight a war without cigarettes? A woman with a neat figure in a thin dress picked her way along the avenue, through the debris, glancing up at him as she passed. He waved but she ignored him. She had a handbag with maybe an umbrella sticking out of it and high-heeled shoes. That was class, dressing like that at this time, ignoring him. He liked thin women. Women with plump arms did not attract him. There were rotted deads in a big pit in France, brought out with their high heels still on. Gestapo boys did that, he was told. He watched them being brought out: thirty, maybe forty. He shouldn't have. There were ribbons on the high heels of the deads.

He shook his head clear and spent a few minutes undressing the thin neat woman, visualizing very clearly her subtle breasts and wishing he had followed her. His lips touched her breasts, one after the other, gently and with reverence. Morrison had a pinup under his helmet, like a Scout card: a page from *Esquire* with a Rita Hayworth flirt stroking her long bare legs and saying, "Would you mind if I took a little time to think that over?" He had another in his map pack: a sweet-and-lovely peeling off her cardigan so you see up to the big round underpart of each breast just short of the nipple. *This is not the season for cardigans.* Parry didn't have a pinup, not one: just Maureen in a swimsuit, which didn't count. His mind wasn't a gas station, for fuck's sake. The closest he had come to a pinup was a postcard of Hiram Powers's *Greek Slave*, which had fired him up when he was fourteen. Something about the chains over the private parts, the incredible smoothness of the marble, the small and lovely breasts. He'd seen it in Washington a few years ago and felt shy, looking at it in public along with women in big hats and fox furs.

Sure, he liked thin women.

There were so many pear-shaped grumpy women with their hair in a coil over each ear and the same pale cardigan over their apron; they were hard-eyed and came back upright like skittles. Whenever the refugees flooded through a village, stumbling in the mud, shouting and bickering, this tribe of dames surveyed them without compassion—though there were plenty of their own kind, grumpy and dumpy and with a coil over each ear, among the refugees.

Yes, but there are some nice-looking women.

In every place they'd passed through. Except for that brick town where it had rained and rained and the enemy shelling and mortars had shot too many men out of their tanks and their lives. And Jack Burgin's head went to hell and gone, so he couldn't grease and comb his wave anymore. And who'd got covered in the mess? That was one of their own goddamn bazookas.

You weren't supposed to fraternize with the enemy. Also, he had a wife-to-be back home in Clarksburg, West Virginia.

You'd have thought they'd have taken off their high heels, looking for somewhere to put them. A lot of people are executed in bare feet. Standing in the goddamn snow. Or not necessarily.

He loved Maureen, yes he did. She was tough, compact, with brown eyes that were too close together but that made her interesting; she was not just your average buttoned-down prettiness, all neat in the pocket. It made her easier to recall. It made it easier to see her face in his sleep, where she was always seated at a piano. Maureen, to his knowledge, had never touched a piano in her life. Maybe when he got back he'd get her to touch piano.

The German girls chased them, in some places.

Didn't they literally run down the fucking road after us, in some places? Yes, please. Didn't they? Too few Heinie apes around, all shot up or away and dying or plain running scared, and these girls were starved and some of them were very sweet and lovely; they'd do it for nothing, nothing but something you couldn't grasp but which might be named comfort. Human comfort.

Others would call it sex starvation. And more things.

The men always gave something afterwards—K-ration crackers or dehydrated pears or a can of Spam. He'd not yet done it. All the lectures and talks had maybe got to him; it was as though every goddamn girl this side of the Atlantic had syphilis, the way the medics talked. Instead, he'd throw his lemonade powder to the kids, or his supper prunes to the grandmothers, or offer his sugar and canned milk to the women with babes in their arms. Partly, it was his uncleanness, his stinking state of uncleanness. As soon as there was water again in the town, there'd be baths. He wanted a hot soapy bath and clean underwear and some kind of miracle bombers to clean out his stomach. And a feather bed in which he could sleep after his bath for forty-eight delicious hours.

Then a hot meal of something nice that wouldn't throw a grenade back in his bowels. And some clean spring water that didn't need boiling and didn't taste of chlorine.

He was so tired it was almost pleasant. If the world revolution happened right now, he would curl over and sleep.

His rifle was goddamn heavy, even. He didn't think he could carry an erection. He needed all the blood for his brain, to swirl around in there and keep him just this side of awake.

The others were probably doing it now, however. Right now, probably.

Morrison, for instance, with the woman looking for Heinrich someone. It probably was Heinrich Himmler and nobody knew it. Parry smiled. He wouldn't mind just being pulled off sometime, over some girl's thin belly, if it came to it. Disease and dirt everywhere. Never mind what the killjoy medics said.

There was this thin breakthrough to survival, his own personal surviving of the war, and he was going to make right for that opening by staying steady. And Maureen would touch piano.

He shifted on the mountain of rubble, looking at his watch. Twenty-three minutes. Time inched past. Your mind kept talking. He pulled out the two labels from his breast pocket: *Waldesraus* and *mit Kanal*. Put them both behind glass. One of the older guys, a PFC from Charlie Company, waved up at him, passing below, giving him a friendly shout. He stupidly stuffed the labels back as if they were valuable loot.

"OK?"

Uh-huh, he was OK.

So who cares about fucking rank?

Stripes are so much chickenshit, targets for snipers. His own had left a faded patch on his shoulder that might not even fool someone, one day.

Parry fingered the cognac, not wanting to shicker some back in such a prominent position.

Yes, it was good being up here, he was thinking, on this mountain, leaning on somebody's broken desk. As if it had always been broken. As if everything had always been broken. He was supposed to be supervising the chow line tomorrow morning, with Captain Cochrane, just after roll call. Between then and reporting back to the CP in about twenty minutes was fluid and off-duty. He felt the exhilaration of the truant. Remembered it from all those years back. The number of those years being ten, because he was awfully young.

Unless some SS son-of-a-bitching bastard decided to exercise his right to defend his wonderfully picturesque and lying country.

He needed to figure what exactly to do with the snowy mountains and golden valley by Mr. Christian Vollerdt. The nice item of salvage. He'd deal with it while everyone else was drunk and sleeping. Chaos is camouflage.

He'd get married and have six kids on the basis of Mr. Vollerdt. And a tank of a Norge refrigerator.

Dusk was settling in, bringing new shadows, casting whole streets into darkness. He scratched his brow, tipping his helmet back and exercising his fingers where the sweaty lining had given him a rash.

And a Gatsby pool.

Hitching his rifle on his back again, he climbed cautiously down the shifting, uncertain slope that had been the museum's tower, the cognac slopping and gurgling in his backpack. He could twist his ankle and be out of the war for a time. Go ahead. Only it is virtually impossible to twist your ankle deliberately, someone said. Anyway, he wasn't a yellow coward. The yellow cowards had to be killed off like rats, that's what the great god Georgie Patton had said.

By the way, sir, he was right.

Parry passed the desk with its folded newspaper and the dead lying underneath and saw how the dead had some kind of a spike on its charred head. Then he was under a length of the museum's wall that had survived up to the roof guttering. It had empty windows like a theater set and a twist of iron balustrade and flowery wallpaper and radiators hanging on. Then it rose to the exposed gable end with the little white Virgin in her oyster-shell niche, like a miracle or someone thinking how she had to jump. That's fine. There were a lot of these miracles in a bombed-out town. A bottle of liquor left whole in a wrecked desk, for instance. Radiators were not miracles; you could have most of a wall blasted into gridwork and the radiators left intact behind like gritted teeth. People had leaned on them. Wet to the skin. Or maybe just a little cold in peacetime.

Looking up, he saw how the roof here must have been glassed; the framework was still there, like inked hatching, ready to fall.

Au revoir, he thought. I'm not such a sucker as to look up and watch you fall.

I see them all: Papa, Mama, Leo, Lily, little Henny, Grand-mama: all my cousins and aunts and uncles. I have just enough buttons—thirty-six—to include them all. Mama is my top button, which keeps me warm around my throat. I could have looked back at the pear tree and seen her in the door and waved.

1 1

Frau Schenkel lit the candle with one of the precious matches, and immediately their position felt better. The flame cast a golden light, for instance, on Hilde Winkel's face, with its soft downy skin and full lips on which the blood gleamed like a careful highlight. The swollen upper lip filled Herr Hoffer's heart with tenderness, although it made him think of a duck. Hilde's thesis was on realism in modern sculpture, the kind of Party sculpture he detested for its heroic bombast and falsity. The swelling was certainly realistic.

"I'm sure it won't scar, Fräulein Winkel," he said, a little breathless from his excursion. "Lips heal very quickly."

It was a flattering light that the candle cast: It made Werner the archivist resemble his younger self, for really he had not changed very much; having so little flesh on him, his cheeks were incapable of sagging. It was even quite temperate down here, and the little golden flame made them forget the discomfort of the hard stone floor, with only an old cushion to soften it.

"I think," said Herr Hoffer, "we are just beginning to get on top of the situation."

"That," said Werner, "is precisely what my sick mother said, two hours before she died."

Herr Hoffer ignored him. He did feel hopeful, suddenly. He had, anyway, adapted to wartime; it had been a long process of insinuation. Even rubble and bodies no longer shocked him. Only shots. Peace would feel strange, like a forgotten smell of biscuits or the inside of an old dresser to which no one had the key.

Frau Schenkel took off her long coat, rolled up her sleeves, and dressed the wounds—she had started out as a nurse in the last war. She was really remarkable. Her son and husband had frozen to death from the feet up. They had died three weeks apart on the Eastern Front and yet she had shown the most remarkable fortitude, coming in to work as if nothing had happened. The only difference was that her hair was scraped back, showing all of her neck and a formidable brow. And the skin was raw either side of every fingernail, which otherwise remained impeccably filed and varnished with something that smelled of pear drops.

Her husband was a train driver and froze at the controls, which seemed odd to Herr Hoffer. He had been at a loss what to say, after the second death (Siggi, the twenty-year-old son's), on the third day of 1943. He had cleared his throat and started a consoling speech, but she had lifted her hand to silence him. She had remained very still like that, behind her typewriter, with her hand up, staring in front of her like a statue—a marble statue, for her face was very pale—and Herr Hoffer had not dared to move a muscle or utter one more word. All he thought was, This woman is now alone. It was as if her aloneness were flowing into her, steeling her, throwing off all exterior invasions.

He thought she might explode, turn hysterical, collapse into a sobbing fit.

Instead, she very slowly lowered her hand, blinked a few times, turned her head towards him, and said, "I dreamed last night of trees, Herr Hoffer. That was enough. I won't describe it, but it was enough. Please, let us carry on as normal."

And so he had, giving her some papers to file. Really, he was very relieved. He was vaguely frightened of Frau Schenkel. If somehow he were to lose his wife and daughters—if a bomb fell directly onto their apartment block, for instance, driving right down into the shelter—he knew he would be in a pitiful state and scarcely responsible for his actions. But Frau Schenkel had dreamed of trees, and now she was in her forest solitude.

Later, perhaps even in the same week, he had found her looking at a painting in the Long Gallery.

This vast clear space, with its glassed roof, had housed the contemporary collection, now dwindled to the harmless, the conventional, the trite. Frau Schenkel very rarely looked at paintings, although she knew the contents of the catalog as well as he did. She was staring at the Paul Burck painting of the birch forest, with its muddy sunken road winding into the shrouded distance through the complete stillness of the trees. It was a painting that had gained from the absence of the great Expressionist works around it, and for that reason Herr Hoffer tried to dislike it. Its only mystery was why it was called *Waldesrauschen*, since the painting gave no hint of a breeze rustling the leaves.

There again, all paintings were trapped in silence, like a noisy fly in amber.

"They grow on eternally," she said, when she heard him trying to tiptoe back out, the parquet creaking. "They are so steadfast, are trees."

She was standing with one foot slightly forward, as if her movement had been arrested suddenly—in extended hesitation—though it was clear she had been staring at the Paul Burck for quite a while. Her position reminded Herr Hoffer of all his favorite sculptures, including those he knew only from photographs. Donatello's *David*, whose bronze he so very much wanted to touch. The same strange tension, between stillness and movement. The colossal marbles of the new Germany had no movement, no hesitancy. No past, and no future. Everything will always be like this. He thought of them as dumb brutes, albeit with swollen veins on their feet and in the crooks of their arms. But he kept this to himself.

And what had he said that time, from the door, while the parquet creaked of its own volition and a fly buzzed against the roof glass in the huge room?

"I think, Frau Schenkel, that one feels protected in a forest."

His voice had echoed. His spectacles had misted up. He had seen again, as if it had happened weeks before and not years, the black-sleeved red-banded arms, taking the paintings off the hooks one by one at a nod from the experts of the Degenerate Confiscation Committee in their gray suits, and remembered what Frau Schenkel had said, watching them: "Between you and me, Herr Hoffer, I was never very keen on those peculiar ones."

But that was several years back, in the previous decade, when he still took the tram to work and Herr Streicher was still technically behind the director's desk, and now (meaning two years ago, standing in the Long Gallery) it was war and Herr Streicher had taken to his bed and Frau Schenkel had lost her son and husband and he bicycled twenty minutes each way, thinking inspired thoughts about art.

One minute you are one thing, and the next you are another.

They could hardly hear the bombing, now the door was closed. It was a special door, constructed following the Ministry's guidelines in 1938.

Herr Hoffer looked up at the low curve of the vault's roof. It really did look invincible. What was it Schiller said about Phidias's Zeus, the crouched Zeus of Olympia? That if he'd stood, the roof of the temple would have shattered? There was strength in curves, and the god was subservient to the makings of man. Yes. The vaults had belonged to the tough old castle, the castle that had reared its rather squat towers on the site for centuries, until the Swedes razed it in 1631, so that you could stand on the rubble and see the sky. As if there had never been any towers at all.

Three coats of size to stiffen the canvas. Amazing, to think that he had bothered!

As if the whiteness was as necessary as the blackness, the entire lack of light that was his secret.

Maybe I am the only person in the world, apart from the demons and the mice. What proof is there that, anyway, everything we experience is not invented by us? But the bread they bring is not invented, nor is hunger. Nor is fear.

12

A typewriter sat on one of the empty windowsills, perhaps blown there or placed for a joke.

Take dictation, Miss Hayworth.

It wasn't all that damaged, although the paint had mostly blistered off. It was a Remington; he could see enough of the name. Like that postcard he'd had in his student rooms at college: a photomontage from the twenties, a crazy Dada picture with this Remington type-writer in the corner and a guy in a suit and a row of pipes and a medical-demonstration head and a picture on an easel and a label saying *Naturkraft*, all thrown together in a photographic collage that must have been revolutionary twenty-odd years ago. He couldn't even remember the name of the artist, but it was a crazy picture and he'd spent a lot of time gazing at it, thinking of other things like girls or grits or the meaning of life.

He stood where the inside of the museum had become the out-side, like a turned-out sock, and looked through the window, pre-tending he was a visitor come to admire the artworks. It was hard to find his balance on the rubble. There was so much glass around, so much old iron.

It did not help much to think of the inside of art museums back home, the way they always felt so civilized and still and untouchable, the air kind of not breathing. Timeless and eternal. Truly true and deep and eternal.

He tapped on the typewriter's twisted keys, but the heat had fused them. He considered a painting he could paint of the typewriter in the bombed-out window, with the smoking ruins beyond, entitled *Survivor*. He was getting so used to rubble and dust and flame and

deads, they were almost average to him, and to see a town with flowers in the windows and people in buses and the smell of bread baking
nicely would be as strange as luxury. Or revolutionary.

When he got back home, that is what he would paint: normal
streets. And from time to time he'd paint a ruin, he'd paint a twisted
typewriter or a little white Virgin in a scorched wall or a newspaper
lying on rubble. No one would buy those; it would be for his children
and his grandchildren in a time when bombing towns had been replaced by world peace and everybody was shoveling shit in Louisiana,
whatever. He couldn't really picture those pictures, though, because
he wanted to ditch his clean advertising style of painting for something more complicated, more from inside him, and when he looked
around him now he saw weird jagged lines and chaotic shapes, more
complicated than a normal street.

He couldn't really figure his pictures-to-be, no, yet he felt an excitement, thinking about them as he walked among the rubble with
the gun on his back, like the regular soldier he was.

He stepped over a dead under a blanket with a hand sticking out
and a helmet upside down beside it with the two little cartoon-
lightning S's on the sides and a lot of stuff from the pockets scattered
about. He turned around and he kicked the helmet. It spun off and
rolled and rocked and kept on rocking smaller and smaller, like it was
talking some.

Every dead is a sad son of a bitch. Even an SS dead.

The emptied pockets meant their men had been down here—
maybe Morrison or the others.

You're looking good, boy, sad and dead. We prefer you like that.
One day in another time I might have said to you, C'mon, let's have
dinner. Too bad I never did or will, because this time is now and is
hauling us all along in the cart.

The secret is not to think too much. I wish I had a gramophone player. Thirty-six buttons. But where am I in the buttons? Papa, Mama, Leo, Lily, little Henny, Grandmama. . . . Where am I?

13

Somewhere in the city they had made woad.

That was what the Romans had seen coming at them out of the trees: woad-painted terrorists, unafraid of death. A great and unearthly scream coming at them out of the mist.

"I think," said Werner—out of the mist, as it were—"we are all living in a hospital."

Frau Schenkel sighed. "A very helpful remark, Herr Oberst."

"It isn't mine. It is Baudelaire's."

"Hospitals are generally more comfortable," Herr Hoffer said, shifting on his cushion.

"Sometimes I think you're all a bit deranged, the things you say," said Frau Schenkel half seriously, through her cigarette.

They slumped back into silence.

Deranged. How very sinister that word was, for Herr Hoffer. It covered such a multitude of sins.

Once they fill you with shame, you are finished.

Woad—and potash. There was Werner's little pamphlet that he had never read from one end to the other. Potash was once the main industry. Now it was thermometers. No, now it was staying alive.

"What are you thinking about, Herr Hoffer?" Hilde Winkel inquired, looking as usual at a point just below his eyes—a touch of shyness that Herr Hoffer found attractive. The lint on her lip was reddening softly like a flower.

Herr Hoffer folded his arms. "I am thinking how difficult we make things for ourselves," he said. The slabs of the wall were cold against his back; he would be bound to get a chill and die just when everything was looking up.

"Men make it difficult," said Hilde, surprisingly.

"Men?"

"Not women. Men."

"The Führer is a man," Werner pointed out.

"He's an artist. He's guided by feminine intuition. And everyone's let him down," said Hilde irrelevantly. "Except the German women. They voted for him, and they have stuck by him."

"German men haven't done too badly either," said Werner, enjoying himself.

"I don't know what you're all talking about, yet again," said Frau Schenkel.

"Hilde is suggesting we expel all the men as well as all the Jews and the Gypsies and the Communists," Werner said, almost gaily. It was strange to see him like this. The broken parts of the record lay at his feet. It upset Herr Hoffer to see them there, as if the breakage was aimed at him personally.

Frau Schenkel bit her lip and looked down at her hands. A spasm went over her face. She blinked furiously.

"Frau Schenkel," said Werner, "I apologize."

"Never mind."

She snapped back into order, like a tablecloth being freed of crumbs. There was another embarrassed silence. The bombardment sounded like a tetchy old man talking into his pot of beer.

"Anyway," Werner went on, scratching his bony cheek, "the women would step into the men's shoes very quickly. Just take a look at Frieda, who hands out the towels up at the swimming baths. She has hairy arms. She makes men cower before her, does Frieda—even the great big Party one-hundred-and-fifty-percenters with huge hams and magnificent biceps."

"Can we change the subject, please?" muttered Hilde.

Nobody had anything to talk about, it appeared. Herr Hoffer was thinking of the wonders of Dresden and the charming old cherry-wood balconies of Lohenfelde.

"It is all such a pity," he said quietly. "Then afterwards it will all go on as before."

"What will?" asked Frau Schenkel.

Herr Hoffer hesitated. "Life," he said vaguely.

"It won't," said Werner, the candle making a curious shadow of his nose. "Life will never be the same again."

"Defeatism," scoffed Frau Schenkel.

"I meant," Herr Hoffer interjected, stalling the argument, "that after all this destruction we will pick ourselves up and carry on."

"Is that bad?" asked Hilde Winkel with difficulty, her lip swelling almost as they watched.

"I didn't say it was bad."

"Like poor Gustav," said Werner.

Herr Hoffer surprised himself by blushing. He said nothing.

"*He* picked himself up and carried on." Werner Oberst smiled, clearly relishing Herr Hoffer's discomfort.

"Really, I don't think that's very kind, Werner."

"That's one thing we can be thankful for," said Frau Schenkel, pulling a face. "Imagine if we had poor Gustav down here with us."

The thought made Hilde giggle. Even Frau Schenkel began to smile. Herr Hoffer felt a bubble of mirth rise alarmingly in his chest. Yes, the thought of being trapped down here with poor Gustav was almost comical, it was so alarming.

"Have you ever read Gustav's thesis on bracelet shading in Raphael?" asked Werner.

"Of course I have, Werner. You've asked me a hundred times over the years."

"Quite brilliant, to my mind. Though I am no expert."

There was a tension between them, softened only by the wavering candle. The shelling and bombing still muttered, rather than roared.

Herr Hoffer did not want to think about Gustav Glatz, of course. Though he did remember the time, some fifteen years ago, just before the Party gained power, when the brilliant young fellow had pointed out the astonishing resemblance between Holbein's portrait of a villainous Englishman called Richard Southwell and the leader of the National Socialists. Gustav even drew a toothbrush mustache on the Holbein reproduction (in the *Steglitzer Anzeiger*), and the unpleasant, self-satisfied, puglike face had become the spit.

"Perhaps," Gustav had said, tossing back his thick locks, "there is a certain physiognomical type."

"What do you mean?"

"Richard Southwell was a murderer, you know, before he was made a sheriff. He helped to execute his childhood friend, the Earl of Surrey, who was a poet."

Herr Hoffer had chuckled. "I thought Herr Hitler is supposed to have the face of a barber."

"Or a waiter."

"A waiter in a seedy café, with grease on the beer and bruisers on the door."

"No." Gustav had laughed. "A waiter in a barbershop who serves you with a cutthroat razor!"

A brilliant mind, sharp and witty. Perhaps he had some Jewish in him. "Glatz." It was quite possible. But he hadn't been taken away; given his state, he ought to have been taken away, Jew or no Jew.

Herr Hoffer tried to stop thinking about Gustav Glatz. He was wishing he had brought the cognac from his desk drawer. But they did feel reasonably safe down here. They all knew how old the vaults were, and the stones that made its walls and ceiling were large and solid. It was a little like burying oneself for safety in the distant German past, which could not be touched. Perhaps he should have taken to his heels with his family like so many others, burying themselves in the deep Thuringian woods. But that was going east, towards the Red Army. Magyars. Woad on their faces. Huge and wild-haired.

Somebody above seemed to slam a giant door, and the walls trembled. The ancient cement between the stones trickled slowly again onto their hands.

They were all looking up with their mouths open.

More doors slammed, exactly as if someone were running wild in the museum. Still, no one said anything, as if talking might attract the shells and bombs. Caspar Friedrich had lifted his head from

Hilde's lap and was looking alert, his one ear pricked, not purring. A bad sign, Herr Hoffer thought. Hilde's lip looked terrible under the patch of lint, but she didn't seem to be in pain. His own lips started quivering, so he tensed them. He often found his mouth tensed like that. Impossible to draw, mouths. Breasts, easy. Buttocks, child's play. But mouths? . . . Waists, too, for some reason. And light on hair. And getting the feet the right size. And the hands the right shape. All those fingers and their shadows. In fact, the whole body was difficult. There were so many vistas.

Leap onto the subject without prior thought! Leap, leap onto the mouth!

It was hard to swallow. Fear was having a physiological effect on him, his heart was tangling itself up with his lungs.

The tetchy old fellow started muttering again, over their heads and far away. God, perhaps, in a heaven of doors.

Herr Hoffer considered that he might have done better with his life. He had left no mark. An artist left a mark, at least. He glanced at Hilde Winkel's maimed mouth. Glass had kissed it and left its mark. He should have kissed it instead. What was he thinking? She was twenty years younger than him! He felt very old.

Forty-two, for God's sake.

War made one feel very small and old, in the end. As if one were lost in a blizzard.

As did the Party. The Party was the most stupid part of oneself made enormous. At the beginning, it had made one feel rather extraordinary because it was pleasant to recognize something in it of oneself that one didn't yet recognize as the most stupid part of oneself. Until then, that stupid part of oneself had been hidden under layer after layer of sophistication and education and trepidation and fornication, and one simply thought, Ah, yes, this is it, after all.

Close my eyes, you'll be mine, serve me summer, serve me wine.

You could die of grief, though. Kirchner, for instance. Kirchner had certainly died of grief. Hundreds of his works had been confiscated, and he had died of grief. Well, one would, wouldn't one? Around the time of the Degenerate Art exhibition.

Naturally.

Really, though, that had been a perverse honor, for Lohenfelde to have been included. In the countrywide tour of Entartete Kunst. A perverse honor! Along with the likes of Halle, Essen, Cologne. Surprising, really. A member of the Kirchner family had actually written to Herr Streicher, telling him quite openly about the tragedy—perhaps his sister. But then, Kirchner was already highly strung. A morphine addict, actually. Two of the confiscated paintings had belonged to the museum. Probably burnt, by now. The bright colors blistering. They had not come back for the exhibition. Others had, other confiscated pictures had returned, to be laughed at. What was that like? It was like a mirage of water in a desert. Torture.

No, it was like seeing a fabulous dish turn into one's own vomit.

Then they were whisked off again, in a dirty furniture van. Having been guffawed at thoroughly. Through the mangle and out again.

The number of visitors to Entartete Kunst (free entry!) at the Kaiser Wilhelm Museum rotated to its total in Herr Hoffer's mind as if in a film: 149,565 . . . 6 . . . 7 . . . 8—149,568! Five times that of any previous exhibition! What a success! Congratulations, Herr Hoffer! That's what counts, the numbers through the turnstile!

Art for the people—149,568 of the people, filing with little steps and jostling through the cramped spaces between the false walls of trelliswork and burlap in the Long Gallery—and they are talking loudly and they are laughing loudly and he's bent double with excruciating stomach pains. For three weeks.

He remembered going back home each day and lying on the sofa while Sabine—O dear loving wife!—stroked his forehead with her cool hand.

"What is the matter, my darling Hein?"

"I don't like people very much."

"You smell of people."

"Exactly. Ugh. There are too many of them, and they are intrinsically vulgar."

"You should be glad, my honeybun. The museum's never been so popular. They're even talking about it in the baker's."

"I'm sure they are. And in the butcher's too. It's because it's free entry, and they can laugh and jeer at my favorite artists. I feel like resigning."

"They say Dachau is very pleasant at this time of year," said Sabine in a strangled voice, tears already filling her eyes.

She would pose for him in the nude, he recalled. Like a proper life model. But his watercolors and charcoal sketches were timid; she would always look too thin. Nothing of her lovely roundness came out in his feeble efforts. He was no artist. Even his oils looked forlorn. Yet he panted after art as the deer for the stream. At one point she wondered, giggling, if he might ask other wives to pose for him, and they were both mutually aroused by the idea, though he never put it into practice. He did, however, imagine her as another man's wife posing for him. His sketches improved, along with their love-making—which normally followed these sessions and frequently damaged the sketch beyond repair.

The Degenerate hanging was an execution. The pictures were crooked and he put them back straight and he was told off.

"Herr Hoffer, you are interfering."

"But you can't hang pictures crookedly!"

"They are supposed to be crooked. That piece of painted internationalist crap is supposed to be on the floor. Take it down and put it back on the fucking floor so it can get kicked. You're getting on my wick, Herr Hoffer. Anyone would think you were a cretin. Have you ever been to Dachau?"

"Yes, frequently. My aunt lives in the town. Very pleasant at this time of year."

What he really said was: nothing at all. It was amazing how severely a picture suffered by being hung at an angle. Its dignity went. So did Herr Hoffer's.

Two Beckmanns, the small Raoul Hausmann photomontage featuring Frau Schlecker's actual Remington typewriter, three Oskar Schlemmers, a small Herzog, the superb early Nolde, and the beautiful Karl Schmidt-Rottluff. All present and correct. Welcome back. Now we will hang you as if you have been knocked by an elbow, sur-

round you with insulting graffiti, and laugh our heads off at you. Ha
ha. Ha ha ha. From the mayor down to the street cleaners. Ha ha ha.
What a lot of bollocks. Deranged, aren't they? Unpleasant. A child
could do better. We're so glad that our instincts were right after all.
Do you paint too?

Of course, Herr Acting Director Streicher was off sick again, another nervous setback. All up to Herr Acting Acting Director Hoffer
to avoid placing his other foot—his only remaining foot—in the concentration camp. Hoppity-hop.

Herr Hoffer, you are a cretin.

He had a sudden need to talk. This silence was awful. One filled it
with accumulated rubble.

He reached across and placed another record on the gramophone,
without looking at the title. It was a waltz, Offenbach's "Souvenir
d'Aix-les-Bains." It had them all swaying slightly, even the Chief
Archivist and Keeper of Books with responsibility for the Fossil,
Town History, and Local Handiworks collections. Who was something of a fossil himself.

"Always Jews," he said, swaying even more.

"That's Herr Streicher for you," said Frau Schenkel.

"What do you mean?" asked Hilde.

Herr Hoffer told her, albeit humorously, that Herr Streicher's
record collection had not been cleansed of infection. He held Caspar
by the paws and pretended to dance, his knuckles brushing Hilde's
blouse. Hilde Winkel frowned.

"I know, but isn't this Johann Strauss?"

"Offenbach," said Werner Oberst. "Strauss is a Jew too."

"Are you sure?"

"Fifty-odd percent of him. Maybe less, maybe more. Ask the rele-
vant authorities."

"Not available today owing to unforeseen circumstances," said Herr
Hoffer. "A pity this isn't the 'American Eagle Waltz,' eh, Caspar?"

"But the Führer likes Johann Strauss," Hilde insisted.

"Well, I'm sure he only likes the right half," Werner said, straight-
faced as ever. "He is an artist, after all."

Herr Hoffer chuckled as Hilde's frown deepened, her eyes gazing at his chin. The record finished but the waltz had gone to his head.

"If the sky is yellow and the grass is blue, what does it matter to me and you?" he sang, as he held the soft paws and danced with Caspar Friedrich. What a good-natured animal he was! The little pads were dry against his fingers.

"I remember that one," said Frau Schenkel. Her eyes were wet with tears.

Werner turned the record over and the music glided on; Herr Hoffer could see all those long-skirted girls and men with huge waxed mustaches swirling about and about in France: polite gaiety and abandon! Yesteryear! Degas, Monet, Renoir! Golden, golden! Ah, my darling Sabine! Ah, Berlin! Ah, life!

The music stopped. Herr Hoffer let go of the cat's paws and sighed. He caught Werner looking at him, as if in intense dislike. But it couldn't be, could it?

"I think," said Werner, pulling a book out of his pocket, "I will read."

"You'll ruin your eyes," said Frau Schenkel.

"'Apropos of the Falling Sleet,'" said Werner. "What a marvelous title."

It was Dostoyevsky's *Letters from the Underworld*. He opened it at the ribbon marker. Werner was peculiarly drawn to Russian literature, although it was banned.

It was annoying, the way Werner was holding the book up to catch the candlelight, reading with a supercilious smile through his thick half-moon spectacles.

"What an appropriate book," Herr Hoffer remarked, though he had never read it.

"I thought so," said Werner. "I read it at least once a year. The bit about the shabby German beaver that is still too dear makes me laugh out loud each time. You recall the passage?"

"Very amusing," said Herr Hoffer.

"And when he thinks his face looks vicious and ugly and stupid and so makes every attempt to make it pure," said Werner, smiling.

"Isn't that wonderful? And then, of course, he thinks everyone else vicious and ugly and stupid."

He glanced over the book at Herr Hoffer, in a way that made the latter feel uncomfortable.

Perhaps Werner has always despised me, he thought, out of pure envy.

"Isn't that wonderful?" repeated Werner, through his glittering half-moon glasses. "Imagine that."

"I like the passage," Herr Hoffer lied, "about a romanticist being a wise man. As a romantic myself."

Werner now gave him a withering look.

"Dostoyevsky is, at that point, describing a specifically Russian romanticism, Heinrich."

"Yes, but—"

"More rounded and practical than the 'stupid transcendental romanticizing' of the Germans, 'in which nothing is ever done by anybody.'"

"I see."

"You're a Russian romantic, then, are you, Heinrich?"

"Of course you know the book very well, Werner."

"I hope he isn't a Russian anything," said Frau Schenkel. "Beggar the thought."

Herr Hoffer closed his eyes for a moment. He saw the cafés and the waltzes and the green Seine.

"Degas," he said, quite irrelevantly, "didn't like Jews."

My chief activity is to potter ["aimlessly wander"?—"herum-schlendern"]. Yesterday about five men came and I only just hid in time. I did not recognize any of the voices. They floated right over me, like big boats. I didn't say goodbye to Mama or the others properly. I didn't look back when I ran past the pear tree and through the back gate and out of the garden, out of my life.

14

There were some big turn-of-the-century houses along the wide street, villas with stone porches and complicated wrought iron on the balconies and some neat gardens. Most of them had been hit or shot up some. Either the Heinies ran like hell or they stopped and brought down trouble on everyone's heads. YOU ARE ENTERING AN ENEMY COUNTRY. KEEP ALERT.

One big house was intact for a couple of floors, though the door was hanging off its hinges. He could see furniture inside. Maybe there were nice wooden beds in there with down mattresses and maybe this was virgin territory, untouched by other squads, and the beds were all free. The map they'd used to work out who was covering which sector was so dirty you could hardly make out the streets anyway. He'd made a rough copy of it as patrol leader, and he looked at it now.

This one must be Fritz Todt Strasse, big and curved. There were a lot of bodies lying about on Fritz Todt Strasse, only one in uniform and not searched; it was another SS dead, with a Hitler mustache of blood that had unraveled down one cheek to the ear and onto the gray collar. Every intact dead in the world looked like they were pretending to sleep. Some looked like they had stomach cramps. The others were half naked, mostly women and kids. A dead horse lay nearby, tied to a charred farm wagon. The smell was bad.

And these were people who said only yesterday, "Our luck will turn tomorrow or maybe the day after tomorrow." Otherwise they wouldn't have bothered to run.

He should go home.

Some goddamn 88s were still whistling, and out to the east there were detonations and columns of black smoke. Maybe the rabbits who'd ambushed them on the highway had pals on the other side of town.

The big houses might have some liquor in them, or stashed food, apart from beds. There were no people. The rich had got out. He didn't bother to go through the pockets of that SS soldier. Who was half-burnt anyway. Instead, he took a closer look at the villa, holding his rifle. All the windows were shuttered and the railings high and the gates padlocked. One of the railings was buckled from the shell that had killed the horse and stuff in the road—he could step right over it—and almost immediately he stopped on the path up.

There were two steps and then the door, only the door had been blown or kicked open. He guessed the rooms had been looked over. There was a shadow standing halfway inside the door and he tensed out of cover as though he was in a wood.

It was a GI.

In fact, it was Morrison. *Hell*, he almost thought, *I love you.* He could tell that stocky stubbled neck anywhere. Also the sloped shoulders and the black linen tape on the barrel of the shouldered rifle and the flashlight tucked into his left bootstrap. And the way the tunic folded at the shoulders. It was all almost beautiful because he knew it so well, like home.

Morrison was talking to someone in the darker shadows of the room.

Parry came up and Morrison didn't even look surprised, he was too concentrated on the immediate task at hand. He was offering a couple of hard candies to a girl. She was standing in the shadows of the hall. Parry couldn't see clearly, but he reckoned this girl was a looker. The ceiling above her head bulged down and the furniture had been kicked or blown over. She was not exactly frightened, more not wanting to make the wrong move. She looked very thin, too thin even for Parry, with a lot of unwashed copper-blond hair.

"Candy?" Morrison was saying. "Candy? Bonbon?" Then he looked around and saw Parry, who laughed.

"I guess she sees there are strings attached," said Parry.

"Hell, she gets the candy *and* the American."

Morrison's lips were as curvy as ever, his eyelids half closed in the square face; Parry could see a sweet-and-lovely going for him. Or a man. A film star's mouth. A female star! That was why he couldn't remember which fucking one it was. Certainly not Tony Martin.

"She may not want the second. I've liberated some cognac. Morriboy, I've gotten hold of some cognac."

"Cognac?"

"Vintage stuff. Like in France. Where are the others?"

"They ain't showing up till they've had themselves some fun, Neal."

"Hell, we're regrouping in about ten minutes."

"Is that so? Time flies. What's *sleep* in German? It's gone clean outa my head. Sounds like a steam train."

"You ain't got time," said Parry.

"Sure I have time. I have so much time. I have more time than you can know. Hundreds of fucking hours."

"Don't mind me, then."

"I don't know this word."

"Maybe I don't know it like you don't know it."

"All right. And you know everything, pal. You're quicker than a speedboat."

"Morriboy—"

"What's that fucking word, Neal? C'mon, c'mon. . . . It is necessary. It is obliged, man."

Parry began to feel nervous about what he'd done. Maybe he'd have to go back alone and invent something. *I lost the patrol I was leading when a spare battalion of Waffen-SS sprang up.* Then he thought, Gentle up, man, time is not sacred. Only warmth is sacred. Outside of the eternal, which is probably neither warm nor cold. Like sleep.

"*Schlafen,*" he said.

"Yup, that's it."

If only he'd known the German for *roundworm*. Or *knitting needle*. He knew *canal*.

Morrison walked forward into the room, waving his candies and saying, *"Schlafen? Schlafen?"*

The girl was not saying one word back. She was standing there with her hands clasped in front of her and her pair of big eyes staring out and saying nothing.

Morrison was going slowly, like she was a rabbit.

Parry looked past Morrison's stocky neck and its stubble folding up against the collar and he saw the girl glancing to her left.

The front door had been blown or kicked open. The house would have been cased but she was looking sideways. She was glancing to her left.

Morrison did a pirouette.

The wallpaper on the side wall started to spot and smoke red along a line, and the sound was a fraction after. He could not hear the shots until there they were, and they were so goddamn loud they slit his mind up like pants.

Parry seemed to take months to get to the point where he was crouched outside by the side of the two steps, gripping the rifle, not even his nose showing beyond the doorjamb.

He waited, his heart in his nose. If he showed his nose he'd be shot up. That's all it took. There were no sounds now, except the buzz in his ears. There was no one in the hallway; he could hear that.

He inched forward until he could see in over the side of the steps, the rifle's muzzle going first with his helmet on it, playing the puppet.

Nobody was shooting him up.

Morrison had got in the fucking gondola and was crossing the line. He was shuddering on the floor with a pink candy in his hand, still in its cellophane. The girl had vanished. Blood was pulsing out from under Morrison's jaw and he had gills in his neck. He had to be thrown back in the water. The splash on the wallpaper was like a hill painted by a five-year-old. It was dribbling down over the pattern of flowers.

Morrison was not saying anything; he was not even calling for a medic or his mom. He was just shuddering, eyes wide open and looking hard at the floor between him and Parry, with his hand under his head as if cradling it. His helmet was rocking on the floor and the pinup was soaked in blood next to it. *Would you mind if I took a little time to think that over?*

Parry was trembling so much he couldn't keep the goddamn rifle still. The sniper must be in the room to the right, its outside shutters closed, a slice of flowery yellow wallpaper through its open door. Ugly fucking foreign taste.

Back of him, out in the street, a few civilians were wandering about, picking their way over debris and the bodies. There was not a single soldier in sight. Morrison was crossing in the fucking speedboat, from the look of his shuddering. There was blood all over his face, like he was staring through fall leaves in a West Virginia wood, and his lips were pulled back and no longer curved.

This was all virgin fuck.

Parry could hear Morrison moan now, little upset moans like a kid. Hell, he could have gone quietly. Parry wanted to shout for a medic, for backup; he wanted to yell but that would give him away to the sniper whereas right now the sniper did not know there was another man, of that he was fairly sure. He didn't have a goddamn grenade. He wanted to keep cool. Nobody must call him *sir* or *corporal*. He was all fuck. He should've had a grenade and chucked it in by the door but grenades were heavy, hanging off your belt, and he liked to travel light when he could. He could only blame himself. He was a jerk. He should drag Morrison out of there but the sniper was in the room to the right and the wounded man was lying in front of the open door to that room. Parry had been in this situation before, but with the boys around him; here he was alone. He couldn't quite grasp this thing: His guardian angel had been hit after seven months of living through everything that was fucking thrown at him in France and Belgium and Luxembourg and Germany. Not at any point on the whole goddamn run had Parry felt so alone and now, he realized, he was scared.

In fact, he hadn't been scared like this for months, even crossing the Siegfried Line and the two big rivers. He'd gotten over the fright that almost paralyzed him, those first days under fire in France. If he kept quiet now and stopped shaking so much, the sniper might come out into the hall. If only he had a fucking grenade or a sticky bomb. All he had was his lousy M-1 and his combat knife and his German fucking phrase book.

I can run for help.

It seemed crazy that there were no Americans around, none of their own guys. He had not disbanded the patrol forever, just for a few goddamn fucking minutes. Maybe they'd all left, his whole company—every one of the companies, whole battalions of them, the whole of the fucking division, the whole goddamn Third Army down to the last cigarette and dehydrated T-juice cocktail, leaving behind just him and Morrison in the ruins, like in so many dreams he'd had.

In which he could never skip rope, either.

There was a strong scent of cognac. His back was wet. He'd smashed the fucking goddamned cognac in his pack, leaping out of the doorway and backing up against the wall. One minute you're in one place and the next another. Day after tomorrow your luck turns, but you're dead by then.

The civilians passed by and kept their distance. They had plaster in their hair, like flour. He must look real worked up and scared, his knuckles white on his rifle. It would do no good if he yelled, even for a medic. It was unnatural, not yelling for a medic. His ears were ringing from the shots. The back of Morrison's stocky neck was still folded up against the collar, still unattractive. Parry felt gripped by a kind of exhaustion, it made him indecisive. His raw ass chafed like hell against his filthy underwear as he sat on his heels and grew indecisive.

He tried to concentrate.

It looked and sounded like Morrison had been hit by a Spandau— a whole shiny machine gun sitting on its bipod, the girl like a fat fly luring the bird. The way those bullets had smacked the wallpaper, it was bound to be a machine gun. Yup. Yup. Yup.

Gentle up.

Then one of the civilians in the road put her hand up to her face, staring in horror. The blood was coming down over the doorsill and over the two smooth marbled steps and trickling down the side like paint and around his heels and kind of making it down the three yards of path because the path was also on a slope and the joints were done awful good and the blood was pooling at the busted gate.

He looked at it dispassionately, as if it were water, as if someone had thrown a bucket of water on the hall tiles to clean them and it was coming out that dark red color he knew so well. It was spilling over his side of the steps and pooling around his big solid soldier's heels. The guy had a lot of blood in him.

Abel Morrison shouldn't have done what he did. He shouldn't have tried to fraternize. To entice the dumb rabbit.

Would you mind if I took a little time to think that over?

Now he—Neal Wesley Parry—must find a solution. The solution could not be found on his own merit.

He was sliding his back very slowly up the wall. He stopped, bent over a little. He listened. It was very quiet. He thought he'd heard something, a movement. The civilians had fucked off, scared. There, again. The sound.

It was a match.

He heard a match being struck in the room off the hallway. The guy was maybe going to blow the house up, a suicidal gesture. Parry tensed himself to run.

Then he smelled tobacco.

The guy who'd shot Morrison out of his life was smoking a cigarette. No, a pipe. It made Parry want one too. Good, rich, three-star pipe tobacco. Sweet tamped-down tobacco, a great deal better than Old Gold.

He was still shaking—more trembling, now. And the blood was everywhere. Morrison was just emptying himself out like a tipped-over bottle. Profound wound, hemorrhaging. The blood had reached the gate and was crumpling up in the dust there. The world was very quiet. Even the explosions and small-arms shit had stopped. He thought he could hear the guy's pipe, leaving his lips. He must be just sitting there behind his Spandau with the girl, arm around the girl, smoking his curved and warty Heinie-type pipe: the fucking heroic last stand of the crazy son-of-a-bitch cocksucking German. Waiting.

Parry felt really scared now. Fear came up and winded him like grief. He'd never met this before, that's why. The only Germans he'd seen were either dead or hurt or walking out with their hands above their heads—mostly Volkssturm guys, the ones walking out with their hands above their heads; mostly old men and kids. The others'd fired at him from woods or distant buildings, but he'd never seen them firing. He'd seen their gunfire sparkle off the sides of tanks or drop his comrades right next to him but he'd never seen the guys in person, actually firing. This is why he was scared. It was a kind of duel.

He was angry with himself for being scared. He was even angrier with himself for having the shits again.

He was pressed up against the wall, his boots in Morrison's good Wisconsin blood, and he was needing to go. He pictured himself rolling into the hall and firing from the hip through the doorway, but this would not translate into action. His face was so tense it hurt; it was creased up and his helmet lining was chafing his eczema and he wanted to cry. The civilians had walked off and away, they weren't even spectating. Yellow cowards. He couldn't handle a Spandau on his own, a whole 23-pounder spitting 800 sharp bullets a minute so there was nowhere to put yourself. He ought to run like hell for help. The others couldn't be far. They shouldn't have gone so far, they should've been heading back to the museum by now, all seven of them.

Morrison was still making sounds.

Not really moans now, more like whimpers, more like a puppy whimpering in the basket when it wants the mother bitch. Parry stopped his desire to take a look or to whisper, "It's OK, buddy, I'm right by you." Instead he mouthed it, which was pointless. He had a picture of Bayou, their old Labrador, in his head, back in Clarksburg. She'd have so many litters, puppies squirming all around her and whimpering just like that, and sometimes his father would have to drown them when they weren't pure-breed Labrador. That was sad. He didn't see what was wrong with mongrels.

He inched his back farther up the wall, but his tunic caught on the roughness of the finish and the collar was pulling at his neck, squashing his Adam's apple. He came away slightly, as if everything were balanced very finely on his head. He heard a laugh. He was sure it was a laugh. From inside the room. A man's low laugh. His belly ached. He looked across at the window but there was no way he'd get that shutter open in time; he'd be shot to pieces through the slats. He was desperate to look through the slats. Maybe he could fire his M-1 straight through the shutter without opening it, through that gap there between the slats, but the window was set too high; he'd have to jump up. It was set so high you could only have seen over the sill on tiptoe; the whole house was set two good steps up—it was to keep the damp ground off, like at home in Clarksburg. Sensible. Against the bugs. For a moment everything went dreamlike and hazy, as if his fear had sleepiness on the flip side.

He all but went to sleep, standing up with his eyes open.

He came to and reckoned he ought to run like hell, but his legs were weak and the ground kept rolling a little. He was fully upright, now, bent over slightly, wanting only to jump out of the blood, his belly aching to let go its weight.

Then his belly let go all by itself.

This was not very polite. Always the left leg, as if he could only shit from one side. It reached his sock. The smell rose up to his nose as steam and smoke from around a locomotive rises and covers everything on the station platform, only this one didn't smell of coal.

*Germans, beware! Do not buy from Jews! Who said, I do not
counsel you to love your neighbor, but to love him who is farthest from you? Could it really have been Nietzsche? Or was it
Schopenhauer? I wish I could ask Papa!*

15

Herr Hoffer was only half surprised by the realization that Werner
despised him. Nevertheless, he could not speak for several minutes.
Silences could be unembarrassedly long in shelters during air raids,
which was why people would take down with them a gramophone or
a pack of cards. People would go to sleep, or pretend to. It was like
sitting in a train carriage for a long journey with others and scarcely
speaking. The soft darkness helped, and the fear that seemed like an
abstract thing behind one's mind, a sort of square of purple or vermilion. This fear united one with the others present; it was a sobering
thought, to think one might die with these people—perfect strangers
much of the time. Strangers who sniffed or mumbled or tapped and
drove one mad.

Herr Hoffer had rarely sheltered in the vaults with his staff before
now—three or four times, perhaps, over the last years. Most of the
raids had been at night or, in summer, early evening from seven-thirty
until midnight; the Allies were very reliable. They bombed the rail-
way line and the factories and installations on the outskirts of Lohenfelde. Many houses and blocks of flats were hit, and now and again
some old and much-loved building in the center, which felt malicious. A year ago the British had bombed on a Sunday morning, and
hundreds of people in the south area of Lohenfelde had stayed put in
Martin Luther Church, thinking it to be the safest place, and of
course it was hit and everyone killed inside it. A whole line of bombs
had fallen out of the sky and pounded the old church and some
buildings facing it to rubble. It was quite deliberate, everyone decided: They always seem to go for schools and churches and hospitals,

it's against the rules, against even the most ruthless usages of war. But there was surprisingly little anger among the townsfolk, only some shrill screams from certain Party members. The war was too large to feel anger. There was instead a kind of detached, rather cool resentment, dignified by the sense that such barbarism was the enemy's invention, the brainchild of Mr. Churchill. One found one's sentiments reflected in the newspapers, which helped. It made one feel superior to the enemy. One knew that the fight against Bolshevism was the highest moral calling, as once in one's grandparents' time it had been the fight against the French Empire and, long before that, against the wild Magyars. Those bombing—the Americans, the British—were greedy and stupid terrorists; they would be pulled down by their false friends the Bolsheviks and pay the price. The German lands had always been under attack, encircled as they were by stupid, greedy peoples like the Slavs, or by the impossibly proud French, those pseudo-Romans with their sneeringly cultivated airs and graces. How the French pretended to be Romans! Napoleon in his toga, that dark Semitic-looking dwarf! And how each of these aggressors—after they had burned a few German cities to the ground—how they came to grief in the forests! How the deep, dark forests beat them back each time, beat back the legions of marauders as something diseased and alien! How satisfying it was to see them beaten back each time, leaving the forests pure and deep and certain! Of such great solace to the native soul was this infinity of trees, the deeps of their slender trunks, the scented balm of their certainty. And now Germany embraced as one nation her infinity of trees, as a mother her suckling progeny. So young was Germany! And if a church collapsed on its sheltering congregation, this was but a mild birth pang to the young nation! The grazed knee of a virile youth! We must look beyond individual grief and clamor to the greater vision, as a tree dreams of the forest of which it is a minuscule part!

At any rate, Herr Hoffer hated the shelters. Often he stayed upstairs, with chairs and pillows around him in case the windows blew in. Sabine, although frightened of the close, diseased air of the shelters in which each cough might carry death to her children (and there was much coughing during the hours underground), was more frightened of being crushed by her own home, and repaired with the girls to the apartment block's shelter every time. Deep in the stifling, airless darkness of the shelters, which were nothing but reinforced cellars, one felt the superiority of being German dwindle to a hard nub, a survival instinct. Up in his apartment, sitting in his circle of pillows and chairs during an air raid, Herr Hoffer would feel it as a glow about him, something psychic and of enormous power. It was the spirit of art, in which his people excelled, that radiated from him. It was deeply spiritual but beyond religion (which, as one knew, had been fatally infected by Romanism). It was the highest good, sublime and timeless, that flowered in art and that, as a German, he was uniquely favored to appreciate.

Sometimes, surreptitiously lighting a candle, he would sit in his circle of chairs and pillows and read his battered copy of Julius Langbehn's *Rembrandt als Erzieher*, seeing where, as a teenager, he had underlined certain passages and feeling a deliciously mingled regret and pride at his youthful idealism. For instance, he had underlined three times, in now-faded red ink: "Bismarck had provided the externals of unification, but a secret Emperor, a great artist hero, would have to furnish and deepen internal unity."

Once, he knew, he had imagined himself, Heinrich Siegfried Hoffer, as that great artist hero, deepening internal unity in the coming years. He had imagined it at the very moment he had read and underlined that sentence; the thought had coursed through him like an electric current, like something fated! What sensitive, idealistic German youth had not thought this, on reading Julius Langbehn? But they kept it to themselves, this secret hope and desire. When Langbehn's artist hero had materialized in the shape of Adolf Hitler, Herr Hoffer had felt almost cheated. But then, in some mysterious and inevitable chemistry of exchange, the actualized artist hero had become his own projection of desire—his, Herr Hoffer's! The man who stood there exhorting the people with his upraised fists, whose shrill voice filled the radio waves for hours at a time, who looked like a waiter in a seedy café or a backstreet barber or like the Englishman who'd helped execute his own friend, was not a man at all but a manifestation of will, of desire. He was (because Herr Hoffer had imagined him before he was a reality) an externalization of his—Herr Hoffer's—own inner spirit and deep will.

This was how Herr Hoffer and most of his friends and acquaintances greeted the Führer in the early days of real power: with a love that was self-love, or love of the highest and finest part of the self.

Once (well into the Party's rule), he had tried to explain this early naïveté to Herr Acting Director Streicher.

"Ah, yes." Herr Streicher had chuckled, puffing on his eternal pipe. "It reminds me of how easy it is to be on friendly terms with those who are not on friendly terms with you, only you don't know they are not on friendly terms with you."

It was quiet overhead now. It occurred to Herr Hoffer that he hadn't yet mentioned the shattering of the Kluge window. He had not planned to tell them, in fact, as he thought it bad for morale, but following Werner's nasty glittery look over the Dostoyevsky and the long silence, Herr Hoffer felt the need to assert himself.

"By the way," he said, "the Kluge window is smashed."

The others were shocked. In fact, everyone fell silent again after the initial shock. It was a kind of triumph for him.

"Of course," said Werner, "you never liked it, did you?"

That was quite unnecessary, thought Herr Hoffer.

"I was sentimentally fond of it," he replied, rather coldly. "It announced itself as part of the soul of the building."

"The soul of a museum is provided by the people," said Hilde Winkel. Her swollen forelip shone like a wet plum in the candlelight.

"The people?"

"Its visitors. Those beings of flesh and blood," she went on, without looking at him, "who animate a building of brick and stone and give meaning to its contents."

"The soul of a gallery," said Herr Hoffer, marveling at the movement of Hilde Winkel's mouth in the soft flattering light, "is in the contact between the works of sublime art and those appreciating them."

"The contact?"

"The meeting of the artist's mind with the viewer's mind."

"And that's the soul?"

"Yes. The meeting creates a kind of spiritual and mental distur-
bance in the middle," said Herr Hoffer, hardly conscious of what he
was saying. "A kind of chemical reaction in the air."

"What, so it hovers in the air," she said, trying not to smile, "like
green smoke?"

There was a rumble from above, more definite than thunder. They
felt it in their backs on the stone, but no cement bits fell.

Werner Oberst was wiping his tiny half-moon spectacles, his lips
creased as if something sour was in his mouth. Perhaps he is afraid
this time, Herr Hoffer thought, feeling the dampness of his own forehead. If only Werner and Frau Schenkel were not here; if only he
were alone with Hilde Winkel and her timid eyes, nursing her lip.

"Well," he said, with a sigh, "put it another way. I like to think that
the works in our care make some contribution, Fräulein Winkel." He
turned to her gently. There was an edge to his voice he could not
help. The stacked paintings stretched into the darkness on their
crude trestles. Hilde's eyes slid over his for a second and he flushed.
"That it isn't all to be found in the animation of the onlooker. That
there is some essence, some energy, like a residue left by the artist. In
the brushstrokes. In the residual smell of the linseed oil and paint
and varnish—"

"What is your favorite painting in the world, Herr Hoffer?" asked
Frau Schenkel suddenly, as if deliberately cutting off his train of
thought.

Without hesitation, Herr Hoffer nominated Altdorfer's *Landscape
with St. George and the Dragon.*

"I saw it as a small boy in a book of my father's, long before I knew
anything about art," he went on, settling involuntarily into the confi-
dent rhythm of his Tuesday morning lectures. "It was not even in
color in the reproduction, and the contrasts were poor, but I was
swept up into the immensity of the rearing trees in which one can
feel the wind, the wind shaking the leaves in the sunlight, the dark

tangle beyond, the enormity of nature in which St. George and the dragon are mere details. Nobody had ever depicted nature like that."

Werner seemed to demur.

"Altdorfer was the first," Herr Hoffer insisted. "It was in Munich, in the Pinakothek—the real thing, I mean. I went to see it when I was twenty-one. It was much smaller than I'd imagined, and rather dark—the light fell on it badly, and I had to step to one side to avoid the shine—but as I stared at it I was similarly swept up into the sublime: the fullness of nature, the organic completeness of the rearing trees as they reach for the sunlight, ignoring the trivial struggle below." Hilde Winkel was at last staring at him—admiringly, he thought. Her eyes shone in the candlelight. "I was very moved," he added, folding his hands.

Werner replaced his glasses and said, "All we need are books, then."

"Sorry?"

"You were as moved by the reproduction as by the original."

"In my childish way, yes."

Werner nodded, in a knowing manner, his face bent and in shadow. It seemed amazing to Herr Hoffer now that he had worked alongside Werner Oberst for so long: The man was an unknown, suddenly. The years meant nothing. He felt delivered to him on a tray, raw and fresh, like a plump fruit.

"But the original always has its own power, of course, Werner. Do you know what happened to Karl Schwesig?"

"No."

"Arrested by the SA in 1933."

"So? Quite normal."

"Tortured for three days in a cellar. He'd offered his attic studio as a sanctuary for refugees, Jews and so on."

"Jews in the attic," said Werner, lifting his face from the shadows. "How shocking."

"Communists, I suppose," Frau Schenkel proffered, with a sour mouth.

"Not necessarily," said Werner.

"Possibly," said Herr Hoffer. "Anyway, they brought all his pictures from the studio into the cellar and lined them up against the walls, facing the room. Do you know why?"

"To burn them in front of his eyes," said Werner.

"No. Frau Schenkel?"

"I'm not opening my mouth. I always say the wrong thing."

"Fräulein Winkel?"

"What does it matter? He was hiding terrorists. I suppose they put their boots through them one by one. I don't know. It's not my job. Someone has to do the nasty jobs."

She was avoiding his eyes again; that shy nervousness was almost more arousing. If he had to be tortured at all, he would choose Hilde to do it. He would be stretched out, naked, totally in her power. He had, in fact, indulged in such a fantasy several times in the small hours, unable to sleep.

"They didn't touch the paintings," he said. "No. Instead, they just left them there, looking on as he was tortured, stark naked. Tortured in front of them. They humiliated the artist before the eyes of his own paintings. Herr Schwesig told me this himself, in private conversation some years ago. He admired the torturers' perspicacity. Now he can't look at those paintings without feeling shame. In fact, he couldn't paint anymore. So you see, the original has an irreplaceable power, like a living person. He wouldn't have felt humiliated in front of mere reproductions."

"Will the Americans bring food?" Frau Schenkel asked, quite irrelevantly.

No one answered, because no one knew. Herr Hoffer was annoyed with her, as much for mentioning the possibility as for changing the subject. He spent most of the day attempting not to think about food, about eggs and cakes and decent white bread and (above all) a cut of pulpy, bleeding meat. He had been hungry for two years, night and day. Frau Hoffer once made lovely cakes, but it had long been forbidden to do such things. Once his mind turned to food he could think of nothing else until some dry morsel had plugged the gap for an hour or two. He had been plump until the shortages, with a healthy appetite; now his skin hung off him, and his face had a shriveled look. Even Frau Hoffer was positively thin these days, her ribs showing under her breasts, which had retained their sturdiness while everything else had shrunk back. Not quite everything; her arms above the elbows had not lost their fleshiness. It was, Herr Hoffer decided, because they were too short; it was a question of proportions, an illusion. He had discovered this while drawing her in the nude, in their private life class. He had never got the proportions of her arms right, because he was always making up for nature. The distance between her elbows and her shoulders was not in proportion to her forearms. He could not record things simply as they were—the objective play of light and shade, from which volume and feeling grew as if by magic. He always had to be interfering, idealizing, meddling with his intellect. True artists were like children. Schmidt-Rottluff, for instance.

Secretly, Herr Hoffer had a passion for Schmidt-Rottluff's work. Its brightly colored daubings, like van Gogh gone wilder, released something in his soul. It had been more than painful for him to see the one Schmidt-Rottluff owned by the Kaiser Wilhelm Museum removed—and then returned in the Degenerate Exhibition, pilloried as the product of "cultural Bolshevism."

Once, he had noted a broad dribble of yellow in the painting. He had been amazed at how extravagant the dribble was, half hidden behind wild strokes of red and green; Schmidt-Rottluff had stroked the creamy yellow on in a liquid manner and left it to run down along its breadth, as if it were so much soap on a window. The painting showed a child on a bench, with a palm tree beyond, executed in the wild free sweeps and stabs of a loaded brush. It had moved and slightly frightened Herr Hoffer, staring at the painting close up and noting the dribble, the carelessness of it, the uncontrolled and deliberate accident of it, fixed for all time as part of a finished work. It might, he thought, be the beginning of some dissolution, some deep attraction in the human mind towards dissolution.

"They will have chocolate," said Hilde Winkel, leaving her lips open over her large teeth as if receiving not a kiss but the impossible extravagance of chocolate. "The Americans will have chocolate."

They were cast in a spell.

The sentence from Hilde Winkel had cast them in a spell. They could hardly breathe, as if caught in the ice of a fairy tale. Bombs thundered distantly. Nothing shook, yet cement dust drifted past the candle flame in soft white veils. They hardly noticed this, frozen in the spell of Hilde Winkel's sentence.

"They won't give it to us," murmured Werner eventually, as if from a realm beyond, as if from behind a sheet of ice, "unless we give them something they crave in return."

The lake is very deep and cold, and I am at the bottom of it. Someone is tugging on the rope. The rope breaks. Why do we live? To remember. And if we die? What happens to our memories then?

16

Parry ran like hell, in the end.

That's what it always came down to: If you weren't hurt, you either ran like hell or you stayed put. No, that wasn't always true, either. Sometimes you walked and fired and kept on walking, like they said they did in the last war. He'd only done that marching-fire deal once, though, when the whole convoy was ambushed outside Dahl with surprise fire from the thick woods either side. D Company was in the rear. It was like the approach on the highway to this fucking shit hole, only worse. There were these thick black woods around Dahl. SS guys tried to hit them in the back from camouflaged foxholes in the woods, under the dead needles and humus, real close—which got the men mad. They cleared out the woods with marching fire, helped by that kid Henderson's jeep-mounted 50-caliber machine gun.

Henderson was put in for the Silver Star, which turned out a few days later to be posthumous.

Now Parry was running like hell up the street with shit down his leg, his backpack full of glass.

He had to wait a few minutes before the others turned up by the museum ruin and then the seven of them made straight for the company CP in the grocery yard. They came back with some more men from his unit, a Browning Automatic Rifle, and a medic smelling of liquor. Parry had told the platoon sergeant, Sergeant Riddel, that Morrison had got hit while they were checking out the house. He didn't tell the sergeant any more. Morrison might not have been hit if the patrol had stayed together. On the other hand, look at it this way: The Spandau and the young bitch had been waiting for someone, anyone not a Heinie. The whole patrol might have been hit, eight men buckling at the neck, the knees, the ankles, sprawling on the ground.

Sergeant Riddel had been drinking and was not too clear in his head about the sequence of events, and the other officers were busy.

The new fighting patrol—twelve men led by Riddel—took up positions opposite the house, behind rubble, covering the front while Parry and a big guy named Jim Webb crept up from the left side. Parry was real scared as he crawled up, imagining a few sharp bullets doing to him what they had done to Morrison. No doubt the sniper could smell him coming and they were right under the window now and the shutters were still closed. Their paint was flaked. He was close enough to see a big flake of paint move in the breeze, like a leaf in washed-out green. It was solid dusk; each time he blinked it got darker. His skin was wincing all over, expecting itself to be torn up.

Jim Webb had a grenade in his hand. The front door was open.

Parry covered Webb as he crept up to the two steps and waved his helmet on the end of his rifle. Nothing.

Then Parry scuttled up behind as Jim Webb looked into the house.

Nothing.

The dead that was Morrison lay there without moving, that was all. The inner door was closed. There were stairs.

Parry glanced back at the shutters, too busy now for fear, too concentrated in the moment. Any movement there and the BAR the other side of the road would rip the flaky wood apart. He covered Webb as the veteran padded in and stood for a moment by the inner door, listening.

Nothing.

Hell fuck, now it was *his* turn.

He had a grenade in his hand. His mind became pure body, as always in such situations. Webb waited until Parry's body had crossed in front of the door, then kicked the door open as Parry drew the pin out and pitched the grenade in and got their ears to whistle.

Once the smoke had cleared, they could see there was no one— just broken mirrors and some spent cartridge cases on a wide bed. It was a bedroom, not a sitting room.

They debated what to do in whispers, pretty sure there was no one in the house. There were other rooms, but the guy would not have hung around after hitting Morrison. He was holed up somewhere else, waiting, just like any sniper. A fucking cocksucking SS son-of-an-asshole-bitch, smoking a good pipe.

All this was said in whispers, as if they didn't want to wake up their kid sister. Their heartbeats were louder than their whispers, however. The mounted Spandau could be pointing at any of the doors from the dark inside of any of the rooms. It didn't even have to wait for the door to be opened; you'd just get a whiff of pipe tobacco and then kiss heaven. Nevertheless, they would have to do their house-clearance drill, or maybe call up a tank to blast the place to fuck at point-blank range and get their picture in all the illustrated papers.

You wanna bet?

What was that fucking black tape on his rifle for, anyway?

Webb signaled to the others to approach with caution, though they were pretty sure the guy had gone. And so had the girl. Morrison had not gone from the hallway. He had not gone anywhere, not even an inch. His blood had turned dark and dead. The others looked at him; they hardly touched him. The film-star mouth was pulled back and very straight and showing the teeth, its curvy nature having to do with the life behind it making it that way. Two of the men were kids even younger-looking than Cowley, with acne on their cheeks and humid upper lips, their helmets seeming a lot too big. Their eyes darted about with anxiety. The back of Morrison's neck was still corrugated up against the collar and showing its gingery stubble, but now it was something else. It was very white, for a start.

The squad, led by Parry, kicked open door after door in the damaged house and went up the stairs covering one another, but even in the attic there was nobody; they were jittery after the death of Morrison and did an unnecessary amount of firing into empty rooms where long mirrors gave them the impression of human movement until the mirrors burst into a thousand stars.

One of the young boys looked out of a back window. He shouted to them like he'd discovered Tahiti.

They looked down and they saw the body down below, lying star-shaped in a flower bed. It was an old guy, with the Spandau under him: he'd thrown himself out of a top window holding the Spandau. They were surprised to see how old he was, lying there in his silk pajamas and his bloodied white hair. Maybe it wasn't him; maybe this was the owner, thrown out by the mad SS cunt who'd chucked out the machine gun and was now disguised as a priest or a three-star U.S. general, and nobody would notice the difference anyway.

They went down into the garden and Parry felt the pockets. There was a warty pipe and some tobacco and a folder of matches. The tobacco smelled very fine indeed.

"He's the one," he said.

Amazingly, when the young kid gave the body a kick, Parry got angry. You didn't kick old guys, especially dead ones.

Now that they were pretty sure that the empty cartridge cases and the body were all that remained of the sniper, they felt better about things. But they were very angry.

Morrison's death was the result of malice. It was unfair. These snipers, these last-ditch crazies—they were malicious; they weren't playing fair. They were licked and they wouldn't stop. This is what the men kept saying, as they dealt with Morrison.

Parry was confused about this notion of fairness; on the road from Kaiserslautern, approaching a small town with some cloth mills outside it and white flags of surrender flying from the windows, they had killed a woman. That is to say, a woman—young, about twenty-five, twenty-six—had come out of a farmhouse adjoining the road and Parry's vehicle had shot at her and she had fallen. She lay there on the shoulder looking very surprised in death, and the convoy had not stopped. No way could a convoy of some eighty tanks and jeeps and half-tracks and TCVs stop because Parry's gunner had shot up a farm girl. The convoy would only stop if it was attacked or to clear out some petty resistance or if there was a roadblock—and there they certainly were, to quote the great God Georgie, going like shit through a tin horn.

It was clear to Parry that the girl had come out of the farm to watch them pass by, it was simple curiosity, but the gunner had shot her out of her apron and she had lain there very dead and very surprised, her eyes wide open, her scarf crooked on her head, and Jimmy Jones the gunner swearing at her softly as if it were all her fault. Jimmy Jones was younger than the girl, probably. He was jumpy after the previous day, when a German tank had driven out of some trees and killed three men in the convoy and then vanished again. Parry was saying nothing. If people popped up without warning they were bound to be risking their goddamn necks, corps commander or farm girl.

Now, looking at Morrison dead as cold cement in a big dark stain, his eyes just visible under the dark lashes, he thought of the farm girl. He felt responsible for both deaths, in some way he couldn't figure.

He sat on his heels and waited for the stretcher while the other men smoked on the street, guns cocked and eyes nervous, addressing passing civilians in a half-joky, half-jeering way. His throat was too sore to smoke. His breeches and sock weren't too wet anymore and the smell wasn't just his.

Morrison being dead meant no one else knew. About it.

Morrison had kept saying, "Yup, you and I, we're gonna go halves on that old painting, being buddies." They were checking out the rest of the vaults and Morrison said this at least five times, in so many words.

Every time he said it, Parry felt sore at him and didn't answer.

"Yup, we're gonna go two buddy halves on that old picture, man," said Morrison. At least five times. Maybe six. You couldn't be clearer.

Now the guy was a dead. He couldn't make a claim. The only claim he could make was on the feelings of his family back home in rural Wisconsin. And no one in the world would ever say *Yup* just the way Morrison said it, with that chicken peck of his head. Not ever again. It had irritated Parry, every time, the way the guy kept chicken pecking and saying *Yup*, like he'd known all along and whatever.

Now it seemed like a great and inexplicable absence.

When the medic had turned over the corporal's body, Parry saw how the neck had been torn open by the bullets and how the pulled-back mouth was all frothed up at the corner. It looked like a bullet had nicked the cheek too. Those bullets were goddamn sharp. And so fast you heard them sing before you heard the report. Kind of a whipping sound.

Parry had never seen death happen so closely or clearly before, not right in front of him like that.

Many men had died on the advance up to here, but it was always when he wasn't looking. Even that kid Burgin getting his head removed by their own bazooka. Each one happened out of the corner of his eye or in some time that ran parallel to his, about ten seconds ahead; he was always missing it or else it was too far away to matter, it was just someone folding at the neck and knee and ankle and sprawling in the distance. Here, this time, it was in an envelope in his skull, to be opened any time he breathed.

The wallpaper still showed the five-year-old's hill but it had been there the whole school year and looked like it needed taking down. Also, it had dribbled so much it was more like a hill with roots, complicated bristly roots searching down and down, the vermilion turned an Indian red already. My guardian angel is gone, he thought. The hill is an angel's wing, in fact, frayed by the winds of death you have to go through to get anywhere.

The candies were still in Morrison's curled hand, still in their cellophane. Parry took the dead wrist—bone-cold but slippery, its small black hairs slicked down with sweat—and tipped the hard candies out into his own hand and rolled them in his palm, thinking how simple were the needs of men and women, and how there is no taste or sweetness at all for a dead.

And for the soul—well, maybe you don't need candies when you're really home.

He pocketed the candies and sat on his heels by the body.

A few minutes later he heard shouts and a girl with plaits in a stained apron was pulled through the door. Her arms were held by two of the squad—the kids with acne and overlarge helmets. She looked very frightened, thin and frightened. He shook his head. It wasn't the same girl. And if it had been? But it wasn't. The two soldiers looked at the girl as if she'd let them down.

"Wait," said Parry.

They looked hopeful. Parry was hunting for the candies all over his battledress. Damn. He finally found them in his breast pocket where the old labels were and he gave them to the girl. His fingers brushed her live hand and he felt something stop his throat. Maybe his heart. She thrust the candies in her apron pocket and ran out.

If it had been the same bitch, what would he have done? Ripped her living goddamned guts out and used them to grease the treads of a tank, to quote Georgie Patton the general? Or what?

Between dreams and waking, there is one difference: the cold. Asleep, I don't feel the cold. That is the one difference. The difference between life and nonlife. Creation and noncreation. Safety and harm. The cold.

17

Herr Hoffer nodded off for a moment.

(He had been extremely tired for three years, ever since the air raids had started. The sirens sounded almost every night, and you could not help but lie awake and think, Maybe they will bomb us tonight, even though they have not bombed us for months. Until this year the Hoffer family had hardly been down to the shelter, but stayed in their beds right through the warnings. The sirens gave a little cough to begin with, to clear the throat. You imagined a small balding man in a glass office, with earphones and papers, operating some kind of control panel. You waited, and then it began. The sirens would whine up and hold their note for longer than you would think possible and then whine down again, and you would be just dropping off to sleep, very tired, when the sirens would start their hideous slow climb upwards once more. The only consolation was that this might be happening over Great Britain too, keeping the enemy awake in their foggy cities. So how could Herr Hoffer be anything other than tired, utterly tired—like the whole population of Lohenfelde, covered for three years in a miasma of tiredness that made everyone sharp and tense with one another, that overcame you suddenly of an afternoon like a thick cloth thrown over the head and body, in which you struggled to keep awake? How many times had Herr Hoffer nodded off at his desk, his elbow on the glass, his face sinking into his hand, his body staying upright in the chair as his soul sank lower and lower into blessèd oblivion? His dream of after the war was to sleep and to eat, if not simultaneously then one after the other: to lie in a feather bed in a pleasant old hotel by the forest and eat all his meals on a tray, to walk in the forest a little and then return to his bed and his great creamy meals of meat and fish and eggs and refined vegetables, washed down by white beers and fine sweet Rhineland wines, topped by firm cheeses and as many chocolate cakes as he could manage, and then sleep in the fresh, unadulterated quietness for as long as he wished—a whole day and night together, if need be—a whole week! This was Herr Hoffer's dream. Frau Hoffer had a part in it too, but not a central one. Her warm nakedness was not as voluptuously desired as food and sleep. There had been a lull in the shelling and bombing—rather a long one into which he woke with a start, conscious of crying out as he leaped from the hotel window by mistake into a deep gorge and now wondered for a second where he was.)

Nobody seemed to have noticed, though he was sure he had at least snorted through his nose. He blew it, just in case. He felt awful.

"Perhaps they have gone away," said Frau Schenkel, looking upwards.

"Perhaps they were never coming," said Werner Oberst.

They listened to the silence. But then a fear that it might be broken by something tumultuous, shattering, that it was merely a prelude rather than a relief, began to be felt in the smoky air of the vaults.

"Who said they were coming in the first place, in fact?" Herr Hoffer asked, after clearing his throat.

Hilde Winkel said that the SS offices had been evacuated.

"They were burning papers yesterday," she said. "I saw the smoke in the garden."

The SS Sturmbannführer himself had left in a big car in a great hurry, followed by members of his staff in any vehicle they could get hold of, including bicycles and a manure cart. One lowly clerk had been spotted pushing a wheelbarrow full of files.

"There were some soldiers in my neighbor's shop yesterday," said Frau Schenkel. "They weren't in uniform. They told my neighbor's wife that the Americans were coming up the motorway in a very long convoy of tanks. She asked them why they weren't trying to stop them and they laughed, I'm afraid to say. They left without paying. They weren't local."

There was a little silence after this confession of Frau Schenkel's—
it was very like a confession, the way she told it. It was a distasteful
story, somehow.

"There won't be any more bombing," said Herr Hoffer. "We'll get a
good night's sleep."

"There'll be Negroes," said Frau Schenkel, with a shudder.

"You've seen them in films," murmured Werner, from deep in his
book.

"Exactly," she said.

Herr Hoffer knew that Frau Schenkel's chief dread was being
raped by a Negro. She had read the articles in the papers and believed them. Herr Hoffer had no idea how the Americans would be-
have when they arrived, but he was fairly certain that even the most
uncivilized among them would not bother with Frau Schenkel. Her
smell alone—a hint of toilets mingling with damp wool and moth-
balls—physically repelled him. In better days it had been covered by
eau de cologne or decent soap, but now even types like Frau Schenkel
avoided washing too often.

He was feeling uncomfortable after Frau Schenkel's little story, in
fact, but for other reasons. Although their Kompanieführer, a grocer
in his late fifties, had fled a few days ago on his delivery bicycle, the
Volkssturm unit could still theoretically have been in the field. Even
fourteen-year-olds had gone off to die for the Fatherland over the last
few weeks. He did not have the excuse that, say, a factory director
might have had, since the Kaiser Wilhelm Museum not only failed to
produce vital parts for the war effort but was also closed. Its rooms
had been emptied of the last of their remaining works a year ago.

He looked across at the paintings on their crude trestles, the
frames glistening gold in the dim light of the candle. He was not
a pessimist. Even through the most difficult moments, he had felt
fortunate.

As a young student at Heidelberg, in the History of Art faculty
with its little round tower and courtyard nestling at the foot of the
hill upon which the ancient Schloss loomed like a ruined god, he had
dreamed of this life: of having the loveliest masterworks in his

charge, of having the power to acquire sublime treasures, old and new, of nursing them as a mother nurses her children, and of being able to talk about them to the masses, to shopkeepers and clerks and factory workers. Of lifting everybody to the sublime, refined level of the History of Art faculty at Heidelberg.

Never had he been more happy than when strolling through the grounds of the ruined castle with his fellow students! All brothers, they were, in the onward march of art and progress, untouched themselves by the horror of war: too young, just too young for the trenches, and never to be touched in the new, reasonable, golden future!

Herr Hoffer closed his eyes and remembered. How the river had snaked away far below them, silvery in the moss-green of the woods, lapping at the pink and red of the illustrious old town, exactly as in the paintings of a hundred years before—how that view united them with the burning, romantic young minds of a hundred years before! Speechless they stood on the lawn, looking down over the parapet— the great castle, burnt to a blank-eyed hollow by the army of Louis Quatorze (they always said his name in French, hating it and loving it!), beseeching them to take up their lives and make them glorious.

It was so very grand and poignant, the castle of Heidelberg. Half a vast tower lay in the position in which it had fallen to the French cannons, like the collapsed part of a sandcastle made by a bucket, its great fallen bulk covered in grass and ivy. It reflected onto them, these callow young men in their modern jackets and coats and hats, the glamour of history. As they sketched it, they felt drawn into the glamour and vastness of history—yet superior to it too. They would not be caught by it, like their elders—their elder brothers, even, who had wallowed in the trenches. They would never be victims.

Herr Hoffer took to wearing a cape and grew a little pointy beard like an artist at the turn of the century, imagining himself a member of a revolutionary painters' group from before the war—*die Brücke*, for instance—looking like Kirchner himself, or Erich Heckel, or Karl Schmidt-Rottluff with his monocle.

He smiled now, to think of it.

Imagine, he wore a broad-brimmed felt hat! Twenty-odd years ago. Impossible. As bright in his head as if it had happened yesterday. Very bright.

Yet it was not an easy time. Not very romantic. And not quite the Age of Reason, either. Oh, no! By his second year, in 1923, he was having to fork out a thousand million marks for a simple meal or hand over a couple of eggs for a ticket to the theater. The streets of Heidelberg were filled with beggars and coke dealers, and his own bare little room was burgled several times. The government fell, there were no more rules, yet every time a revolution was announced, nothing happened except that somewhere else the workers were shot and food was even scarcer. Friends of his speculated each day with shares and grew immensely rich; Herr Hoffer drank more champagne at that time than at any time since, yet went hungry like other Germans when a party wasn't thrown. And the girls! They were so free with their favors! He would sit in his room, the God-fearing fellow from Eberbach, rather terrified of the licentiousness—even dreading the girls who came along to the parties in their white pancake makeup, stripping to show their surprisingly clean breasts. They could not all have been actresses or cabaret dancers, surely!

And how quickly all those young men's ideals melted into believing in nothing at all except the next speculation, the next stock market tip, the next girl! Yet ideals were all they really had, as they looked out over the plain from the ruined Schloss at eventide, when all was golden below, and quoted Schiller and Benn and Hofmannsthal and believed they were passing through chaos into a fresh era of beauty and refinement.

"A spot of natural housecleaning," they would say. "That's what it is. Without destruction, no creation. Without the blank canvas, stiff with size, no masterwork."

And their young nation was to be a beacon for the whole world!

He smiled inwardly to think of it, yet it also filled him with dread. He had so wanted a pleasant, stimulating life—and it had been given him, it really had, yet with this absurd shadow, this torment of an outer reality to which, nevertheless, he had subscribed as one pats an angry tiger on the head, hoping it will not eat you. He was forty-two now. Forty-two! He had walked as a young man in the untended grounds of the ruined castle with his companions, and, yes, he had dreamed of so much.

He was not a pessimist. He had his wife, his two darling daughters. This beautiful museum.

He should be back at home.

Werner had wound up the gramophone again: Schumann! "Die alten, bösen Lieder," another poem by Heine! The piano thumped its first fierce notes and then—ah, yes, let us bury the old bad songs, the wicked dreams; fetch a big coffin! Werner was softly singing along, but Herr Hoffer thought it prudent not to, catching Frau Schenkel's look; instead, he closed his eyes and returned to Heidelberg and their dreams.

The uncouth rule of the vulgar—the direct consequence of science, technology, and urban industrialization—was unnatural. How far off did science, technology, and urban industrialization seem from the heights of Heidelberg, in the scent of wild spring flowers or the unmown grass under the boughs! Against that evil trinity they set the golden measure of art, whose spirituality was an unspoken mystery, a fragment of the divine, a sacred yearning impulse that conferred dignity on human endeavor and had been almost lost in the lying vulgarity of the modern world.

"I hope they don't have dive-bombers," said Frau Schenkel, from another realm.

"Bless my heart," said Werner. "Right in the middle of Schumann."

Yet revolutionary newness inspired him too; he would even feel the sharp international mockery of the Dadaists as something invigorating, if not altogether healthy. On seeing his first Cubist work for real, one summer—a vast swirl of color by Delaunay in Berlin, in that fashionable gallery in Potsdamer Strasse—he felt really as if he were starting out on the most tremendous adventure! He stood in the glamour of it as he had stood in the glamour of the fallen tower and the hollowed grandeur of the Schloss; it helped that he was in Berlin, of course, and that the gallery hosted dances featuring girls naked from the skirt up. But he was enthralled. There was the death of money. There was the breath of art.

Those were heady years for Herr Hoffer.

And he fell in love, in the end, with a lovely vision in a hat shop: Sabine Tressel, who knew nothing about art but who lifted her hands to her hair and sucked Herr Hoffer's breath away in one gesture.

Werner was mouthing the words now, as they faded in that deliciously ironic and profound manner into the last, sad, delicate notes on the piano.

> Knowest thou why the coffin, then,
> so large and weighty be?
> I lay both my dear love within
> and my hard agony.

Could Werner ever have been in love? Might not some long-buried pain from his youth explain it all, explain his skeletal dryness? Could Werner ever have been young? Even when Herr Hoffer first arrived some fifteen years ago, Werner had looked just the same: pickled, fossilized, dusty. Yet he must only have been in his thirties.

Hilde Winkel was talking as Werner replaced the record in its sleeve, the brown paper spotted with his blood. The lull in the shelling made her wonder if they shouldn't go up and see what was happening.

"Maybe they've arrived from the motorway," said Werner, "and that is why they've stopped."

They took this in.

Herr Hoffer could not really imagine it, except in the silliest toy-like terms. The column of tanks snaking up the clean white motorway, with its square slabs of concrete, between the huge bare fields around Lohenfelde. He knew that their motorways were modeled on park footpaths in America—and now he saw the tanks like a boy's toys on an American footpath, arriving in a model of their town, like the model on display in the Rathaus, and knocking some of the little buildings over.

"Then they will go on and meet our boys marching back from the east with the Russian prisoners," said Frau Schenkel, "and they will have a very bad surprise."

"What will the Russian prisoners do?" asked Werner Oberst, as if it were amusing.

Frau Schenkel glared at him out of the corner of her eye.

"They will cheer," Hilde Winkel suggested. "While we are crushing the capitalist enemy that is also their enemy."

"That's right," said Frau Schenkel.

"The Bolsheviks will cheer," repeated Werner, a touch caustically.

"That's right. You just wait and see."

"Anyway, there won't be any Russian prisoners—cheering or not cheering."

"You mean we will have shot them all?" asked Hilde Winkel, as if surprised.

"There won't be any Russian prisoners," Werner repeated, with a grim smile.

Herr Hoffer knew exactly what he meant. A cousin of Frau Hoffer's had a neighbor who listened to the BBC.

This frail contact was a source of great anxiety to him, in fact. He retained a neutral expression while Frau Schenkel frowned, looking upset.

"They are decent men, our boys on the Eastern Front," she said. "They never shoot prisoners, not even Bolsheviks. Slavs and Jews, maybe, but not Bolsheviks. I should know. I can show you my dear ones' letters. They give black bread to starving Russian children in villages. They've got a Jew as interpreter, even—a Russian Jew. They're certainly not relying on rubbishy lies while sitting very comfortably at home with proper socks."

She talked about her son and husband as if they still lived.

"I for one am not very comfortable," murmured Werner, shifting on his cushion. "And my socks need darning."

"Well, don't ask me to do them," said Frau Schenkel.

Hilde Winkel and Herr Hoffer were smiling. The mutual antagonism of Frau Schenkel and Werner Oberst could be quite amusing at times.

A distant detonation. Then silence again. Perhaps the Americans couldn't be bothered with Lohenfelde and had passed it by. It was almost an insult, if so.

Werner put his book down and closed his eyes.

I'll bet he's got a headache, thought Herr Hoffer. It's too flickery and dark to read. This could be a dungeon, a dungeon for the deranged.

Watch out for that word *deranged*. It has very nasty associations.

Sitting in the vaults seven years later, Herr Hoffer remembered the opening as if it had happened last week. The Party official had not quite frothed at the mouth as the Führer had done when opening the exhibition in Munich, but he had very much adopted the same line.

"Ladies and gentlemen," he had said, leaning towards the microphone at one end of the museum lobby, "these works on display show natural forms horribly distorted, the sky as yellow rather than blue, and the world of dreams and hallucinations as more real than reality. Medical science would say that the creators of these works are suffering from a mental derangement. But the veil has been drawn over our eyes by so-called experts in the pay of Jewish capitalists. Soon, we may all be suffering from mental derangement if we do not speak the honest truth and say, Enough!"

Everyone had clapped. Herr Hoffer had fiddled with his spectacles, head lowered.

"And now," the official had continued, in his strong Bavarian accent, "I must say *enough* to myself, or there won't be time to let you see for yourselves what rubbish has been foisted upon us all these years, contaminating our Germanness! Herr Hoffer?"

There was laughter at the little joke. Everyone felt very clever and rational and good-humored.

How stifling the cramped lobby had felt to Herr Hoffer, the fur collars and heavy coats giving off a pungency of stale scent and nicotine and sweatiness! He could smell it even now, seven years later.

Then it was his turn. It was one of the most difficult moments of his life. He thanked all those present and hoped the thousands of anticipated visitors to the exhibition would learn something about "the central importance of art as something to be taken seriously." A sea of faces: important faces. A couple of coughs. A sneeze. His collar was soaking wet. "That these visitors might understand art's great value as a force representative of the highest good, sublime and timeless. As containing profound healing properties that might furnish and deepen internal unity, rather than demolish it."

These ambiguous abstractions, mostly borrowed from a few pages of Julius Langbehn, cascaded harmlessly over the illustrious gleaming heads and met with a polite round of applause.

The Party official had looked at him afterwards with suspicion.

"You did not once mention the word *degenerate*," he said. "It was almost as if you were standing outside our collective indignation and smirking. Like a Jew. I do hope that is not the case."

"Oh, I think they knew what the exhibition is called," said Herr Hoffer. It was fortunate, perhaps, that the official was short and fat and balding. "No one could have missed it, my dear sir, coming in."

The official curled his lip and Herr Hoffer had gone on to say, with a caustic smirk quite alien to the muscles of his face, how the city's burghers liked nothing better than to be titillated now and again by spiritually uplifting sentiments. This made the official feel superior. Herr Hoffer rounded it off by offering him a thin expensive cigar.

The worst moment of the whole sorry episode came when the museum's own humiliated pictures were once again carried out of their natural home, like a robber's swag, on their way to Halle. That time it truly felt like theft. Herr Hoffer, out of sight of the janitor, cried real tears after Degenerate Art had departed in two dirty furniture vans, leaving only the words *Entartete Kunst* and *Eintritt frei* in great swooping letters of red-painted wood. A large banner had been draped along the wall facing Count von Moltke Strasse, showing a booted swastika crushing some Semitic-looking artists: This was the work of the local paper's cartoonist. It flapped and snapped there for a few weeks until repeated letters to the local Propagandaministerium official got it taken down.

Of course, everyone congratulated Herr Hoffer on the triumphant success of the exhibition. And then he had a migraine that lasted ten days.

Werner opened his eyes and asked Herr Hoffer what he was thinking about.

"Nothing much. My family, mostly," he fibbed. "And a soft bed."

"I am thinking of Irminfrid," said Werner.

"Who's she?" asked Frau Schenkel.

"The great king of the Germanic Thuringians," Werner sighed. "Defeated by the Franks at Burgscheidungen in 531. Thereupon the kingdom was ruled by Frankish dukes, as we will be ruled by the Americans. You see, nothing is new in history if one takes the trouble to delve. And we all come through, somehow. Again and again."

"I was thinking of coffee, I'm afraid," said Frau Schenkel. "Sorry to be nonintellectual."

"Well," said Herr Hoffer, "as Kurt Schwitters himself remarked, in times of acute shortage, one's heart hops from sugar to coffee."

"Schwitters is working in a lacquer factory in Wuppertal these days," said Hilde Winkel, with a satisfied smile.

"That's Oscar Schlemmer," said Herr Hoffer. "Schwitters is in exile in Norway."

"Even better. It's cold up there."

"We had one of his piles of rubbish," said Frau Schenkel, "and Frau Blumen chucked it out."

"Not quite, Frau Schenkel," said Herr Hoffer, lifting his finger like a teacher, nettled by the comments. "We had one of his assemblages, *Small Cathedral*. Clearly related to his *Cathedral of Erotic Misery*. It consisted of a lock, three pieces of driftwood, a shred of cloth, and a metal grill. It illustrated the artist's belief that life is an aesthetic phenomenon and that art and life are one glorious fusion. Frau Blumen simply objected to having to spend ten minutes dusting 'something

off a rubbish heap.' Her words, not mine. We gave her a little extra
each week, a new feather duster, and the work was spotless. Did you
know I went to see Schwitters's huge *Merz* sculpture in Hannover?"

Nobody looked impressed.

"It had little grottoes to his friends, and in them he had placed mementos of them, things found in their homes. Moholy-Nagy's was a
sock, a pencil, and, as far as I remember, a cigarette stub. One grotto
had a guinea pig running about in it. I was very jealous of Hannover.
The Degenerate thickies took ours and no doubt stamped on it with
their big black boots."

He was enjoying the illicitness, the attention: Hilde seemed to
tingle beside him, very cross. He had never been so frank.

"Whatever, we're best shot of them," said Frau Schenkel. "It wasn't
what I call art. He can stay in Sweden, as far as I'm concerned."

"Norway," corrected Herr Hoffer.

"He can stay wherever, as long as it's not Germany."

She studied her nails, which had not been varnished for a few
weeks; varnish was kept back for the Luftwaffe.

"At the bottom of a fjord, preferably," she added.

"Tell that to the Americans," murmured Werner.

Hilde Winkel snorted. "You think they care about a clown like
Schwitters? Or any kind of proper art? All they care about is blowing
our cities to bits—and their chewing gum!"

Blood beaded around the lint on her swollen top lip.

"The fusion, my dear Fräulein Winkel, of life and art." Werner
smiled.

"Do be careful of your lip," said Herr Hoffer.

"They'd only care about the so-called fusion of life and art if it
made them money!" Hilde snapped, not even wincing. "Just like the
British! And what are we *doing* about it now?"

She glared at each of them in turn, but again at their chins, as
if there were something interesting crawling there. Her nostrils
were flared and her jaw stuck out. Despite her top lip, Herr Hoffer
thought she was a little like the fearsomely lovely Brigitte Helm from

his youth. He hoped she wouldn't be this angry within earshot of the Americans.

"We are staying alive, Fräulein Winkel," he said softly. "There is no point in doing anything else, right now."

She shook her head, as if in despair, and caught a drop of blood on her hand.

Herr Hoffer consulted his watch. It was not yet half past eight in the morning. It felt as if they had been there for hours.

The shelling resumed, but farther off now, just a distant grumble.

Werner put on another record: an ancient jazz number that Herr Acting Director Streicher would play very often in his office, purely in defiance of the Party. Now it was in defiance of Hilde, who shook her head again, in disgust this time. The music jigged about madly for a minute and then hit a terrible scratch that sounded like a train failing to get going. Werner moved the needle on, but the scratch continued to the paper label.

"What a pity," said Herr Hoffer.

"Danced to that, in my youth," said Frau Schenkel, pouting her lips around her cigarette and touching up her severe gray hair.

Werner slipped the record back into its sleeve and closed his eyes. The silence was more noticeable after the raucous jazz. Herr Hoffer's thoughts went from sugar to coffee and back again. The minutes dragged. He tried to imagine Frau Schenkel as a young woman, dancing to jazz. The cathedral of erotic misery!

His stomach made noises like a creaking door. He shifted and coughed, touching Hilde's shoulder with his. She moved hers away slightly, until they no longer touched.

"Maybe we've beaten them back," said Frau Schenkel.

Hilde Winkel laughed caustically, then winced. She held a hand over her mouth. "I think I need stitches," she said. "I hope the Americans will treat me, at least."

"They'll treat you, all right," muttered Werner, without opening his eyes.

No one said anything, because no one really knew one way or the other.

Why do they look after me? If they are caught, they will be shot.
When I hear one come up the ladder with my food and water, I
am never sure. Only when I hear the three knocks followed by
a silence followed by a fourth do I know it is one of them.
Sometimes they don't come for days. Then I believe I am dead,
and that being alive is a dream. Except that when you are dead,
you do not think all the time of sugar and coffee.

18

The stretcher guys took Morrison away and the fighting patrol did
their house-clearing drill up the whole wide street, and then Parry
gave his report. It was not hard, lying. The others stayed in the billet,
drinking and smoking and playing cards. They'd lost their taste for
girls now. They weren't about to blame the patrol leader, they were
too callow, but Parry did not want to be around. He had a new E-Z-
Flow double-edged razor and a fresh fat tube of Barbasol and he took
his time, pressing his chin and his cheeks with his fingers and then
shaving some more just for the hell of it. He had a fresh towel
wrapped around his middle after his bucket shower and he wouldn't
have minded a girl's hand down there just then; he didn't need to be
in bed. Her skin would also smell of pine from the soap and her thick
hair, too. He was issued a clean pair of German underpants and socks
and an absent buddy's green trousers from the stores. Its pocket flaps
were frayed. They smelled of laundry. He didn't know the buddy. The
pockets were empty.

"This man is something else now," he said, almost a question.

"Yeah, he's maybe undergoing treatment in Honolulu," said Riddel. "Try not to muss them. He may want them back."

Parry spooned down a little hot chow and swigged some soda, and
then he hunted around for a battery for his flashlight. He had a problem finding one however—one that worked. Almost everyone who
might have helped him was drunk. He felt good, though. He didn't
need to be drunk to feel good, and his face was smooth and glowed

and the back of his hand smelled of pine. He had not had a new pair of pants in seven months.

He went over to where Morrison's body had been taken and took the flashlight out of the bootstrap. No one had yet taken Morrison's boots off. Deads weren't a priority. Morrison was lying in a room with about ten other guys under what looked like old curtains, and there was his dog tag to show which one he was because they were a row of covered strangers, but Parry was only interested in the boot with the flashlight tucked in. The light worked.

The strange thing is they were all strangers to themselves now.

He thanked Morrison and made the sign of the cross over his chest in case the chaplain wasn't around; then a wave of sorrow came over him and he let the tears drip onto his hands. Soldiers spent so much time sobbing, he thought, that there wasn't too much time left to fight.

He blew his nose and hurried away without lifting the old curtain's shroud and taking a last look at his guardian angel's face, knowing it wouldn't be the same and that the new dead one would replace the old live one in his memory.

He slowed down, calming himself, feeling hollowed out but not too sad now. He had kept his rifle on him. The town was secured to the last-but-one laundry basket, as Sergeant Riddel put it, but in that basket is a Waffen-SS colonel with a Spandau and in the very last basket is a bomb.

Also, he had his plan.

It was dark by now. There was a light mist of dust and smoke that thickened into floating ripples here and there, like fog in a vampire movie. It made things easier on the eye. Chickens were bubbling over campfires that were blurred and beautiful in the mist. Artillery shells were still falling, but no one knew where from and no one cared. Wires hissed and sparked, and now and again something small exploded, as if waiting for the right moment. Small fires burned away at the tops of ruined apartment blocks, like beacons to immortality on Grecian temples. He had done a picture of a Grecian temple and its blazing beacon to immortality for Texaco, and the colors got printed all wrong and it looked sullen. There were sweet whiffs of brandy and beer through the dust and smoke and stink of rubber; his tongue had gotten furred with this unclean air. Bigger fires still glowed, especially from the wrecked thermometer factory.

He was told to go take a look at the thermometer factory. It was almost on his way. The mercury tanks had been torn by a shell and splashes of mercury were skidding in their weird rolling way over the yard, quicksilver reddening in the twilight, poisonous and lovely, welling up against corpses and slipping around them and then breaking apart again into quivering silvery constellations and splashes of tiny beads that met up and merged and grew bigger. It left no stain on the ground, like blood or water or gasoline did; it didn't seem to touch the ground at all. No one wanted to put a finger in it, or even a toe. They threw bricks at it instead to make it shatter and move.

The girls in town were friendly, he'd heard; they kept saying they hated the Russians but not the Brits and the Yankees—they especially loved the Yankees. Some were angry that the mayor or whoever had not put out a white flag despite the SS guys; others were proud. They were so hungry, but then so were the soldiers hungry: most of the supply trucks had not kept up with their advance, which was why they were sticking around for a couple of days. This was what he had picked up from Lieutenant Howard, who had ulcers from worrying about things. The only crates in the canteen were breakfast rations: dehydrated T-juice cocktail and whole-wheat cereal and canned bacon. The hot chow had been canned bacon floating in some dehydrated bean soup that hadn't wholly liquefied. There were, however, plenty of cigarettes. If the cigarettes ever ran out, the whole goddamn Third Army would give up.

He lit a Chesterfield and picked his way through rubble and over deads looking immortal for a day. They looked as if they had just started but you had to remember they had also just finished. Dazed old men with suitcases and bundles didn't even notice him. They were sadder than anybody because the blood on their hands was their own past; it was all they had. Mothers with silent kids were not finding it easy to push their piled-up baby carriages. Men from other companies were celebrating victory over yet another strategic point, their hearts still beating. They were laughing and shouting and whistling in the ruins. Some guys had cut the head off a chicken and were watching the body run up and down like a windup toy.

Morrison was missing all this, he thought. He'd never know it again. It was as irrelevant to him now as any goddamn thing was, including the Milky Way.

The picture of the moment of Morrison's death kept coming up in Parry's mind, as if he were at the movies only it was dark, and then all of a sudden a couple of seconds of the movie was shown but no more.

He needed to make jokes and hear them. Good jokes.

The back of the stubbled neck, the spinning around, the gills in the neck, the weird little puppy whimpers. Then darkness. Darkness in his mind.

Parry badly wanted to live, but so had Morrison wanted to live. A square-headed patriot from rural Wisconsin with a curvy girl's mouth who moved his head forward and back like a chicken as he said *Yup*.

No one else did that; it was unique.

And the family would not yet know.

Morrison Senior was a leather worker, worked hides in a stinking concrete shed. That's what Morrison had told him, several times. And he always won at pinochle.

Parry passed a broken-up shop; there was kitchen stuff, whisks and graters and pans and a whole cooker, in the rubble blown out over the road. It amazed him that such shops still functioned at the end of time. A few hollowed-out civilians were picking at the mess, filling their pockets, cutting their fingers on the broken window glass. Heaps of bricks and old beams, smoking. They had really dumped a lot of ordnance here. They had bombed the rubble, probably. He wondered why burnt buildings always smelled so thick and sour. And the stubbornness of radiators.

He walked on towards the wreckage of the museum a few big streets to the east, looking innocent. He was an artist. He was the only artist around here, he felt. One day he would certainly quit doing advertising copy and aim for the purity of true artistic inspiration. He saw himself in a big airy studio filled with a crisp northern light, but he still could not picture the kinds of paintings he would create. Did that matter? He never had that kind of problem with advertising copy—with peanuts and chocolate cookies and chewing gum and automobiles. It came to him whole and complete, the image, even when there was very little instruction from on high, from the firm itself or his boss. His lines were always clear and neat, and he was exceptionally good at faces.

Some said he was a little like Grant Wood.

There were gleams of sweat on his corn gatherers and dusky coffee pickers. It was a blend of social realism and something dreamlike and easy, like a childhood memory. If it hadn't been for the war, he would now be in New York, almost certainly, with one of the top firms. It helped so much to have money. He had no money. He couldn't seem to hang on to what little he made in his job. All he needed was a good sum as a kind of starting fund. This was why he was heading back to the vaults. It was for art's sake he was doing this. He didn't need to try to look innocent; he felt it. He felt OK, doing what he was about to do, although he also felt self-conscious about being alone and made sure he looked like he was a soldier with a strict military objective, heading someplace.

A lot of streets, even the wider ones, were neck high in rubble, as if a river of brick had flowed down them and settled up to the middle of the ground-floor windows; no path had yet been cleared by the prisoners, and only a very few people ventured on them.

They were streets of death, he thought; that's how you walked to the other world, over a sea of loose bricks and lumps of masonry, stumbling, taking a helluva long time.

A lone tank ground its way up and over the debris and passed him in a choking cloud of plaster dust where a group of civilians stood at the base of a tall ladder. At the top of the ladder was a man attaching a rope around a giant Nazi eagle bolted to the building. He wanted to stay, to watch the Nazi eagle get pulled down so it would remain as a mental sign for him in the chaos, a sign of the end of evil, but it was getting dark and the guy was having problems knotting the rope and dust was hanging in the air.

Anyway, the end of evil will only come with the end of the profit by it. No way will it come tomorrow, or the day after.

Apart from small-arms fire and some sporadic artillery, there were machine guns going off somewhere, in short bursts. The Brits called them chatterboxes, and that was the right word; they talked too much and too easily. These sounded like big Browning MMGs, the ones with a four-thousand-yard range, maybe clearing some trouble on the outskirts. He hoped there wasn't too much trouble.

Maybe they had found another guy with a Spandau in some upper window and that noise was a tank spraying fire at him until he danced and screamed and fell forward like a puppet.

He flashed his light in the dark pockets of the rubble as he passed it. There was a blanket hanging off a smashed wall next to a broken bed with a doll beside it, the type whose eyes open when you stand it up. Sometimes dolls were booby traps so he didn't touch it and it reminded him of a dead kid he'd seen. He rolled the blanket up and carried it on his shoulder.

He had this idea he'd need something soft to sit on, waiting.

When he saw the exposed gable end and its surviving wall with the typewriter in the window and the hatch of skylight at the top and the tiny Virgin hanging on in there and the hillock of rubble with the desk halfway up, he felt an excitement such as he had never known before.

It was almost a sexual excitement, and he had to force himself to look calm, to wait again like a guard with his gun across his knees until the coast was clear.

It took some time.

There were a lot more people around now, as if they'd suddenly emerged from hiding, and they came towards and past him like a dream of being somewhere abroad and strange: civilians with suitcases like they were tourists or wheeling bicycles loaded with linen or pushing handcarts spilling over with china and deck chairs and mattresses. Nobody acknowledged Parry, which made it even more like a dream. He saw a hand in the rubble, a girl's hand, and kicked away at the stones and stuff until he saw a white breast and shoulder and realized it was a statue, a marble nude without a head, maybe the one the boys had pretended to screw. But it had found itself under rubble again, as if it had sunk in under its own weight. Maybe it was old and Grecian. It had sharp nipples, exaggerated. Maureen's were not like that.

This is not the season for cardigans.

He sat on his heels a little way up the rubble hillock again and wondered where life went to. He somehow thought it was tougher being dispossessed than being bombed out. He couldn't imagine, back home, having his door kicked down by strangers, the rooms looted, his family told to go. It must have happened in the Civil War, along with massacres. For that matter, he couldn't imagine Clarksburg being bombed.

Clarksburg had a small museum with some Indian flints and mementos of the early settlers and a room dedicated to Stonewall Jackson, with his uniform in a glass case and his stuffed war horse. Imagine that museum turned to rubble.

When he was in England a year back, training for the invasion, an RAF guy told him the slang term for hitting museums, schools, hospitals, and any other soft civilian stuff.

Sex-appeal bombing.

That was British humor, he guessed, you had to say it in that weird British accent to make it funny. *I say, old chap, let's do some sex-appeal bombing, don't you know. Bloody good show, what?* But the Brits had done as much as the Americans or the Canadians or anybody else on D-Day and lost fewer men; for all their weird accents and behavior, they were pretty good at fighting.

A group of GIs passed below him with linked arms, helmets askew, like a dance routine. He did not know them. They were singing "Good for Nothin' Joe."

The burnt bodies farther down, around the dead horse, hadn't been cleared; he could see them as rocks in the gathering darkness. Stones in a river.

He kept quiet.

He fingered the labels in his breast pocket. *Waldesraus*. And the other one that said *mit Kanal*.

Do people who don't speak English picture the same life? If you know what I mean.

He got up slowly and slipped down into the vaults. (He'd waited until there was a gap in the passersby, so no one saw.)

Something big scuttled away from the bodies down there as he lowered himself in. Maybe the rats were hungry too. He switched on Morrison's flashlight and avoided doing more than glancing at the four cadavers with their purple agonized faces, almost like Negro faces, lined up on either side next to the wreckage of the artworks. Deads don't have themselves any fun.

He'd been nervous about not finding the snowy mountains and golden valley in the slit that was maybe a niche for a rushlight, but the painting was still there. The four guardian angels had protected it. He smiled to himself as he took the salvage out of the niche. He loved this painting more and more. Mr. Christian Vollerdt. You and I.

He stood the flashlight upright in the niche and studied the painting again. The late-evening light flooded the valley beyond the silver birch trees, beyond the pool and the high rock: amazing, how the painting was the judge of its own light.

There was a dog; he hadn't noticed the dog before.

The tiny shepherd still leaned on his stick and the sheep were bunched up around him. The light's beam fell on the label and he savored it again. Something, maybe John, *John Christian Vollerdt (1708–1769), Landschaft mit Ruinen*. Landscape with Ruin. Or maybe Ruins. He hadn't worked that out with Morrison around; alone, he felt more intelligent.

Vollerdt must be famous. He wished he knew how to say the name as it really was; his way rhymed with *dirt*. At any rate, it was a beautiful painting. That high rock wasn't a rock, it was the side of a ruin, maybe a big church or a castle, with the broken columns in the foreground also a part of some big joint.

Good for nothin' Joe, huh?

The splendor of the snowy mountains, like the timbered back-country of home where the trout flash in the shallows and all that crap he had to illustrate. The peaks are catching the last of the sun beyond the golden valley. Like ice in the bucket at Pompeii or whatever, this thing had somehow survived the conflagration. He felt almost religious about this picture. It was blessed. It had tiny hairline cracks in it, like the joins of a jigsaw. Maybe in one corner there was some blistering. Or maybe it was age.

He was touching the painting softly with his finger and feeling the faint corrugations of the varnished brushstrokes when he heard a noise.

He heard this scuffling noise and he grabbed the light clumsily from the niche and the beam caught a movement in the head of the guy who was not Himmler.

We're all here for the night, man.

The guy with the round spectacles and the yawn. He was shaking his head.

He was staring at Parry with his blind spectacles and shaking his head.

Keep quiet and hope the demons don't notice you. I didn't look back, but I'm still [in] hell.

19

The bombardment could no longer be confused with Herr Hoffer's stomach. The walls now shivered against their spines. The candle flame was surrounded by a misty aureole that was not smoke but dust, and the air definitely smelled of a bitterness that even Frau Schenkel's dirty cigarettes could not be manufacturing.

Herr Hoffer closed his eyes, keeping his mind very still. He was trying not to feel nauseated. He had not had a migraine for six weeks.

He would lie in his bed with a sock over each eye. Buried in complete darkness, like his secret. It was all he could bear. Light was torture. Poor Sabine would have to whisper comforting words, empty the pail of his vomit, and keep the children quiet. The attacks usually came when he relaxed after severe tension, but the last one, in February, was the result of shock.

Dresden.

He must not think of Dresden. There—he felt worse now. A sort of disbelief that winded him. He undid his top button.

"Are you all right, Herr Hoffer?"

"Very well, thank you, Frau Schenkel. Just the air."

When he'd heard the news about his favorite city, he had immediately wanted their air boys to pulverize Oxford. He had spent a week in Oxford in 1928, examining its treasures (particularly the Ashmolean's Claude Lorraine). He had punted on the Isis under the willows and taken tea in Iffley. Completely smitten, he'd been. He had visited Bath, too, and marveled. When, earlier in the war, he had heard about the air raid on Bath and the destruction of the Assembly Rooms, he had cried. On hearing the news about Dresden, he had wanted Bath to be smashed again and Oxford, his beloved Oxford, to be completely flattened.

Then he felt like killing himself, but the migraine had taken over.

Sabine was a little impatient with him, but he could not move from the darkness of the bedroom for three days, not even to end his life.

He must not think of Dresden.

Being down in the vaults during an air raid horribly resembled a migraine attack anyway. He had suffered a bad one early in the war, during a heat wave, after a phone call from the SS Standartenführer in Berlin accusing him of defeatism. This was because he had suggested, in a letter to the SS Sturmbannführer, the return of *Mademoiselle de Guilleroy au Bain* to the safety of the museum's shelter.

Sabine had not been altogether sympathetic. In fact, she had suggested yet again that he do as everyone who was anyone in Lohenfelde had long done and join the FRIENDS OF THE REICHSFÜHRER SS.

"It doesn't cost a thing," she had pointed out. "One mark a year. All further contributions are voluntary."

"No," he had replied. "No no no no."

"In fact," his dearest love went on, completely naked, combing her long fair locks in front of the mirror, "the best thing you could do for me and the children is to join the organization itself."

"What do you mean?"

"Become a Schutzstaffel officer."

"I'd rather become a pig."

"Oh, thank you, Heinrich, for being so thoughtful about your family."

Her bare buttocks squirmed on the embroidered stool.

"I don't want silly aluminum badges stuck all over my chest," he said feebly.

"It's ever so classy and fashionable," she insisted.

"I hate class and despise fashion," he said.

It was turning into an argument. She finished combing her hair and slipped into bed beside him.

"The uniform is very sexy," she said. "Especially the black belt and black jackboots."

"I would look ridiculous."

She stroked his midriff as he lay there in his damp nightshirt, her breasts taut and glistening. He touched them, and they were surprisingly cool.

"I was thinking of wearing them myself," she said, "and nothing else, Heinrich my cherry."

She was most amused by the abrupt and surprising reaction of her favorite little man to this information. How straight the little chap stood to attention, in his shiny red helmet—as if Herr Minister Himmler himself were inspecting! The little chap surely deserved a kiss! There, there and there! . . .

"Herr Hoffer, would you like me to open the door?"

"No, thank you, Frau Schenkel, I'm quite all right. Really."

He shifted on his cushion and sighed. The best way to escape fear was to think of sex; it was well known. He tried to make his face look priestly and profound and kept his eyes closed. The dust was getting up his nose, stinging it slightly. Lime dust, perhaps. Just the beginning.

Actually, the mere sight of an SS uniform curdled his stomach. The purge of the modern works back in '36 was all done by SS henchmen, ordered about by the horrible Ziegler and the madman Willrich, with Herr Hoffer—having been asked by Herr Streicher to do so—wretchedly accompanying them through the galleries. Fortunately, the Degenerate Confiscation Committee did not have an independent inventory and did not notice the missing works (those already secreted in the vaults). It was all done in such a hurry, for there were hundreds of collections to disembowel all over the Reich.

"The worst day of my life," he had said to Sabine, afterwards. "I should have done something."

"And get yourself arrested, Heinrich? Don't be foolish. They are only paintings, my pumpkin."

The trouble was, the museum was supported by local businesses and company branches whose managers and chairmen were certainly members of the Friends of the Reichsführer SS: the Deutsche Bank, I. G. Farben, Robert Bosch, Kreipe Thermometer, Siemens-Schuckert, Lohenfelde Druckerei—the list was very long. Their contributions, as part of their civic responsibilities, were vital to the museum; the superb van Gogh, for instance, would not have been acquired in 1923 without their help, even at its bargain price (Vincent was not yet quite a legend in 1923).

"The SS is all things to all men," Herr Streicher had said, scowling. "Like Christianity."

Then the Degenerate Committee had swept through and torn a great hole in the modernist collection, and the elegant black uniform became suddenly hateful to Herr Hoffer.

In fact, that terrible day back in '36 left him with a great desire for revenge. One day he would combust, he reckoned, if his fury and his guilt had no outlet in action. As action was impossible, he would fantasize. His favorite invention was the "Degenerates Exhibition": groups of bedraggled men and women tied up in bundles, with

SS Degenerate written clumsily on placards hung about their necks. This exhibition would be continually extended by order of the Director! He was sure the Americans would allow this. Perhaps not the British. How had Treitschke described an Englishman? He'd learned it at school: "The hypocrite who, with a Bible in one hand and an opium pipe in the other, scatters over the universe the benefits of civilization."

But who would come to mock and jeer, apart from the Jews? The tens of thousands who mocked and jeered at the modern paintings just a few years before?

It frightened him, thinking this.

And what about the hundreds of thousands of decent citizens who were just SS office employees or honorary members? There would be no room for them in the museum, with placards around their necks. He would have to use the third floor and the attics, and still it would be crowded compared to the handful of visitors. And then the Americans would go home, leaving him stranded.

But it was only a fantasy, to stop him bursting.

Werner had lit a cigarette and handed the pack to Hilde Winkel. Like Frau Schenkel and Herr Wolmer, he had hoarded cigarettes in a drawer for two years. Herr Hoffer took one too. The vaults filled with the delicious scent of quite decent tobacco.

Frau Schenkel said, out of the blue, that she had locked up all her valuables and objects of sentimental value in a cupboard in her apartment and the key was in her pocket. She said this with a cool official air, as if she were entrusting them with something.

They all nodded, enjoying their cigarettes too much to speak. Herr Hoffer did not smoke very often—Sabine did not approve—but he was savoring every mouthful, drawing it deeper into his lungs than ever before. It allowed one to think.

Of course Werner did not despise him. How ridiculous one's thoughts got in these situations! Better to dream of Sabine naked.

A sudden stab—of jealousy—made him all but cough.

Bendel.

Bendel had only smoked Turkish cigarettes, herbal concoctions.

He actually thought, like the Führer, that ordinary tobacco was bad for you!

Bendel *certainly* looked good in black, according to Sabine.

"Maybe. But the wrapping is not the goods."

"It helps" had been her reply.

Ah! Herr Hoffer wanted to cry. He squeezed his eyes tight and kept himself from moaning. He must not think of Bendel. Or Dresden. Or sex. Or plump pork chops. Or the Degenerate Committee. Picking wildflowers in a meadow with his mother, the scents of the forest all around; that's more like it. Bendel could go to hell. He, Herr Hoffer, would stay with heaven. Searching for wildflowers near Bad Wildungen, the sun warm on the meadow grass and the hills brimming with firs, butterflies, his mother laughing in her bright dress. . . .

The trouble with Bendel was that he took you in with his charm.

Herr Acting Director Streicher, who kept his ear very close to the ground, was the only one not taken in by SS Sturmführer Klaus Bendel.

Mind you, Herr Streicher was already a nervous man when Bendel first popped up. When was that, '35? The screws were already tightening. Dismissal (or worse) was normal in the art world. Dismissal never came for Herr Acting Director Streicher. But the expectation of it screwed his nerves up like violin gut.

"It's the Bismarck method," he would joke. "Keep all Europe in a state of nervous apprehension by hinting at war. They hope to wear me down."

"You mean the Führer method."

"Oh, he just inherited the mantle."

It might have been easier for Herr Streicher if he had been dismissed—like his predecessor. But Herr Director Kirschenbaum was a Jew. And he had, through his contacts with other wealthy Jews, falsely increased the value of certain mediocre artists to the benefit of his personal collection—or so it was claimed in the local gazette (reprinted in the prestigious *Deutsche Kulturwacht*). That was enough to get old Kirschenbaum off his seat. Don't believe a word of it!

Scholars and curators fell like ninepins—Justi, Schardt, the lot—but Herr Acting Director Streicher kept upright, despite his support for "long-haired swindlers" and "lunatic sensationalists."

"Perhaps," he said one winter's day, lighting the office fire with a copy of the Nazi paper *Der Volkische Beobachter*, "it is because they have never officially appointed me as Kirschenbaum's successor, Heinrich. I fit into no category. I am invisible."

Herr Hoffer thought that very unlikely.

Sitting in the vaults and relishing his cigarette, he remembered his first proper encounter with Bendel. Herr Streicher had encouraged it. It must have been early '36, just before the purge of the modernist collection. There was snow. Herr Streicher had called Herr Hoffer into the office and started off almost in a whisper, since it was well known that Frau Schenkel in the room next door had very good ears and was married to a train driver—a man of no great importance except that he was a Party member of long date, had attended its training institute at Sonthofen, and subsequently organized "Saxon" forest camps for boys where he taught them how to grind corn and throw spears and build huts out of branches and bracken.

The Acting Director asked that the Assistant Director make the SS officer's acquaintance.

"His name is Klaus Bendel. A lieutenant, but only a pen pusher. He has signed the visitors' book twenty times in one month," said Herr Streicher, under his breath.

"Twenty times! Goodness me. I didn't think it was that many."

"Ever talked to him?"

"No. Not more than a polite greeting."

"Very wise. I want you to talk to him. Unusual taste for an SS man. Spends a great deal of time in front of the van Gogh."

"Hardly surprising. The jewel of our collection."

Herr Streicher frowned. For him, it was the small Poussin figure study.

"The jewel of our nineteenth-century crown, then," Herr Hoffer qualified. "As the Kandinsky is of our modern collection."

Herr Hoffer had purchased the Kandinsky at auction the previous year. Its owner, a wealthy Jew, had emigrated to America in a hurry, and his entire collection went piecemeal for an absurdly low price. It was the museum's first Kandinsky, entitled *Blue Circles II* (although there were no discernible circles in the painting, only wild sweeps of violet that never joined up).

Herr Streicher, missing the point, said that Bendel showed no interest in the Kandinsky. He stroked his bushy white eyebrows with a yellowed forefinger. "The Dark Dwarf, for one, likes van Gogh. I have this on the highest authority."

"I see. But Herr Minister Goebbels has nothing much to do with the SS, Herr Streicher."

"This fondness for the Dutch genius is not a peculiarity the Dark Dwarf would be eager to make public, Heinrich," the Acting Director went on. "Like a sexual maladjustment." He puffed a few times on his pipe. "The Führer disapproves of insanity in artists. Although personally I have seen plenty of yellow skies. Fewer blue meadows. Though cornflowers, like poppies, can turn a field blue. His drawings are more convincing than his paintings, I've always thought."

"The Führer's?"

"Van Gogh's, Herr Hoffer. I would not presume to judge the Führer's work. It is presumably above judgment. Watercolors of Vienna monuments. Snowy peaks. Pretty little Alpine valleys—"

"There are two words for color in Dutch," Herr Hoffer interrupted, adjusting the subject before Herr Streicher said anything silly. "*Verf* and *kleur. Verf* is the material and *kleur* the effect. Vincent kept mentioning *verf* in his letters."

"So?"

"Vincent started from the colors on his palette, the *verf.* Not from nature. Yet the effect is to bring one closer to nature."

"Do you have to call him Vincent? It sounds as though you were a friend of his."

"Rembrandt? That's a first name."

The Acting Director sighed, as if his assistant was being quarrelsome. The pipe in his mouth made a bubbling sound.

"Van Gogh may be an extraordinary genius," Herr Streicher conceded, "but he hasn't the talent to go with it. However, this painting of his is an important and extremely valuable item in our collection."

Herr Hoffer, instead of taking up the cudgels, pointed out that van Gogh had never been the subject of official abuse, perhaps because he was nineteenth-century. There was no reason for alarm, surely.

Herr Streicher shifted behind his desk, not listening. He then leaned forward and fixed Herr Hoffer with his ice-blue eyes. His white hair looked very wild.

"Whether or not the fellow's acting from the purest personal impulse, Heinrich, I would like you to make his acquaintance. You can always spray yourself, afterwards. I once met the Director of Television and shook his hand. Then I scrubbed it with bleach. It came up in a rash."

The Director of Television was Göring. Herr Streicher liked to call him by his least important title. Herr Hoffer wished the Acting Director would keep his voice down.

Up until then, they had left SS Sturmführer Bendel alone. It was best to leave members of the SS alone, especially young ones.

A week or so later, with the snow still on the ground but dirty and wet, Herr Hoffer was passing the SS administrative office on his bicycle and recognized Bendel. He was in uniform (without a coat, though it was cold), chatting up one of the girl auxiliaries. The Waffen-SS was not yet installed at Lohenfelde in 1936, for there was no call back then to defend the city with arms, but there had long been an SS administrative office in leafy Joseph Goebbels Strasse. It was a few doors up from the regional Gestapo office, where plainclothes detectives serving with the Kriminalpolizei would also come and go. The SS office's black-capped female auxiliaries in their pretty gray gloves would flounce past the spotty-faced sentries in a most provocative manner.

Turning his head to view the man better, Herr Hoffer wobbled on his bicycle and struck the curbstone, which was old and high in that lime-shaded street. He fell off, but not badly. Ignominiously, as he later put it.

SS Sturmführer Bendel ran up and helped him to his feet. Herr Hoffer, brushing the snow off his coat, thanked him, and they walked together up the long street. Klaus Bendel was charm itself and congratulated Herr Hoffer on the excellence of the museum's picture collection, adding that he was sure the medieval pieces in wood were excellent too but they were not his field. His field was broad, however: He had studied Art History under Herr Professor Pinder at the University of Berlin, followed by Applied Arts at the Vienna Academy (not to be mentioned, dear sir, in front of the Führer, who had failed the entrance examination twice), had spent a semester in Harvard as an exchange student, and was several months in the Louvre, researching for his thesis, "Form as an Aesthetic Principle in Georges de la Tour."

What an interesting fellow, thought Herr Hoffer.

"Too busy to paint, these days," said Bendel.

He explained his job as they walked (Herr Hoffer wheeling his bicycle along the mushy pavement). He was the official coordinator between the local SS subdistrict and the art and architectural section of Reichsführer-SS Himmler's personal staff. The subdistrict included a large area around Lohenfelde but was of course a great deal smaller than the total SS district, whose headquarters were naturally also in Lohenfelde and which was in the hands of his superior, SS Sturmbannführer Wedel, who had a gold tooth. The physical proximity of Bendel to Wedel—their offices were on the same floor—meant that the gold tooth often sought the lieutenant's advice in artistic or cultural matters and thus irritated the staff members who held similar positions in the other subdistricts under Sturmbannführer Wedel's aegis.

It was, conceded Bendel, a bloody pain in the wick.

Herr Hoffer was no longer nervous. In fact, he was rather enjoying (by proxy) the nervous glances of people passing the other way. Bendel was in uniform. Something about the SS uniform, with its blood-red armband and shiny black boots and belt and gloves, and the strange note of brown in the shirt behind the black tie, and the disparate highlights of silver, made you think of the wearer as a particularly expensive type of ornament, not as something living at all. A lacquered Japanese table, perhaps.

Making conversation in a sudden pause, he asked after the significance of the number stitched on the officer's cuff and on one of his collar patches: XIII.

"The number of the subdistrict," said Bendel. "We are Lohenfelde Abschnitt Dreizehn." He lifted his arm almost to Herr Hoffer's nose and displayed his cuff, the number raised in white thread. A smell of sweet Turkish cigarettes hung about the cloth, as if the young man still spent his evenings in student rooms. "I am not superstitious," Bendel added, bursting into laughter.

He had an oddly loud laugh, coming in a little late.

Herr Hoffer tentatively asked what Bendel's task consisted of, as coordinator between Reichsführer Himmler's personal staff, dealing with art and architectural matters, and their own Lohenfelde Abschnitt XIII.

Bendel sighed. "Do you know, I'm less sure every day. Bombarded with papers, I am. For instance, the Combat League for German Culture writes SS Sturmbannführer Wedel yet another damn letter complaining of certain Jewish-Bolshevist works in your own fine collection, Herr Assistant Director. He sends it across to me. I forward it to the appropriate authority—in this case, either the Reich Ministry for National Enlightenment and Propaganda, or the Reich Chamber of Visual Arts, or Herr Minister Rust at the Education and Culture Ministry. Perhaps all three, if I'm in doubt."

Herr Hoffer gulped and turned pale. He tried not to, but he could not help it.

"And then," the cheery young man went on, "I might do as Herr Schultze-Naumburg did a few years ago."

"Oh? What was that?"

"He approached the Führer himself, with photographs of the modernist collection in the Kronprinzen Palast. The Führer cares more for art than anything else apart from buildings, motorways, and dogs, Herr Hoffer. We have photographs on file of the Kaiser Wilhelm collection. Poor quality, but sufficient."

The fresh handsome face under the black-peaked cap seemed to

Herr Hoffer, as it smiled at him, slightly sinister in its bonhomie. The silly death's-head badge didn't help.

"Has this example of your daily work—has it actually happened?" he asked, unable to resist a tremble in his voice. His arms felt very stiff, wheeling the bicycle. The street seemed wide, dark, and endless. He had not come across any nasty letters from the Kampfbund für Deutsche Kultur, although it was possible Herr Streicher had hidden them from him.

"Oh, yes," said the young man. "It has happened because I have imagined it happening."

"I don't understand."

"Everything I have imagined happening, happens in the end," Bendel said, smiling again, his breath pluming the air.

Ah, they were at the end of the street at last. Cars passed on the main boulevard before them, turning the snow to black filth. A wagon was being unloaded of its barrels in front of a tavern. Bendel was watching the men unloading the barrels with an intense, absorbed look. Herr Hoffer had butterflies in his stomach. Surely the Führer would not be bothered with a provincial art museum, however fine.

"I imagined the Führer when I was a child," Bendel said, as if reading his thoughts. "Before he was even well known. Then I imagined, as a youth of fifteen, a time when things would be pure, with all corruption and trivial elements burned away. As an art student, before the Führer became the Führer and changed everything, I imagined that high art would fill our towns and cities and the daily lives of the masses, vulgarity would be banished, and Germany would be the new Athens. In each case, my imagination has been ahead of reality. My dreams were always of knights and maidens and high castles in a land with no cars or factories or electric wires. Perhaps they were not empty dreams at all but a glimpse of the future."

He's one of those SS lunatics, thought Herr Hoffer. That's what he is, for all his handsome charm. Ambitious and lunatic.

Then Bendel turned to him, and Herr Hoffer blushed. The fellow still had youthful red pimples on his pale chin. Middle twenties, perhaps. Precocious.

"So that is why, when I am passed a letter concerning your excellent museum from those lower-class cretins in the Combat League for German Culture, I write back directly with what I have just said to you, in so many words, and file their stupidity away in my private drawer." His face, impassioned now, came closer to Herr Hoffer's. "The vulgar masses are still in control, Herr Assistant Director. Do you understand?"

Herr Hoffer nodded, albeit weakly.

"By the way, I am invited to a function in the presence of Herr Minister Goebbels next week. I have decided not to tell him about your van Gogh. You know he is very fond of van Gogh, despite the Chief's disapproval. Your secret is safe with me."

"Secret?"

"The van Gogh is unique. Yours, I mean. *The Artist near Auvers-sur-Oise*. Where else does the artist show himself at work?"

"Debatable," said Herr Hoffer. "There's a monograph by one of our former employees, Gustav Glatz—"

"Herr Hoffer, of course it is as the title says. As *Hamlet, Prince of Denmark* is a play about Hamlet, Prince of Denmark. So few people are aware of this uniqueness that it is like a secret. For now, I prefer to keep it that way."

"You sound as though it's your decision, not ours."

"Well, in a way it is. As the ogre said in the poem, after he had eaten the fairy princess's baby, 'But I was hungry!' Victor Hugo. Most amusing, especially in the original French."

Herr Hoffer failed to understand this reference, yet the tone was not at all menacing. The young officer bid him farewell with a friendly if slightly arrogant squeeze of his shoulder, crossed the street, and disappeared into the crowds. His self-assurance was most unusual for one so young. It had the effect of making Herr Hoffer feel like a schoolboy.

Herr Hoffer's report to Herr Acting Director Streicher was confused, he now recalled. It did nothing to appease Herr Streicher's anxiety. Confusion is worse than clarity. Clarity was all the Führer had wished for: the air clean and spacious and full of sunlight, as in Athens of old. Herr Streicher had the strange impression, as he put it, that in the three years the Führer had been in power, things had got yet more confused—even after the Brownshirt thugs had been dealt with. No one from the Combat League had ever complained, he said.

Apart from a few Party philistines, the museum's modernist collection at that time attracted no derisory laughter, let alone sputtering fury.

This was unusual but by no means unique. The beating-up of poor Gustav Glatz in 1933 was by the SA, who were liquidated the following year. This nastiness happened the day before the people's election, in March, which was why the poster had been pinned to the delivery door. Gustav Glatz, the museum's Baroque specialist, author of the brilliant thesis on bracelet shading in Raphael, was beaten to a pulp by men of the SA. Most of the staff blamed the SA, not the new chancellor—who dealt with the SA problem himself.

The talk at the museum had always avoided politics for the most part, even in the Party's early days. When, one morning, they discovered an unpleasant Party notice pasted on the fence opposite, Herr Director Kirschenbaum merely pointed out the brilliance of the collage effect. Since it had not quite covered the poster underneath, it said, in big black letters visible from the museum:

GERMANS!

BEWARE!

DO NOT BUY FROM JEWS!

BABYLON

GRETA GARBO

When some filthy anti-Jewish graffiti appeared on the museum's front wall, they simply discussed the best way to clean it off. Even when Herr Director Kirschenbaum was dismissed after the defamatory article in the local paper, comments were kept to a minimum. It was a very dingy February day in 1934. He was given fifteen minutes to clear his desk, and the others shook his hand shyly (except for Frau Schenkel, who had always found him "typically" Jewish). "Do not buy from Greta Garbo," he said. And he was gone. They all kept their heads down and carried on. Werner was not yet on the staff, of course.

Herr Streicher helped matters by always attending Party functions to which he was invited, as Acting Director of the region's principal museum, and by remaining on best terms with those who were something in the town. People knew about Herr Streicher's Iron Cross, which he wore on all possible formal occasions. And (sadly) the final and perhaps most important reason for their modernist collection's escaping criticism was that the museum was very far from being a central feature of Lohenfelde's civic or social life by the 1930s. A brand-new and rather oversized jewel in her crown when opened in 1904, the Kaiser Wilhelm was now of another epoch, like its name, a little chipped and dusty. Its architecture, mixing styles and references, was regarded as quaint, even embarrassing, in an age of strict classicism and heroic pomposity. Locals would show you the town hall (or at least its amusing clock), the gleaming new thermometer factory, the crooked old pink-tinted inn from 1632 (recently restored), and the town park with its huge oaks and attractive ponds very much before they would show you the museum and its fossil, book, and art collections. The general wealth of buildings from the seventeenth and eighteenth centuries, gathered at the center of town, with their lovely carved cherrywood balconies, eclipsed the eccentric thirty-year-old construction situated just a street or two too far for an easy stroll, in a morbidly quiet quarter where the bourgeois villas and gardens sat like overstuffed dining-club members behind ornamental trees.

That is why, after the "dismissal" of Herr Director Kirschenbaum in 1934, no one took much notice of the museum and its illustrious contents—and this, although in some ways its salvation, annoyed Herr Streicher and saddened his assistant. They were torn between encouraging attendance—by special exhibitions, posters, and leaflets—and attracting as little notice as possible by merely keeping the correct opening hours. In the end, they settled on the latter; even the purchase of the Kandinsky was not announced in the local gazette. It was always best to keep your head well down in difficult times.

This gave their achievements the air of felonies, which was why the frequent visits of the same SS officer had given rise to anxiety. Herr Hoffer quite understood. Concerning Herr Hoffer's report, the Acting Director was oddly gleeful; SS Sturmführer Bendel's enthusiasm for the van Gogh confirmed all their suspicions. Herr Hoffer had not even mentioned the business about the photographs being shown to the Führer, as it was only a joke.

"*Unique,*" said Herr Streicher, "is a worrying word. I don't like that *unique*, not at all."

"Really, I think there is nothing to worry about. He wants to be Culture Minister, I think, like a lot of other bright young men, but—"

"There is a great deal to worry about," cried Herr Streicher. He thrust a copy of *The Times* in front of Herr Hoffer's nose. It was yesterday's edition. It moved the smoke into swirls in the stuffy office as Herr Streicher waved it around.

"I can't read English that well," Herr Hoffer admitted, as he did frequently, usually following up with a joke about having been to Oxford. Herr Streicher was always waving *The Times* in front of his nose, just as he was always calling Herr Minister Goebbels the Dark Dwarf and General Göring by his least important title, Director of Television.

"The Kronprinzen Palast has been closed. On the orders of Rust," Herr Streicher growled, tapping a tiny article on an inside page, circled by him in red.

"I see. Because of the Barlach?"

"Because we are dealing with maniacs, Heinrich. They would be fine behind a grocery counter where their mania would be confined to bags of dried peas, but they are far from fine behind a ministerial desk."

Herr Hoffer had planned on visiting the brand-new Barlach Gallery, as well as the rest of the refurbished exhibition rooms. He had looked at the timetable for Berlin trains and discussed it with Sabine—she wanted to go to the big stores. Ernst Barlach was one of his favorite avant-garde artists. This was very bad news all round.

"One hasn't been able to see the Schlemmers for years," Herr Streicher said, pacing up and down. "They got rid of their excellent Beckmann room entirely. One Klee left on show. And Herr Director Hanfstaengl is cousin to Ernst Hanfstaengl, the Führer's favorite. And still that isn't good enough for the maniacs!"

"Oh, dear. And Kandinsky reckoned this was the Epoch of Spirituality—one of the greatest, as he put it, in Evolution."

"I was told on the phone yesterday, in fact."

"Mind you, that was in 1912."

"Please concentrate, Heinrich!" The Acting Director slapped his hand on the glass-topped table; Herr Hoffer half expected it to break. "Dresden phoned, but I wouldn't believe it until I had read it in black and white. And not in Party black and white, if you please!"

"I do suggest you keep your voice down, Herr Streicher."

"Our van Gogh is the most at risk, Heinrich. As for that Bendel fellow, for God's sake keep an eye on him. I don't like that *unique* at all."

"You didn't hear him say it. Maybe he said it as other people say it. A lot of people like van Gogh, quite respectable people. He entered the German bloodstream via the group *die Brücke*, and now everyone of taste likes him. I like van Gogh too, as a matter of fact. After all, he *is* unique."

"But not everyone stands, my dear Heinrich, for half an hour at a time in front of one of his paintings!" Herr Streicher was knocking out his pipe's dottle into the metal bin. The noise made Herr Hoffer wince. "It's not normal. An obsession. The fellow's got his eye on it. The Dark Dwarf knows, I'm sure, that our van Gogh is twenty times more unique than the usual unique. The only one, for God's sake, that shows the painter at work!"

"That's the subject of some debate, of course—"

"Heinrich, don't be naïve. Does the Dark Dwarf care about debate? He writes novels, after all."

Herr Hoffer wasn't sure whether or not this was one of Herr Streicher's obscure jokes, but he smiled anyway.

"Bendel promised not to mention our van Gogh to Herr Minister Goebbels. He's meeting him next week."

"So you *did* talk about the Dark Dwarf!"

"Please, do try to keep your voice down, Herr Director!"

Hilde Winkel, through the darkness of the present, had begun talking. Herr Hoffer opened his eyes. The blood was dry and black on the lint and on her lip, as if painted on with a full brush.

"My sister, she lives in Giessen," Hilde was saying. "She's a science student. On Saint Nicholas Eve, last year, she and two friends had been cramming for a histology exam, so they rewarded themselves the day before by buying two pork chops each. They used up all their meat stamps on those chops. The air-raid siren sounded just as the chops were ready. Her two friends snatched their chops to munch in the cellar, but my sister said she would enjoy them properly, with a knife and fork at the table, after the raid. She left them in the pan and went down into the cellar."

"I hope this isn't depressing," said Frau Schenkel.

"No, not too depressing. When she came out of the cellar, the house had gone, along with the pork chops. In fact, the whole of Giessen had gone, completely smashed to bits."

"That's not depressing?"

"Let the girl finish," growled Werner.

"All she thought, as she looked at the miles and miles of rubble, was, 'My God, why didn't I eat those pork chops?'"

They all laughed.

"At least she wasn't suffocated," said Frau Schenkel. "A lot of them were suffocated in the cellars in Hamburg."

"That was the firestorm," said Werner. "Carbon dioxide."

"I don't care what it was," Frau Schenkel said. "They were still suffocated."

"That's why we aren't sitting round the corner," said Herr Hoffer soothingly. "We can get out quickly, if need be."

Werner snorted. "I don't imagine for a minute those poor folk were not harboring similar illusions," he said.

"Which folk?"

"In the cellars of Hamburg."

"I don't know what you're talking about, Herr Oberst," said Frau Schenkel. "I wish you'd speak plain German, sometimes."

"Let's change the subject," Hilde Winkel sighed.

Nobody proffered a new one. Herr Hoffer had finished his cigarette. Now all he could think of was chops: fat and juicy, with a touch of mustard. To hell with Bendel, anyway. Fried, seasoned, served on a lettuce leaf. His dear mother, before her illness, would spread them with chopped tomato and black pepper, but never mustard.

My God, he was so hungry. He was shaking his head from side to side, amazed at his own hunger.

I will become wood. The wood will start off in my feet and creep up to my head. Once the last knot of timber has appeared on my scalp, I will then cease to feel fear or hunger. No one will notice me, though they walk straight past—not even the bombs will notice me. I will join the universe of dead wood that pretends to be alive, pretends to be a forest creaking in the wind, in which I will be nothing but a small thin tree you walk straight past. A forest the woodcutters have missed completely.

20

It was shaking its head. Telling him not to.

Hear that?

Yup. He knew that now.

The flashlight was throwing its beam and the beam was quivering like hell and then a rat showed up in it. The rat was tugging at the dead's leg. There was a glitter of two tiny disks as it thought about things, and then a long black tail was slipping away into its own darkness.

The guy in the round spectacles, stiff as money when you ain't got none, had shifted from toe to head because a rat was tugging on his leg.

He moved the light around until the face of the dead on the other wall showed up, with the arm on his girl; it also had spectacles, but they had fallen forward over the mouth. The heat had twisted them, fused them to the flesh; it must have been very great, the heat.

He would've liked to have preserved these people in some way, turned them into an exhibit for a big gallery someplace back home, perhaps in the violet-painted gallery on Hewes Avenue belonging to his boss's rich bohemian niece: the weirdest sculpture ever, this would be, entitled *The Four Fates; or, Is This Your Enemy?*

His chicken heart resumed control. There was nowhere in the mess to lay the painting down. He went farther into the vaults, probing with his light around the corner. The place showed up where he'd shat and covered it after and then the old wood statue showed up that Morriboy had shot the head clean off of and then the dead in the blue cardigan showed up and then a clear space nearby. Rats had been at this dead's face again, and the other cheek was torn away to the back teeth. It was not a nice place to be, but he had no choice. The dead was not grinning and showing his back teeth, he'd just lost some of his face to that goddamn rat as hungry as hell.

Those guys like Bosch and Goya, they must have been nuts.

Life itself is a nightmare a lot of the time; you don't have to add to it pictorially. Nobody's going to put stuff like that on their walls. They need snowy mountains and shepherds and golden valleys.

He took off his jacket and laid it down on the stone floor and then took out his little mountain knife and eased the nails so the picture came out of its gilded frame. This was not difficult. He kicked away the frame, which was now kindling.

Hell, none of it was difficult. The back of the painting was rough as a hessian sack, with a little numbered ticket stuck on it maybe a hundred years ago, like the painting was a piece of merchandise. The stretcher was just four ordinary lengths of wood, like it would be now, so you could not believe that something so beautiful was on the other side.

The canvas was fixed to the outer sides by about a hundred ancient thumbtacks.

Setting the light with difficulty on the uneven slabs, he proceeded to cut the canvas. He held the picture vertical with a steady hand but the slab under it wobbled, as if it wasn't cemented down, so he had to move to the slab next door. He worked slowly, and his hands were now shaking. This was not the first time. His hands had shaken badly the first time he had aimed at a man in a bombed-out French town called Faulquemont, back in late November, through thin sleet. The man was a German soldier wearing a huge tarpaulin with holes for the arms and he had jerked and folded like a deck chair.

Maybe it wasn't his own bullet, because there were others firing.

He remembered that name: Faulquemont.

The man was dead by the time they reached the wrecked shop from where he'd been shooting at them and yelling. They stepped over him and moved on. He'd looked just like a dead should look, with his mouth open and blood on his nose, but more individual than Parry would've liked. He was small, rat-faced, with pouches of exhaustion under his eyes and graying stubble, maybe in his forties. He didn't look like a German soldier. He'd made the tarpaulin coat to keep himself dry, or maybe it was a kind of gas cape. Now it lay on him like his death shroud, flapped up over his head so Parry'd had to lift the corner back with the snout of his rifle to take a look. He wished he hadn't, because the first man you kill will always hang around.

The knife made slow headway in the canvas; he was cutting against the thin weak wood of the stretcher. His hands were still shaking, but less so. He didn't like being down in the vaults anymore, with rats and deads and mess.

But this was salvage.

The stink of burning still hung heavy in the air; the stink of burnt varnish and burnt oil paint and burnt canvas and burnt gilt and burnt people in their clothes. The flashlight made a tiny thrumming sound for some reason; otherwise there was only the scrape and squeak of the knife as it made its way through the thick threads of the canvas. It would have been so much easier to have slashed through the canvas flush to the edge, letting the knife have all its play, but he didn't want to damage the painting itself; so he took it an inch or two back, which was harder.

Maybe the fumes given off by the burning paint and linseed and varnish had suffocated them first. It was a chemical reaction.

If he pressed too hard, the stretcher started splintering or the canvas got kind of pushed into the wood and messed up. Oak, it felt like. Or maybe it was pear wood, like they had always used for palettes. You could never be sure. A great deal changed, though not pear for palettes. The strange thing was, he himself used a butcher's tray.

His army-issue knife was not the ideal instrument; he'd have done better with a surgical instrument. He should have raided the medical truck; there was a complete operating kit in there. They could saw and suture all day and night, and sometimes they did. The knife slipped and nicked his thumb. A bead of blood welled and he had to suck it for a few moments, his shadow leaping behind him as he moved his arms.

He didn't want blood on the painting.

He tried, at one point, to prise the canvas free from the rusted thumbtacks with the point of his knife, but the canvas tore and he abandoned the idea. The shadow of his arm kept obscuring things, but he made progress. He did make progress. He sawed away delicately with the serrated underlip of the blade. He looked up and caught the dead young man's grinning face, thrown into something worse by the harsh light.

A dead cannot hurt you.

He wondered who had shot the guy, and through the chest, taking the blue weave into the ribs and then the heart or lungs; he couldn't have gotten down here himself, not with a wound like that. Two wounds. Neat holes. And the only blood was around his body. He must have been shot here, or at least in the vaults. By whom? Hell, who cares? There are so many deads, probably millions, that it doesn't matter at all.

Parry knew what he was doing was wrong. It was a small wrong in the huger evil . . . but he had a bad feeling about it. The kind of sexual excitement was gone. He kept teasing himself—whispering the words—about his moral conscience. The world was going to be a very tough place for a while, even far away in America; the war was nowhere near over in the Far East, and the Russkies weren't just going to lie down and be tickled in Europe. Some of the men were talking about the next war, the big war between Communism and Capitalism. All hell was going to break loose, and a man had to be well set up for that. He had to be very well set up or sink without a trace. Parry did not want to sink without a trace.

He cut through the remaining fibers and lifted the goddamn canvas away. It kept its shape. The only weight was the paint. A couple of the wedges were stuck to the back and he had to peel them off.

The varnished painting shone in the flashlight's beam. But the work looked frail, even a little undressed. When the light fell on it in a certain way, hiding the image in glare, it looked like the surface of the sea as he'd seen it from the troopship, high up, when the sea was calm but marked by tiny lines and pockmarks; that was age, he thought. In the end, it was only a material, like iron or rubber. He'd never before been so aware of this.

Everything is material, he thought.

It was a beautiful painting; he was getting used to it without its frame, with only the thin strip of bare canvas all around, still folded back a little. Carefully, he flattened out this margin, where the paint gave out like the edge of a scabbed wound.

This painting reminded him, as he stood there some twenty feet below the ruined town, of a deep dark wishing well near his uncle's place in Vermont. He would look down into the well as a child, exult-

ing at the circle of light far below, in which his head was visible as a
kind of notch. He'd see another realm down there, in which a lot of
good things might come true. *I am on vacation, and I am going fishing.*

The antique painting gave him that kind of feeling, looking at it in
the beam of the flashlight. It was his painting. He was part of its history. He could not imagine this painting surviving him and he sank
down into its landscape in blessèd relief.

*Papa, Mama, Leo, Lily, little Henny, Grandmama, you are
alive, I am alive—so we are all still alive, thank goodness! Yet I
am not here. I am a trick of light. I am not even a ghost. I am
not even in your dream [Traum]. I am marking the days on a
beam. The beam is longer than my life.*

21

Herr Hoffer suddenly imagined himself in the hold of a large airplane, fleeing war-torn Europe. The vaults were the right shape, long
and with a curved ceiling (he ignored the fact that they turned the
corner and continued for the same length), and everything was vibrating and rumbling as it did in an airplane. The vibrating stopped
as the rumbling stopped, but the plane flew on. Where to, with its
precious cargo? Into the past, where everything was better. There
was a brief period when, really, the Führer had seemed to fulfill all
Herr Hoffer's student dreams of the artist hero that might have been
himself, emerging from the dark mysteries of the trees as Hermann
himself did before the aghast Romans—invincible Hermann himself, whose towering copper-sheeted statue Herr Hoffer had wondered at, as a boy on a school outing to the Teutoburg Forest back in
1911. He chuckled silently to himself, remembering how he and the
other boys had climbed up the spiral stairs inside the statue's base to
the viewing platform, still far below Hermann's feet, and gazed over

the trees towards Romanish France, towards the Arch-Fiend France, and had shaken their small fists. It was the time of the Moroccan crisis, when feelings were high against France and many people were talking of war. There was no war, not yet, but to Herr Hoffer's mind everything went wrong from that moment—not his own trivial visit to the monument, of course, but the French invasion of Morocco. How huge and defiant was the statue rearing above him, the muscled legs sheathed like boilers, the bolts like a warrior's stitched scars on the bare arm with its upraised sword, the blade actually hidden in the low misty clouds that hung over the forest, as a real god's might have been! How proud of being German he had felt, and how impossible to imagine himself as anything else!

He chuckled silently again, before noticing Hilde Winkel's glance beside him. He smiled at her gamely and settled back, wishing he had a cushion. He crossed his legs at the ankles and folded his arms.

Werner put the other Mendelssohn on the gramophone, winding it up with a grunt. It was Goethe's loving woman, writing to her absent love, only now she was singing it. Why was she estranged from her own people? Was her husband away in the wars and she far from her family, or was she in exile? A single kiss, yes, was all her delight, and the singer put everything into the yearning. Letters were strange things, both distant and very close. Herr Hoffer could quite clearly see her with a plume in hand, writing as her soul sang, yearning.

There was a scratch on *Stille*, as if Herr Streicher had done it deliberately; the word caught on itself three times before Werner jogged the player. Music was vulnerable too, in the end. He had a great desire to remove his shoes, but the others would see his darned socks, even in the weak light. Frau Hoffer had darned these socks several times. Also, they might have to evacuate the place very suddenly. That was an odd thing about bombs—they blew people's shoes off. A lot of the dead would be scattered about in their socks, with their shoes nearby. Before the war, he had never seen a dead person—not counting his grandfather in the coffin in 1908, who hadn't been real. After a raid, the bodies were quickly covered in blankets and the grisly bits and pieces recovered by special volunteers with sacks, followed by men with brushes and buckets, so that often he might cycle to work with very little to show for the raid but the odd blasted building. Strange, how burnt people were purple, not black. Another peculiar thing was the way in which the blankets never quite covered the bodies; there was frequently a hand or a foot protruding. It was disturbing. It often looked as if they were reaching out, about to remove the blanket and stand upright again, blinking, to walk back into their lost lives.

People standing in front of their ruined homes would sob, and it was like gales of laughter from a distance. On the other hand, Gustav Glatz would laugh, and it sounded like sobbing. Gustav would wander into the museum at odd moments and laugh and show the staff his lacerated tongue, mumbling and snorting. His front teeth had been knocked out and many of the others loosened, so he'd had a false set made which were slightly too big. He would remove his false teeth, wincing, and open his mouth and show his tongue—which seemed, yes, to have scars across it. The staff would look suitably shocked, but since he wandered in at least once a month, their looks became less convincing. His right eye remained black; it was not a normal black eye, apparently, it was something worse. Poor Gustav; he had been such a promising scholar, their expert on the Baroque. One felt sorry for him, wandering about like that, a real wreck after the SA thugs set on him, but after a while one dreaded his visits. There was no single painting or sculpture that could convey poor Gustav Glatz's suffering or the horror of a mother's grief, let alone the horror of being boiled alive like a prawn—as had happened in shelters when the boiler burst. Even Grunewald would not be up to it. And now he was scared. The museum had a very large boiler. There had been gas and electricity right up to today, apart from the odd interruption after a raid. He could not imagine the horror of being boiled alive, of clambering as high as one could, holding one's children above one's head as the steaming waters blistered one's ankles and then one's knees.

He shuddered, and the others glanced at him.

I'm quite all right, he wanted to say, but he swallowed instead and closed his eyes. Then he yawned, a huge yawn he could not stifle. He heard the others follow him. That was the thing about yawns. They were catching, just as being scared was catching.

A painting could not convey being scared, either.

"These silences are excruciating." That was Werner Oberst. Who had not yawned, it seems. "Anyone would think we were ghosts."

"Sleepy ghosts," said Hilde Winkel, holding a finger to her bad lip.

"Then put another record on," said Frau Schenkel.

"We're not a dance hall," said Werner. "There are only five records, anyway. You only brought five down, Heinrich. Maybe you thought defeat would come sooner rather than later."

Herr Hoffer blinked and apologized and then Hilde Winkel started crying. She covered her face in her hands and shook next to him. He placed a hand on her back and felt the thinness rippling and a certain unevenness he assumed to be her undergarment.

"Thank you," she said, blowing her nose. "I was thinking about those chops. My sister caught a chill in the rubble and passed away in January."

"My sister liked to sing," Werner murmured, for some reason. "She was nine years older than me."

"I said it would be depressing," said Frau Schenkel, with a satisfied nod.

Herr Hoffer kept on rubbing Hilde Winkel's back for a few moments, feeling fatherly. He was, after all, the head of this little family. He had been so for four years, since Herr Streicher's last collapse. He was not only the head but the savior; he had saved the remainder of the collection. The Americans would acknowledge him as the savior.

The silence grew weighty, though it was better not to talk. The tetchy old man overhead had nodded off, for the moment. No— there was a little stutter, like stones cast in a bucket. Those were shots.

Even Sabine had never known anything about it. Even that damn Bendel; even he had been foxed.

Herr Hoffer had really been very agile. When the call comes, you are ready. He had already started to secrete a few of the more sensitive paintings by the time the Degenerate Confiscation Committee wreaked its terrible harvest in '36: Herr Streicher was fully supportive of this precautionary measure against Party looters.

"I insist," he had said, knocking out his pipe for emphasis, "that the Poussin figure study be the first guest of the vaults."

"Not the Bernini marble?"

"We don't have a Bernini marble."

"My joke, Herr Director. It is very important at times like these that we keep a sense of humor."

Herr Acting Director Streicher had frowned, scratching his wild shock of white hair. It had grown whiter very quickly, in Herr Hoffer's opinion.

"Nothing," Herr Streicher had replied, "is more grotesquely amusing than seeing these barbershop cretins try to run Germany, if you are of a cynical disposition like myself."

So the little Poussin went down that night into the darkness of the vaults. A dozen others followed over the next few years. But this piecemeal, haphazard maneuver turned, in Herr Hoffer's hands, into a sophisticated operation of which he was very proud.

One answers the call when one has to.

The key was having had four years to do it in, since Herr Streicher's last collapse: reducing the collection not stolen by the Degenerate louts to a skeletal sample and storing the rest quite openly (as it were) in a room on the ground floor. Next to the toilets, yes, and only on the ground floor, but windowless, steel-plated, and sandbagged. Their official air-raid shelter, as demanded by the authorities long before the war. LUFTSCHUTZBUNKER said the stenciled red letters on the door, in case anyone was in any doubt.

And all these paintings in the vaults? What the hell are they down here for?

Well, Captain Clark Gable of the U.S. Army, that was my masterstroke, for which I was taking a great risk. These were the ones I slipped a little deeper, you see. Over a hundred of them! Personal favorites or in particular danger from the Nazi cretins. This paper in my pocket is the inventory, but it includes only those works visible in the Luftschutzbunker. And (this is the brilliance of it), it is full of mistakes. It is what I jokingly refer to as my imprecision relation. Heisenberg, you know? Anyway, the most flagrant mistake was the listing of *Mademoiselle de Guilleroy au Bain* as present in the Luftschutzbunker when she was, of course, in the SS Sturmbann-führer's office, that building you are now using for storing your chewing gum and chocolate and excellent fruit drink. So the other mistakes were covered by—well, my own apparent idiocy. It foxed everyone.

Thank you, Captain Gable. But, you know, I believe in the supreme value of art. We must all make our humble sacrifice—

"Heinrich."

"Yes, Werner?"

"What's that supercilious smile about?"

"Was I smiling?"

"It was most unattractive."

"Sorry to offend. I was thinking of those lamb chops."

"Pork chops," murmured Hilde. "If only she had enjoyed them, before she caught that chill in the rubble."

"If only," said Herr Hoffer, "I had gone by way of the park to see the blossom this morning. It is a clear, bright day out there, beyond the smoke."

"You're not suggesting a calamitous outcome in regard to our own sweet selves, are you, Heinrich?"

"No, Werner, but I wouldn't have minded seeing the blossom, all the same."

Hilde started crying again, very quietly.

Frau Schenkel said, "My hips hurt. I'm not up to sitting on the floor."

"That's age," said Werner gruffly.

"I know it's age," said Frau Schenkel. "It takes me longer and longer to get up in the morning."

"You think it's a long way off," said Werner, "and then suddenly you're in it."

"My philosophy," said Frau Schenkel, "is that you never know what's around the next corner. You just never know."

"Even though one gets plenty of warning." Herr Hoffer smiled.

"You're not old," said Frau Schenkel.

"Neither are you," he replied gallantly.

He glanced at Werner, who had always been old. Werner said nothing.

"Thank you, Herr Hoffer," said Frau Schenkel, "but it isn't all appearances, I'm afraid."

Herr Hoffer was too tired and nervous to continue a conversation he had had in the office many times before. He crossed his legs at the ankles and folded his arms. He calculated that Frau Schenkel must, in fact, be nearing sixty. She had been in her mid-forties when he first met her, with a decent figure. Although she'd resembled a hungry cormorant, even then. In fact, she'd reminded him of Botticelli's cruel young Medici in the Kaiser Friedrich collection—a painting that had struck him with great force on his earliest visits to Berlin as a young man. The first portrait to show an interior psychological truth, he had read; at an age when interior psychological truth seemed to belong only to oneself, he had been so excited by it! Ah, so near and yet so long ago, he had reflected. And now he might say the same of his own youth!

The cloudy candlelight was exaggerating his secretary's features. Her long nose with its wavering shadow came almost to the level of her upper lip, and she had a habit of raising her right eyebrow, so that she really did look quite cruel and self-satisfied at times, as did the Medici youth.

Sometimes he had dreamed of a young smiling secretary with nice teeth, instead of Frau Schenkel. He had even, sometimes, half wished she would have some health problem and retire early. Vanish from his life.

If people knew one's inner thoughts, society would become intolerable.

Hilde Winkel blew her nose and wiped her eyes, apologizing. No one even bothered to comment. People were not made by God to sit underground in the darkness, hungry and cold, while other people tried to destroy their homes with high explosive. These sudden bursts of despair were, in fact, a sign that you had recognized the situation for what it was. Most of the rest of the time you concentrated on details, such as the most comfortable sitting position on concrete or whether the darns in your socks were showing. Herr Hoffer recalled spending an entire session in the air-raid cellar at home wondering why coffee was ruined when it was boiled in the pan and yet could not be made properly unless the water poured over the ground beans was at absolute boiling point. The fact that he'd not had any real coffee in the house for two years did not enter into the discussion, which was conducted entirely in his own head, accompanied by the appropriate sensations of smell and taste and so on. Sabine commented afterwards that she believed he had been having sexual fantasies, which he vigorously denied. The noise of the raid had gone on and on above them, rather like a stream of overloaded lorries racing and banging over potholes, and yet he had continued with this inner debate about coffee. At other times in the shelters he had been stiff with fear, though the raids were either nonexistent or much farther off: This is why he preferred sitting in his flat wadded by cushions.

Hilde gave a shuddering tear-filled sigh and Herr Hoffer placed his hand again on her back, in that fatherly way. How slim her back felt under the nobbly bit of the undergarment!

Bendel had put his hand on Sabine's back, of course. But with quite different motives.

I can't speak, as if I don't have a tongue, but my head sings. Ex-actly like a tree at dawn, in spring, in the depths of the Spree-wald. One of the three speaks to me in nonsense that rhymes, sometimes. I think I understand him. He shows me his tongue. Life is nonsense that sometimes rhymes.

22

Parry looked down at the snowy mountains and golden valley for some minutes. His hands had stopped shaking. He'd lowered his whole soul into the world down there, a much better world in its purity and innocence.

Then he rolled the picture up, slowly and carefully.

It was incredible that you could roll up such a thing. It was stiff, but it rolled up like cardboard. He didn't roll it too tight, as that would have cracked the paint; he imagined it shelling off like old skin, the hairline cracks forming into plates and shelling off, the little blisters in the corner bursting. He had the impression, down there in the vaults, rolling up that old picture by Mr. Christian Vollerdt, that everything he was doing in his life had some greater purpose, that all his actions would eventually make up into one great construction, and it would only then be clear what that construction was, what it represented.

Back in Vermont they'd had a neighbor who'd construct giant dolls out of bits and pieces he'd pick up in yards and farms, with the help of chicken wire and plaster and paint, and until the paint went on you couldn't see what the hell it was meant to be, it was just like a tall pile of garbage. The paint kind of made sense of it all, tied it together, and the giant doll would be added to the other giants in the field behind his house. The guy was not an artist, he was just crazy, but now Parry could see how one's life could appear to resemble a tall pile of bits and pieces, of garbage, until the last stroke of paint made sense of it all, the last breath.

He held in his hand a thick tube: like hessian, like sackcloth. The painting might never have been. He wanted to burst into tears, although he had triumphed.

My pencil is almost finished. [. . . ?] At some point in your life you become separated from your luck. Then everything gets difficult.

23

Even Bendel had been foxed.

The young fellow would pop round to the museum very often, but he was kept sweet by being shown the stored works in the Luftschutzbunker. If anyone mentioned the vaults, Herr Hoffer would claim they were too damp and full of rats. SS Sturmführer Bendel would gravitate without fail to the nineteenth-century gallery and stare for a long time at the van Gogh.

When, in late 1941, it was taken down from its hook to join the other works stored for safety in the Luftschutzbunker, Bendel would ask to see it there.

Herr Hoffer obliged but kept a close eye on him. He really wanted the van Gogh to slip straight down into the vaults, but it could not "vanish" while Bendel was around. *The Artist near Auvers-sur-Oise* held the man entranced.

"Now I understand, Herr Hoffer."

"What do you understand?"

"That what matters is the vision a man has—above and beyond his fellow creatures."

Herr Hoffer, looking at the painting, felt rather proprietorial. The windowless Luftschutzbunker had been installed with a fan, but it still smelled of linseed oil and the toilets next door.

"He anticipated the Expressionists by fifteen years or more" was what he had said in his gallery lectures in front of this painting. He no longer said that, nor did he mention van Gogh's mental breakdown.

"All great artists are blessed with an inner vision that is unique to them, Herr Bendel. It is a gift they must respect, as an artist must respect the surface he draws upon."

"How strange," said SS Sturmführer Bendel, his boot heels squeaking as he swiveled Herr Hoffer's way, "that you liken an inner vision to the outside surface of a canvas."

"Not just canvas," Herr Hoffer replied, slightly piqued. "It might be the side of a clay pot, a newspaper, anything. Even an old crumbling wall."

Bendel gave one of his boyish laughs. It was always a bit too loud.

"You are very literal," he said. "I am not sure this particular great artist would have approved."

"To his mind," said Herr Hoffer, "as to the ancient Chinese mind, the inner and the outer were seamlessly joined. Are we looking at a field of wheat in northern France or an individual's soul refracted through so many agitated strokes of the brush?"

SS Sturmführer Bendel kept very still for a moment. "I see something else entirely," he said, and walked out.

They never talked politics; they strolled together through a sort of sealed parkland of high art, immune from interference. Occasionally Bendel would mention the Führer, but only with reference to the latter's taste for such-and-such a painter (generally nineteenth-century). He never mentioned his boss, Reichsführer-SS Himmler, and he rarely appeared in uniform. He told jokes about General Göring that were genuinely funny. For instance, Göring was visiting a steel factory when he suddenly shot up to the ceiling; an electromagnet had caught his medals. (Apparently, the general found them funny too, which spoiled Herr Hoffer's enjoyment while it soothed his nervousness.)

Once, Herr Hoffer had called him an extreme romantic.

"Do you know what Dostoyevsky called the romantic, Herr Hoffer?"

"I'm afraid not."

"A wise man. In *Letters from the Underworld*."

"Yes," said Herr Hoffer, who had never read it, "an excellent book, but very Russian."

Bendel had laughed his loud high-pitched laugh. It was fashionable, among SS officers, this laugh, probably because of Reinhard Heydrich.

"How right you are, Herr Hoffer. Very Russian indeed."

Klaus Bendel was, in short, an agreeable and stimulating young man whose engaging boyishness was only slightly marred by a shrill note that crept in from time to time. This reminded Herr Hoffer of his own youth. The shrill note was usually philosophical, an extreme or sweeping statement that came out of the blue and rendered the careful discussion null and void. The last two thousand years of Western civilization would be dismissed in a sentence; Bendel was drawn to prehistory, in which he found "the truth of beauty allied to nature, something instinctual and true." Flint tools and arrows of barbed bone or whale ivory were the artifacts he held in special esteem; he was involved in various archaeological digs run by the SS, and this had changed his view of art. Art, he would maintain, was at its most truthful when it was unconscious: when a bone arrow achieved, in its anonymous, unconscious simplicity, the expression of man's innermost soul. The prehistoric hunters would not have called it art. Art was the product of a lapse, a decline into a sedentary and urban form of life. Paintings were a frivolity, a decadent corruption of the essential millennial effort of prehistoric or primitive man to unite the utilitarian with the sophisticated aesthetic of art. This made art a subtle companion of nature; the shark and the bone arrow combine aesthetic and practical perfection. Both are beautiful because they are perfect. We are living, Bendel would go on (his eyes shining with excitement), in an age of imperfection. We have lost the instinct, the unself-consciousness that was our natural birthright. The intellect has taken over; our movements are awkward and ugly. Look at the terrible ugliness of cities! Look at this room, this gallery—how absurd it is, when you think about it instinctually! These are our sacred objects, this our modern church—but isn't it absurd and unnatural when you look at it coldly, like a timeless god? Wouldn't you prefer the terrible mask burning in the fire?

"Personally," Herr Hoffer said once, after one of these fits of enthusiasm, "I would prefer a drawing by Raphael to the mask in the fire."

"Herr Hoffer, you have missed the point entirely. If you don't mind me saying so, you are being naïve."

"Candid, perhaps. Did you know that Leibniz, that great man of Reason, started out as a member of a secret society, dabbling in magic and alchemy and Rosicrucianism? Apparently there was a lot of that sort of rubbish following the Thirty Years' War."

"What are you saying, Herr Hoffer?"

"I'm not sure."

There was a pause. Bendel was in uniform, looking tall and elegant and restrained. He folded his arms abruptly, and there were tiny creaks and clinks from the blackness.

"If you're suggesting I am not an antirationalist, then remember what Leibniz said about primitive truths of fact."

"I don't remember, Herr Sturmführer."

"That they are the immediate internal experiences of an immediateness of feeling."

"Did he? I see. At any rate, if you're saying all art is the vanity of illusion, then the still-life painters of Holland said it some three hundred years before you."

The mistake, of course, was to have invited him home. What an idiot one could be!

It was at Sabine's suggestion, now he came to think of it. She was keen to meet this young fellow she had heard so much about. It was '39, a wet March.

"Invite him over? But I can't."

"Coffee and cakes, Heinrich. Stop pacing up and down."

"No."

"Why not?"

"He's SS."

"So?"

He mimed pictures being taken off the walls; he was never quite sure that the apartment was not being listened to in some way. Elisabeth (she was seven, then—how fast they grew!) came in hand in hand with little Erika and laughed.

"What're you doing, Papa?"

"I'm—I'm—"

He couldn't think.

Erika pointed at him and piped, "Papa's a strong man."

"That's right. I'm lifting a whole house, my poppet. Oof. Now a lorry. Oof."

The two girls shrieked with laughter. Herr Hoffer had once seen a strong man in a Jewish café theater in Vienna, on Praterstrasse. He told them about it, how the man had bent a thick steel bar. The girls' mouths were open in awe.

"Papa and I are talking, you two," said Sabine. "There are almond biscuits in the larder."

They scampered out.

"You like him, Heinrich."

"I'm humoring him," he replied, keeping his voice down. "I'm keeping to the right side. It's a game. Part of my job."

"Exactly, my honeybun. Make sure he comes in uniform," she added, planting a sloppy kiss.

And so he came. In uniform. Smelling of herbal cigarettes.

Sabine's eyes sparkled. The SS had a lot of cachet in Lohenfelde. And he was very handsome, any fool could see that. He asked Sabine all the right questions and complimented her on her cakes. (Ah, how they had taken those cakes and that coffee for granted, six years ago!) Herr Hoffer's heart never quite calmed, however, the whole time Bendel was in the apartment; he was more like a raven than a lacquered ornament here. Also, he was sharing the sofa with Sabine, which did not seem quite right.

"Do you meet the Führer on your trips, Herr Bendel?"

"I have spent an entire afternoon in his company, Frau Hoffer."

"No!"

"In an airplane, flying from one end of Germany to the other. The Herr Reichskanzler never spoke a word the whole time."

"But they say he talks for hours without stopping."

Herr Hoffer felt a flush of fear, but Bendel only smiled.

"I'm sure he can. But people tend to contradict what is reported of them, don't they? Or what one expects. You, for instance, Frau Hoffer, are not what I was expecting."

Sabine blushed, perhaps because their shoulders touched at that moment.

"Worse or better?"

"Oh, much better."

"You mean you were going by my husband's reports?"

"Not at all. It's just that one has a certain received idea of housewives of a certain age married to bespectacled functionaries."

His playful smile disarmed what might have been insulting; Sabine laughed, and Herr Hoffer served him more cake, feeling a flush of pride rather than annoyance.

"Anyway, the Führer just sat there, across the aisle. He didn't even smile. He didn't move a muscle. He was awake, or at least his eyes were open. No food, no water. Nobody smoked, of course."

"You must have been disappointed," Sabine said, her eyes widening, chin cupped in her hand. "I mean, not by the Führer himself, but by the fact that you didn't hear his conversation."

"Not at all, Frau Hoffer. I understood his power." Bendel's neck seemed to stretch above the brown collar, a glint coming into his eyes: Sabine's wide eyes caught the glint and sparkled in return. "I once went to the zoo in Berlin, as a child, and stood for a long time in front of the lion cage. I wasn't interested in anything else. The lion lay like a cat, with its head on its paws, its eyes slightly open. Apart from the flicking of its ears, for the flies, it never moved. I wanted it to move, because I was stupid and thought power was in movement." He turned his head and glanced at Herr Hoffer before returning to Sabine. "Real power is in stillness, Frau Hoffer. Have you ever noticed that I try to keep my head still when talking? It gives one more authority. A man who moves his head about when talking has no authority. I have to learn it, because it doesn't come naturally. For the

Führer, it is completely natural. To tell you the truth, I was terrified on that airplane. It was like being inside the cage, not outside; one certainly wouldn't want the lion to move. Although I have to say that the Führer was completely unaware of my existence. He has changed all our lives, but he doesn't really notice us. We are extensions of himself and nothing more."

"I suppose we are," said Herr Hoffer, his heart beating far too loudly. "As one is a tiny vertical extension of Germany."

This made Bendel laugh as he bent to his coffee. Sabine laughed too—breathlessly, like a young girl.

Herr Hoffer changed the subject.

"Herr Sturmführer Bendel and I had a great argument last week, didn't we?"

Bendel frowned.

"He thinks our charming Jacob Beck, *Hausandacht*, should not be hung next to the Johann Christian Vollerdt, *Landschaft mit Ruinen*."

"An indifferent copy of the original, which is in Magdeburg," Bendel explained. "The Vollerdt, not the Beck."

"Won't everything have to be stored away in the shelter, if we're forced into war?"

"Exactly where we had our discussion," said Bendel. "We were planning the future, my dear Frau Hoffer. Your husband and I look forward, not back. The Kaiser Wilhelm Museum will be a brilliant little jewel in the vast and glittering panoply of the Reich's cultural life."

"He believes the landscapes should be separated from the genre paintings, Sabine. It's not a question of quality. At least we have a visitor who cares, even if we do not always agree with him."

"Please don't talk about work, Heinrich. It gets terribly boring if you're not part of it."

She smiled knowingly at Bendel—who, damn him, smiled knowingly back! And then, if Herr Hoffer remembered correctly, Bendel had placed his hand on her back.

"You know we have just got hold of Prague, Frau Hoffer?"

This is my kingdom. I have no subjects. The old thin one with spectacles brought me a new pencil and put his arm round my shoulder. Maybe I will use up all their pencils, every pencil in Germany, every pencil in the whole world.

24

Parry relieved his full bladder in the farthest, darkest end of the vaults, against the big flat stones. It always took him a long time; it had to be eased out. It would stop and start. Maybe this was nerves. The dead on the floor, with its torn cheeks and wide-open eyes, was frightening him some, he had to be honest. Also, the smell—including what he reckoned was his own call of nature—was very nasty, although he was used by now to smells of all thicknesses, especially underground: gun oil and sweat and damp plaster; dried meat and pissed-in ration tins and smoky oil lamps and wet potatoes.

Wet fucking potatoes!

And Holland, where they were sent, right on the border before they saw any action, full of drying tobacco leaves in farmhouses with interiors like de Hooch or Vermeer, if only they hadn't been smashed so bad.

Yet the light still fell on wood and cloth and glass like it did in de Hooch and Vermeer, making the moment eternal, though the wood was splintered, the cloth ripped, the glass broken. Nowhere else did he find the moment made eternal by the way the light fell as he found it in Holland.

Maybe it was his art studies that made him see that in Holland and nowhere else, rather than something about Holland. Nobody else saw it that way, because all they read was cartoons and *Yank* and *Stars and Stripes.* If they didn't just look at the pictures. He felt like a professor, sometimes.

Then they were shoved back west and south as if someone had made a mistake, straight into Belgian snow and blood, while other divisions along with the British carried on into northern Germany. And

sometimes he could not figure what country he was in or what time
he was in, whether dream time or awake time.

He wanted to wait an hour or two before venturing out; things'd
be calmer. He didn't want to get caught up in the riot, in the hunt for
liquor and eggs and girls and stuff, not with his future rolled up in his
map pack. He was due to be back with his unit at dawn. Nobody was
sure how long they were staying in this city. They could be rolling out
tomorrow, for all he knew. Even the captain wasn't sure, talking to
the major on the sound power phone in the grocer's yard where their
CP was. Berlin was going to be hot, when they got to it. He hoped
the Russkies wouldn't turn on them, like Siberian wolves. Were there
wolves in Siberia?

"You know what I mean," he said to himself in a whisper, as if he
were two people (easing his bladder). Which was his right.

He felt very on his own down here, but he would whisper to himself a lot; it helped him. He wondered if Morrison had managed to
talk to that woman who'd called down a name—Hermann? Heinrich?—through the hole in the ceiling, before the boy was chalked.
He had an infection from not changing his underwear. His piss was
pepper; it hurt and he was grunting like an old man.

This infection could creep up and enter his bladder and his kid-
neys or even his liver and then he'd be dead, probably, because the
medics were too busy to sort out some guy with a minor infection.
Probably why he kept feeling as though he had a fever.

He thought of the thermometer factory and its gallons of mercury
spilling out, leaving no trace on the ground. It'd be good if you could
go through life like mercury, touching but not touching, not staining
anything or being stained.

His little wad of toilet paper was a joke. He used it to pat his glans
dry so it wouldn't sting so much, and then he buttoned himself up
again and left that part of the vaults until the dead guy was hidden by
the corner and the others were still on the far side of the burnt stuff.

He had placed the rolled-up canvas in his map pack; it just fitted,
but he had to leave the pack's flap unclipped after throwing out some
dirty maps and the French phrase book and the *Pocket Guide to Paris*

and Cities of Northern France. He wouldn't be needing them now. One day he hoped to go to Paris and climb the Eiffel Tower and see the beautiful slim dames of the Folies-Bergère and maybe have a girl with full lips as his life model.

He'd wait an hour or two.

He slung the pack over his shoulder and cleared a space and spread the torn blanket where the vaults turned, and he sat on the blanket, wondering whether to extinguish Morrison's flashlight. He did so, and the blackness was very bad.

Democracy on the march.

In blackness.

I am ill. Therefore I exist. Therefore I am visible and that is dangerous.

25

There was a sudden ugly splintering sound, followed by a louder ringing in his ears. No vibration of the walls. The others seemed unaffected. People prided themselves on their coolness; it was a way of surviving. He was glad they could not see each other very well in the candlelight; it made the lack of conversation easier. They were all so tired. No one had slept properly in two years, not one night. It became an effort simply to drag oneself from moment to moment. He must stop thinking about that damn Bendel. The fellow had not reappeared in years; he might even be dead.

Hilde Winkel next to him had stopped crying and was wiping her eyes on her handkerchief. Herr Hoffer removed his hand, smiling shyly, the palm hot and damp from her back.

The vaults rocked very slightly. They might almost be in a tram, in facing seats. A deep percussive note washed through them. It was a curious sensation: sound become tactile. It worried all of them, by the look of the eyebrows.

Frau Schenkel opposite broke the silence.

"I think you're in the wrong place, Herr Hoffer."

"What do you mean?"

"I've been thinking about it. You should not have abandoned your family."

"Abandoned?"

"This isn't just a normal raid, is it? It's the end of it all, whatever that means. Anyway, what I want to know is, why are you here, instead of with your wife and children? It's not natural, if you know what I mean. Isn't it one of their birthdays soon?"

They were all three staring at him. He was frowning, greatly bewildered.

"My duty. As Acting Acting Director, Frau Schenkel."

My God, it was Erika's birthday next week! Eight years old! She wanted to learn the harp!

"There is nothing in the building, Heinrich," said Werner, as if they had all three discussed this beforehand. He was just like a crazed waiter, with that blood-spotted handkerchief draped on his shoulder. "It is an empty shell, a ghost. Even Herr Lohse is not in his thermometer factory."

"Then why are you three here?"

"We have no family," said Werner.

"I do," said Hilde.

"I mean, no family in Lohenfelde."

Herr Hoffer looked across at the paintings ranged in the darkness on their crude trestles. The candlelight gleamed on the gilded wood of the older works. A harp would be quite impracticable in their apartment and very expensive. But he would buy little Erika a harp. One day she would be a great harpist, thanks to their perseverance.

"Yes," said Frau Schenkel, before he could speak, "but those paintings are not really here, are they?"

"Yes, they are," said Herr Hoffer.

"They are not listed," said Werner, for once siding with Frau Schenkel. It was as if he had been waiting for this opening for years.

"Oh, somewhere they are," said Herr Hoffer vaguely, feeling cornered without due warning.

"In your head," said Werner.

"Well, I am actually in charge here, Werner."

"Supposing I had secreted the books as you have secreted the paintings?"

"You would have placed them in the vaults for safety, that's all."

His heart was pounding.

"No, I would have expropriated them without official sanction," said Werner, crossing his arms and smiling grimly. It was hard work being pompous and sanctimonious while sitting on the floor with a bloodied handkerchief on your shoulder.

"I think, in Herr Streicher's absence and with his full permission, I had the appropriate authority to take all necessary measures, Werner."

"Are you sure?"

"Yes."

"Is it really true," said Frau Schenkel, "that no one else but us knows about these paintings here, Herr Hoffer?"

"I sent a copy of the inventory to Berlin and another to our bank," Herr Hoffer replied, wrestling to find his authority without succumbing to petulance. The third copy of the inventory—a single sheet of thin-lined pinkish octavo paper—was burning a hole in his inside pocket. He wished he had brought the cognac now, of course, if only to settle his stomach. "What a time to start an interrogation," he added, glancing at Hilde for support.

"That inventory did not include these works here," said Werner flatly. "Almost a quarter of the entire collection."

Herr Hoffer looked at him. "No. And you know perfectly well why."

"It was not a proper or a full inventory," Werner went on, like a stenographer's typewriter.

"Exceptional times demand exceptional measures."

"I made a full inventory of the library's contents, volume by volume, and they were all taken away," said Werner, rubbing his nose and wincing, because there were little cuts on it made by the glass.

"To the salt mine," said Herr Hoffer, as if that was reassuring.

"Taken away," repeated Werner, with a hint of mournfulness.

"That is books," said Frau Schenkel.

"So?"

"We're talking about paintings, Herr Oberst."

"The books were placed in the salt mine for their own good, Werner," Herr Hoffer insisted, seizing his advantage. "I have checked them since, at least once a month, as you are well aware. The conditions are ideal. It is perfectly dry at 460 meters down; the salt absorbs excessive moisture and there is no groundwater circulating. There is not a hint of any change to the books, even on the oldest pigskin bindings. I regularly leaf through a sample, and the pages are entirely clean. Here it isn't so dry, as we know. In fact, it's even a little damp in certain atmospheric conditions. And the rats—"

"Exactly. These paintings have suffered over the last year. That frame has been nibbled."

"Nothing compared to the treatment they might have received had they gone off with the others. You saw the way they were bundled into those dirty furniture vans by those sloppy men from the Self-Protection Service."

"Thank God they were sloppy. If they hadn't been, they would have checked the inventory properly and suspected something. Imagine that."

"Those boys weren't sloppy," said Frau Schenkel. "They had been up all night pulling out bodies from that orphanage."

"That doesn't affect my point," said Herr Hoffer. "And you know perfectly well, Werner, that any inventory was a farce, since the museum's contents belong entirely to the Reich. I'm sorry, but I don't understand why you are suddenly attacking me on this subject."

"I am not attacking you, Heinrich, I am informing myself. As Chief Archivist and Keeper of Books, with responsibility for the

Fossil, Town History, and Local Handiworks collections, I think I have a right to know. I can't speak on behalf of my missing colleagues, God rest their souls."

Herr Hoffer coughed involuntarily. The reference to the eight members of staff, from gallery guards to trainee curators, missing or killed in action was couched as an accusation.

"At no point did you ask me, Werner," he said.

"I was waiting to be told."

"We had several meetings at which the storage details came up. You could have asked then or under Any Other Business."

"Yes, and you would have started by lying to me," said Werner. "As you did just now to Frau Schenkel."

"Lying is too strong," Frau Schenkel broke in. "Herr Oberst, this is really not the moment—"

"Frau Schenkel, keep quiet."

"No, why should I?"

"Listen," said Herr Hoffer, raising his hands, "we act in the most intelligent and reasonable manner with one aim only in mind, like a sacred calling: the safety and protection of the collection for which we are all, in our own ways, responsible. The collection has been much damaged and dispersed over the last seven or eight years for reasons beyond our control. This unofficial storage in the vaults is, in a way, a rearguard action to protect the remaining works at special risk, solely for the future benefit of the people of Lohenfelde, after this nightmare is over."

"What nightmare do you mean?" asked Hilde Winkel, frowning.

Herr Hoffer felt all their eyes upon him in the frail yellow light. His injured hand hurt. His face stung.

"The war," was all he said.

"Surely a salt mine 460 meters deep is preferable to some old town vaults with rats and condensation?" Werner scoffed.

"I couldn't be certain that the paintings would reach the salt mine," he said.

"And the books?"

"I did not feel the same danger."

"The Führer collects books, Heinrich," said Werner, taking off his half-moon spectacles and resting the ends of them in the corner of his mouth. They came out and waved a little when he talked. "Thousands of them. For Linz. Tens of thousands of them. It was to be the greatest library in the world."

"And you wouldn't have felt honored, Herr Oberst?" asked Hilde Winkel.

Herr Hoffer felt the heat was off.

"Honored?"

"By the inclusion of some of our volumes in the Führer's great library?"

"A librarian has the care of every volume at heart, Fräulein Winkel," said Werner. "Ours is not a lending library."

The women's eyes widened. For Herr Hoffer, the idea of the Führer filling in a library ticket was more surreal than shocking.

"The fact is," said Werner, the spectacles at his mouth flashing in the candlelight like a warning, "you started secreting them down here long before the war. That air-raid shelter next to the toilets was a decoy."

"Yes, certain examples especially at risk were placed down here. Herr Streicher and I started with a few works, but I developed—"

"Degenerates?" Hilde Winkel interrupted.

Werner replaced his spectacles and sighed.

"Paul Burck isn't a degenerate," said Frau Schenkel. "Far from it. You can understand what you're looking at. You can hear the rustling of the leaves."

"Is Burck's painting here?"

"Yes, Fräulein Winkel, mainly for Frau Schenkel's sake," said Herr Hoffer. "As well as certain modernist works. Takes all sorts," he added, unnecessarily.

"I didn't know it was just for my sake," said Frau Schenkel, looking pleased.

Hilde opened her damaged mouth to speak.

"And what about the Teniers?" Werner said, staring at him, his glittering lenses like an awful vision in a mirror.

"The Teniers?" Herr Hoffer echoed, feeling his face draining of blood.

"That's with the SS Sturmbannführer, in his office," said Frau Schenkel.

"That's the Nattier," said Werner, keeping his gaze fixed on Herr Hoffer, "the Jean Marc Nattier: Mademoiselle de Guilleroy splashing about in the tub. I'm referring to the Teniers. David Teniers the Younger. *Venus Bathing.*"

"If you want to split hairs, Herr Oberst—"

"Different scalps, Frau Schenkel." Werner smiled. "Different style, different period, different nationality. They both show females bathing, that's all. One in a tub, one in a pool. One's a goddess, the other's a French lady of the court showing her legs. The Jean Marc Nattier was openly borrowed, as it were, by the SS Sturmbannführer, and one day we will get it back. I'm talking about the David Teniers. David Teniers the Younger. His nude."

"I don't think I'll be bothering either way," said Frau Schenkel, with a sniff.

"Venus Bathing," Werner continued, with a patient sigh. "A work dated 1653, from his middle period. As is typical of David Teniers the Younger, the figure has strangely disproportionate arms. He is more used to painting drunk Flemish peasants. Venus is dressed in nothing but jewelry. Purchased for the collection in 1906. You know the one I mean, Heinrich. There is only one in the possession of the museum. Of inestimable value to future generations of art lovers in Lohenfelde and beyond. What has become of our Teniers, Heinrich?"

And Herr Hoffer, although he had been mentally rehearsing this scene for several months in the small hours of the night, could not find enough moisture in his throat to utter a single word.

Papa, Mama, Leo, Lily, little Henny, Grandmama. I am alive,
you are alive, so we are all still alive, thank goodness! Or is it
that we are all dead? I have nothing to say. What is there to say?
Nothing is nothing is nothing. The huge beam disappears into
the shadows and I can't see the end. I wish I had one of my old
dolls. Emilie, for instance.

26

Parry tried to get used to the blackness. The blackness felt safer. This
was what God started with on the first day. In the beginning was the
blackness and then the Word.

He reached into his left pocket and fished a cigarette from the tin
and then lit another before the first was halfway through, keeping the
glow hidden in his hand.

He unwrapped a candy from its cellophane and the noise filled
the vaults. It turned out to be fudge. It tasted of the Ardennes. His
new trousers felt strange against his thighs.

He was sure that if he switched on the flashlight someone would
notice aboveground: When a town lost its electricity or gas, any
flicker attracted attention. If someone found him down here, they'd
wonder what he was doing staying with a crowd of deads and they
would smell something suspicious.

He tried not to think too much about the deads, or about rats as
hungry as hell.

The Pied Piper of Hamelin.

As a kid, years ago, he'd think too much about the boy with the
calliper who was too lame to keep up and who watched the earth
swallow his friends where the Pied Piper had led them in like rats.
He didn't realize then that everyone who read that story identified
with the lame boy, because the others had gone away forever and no
one likes to think of themselves as going away forever, disappearing
forever. It was nothing to do with Freud, it was just that no one can
think of themselves as not existing, as being in a kind of blackness for

eternity, like this blackness—except that here there were sounds.
Here there were sounds.

He heard a tiny grating noise from around the corner where the
guy in the blue cardigan lay. Scritch scratch. Teeth against bone.
Something malevolent and intelligent gnawing away. That was unpleasant.

Against the black canvas surrounding him, his eyes started painting pictures. That was bad. The pictures were not good. They were
rushing things of war, of dead faces and bad moments of fear, of bodies falling and bodies showing how messy and wet and evil-smelling
they are inside. Even children's. Of smashed equipment and fire and
dead horses. A lot of dead horses. Men laughing by broken trees
while the ice did not break and the rivers were like the river in Dante
he'd had to draw for the art-class exercise back home in red and
black wash—*and use the paper, Neal, let it show through for highlights
and dramatic contrast. The secret of art is economy, Neal. Minimum effort for maximum effect.* Morrison, who'd been with him right from
England for fuck's sake, laughing like he was there right in front of
him now. That SS guy outside Dorsten who didn't want to be helped,
lying there bleeding from his stumps in the pillbox, his sleeves in
rags, who didn't want to be helped and screamed at them in Heinie
lingo to fuck off, it sounded like, while Morrison laughed because
the guy looked like a glove puppet.

He didn't feel all that well. The blackness was bad. He was in sad
shape. He was fagged out.

Morrison?

You're fagged out, Morriboy?

Yup, I'm in sad shape. I'm in sad shape, Neal. Do you have a
cigarette?

*Today the one with the big mustache brought a mirror, but I am
not to keep it. It is the lovely lake of Königssee, in which I look
at myself and drown.*

27

"The Teniers," Herr Hoffer said, finding his voice after swallowing,
"is in the salt mine."

"No. It had already left the museum."

Frau Schenkel tutted. "Herr Oberst, is this the time or place?"

Tiny bits of masonry pattered down. The candle's flame was
sucked into the melting wax and then enlarged, turning Werner
Oberst's half-moon spectacles into two headlights taped for a black-
out. They seemed to be driving straight for Herr Hoffer, mesmerized
in the road like a rabbit. There was a distant boom.

"Yesterday morning," said Werner, "I had an appointment with
Herr Kreisleiter Fest, in his gymnasium of an office. I was attempting
to recover the unique town plan of 1701 that the district Party office
had borrowed from the archives, if you remember, two years ago."

"Did you get it back?"

"That, Heinrich, is beside the present point. Everything was in
chaos, with Fest sitting in the middle like a pumpkin. They were
packing everything into boxes, everything except the telephone.
Funny, they all knew before we did. I was wearing my wound badge.
Fest asked me what kind of wound it was. As if I was shirking."

Werner lifted up his right arm, the one that was always rather awkward in its movement. "It splintered at the elbow from a single bullet
on the Somme," he said. "The nerves were smashed. It gives me pain
every day. If I am sometimes short-tempered, it is the pain."

"Ah," said Frau Schenkel, "so that's all right then."

"The buffoon was called out to greet some woman in a fur. At any
rate, through all the comings and goings of men with boxes, I noticed
something extraordinary through a door at one end. Pink flesh."

"Nothing surprises me." Frau Schenkel sighed. "You never know what's round the next corner."

"I went closer," continued Werner, "and peeped in. It was the Kreisleiter's private drawing room, not yet packed up. The pink flesh belonged to the torso of a painted Venus. You'll have guessed by whom. She was hanging above the fireplace. I was very surprised; I had thought *Venus Bathing* was here, in the vaults. At that moment the buffoon came back into the room. I was a little vexed, I have to admit. 'Ah, yes, a wonderful painting,' he said, leading me into the private drawing room. 'Look at the ass on her! That's genius, that is. They knew how to paint skirt in those days.'"

Frau Schenkel giggled. "You've got him very well, Herr Oberst!"

Never, in twenty years, thought Herr Hoffer, has she complimented him before. I am in trouble.

"'But this wonderful painting, my dear Oberst,'" Werner went on, pitching the Hannoverian accent even thicker, "'like all your wonderful paintings, is the property of the Reich! As you bloody well know. Anyway, I did not even expropriate the bird. She was a gift.' 'A gift, Kreisleiter Fest?' 'And stop pissing blood about it, Oberst—the bird's to fly to safety this very afternoon! In the boot of my personal car, under my personal bloody protection!'"

Werner was almost pop-eyed. He had become, despite his dry thinness, Kreisleiter Fest.

"Very good," said Frau Schenkel, nodding and smiling.

Hilde was frowning, however.

"And what was our Kreisleiter Fest before the war?" Werner growled, himself again. "A greengrocer in a white coat. In Ebstorf."

"My brother-in-law was stationmaster at Ebstorf," said Frau Schenkel. "Trains run in the family."

"Why don't we put on a record?" murmured Herr Hoffer. "Offenbach. *Orphée aux enfers.*"

"Kreisleiter Fest collaborates closely with the Gestapo," Hilde Winkel said. "You have to tread carefully with Kreisleiter Fest."

"My sister, mind you, hated trains," said Frau Schenkel. "She was standing on the platform, age five, when she was suddenly covered in steam and smoke."

"Heinrich," cried Werner Oberst, in his thin, rather high voice, "why did you have to do it?"

The bombardment paused. They could almost imagine the gunners stilled like themselves in astonishment, poised over the ordnance. Herr Hoffer closed his eyes for a moment. In all his life, he had never got away with anything. God somehow saw to it.

"Do what?" asked Frau Schenkel.

"You tell, Heinrich, you tell," said Werner Oberst, in what might almost have passed for a sad voice in any other circumstance and from any other mouth.

"He said he would kill me," murmured Herr Hoffer.

"Correction. Send you to the Russian Front."

"Exactly."

Herr Hoffer swallowed back nausea.

"I did not want to be absent," he continued, without opening his eyes. "I had responsibilities."

"Responsibilities?"

"We're talking about January last year, before the evacuation order was given."

"So?"

"Let me finish." He tried walking through the wildflower meadow with his mother, but all he could see was Bendel walking with Sabine. Hand in hand. He took a long, profound breath which didn't seem to get very far in his lungs. "It was an icy day, actually. You recall how awful the winter was last year. I was summoned to see Fest and I was, naturally, a little nervous. He's not, I think we agree, the most polished of individuals. Anyway, he came straight to the point. The Bolsheviks were about to win back Leningrad, he said, and they were very short of mature, intelligent men out there. I replied immediately that it was vital I remain in Lohenfelde. Fest said, 'Vital for whom, Herr Hoffer?' That was when I made my error. I said of course it was vital for the Kaiser Wilhelm. 'Ah,' he said, 'but not at all vital for the Reich, Herr Hoffer.'"

"You haven't quite got him," said Frau Schenkel.

"If I'd said that straight off, about it being vital for the Reich—"

"We get the picture," murmured Werner. "Your error."

"The next thing he said was, 'Is it to be Leningrad, my dear fellow, or Dachau?' The Dachau business was just ridiculous, of course. Just threats and bullying. Why should I be sent to Dachau? What had I done?"

Werner grunted. The others looked away.

Herr Hoffer closed his eyes again. It was like trying to tell his restless daughters about paintings and myths. He was not very good at it; he couldn't do the voices. They liked the museum only because they could run up and down the galleries, making an awful noise and irritating Werner.

"Well? We are all ears, Heinrich."

"I'm sorry. The only pictures in his oversized office were photographs of racing horses and some postcard watercolors of the Hannoverian countryside. And a Siemens calendar. As you know. Apart from the Führer's portrait, of course."

No one said anything. The golden stems of the willow. A mandolin. Ah, for your moist wings, O West, how sorely do I envy you!

"Heinrich?"

"I said I must be present, as Acting Acting Director, when the contents of the museum were removed to storage in the salt mine. He came over to my side of the desk and sat on the edge of it, swinging his black boots. They're the only bit of him that's polished."

"I think we've got that point, Heinrich."

"I don't know how the desk took it, in fact. You know how overweight he is. My chair was a long way from the desk, in the middle of the floor. It was very quiet."

Herr Hoffer opened his eyes, closing them again almost instantly on seeing Werner's fixed gaze. He pictured the fat district leader staring at him over the shining sweep of parquet, the man's brown breeches like a clown's trousers, a hint of sweat drifting over with the expensive cologne. It had made Herr Hoffer feel very small, stranded in the middle of the parquet.

"And? Heinrich?"

"I knew what his next words were going to be. Everyone knows our Kreisleiter. He said to me that we could make a deal."

"Ah, yes."

"I pretended to be bewildered. He got cross. 'I think Leningrad rather than Dachau,' he said, 'as you look so hot and sweaty, Herr Hoffer!'"

All three of them found this funny; Herr Hoffer gamely squeezed out a smile.

"Yes, if only one could find him amusing. Having despatched me to the Russian Front, he would have helped himself to the entire collection."

"You could have reported him to a higher authority," said Werner. "For felony. That Orstgruppenleiter in Bavaria—where was it? I can't remember—anyway, they nailed him. For embezzlement."

"And my family?" said Herr Hoffer, nettled now. "That's Party policy, that is. Think of my family, please, Werner."

"So you let him," said Werner.

"If you want to put it like that. Which I'm sure you do."

"And that's putting it kindly, Heinrich."

"At least let me finish, Werner! Thank you. Fest visited us the next day. He was plastered, as usual. He insisted on examining those paintings stocked in the Luftschutzbunker. We went through them together. He complained about the smell from the toilets. We came to the Teniers *Venus*, and then the von Bohn *Kleopatra*, and he slobbered over them. He made the most vulgar remarks about them. I pleaded with him not to take both, and because he was plastered he put his arm around my shoulder and agreed to take only one. Unfortunately, he chose the Teniers, not the von Bohn."

"So he does have taste, after all," said Werner. "As Max Friedländer once put it, 'An artist loves nature, not his art. The art is loved particularly by dilettantes and amateurs.'"

"I don't see the relevance of that remark, Werner."

Werner smiled thinly. Another of his jokes.

"I brought the Teniers to him a fortnight later," Herr Hoffer continued. "Being already in the Luftschutzbunker, it was not hard to conceal the removal."

"You told us it had been slipped down to the vaults, Heinrich."

"It was only for the good of the museum," he said, not quite sturdily enough.

"Oh, come on," said Werner. "It was to save your own skin. Anyway, Fatty Fest gave me a different version. He told me you had been the first to offer the deal."

Herr Hoffer nodded, looking up at the big square stones in the ceiling and trying not to wince. "But it was quite clear what he was after, even if he didn't state it openly. Agility is the thing," he added, and pursed his lips.

Frau Schenkel raised her chin and looked down her long nose at Herr Hoffer.

"Do you mean to tell me, Herr Hoffer, that you bribed the Kreisleiter with a painting from the museum in order to avoid the draft?"

"That's putting it too crudely, Frau Schenkel—"

"Making me an unwitting party to the deed?"

"I don't understand."

"Who typed the false inventory, Herr Hoffer?"

"Frau Schenkel," Werner interjected, "nobody cares about that."

"I do!"

"Please," came Hilde Winkel's pleasant young voice, "do we have to quarrel at such a time? With the barbarians at the gate?"

"Ah, this is your adored realism, my dear Fräulein Winkel!" cried Werner Oberst.

"Naturalism, not realism. I prefer the term naturalism, Herr Oberst."

"Is there a difference? I had always thought the terms interchangeable."

"I prefer to keep them distinct. Up to a point, Herr Oberst."

"Philosophically speaking, I suppose."

"Let me illustrate. The thrust of my thesis. The difference or, rather, distinction," Hilde went on, with the harmless if slightly aggressive intensity of youth, "is exemplified between early and late classical Greek sculpture. That is, the manner in which the later period departs from the norm of perfection through imitative naturalism. The influence of both periods on our own contemporary masters such as Breker, Thorak, or Albiker is extremely illuminating. It is my conviction, you see, that they are combining both periods in a new revolutionary manner. I mean, by showing the swollen veins that denote struggle and effort, but without sinking into the decadence of imitative naturalism."

She was blinking, as if someone were throwing dust in her eyes. It was intellectual excitement.

"All very disappointing," Frau Schenkel sighed.

"And how do they achieve this?" Hilde Winkel continued, although no one was listening. "By never forgetting the suprahuman ideal to which great sculpture must always aspire, in the true Platonic tradition!"

"We live in disappointing times, Frau Schenkel," said Werner.

"At least I saved von Bohn's *Kleopatra*," Herr Hoffer said. "I slipped it down here straight after Fest had left, in case he came back for it. I don't know what I'd have said, mind you."

"Yes, at least you did that, Heinrich," said Werner, folding his bony hands around one knee and nodding very slowly. "At least we have the von Bohn *Kleopatra*."

Maybe you are the ones pulling on the rope.

28

"Heinrich? Heinrich?"

Morrison was talking to him. The voice was high, now, because death did that to you. No phantom had a low voice. You returned to childhood.

The livid movement of flame light wavered over the vaults. It wasn't the fluttering that he felt all over his body but something separate, not him. There was an angel, in fact, a woman. It wasn't Morrison. It wasn't hell—unless it was a demon. A demon of the deep Germanic forests they'd been told about in England, that gave Hitler his satanic power.

Parry struggled against his fever and his colossal exhaustion, as if it were something separate. He separated it as he'd separate his fear. This is how most of the men died: not with a bullet but with sickness.

A cigarette hung from his lips. Maybe the airlessness had extinguished it, or maybe he'd forgotten to light it.

The woman was holding her lamp near the four deads by the exit hole. He made sure he kept still as she started to wail. She was grieving. One of those deads was called Heinrich. From the look of the way she stood, bent over a little, it was the guy with the Himmler spectacles still on his nose. The hell with her.

The one who'd been cradling that cross, he thought. The hell with her. That painting burnt to a cross. Like crossed keys or a mark of the plague on those doors back then, whenever, in ol' London. Nope, he'd not been there. Not back then. It was all rats.

Parry patted the wooden labels in his breast pocket and remembered; he'd try to ask her what *Waldesraus* meant. It was a word that would heal him. Certain words were good medicine; you could chew on them like sweet, wholesome bread with healing herbs inside. This was the quart of Indian blood coming up in him: that Apache grandmother who'd given him his slant lower eyelids and swarthy skin. He was joining up the dots with difficulty, making a great effort. Good. The woman was standing there shaking all over, and the lamp—a kerosene lamp, it looked like—was shaking with her. There is no wind down here, he thought. Is there wind overhead? He couldn't remember.

Maybe.

He shrugged. I figure, he thought, that if she collapses with her grief, the kerosene lamp will fall and smash and we'll be cooked to a couple of deads no one will take into account, with all the other deads around in this world conflict.

This was why he would just have to get up and make it over to her, before she let go of the lamp like a goddamn phosphorus blanket bombing. He made a great effort and stood up. He was stumbling over to her and she saw him and screamed and he thought she was going to drop the goddamn lamp.

Then he came up close and she just stared at him with big eyes, one hand over her mouth.

Said nothing. Dirty, bruised face.

He took the lamp from her and fished around in his pockets and found the last candy he'd been given by Morrison. No, Morrison was already dead and he'd never again win at pinochle. It wasn't the fudge, it was a hard clear candy with a flavor of strawberry, almost. But not quite.

She took the candy and unwrapped it and put it in her mouth, shaking, her body shaking all over, and then she did an unexpected thing as Parry stood there with the lamp, feeling weak and ill.

She placed her hands on his chest—on the dirty tunic, to be precise—and laid her head between the hands so it touched where it buttoned up and he felt it as weight, though not much. She had a mess of fair hair, which he stroked. It was as if she were listening to the beat of his heart, except that she was moaning softly. Her hair smelled not of spring but of autumn. It was a little rank and smoky, but he didn't mind that. It was a juicy kind of rankness, like those rotted windfalls in the Normandy orchards, and the hair was thick and soft against his mouth. He let the hair soften his face, rubbing it with his mouth and nose and chin and eyes. It was so nice, so soft.

He even took some inside his mouth and chewed it for a moment.

As kids they'd believed that if you ate a girl's hair she would certainly have a crush on you. This clever kid called Larry Spinks had given him some nice blond hair and he'd almost choked swallowing it, and then he was told by Larry and the others, who were laughing, that the hair had been cut from Sophie McConnell's corpse—she'd been run over by a car and killed the previous week and now she would come and crave him in the dark of his bedroom with her glowing eyes and her face all messed up from the car.

He couldn't sleep without a light for two years. This is probably why he'd been numb to girls until Maureen had come along and rescued him with her sweet kindness.

All living heads have warmth.

Something flashed nearby, but it was only the spectacles on the dead's nose, catching the light. The dead wasn't moving, however. It was the lamp swinging in his own hand.

He put the lamp down carefully on the floor of the vaults. Then he held the woman as if without her he might fall over. He held her tight enough so as his own chest didn't start shaking, because there was so much he had to let go.

If you'd kiss me good night at night, in your usual way, that would be better. One day kisses will mean something else to me. Thirty-six buttons. I kiss each of them in turn. One by one by [one].

29

Herr Hoffer knew why Werner was so cross, why he'd harbored the knowledge with such delicious hate, waiting for the right moment.

My God, it was that auction in Munich, near the beginning of the war. Werner Oberst had come very close, in that auction, to acquiring a handsome second edition of the *Theatrum Pictorium;* one theory held that the Teniers *Venus* of 1653 was a copy of an unknown Italian master in the collection of the Archduke William. Certainly one of the 244 engravings in that famous book was identical to the (reversed) Teniers. Poor Gustav Glatz had written a paper on it in 1931, translated for the *Gazette des Beaux Arts* in Paris, for which triumph he had received a sum equivalent to a meal for two in the shabbiest restaurant in Lohenfelde (without beer). Or so he claimed.

Werner had been outbid by Friedrich Wolffhardt, in charge of developing the Führer's library in Linz. Wolffhardt purchased the entire collection that day, just like that—mostly first editions from the seventeenth and eighteenth centuries.

Werner was furious, given the possible connection with their own Teniers and the fact that the book, as part of the vast confiscated private library of Nathan Gutheimer, would have gone for a relatively low price. He had decided that if that devil Wolffhardt ever tried to plunder, for Linz, their own excellent book and manuscript collection, he—Werner Oberst, Chief Archivist and Keeper of Books—would defend the library with his old trench pistol and make the ultimate sacrifice. He had told the Acting Director this, as well as his deputy, pointing out that he had been an excellent shot in the last war. Bullets seemed to go where he wanted them to, he claimed, as long as he didn't think about it too hard. Neither man had objected, nor had they approved.

This was long before the Chief Archivist was recruited into the Volkssturm, last autumn, from which point he felt that his position was compromised. Luckily for everyone, Wolffhardt's greedy prowling through the Reich had never passed through Lohenfelde. Werner sometimes fancied he knew the reason, which was absurd. They were lucky, that was all. The Reich was vast.

At any rate, Herr Hoffer now understood why the Teniers painting meant so much to Werner Oberst; why it sparked such anger in the general waste. Otherwise it didn't really make sense, this reaction of Werner's; at least half their collection had been "confiscated," and the Jean Marc Nattier had been simply plucked off the wall by the last SS Sturmbannführer—hardly a "borrowing"! David Teniers the Younger's voluptuous *Venus* was just another brick in the awful edifice. It was only a painting! It was not a human life! He wasn't guilty of murder!

Anyway, back in the heady days in Heidelberg, certain of his

fellow students thought painting pictures was no longer even possible in a world with such awful social problems and after such a
terrible war. If paintings were to be painted, they must be painted on
the sides of buildings or jugs, not left to the art dealers and the rich
Jewish collectors. Herr Hoffer had scoffed then, but he might agree
with them now. He would rather art vanished completely for a hundred years than bear the likes of Party daubers like Ziegler or Troost
or Gradl at its helm. He wanted to say all this, but of course he could
not. No wonder Werner despised him.

He felt sorry for Werner—he did not despise the man in return.
Werner had no wife and no family, only his books and fossils and war
wound. And now the books were gone, down in the salt mine where
Werner could not stroke them. He, Herr Hoffer, had a wife, a loving
and attractive wife, and two adorable children.

His stomach suddenly turned. Why was he not with them? What
did all these masterpieces matter (though he was the first to admit
that many of them were minor works) compared to Sabine, Erika,
and Elisabeth?

The thought that they might already be dead flashed through his
mind like an obscenity.

It was simply not possible.

I will grant you, dear Lord, all these paintings, if you spare my wife
and darling girls.

Another deal. Another negotiation. He had been negotiating for
years. He had saved at least thirty modern works, although he had let
the Schmidt-Rottluff and the Kandinsky and the Hausmann photomontage slip through his fingers: his favorites. Not the Vincent,
however. Not the Vincent van Gogh. He was the only one who knew
where it was. Herr Streicher did not know where it was. Even
Werner Oberst did not know—and therefore did not know everything, after all.

But Herr Hoffer knew, because he had put it there.

He had SS Sturmführer Bendel to thank for that. If SS Sturmführer Bendel had not shown an almost morbid interest in the painting, Herr Hoffer would not have acted as he did. It was his chief

victory. It was the one painting most at risk, and he had saved it. The museum's jewel. In the unbefitting place of darkness. Without light, there is no glory.

Umbra. Pure umbra.

So why had he bothered with three coats of size?

Machine guns, now. A mortar or field gun, burping every so often. The cretinous Kreisleiter was fighting back, or perhaps it was the Waffen-SS on their own. It was all lost, but they would carry on until Lohenfelde was leveled and the Americans were very angry, shooting at everything in sight.

Captain Clark Gable, my name is Hoffer, Heinrich Hoffer. Please don't believe what you hear from certain quarters. I did what I thought was best. Most of us, especially myself, prayed for your arrival every day, if only to get some sleep.

He kept his eyes shut, feeling what the three others now thought of him as a hot, sour breath on his face. He began, not surprisingly, to remember that day in 1910 when he stole a pear from the market stall and was beaten with a cane by his father. It was a large, round, shiny pear, and very sweet. He was sure it would have been very sweet, but he did not get to taste it. The stall owner had spotted him. He could not say why he had stolen it. He was a good boy and feared God and went to the bare, white, wax-smelling church at least twice a week with his family. But he had stolen the pear. And his father had thrashed him. His father was not even a violent man. But he was keen to nip evil in the bud; it saved trouble later. That's how he'd put it. And Heinrich Hoffer had grown up straight, not crooked, and passed smoothly into adulthood as a student beneath the ruined Schloss of Heidelberg, acquiring his scars and glory. But the untasted pear haunted him.

Always there was the feeling in his life—even in Sabine's succulent embrace—that some ultimate happiness was eluding him, that he had not quite managed to sink his teeth into the ultimate sweetness.

"Herr Hoffer?"

"Yes, Fräulein Winkel?"

"Hilde, please. I believe you acted out of integrity, Herr Hoffer. With Fest."

"Thank you, Hilde."

He heard a snort from Werner. Herr Hoffer kept his eyes closed, as if he were on a train and dozing.

"The times are very difficult," he added.

"Through no fault of the Führer's," said Hilde quickly.

He didn't reply. No one replied. Hilde, for all her naïve enthusiasm and shy loveliness, might easily be a Party block spy. The Americans might yet be repulsed. People were dealt with until the very last moment. Summarily. They didn't even bother to send you off to a camp. Too much trouble. No time. They just blew your brains out or throttled you on the spot, without even removing your shoes or your jacket. Right up to the last minute. Most especially in the last minute. The play was not over until the curtain fell and bumped on the stage.

He looked at his watch for something to do, peering at it in the candlelight. The hands got confused under the glass. It could have been quarter to eleven or five to nine. For a few seconds he actually forgot where in the twenty-four hours they were situated. The air here was always the same, the temperature unvarying in the blackness; you could live here in the winter and not die of cold, and cool off in the summer. Night and day were identical.

Five to nine in the morning, obviously.

He listened to the watch's movement for a moment, holding it up to his ear. It comforted him, the tiny grind and click. A birthday present from Sabine, and rather fine. Werner had a fob, of course, and had to produce it.

"Two minutes to nine o'clock," said Werner. "I doubt we'll hear the bells."

"As my dear mother would say, 'We've got the whole of today to arrive at tomorrow,'" said Frau Schenkel, who was in fact a notorious stickler for time—and the main reason Herr Hoffer would always try to get the earlier tram in the morning, when there were still trams. Once, when he came into work five minutes late, after baby Erika had coughed all night, Frau Schenkel had looked at him as if she knew some awful moral disintegration had already begun. Even after he had explained, out of his exhaustion, she had given the air of not quite believing him. The key, of course, was not to care what she or anyone else thought.

But he did care, and much too much. Three coats of size to stiffen the canvas! Ridiculous!

They stayed quiet for the bells, in case. Ten trucks loaded with iron rivets passed full pelt over a trench in Otto von Guericke Strasse, or so it sounded. That was followed by a lot of burping and smaller thumps. There was the distinctive bitterness of smoke, which was more disturbing than the noise. It had leaked down here off the street, Herr Hoffer decided, feeling a little breathless. There must be a ventilation hole somewhere.

Damn, he needed to go to the toilet; his bowels were loosening. It was nerves, mainly.

It was unfair of Werner to bring up such matters at this juncture. Extremely unfair. It was sadistic. It came of an embittered nature.

"I've been thinking," Herr Hoffer said, adjusting his armband, which had a tendency to end up by his elbow. "As a member of the armed forces, I should go on patrol, should I not?"

"What do you mean?" came from Frau Schenkel.

"I mean I should do a tour of inspection above. The museum, not the streets."

"You've only just come back down," said Frau Schenkel.

"Herr Wolmer might need help," he said, too weakly.

He couldn't possibly tell them he needed to empty his bowels. Some people used a bedpan in front of everyone else, shielded only by a relative holding up a coat: one of the main horrors of the public shelters, in his opinion.

"Don't get too close to glass," said Hilde.

"You're better off down here," Werner growled. "You might not want to come back."

"You'd be best off with your family anyway," Frau Schenkel muttered, scratching her scrawny neck.

"Of course I'll come back, Werner," said Herr Hoffer, a touch crossly.

Hilde stretched her arms up and gave a little grunt, having grown stiff; she was an active sportswoman, apparently, exercising the body as well as the intellect. She linked her fingers together, turned her hands palms upwards, and stretched, very gymnastically.

Herr Hoffer suddenly caught a sharp scent of sweat, almost fierce in its sharpness. Hilde's sweat.

He experienced the most extraordinary animal desire.

It was as if this desire were emanating from the very pores of her body and entering his insides with its animal strength, bypassing his mind. There was nothing even sweet about her sweat; it might almost have been a man's. But the mere fact that the lovely Hilde could smell so fiercely and frankly was itself stirring. No, that reflection came after; that was his mind catching up. Her face was hidden by her arms, but he could have drunk her smell to the last drop.

She lowered her arms with another grunt and let them rest in her lap, her head tipped back.

Herr Hoffer stood up with difficulty, deeply uncomfortable and at the same time very glad. There was almost a moral power in that attraction. And he hated the fuggish odor of gymnasiums! He didn't like the smell of people at all, in fact, and the lack of decent soap—soap that lathered, that didn't just swim uselessly about on top of the water—meant that people around him had smelled a lot more in recent years. The revelation of Hilde's smell made him embrace humanity again.

This was his main comforting thought a few minutes later, on passing through the bare galleries above. The hazy air was bitter and the parquet crunched underfoot like sand, though Herr Wolmer had tried to sweep up, even here. The man was a marvel! The bombardment seemed muffled by the museum's emptiness, in fact—or maybe they were shelling farther off. He pictured the shells falling on Hermann Göring Strasse, where his apartment stood.

He felt an enormous relief, getting out of the vaults.

Though he had never really got used to the emptiness of the

museum, of all its huge rooms. It seemed to deny his very right to exist, this emptiness. If he opened his mouth now it would be only to scream. To scream is at least a denial of futility. He felt so like screaming.

Instead, he coughed. He really did need the toilet rather urgently.

He hurried on, his steps echoing over the rumblings beyond—on the other side of life. He thought, for a moment, there was someone else in one of the galleries—or rather, he had the sensation that someone had just left seconds before—but it was undoubtedly the echo of his own steps. In the seventeenth-century gallery, in the corner next to where a lovely Marell flower study had hung, a large black spider waited, its web already dingy from the dust and smoke. The point, he thought, is not to lose faith. The pictures will hang again from the picture rails. German culture will be restored. Its essence is depth and spirit: Such things cannot be shattered by bombs or soiled by cretins like Fest. The French will understand this, in their calculating, sharp way. Even the British, with their purely mercantile instincts, will understand this in the hour of victory. He was not so sure about the Americans. He somehow saw them as a force, quite shallow, that would flow over and depart, leaving only a litter of gifts: chewing gum and Coca-Cola and chocolate bars.

He must be mad. The Americans were pummeling his town to bits. That was not very shallow.

He stopped in front of the marble hulk *Defiant*, guarding the library: It was the work of Willy Meller, no less. Herr Hoffer privately nicknamed it Trotsky. Here he had found Hilde on several occasions, sketching the fellow's toes, biceps, absurd tendons. He had to admit, now, that her presence over the last year had added a spring to his step on the way to work. But at no point had he ever dreamed of trying anything. He simply admired her, that was all. She had beauty and a youthful intellectual passion. How she could see anything in this tripe defeated him. The Party had somehow possessed her, like a demon lover.

The library, holding antiquarian volumes up to 1850 and intended only for scholars, was like a granary without so much as a husk of corn; at least the shelves were there. At least it smelled of beeswax and leather. The galleries, however, with their bare whiteness, were like brains without a thought. He could still feel the concentrated silence of intellectual effort in the empty library, like a firm-set jaw.

The Führer scowled down at him, though. His huge photograph hung above Werner's desk on the podium, scowling down on the long empty tables where Herr Hoffer felt like the last scholar in the world. No one had thought of saving that picture! He could not work out Werner Oberst, whether he was on one side or the other. Anyway, there were no longer any sides, just those that surrounded them like high prison walls.

The shells had paused. His bowels constricted, in anticipation of a sudden loud bang. The pauses were worse than the noises.

He used the toilets off the library, as he always did in the past. The official staff toilet off the office had very thin walls, you could hear Frau Schenkel's typewriter as if she were in there with you. *For the use of library members only*. The small private space was a relief, even before he had emptied his bowels, his piles more irritating than painful today. It was such a relief to be alone, to let oneself go. Did Hitler shit? He couldn't imagine it.

And the graffiti was scholarly, in Latin or Greek or English or French.

Quas dederis solas semper habebis opes: Martial.

J'en ai trop prolongé la coupable durée: Racine.

Something by Talleyrand, blacked out.

There was no paper. He checked the color of his turds (black) and pulled the chain. There was no water, not even from the taps. His face in the mirror above the handbasin surprised him; his thinning hair was all over the place. He had run out of cream, and Sabine cut with blunt scissors. He took off his spectacles and pressed his face with his fingers—smoothing out the violet-tinted eye bags, the lines around his nose, the folds at the corners of his mouth. The tiny wounds made by the glass were a stipple of dark spots; they stung when he moved his skin about. Lack of food made him both more youthful and more elderly. He replaced his spectacles and kept very still for a moment, as if posing.

Portrait of a Gentleman, 1945
Oil on panel, 25.6 x 30.4
Private collection.

The light fell on one side of his face, dividing it along its contours like the colored relief in an atlas. The artist had rendered the skin in thick impasto—no, with the careful, methodical brush of an old Flemish master. Ladies and gentlemen, see how the inner life is suggested by the physical verisimilitude of the painted flesh, the highlight on the glistening eyeball!

He smiled, and his living portrait startled him. He must paint, when the war was over! He must devote himself to painting, even if he was appointed Director! Pencil, chalk, and watercolor: his favorite combination. Oh, if only he had taken up the true bohemian life in his youth, peeling potatoes for his supper in the corner of a Berlin attic, washing now and again in a tin basin, drying his shirt on the roof!

He felt safe in the little washroom. The bombardment had eased. And then a sudden chill took hold of him. Werner would tell the Americans about the Teniers. Venus would rise from her bath, dripping and naked, holding Werner Oberst's hand. Werner, whose record had been spotless in all regards, would tell them all about the Acting Acting Director's collusion with the Regional Party Leader, that fat buffoon Fest.

Would they care? They might. Plenty of men released from the camps or returning from exile to replace the Acting Acting Director. The Jews, for instance. The Americans would be very keen on helping the Jews, making up for the abuse. The mere fact that he had remained in his post, thanks to his agility, would count against him. Deep down they would be jealous of his agility, his pluck, and so seek to destroy him with lies about collusion and betrayal. All he had cared about was the museum and its contents, as an officer must care about his ship and its passengers and its cargo and its crew. But how much would that count for in the face of all those self-righteous exiles and camp inmates and vengeful Jews—those who had either fled to save their skin or been careless enough to tread on the Party's toes?

His expression in the mirror was pitiful, ravaged. A smell of sewage was seeping up, thicker than his own smell: The pipes had probably burst. He watched his lips shape the words, as if in a film: *All I have wanted in life is beauty. Is there not a moral force in beauty? Kant thought so, for one.*

Now he looked like a clown, one of those sinister cabaret clowns with white faces and black lips. Kant had lent the face no extra dignity whatsoever. It twitched in surprise, suddenly; the little window in the washroom, glazed and ribbed, showed the shadow of something large moving in a strange way beyond it.

He hesitated, then opened the window with difficulty and saw the edge of a large cloth fluttering and billowing in the wind. It was the big red swastika banner, draped the length of the museum's back brick wall facing Count von Moltke Strasse. The banner had come loose. The cloth struck his face as he tried to take hold of it, stinging his eye. There was no one on the long street, its dingy buildings— some of them warehouses—not at all damaged. Everyone must be underground, he thought.

He closed the window again and wiped his wet eye. The banner should be taken down, or the Americans might see it as a provocation. But who would volunteer to remove it before the Americans arrived? The very idea contracted his stomach. A burst of mortar shells, quite near, announced the renewal of the bombardment. It was as if the whole business had an independent brain, like an ogre having its meal.

He left the toilets and crossed the Thoma flower mosaic to the great flight of stairs. He might as well do his duty and check the upper floors again. It stopped his brooding. He passed the superb white-glazed Allach milkmaid in the oyster-shell niche halfway up the stairs: It was a gift from Reichsführer-SS Himmler himself, via SS Obersturmbannführer Professor Diebitsch, the fine-porcelain manager in Dachau. It was expected, in return, that the museum should exhibit one of Diebitsch's quaint pastoral paintings—which it did. Herr Hoffer had left the milkmaid there during the evacuation, moving it quite close to the edge: Each vibration moved it closer. And closer.

The sweet little milkmaid would fall and shatter. Then she would be free.

He moved it again, placing it right on the lip of the niche. A sudden fit of giddiness overtook him. He made it to the top of the stairs and a cushioned bench next to the marble *Dawn*. He was short of breath and felt his pulse. It was irregular. This was not a heart attack, it was an anxiety attack. He calmed himself down with some yogic breathing exercises Sabine had learned at the gym. It would be terrible to die next to *Dawn*. This particular rubbish was by a young and clever disciple of Klimsch, Thomas Rotmann. The breasts were absurdly pert over the narrow waist and shone like door handles from being touched. It was the only erotic Party nude he knew, and for this reason he particularly disliked it.

He placed his fingers on its shoulder. It was cold, of course.

Ah, Sabine, my dearest darling. You are never cold.

Mama, Papa, have you forgotten me? Please don't forget me. I am ill. You haven't said good night to me yet. Someone is coming, like a bad dream. Maybe he will show me his tongue again and it will blossom into a flower, or sharpen to a point and sting me. The lake is very deep when I look in the mirror. That is why I am not to keep it.

30

The dame was warm.

She was in shock, and of course she didn't know she was in shock. That's the whole thing about shock. You can even be a corporal in the army of the United States and not know you're in shock.

Parry had got her up to the surface. Now he tried to sit her down on a big wooden beam that was almost horizontal, but she just repeated her name—*Frau Hoffer, Frau Hoffer*—and kept on clinging to him. In the end he sat himself down and let her cling to him.

He'd got the map pack on him too, with the rolled-up canvas inside. It was against his chest now, pressed to him like an extra muscular heart. He shifted it to his side so it wouldn't be mussed up and thought how he needed to wrap the canvas in something, given that the pack's flap couldn't be buttoned shut. Brown paper. Newspaper. Newspaper was what he needed.

He remembered there was some newspaper scattered next to that SS dead in the street nearby, as if the pages had been blown away from his face. But she wouldn't let him go! Parry was not a boy, and he'd have had no trouble throwing her off, but he couldn't do it. He tried to unstick her from his chest, but she just grabbed his mackinaw's lapels and hung on, sobbing.

He was used to this, he thought, and almost laughed.

It was like those times in France and then in Belgium. They arrived in Normandy in late summer and in every village the back of the troop truck would be waist-high in girls and flowers, the truck's floor a pungent mush of fruit. They'd roll with the girls in fruit like

Roman emperors as the truck rolled on through some town or village
and then they'd drink themselves stupid, wrapped in the tricolor,
faces smudged with lipstick, and they'd reckon in those first few days
that war was OK, very OK, despite those burnt hedges and tanks and
crap that hadn't been moved after D-Day plus sixty and that told
them what the action was really about and that they kind of imagined
now would be manageable.

And after his first daytime patrol a month later, when they'd broken every goddamn rule in the book and yet survived a burst of mortar and the first live noncaptive German they'd seen so far (he stood
in the middle of the lane before he ran like hell), every man had
come over with the shakes and then they'd thrown up, one after the
other, like dogs.

Good for Nothin' Joes.

He managed to spread the folded blanket over the beam in the
rubble with one hand and leaned back on it with the hausfrau clinging to him. He wriggled his back against the loose stuff until it wasn't
too uncomfortable.

He hoped no one would come up to them in the darkness.

This was not sex, this was grief. He respected her grief. He
stroked her hair. It was part of the job. She was not beautiful, in fact.

All he could see was the torn gable end of the museum looming
above them, darker against the night sky, with that crosshatch of skylight hanging on nothing and a little pale spot where the miracle Virgin stood. They were inside the museum, not outside, only there was
no inside now, it was all outside. Voices singing, but nothing too
close. They were out of sight of the streets, the animal tracks.

"We could play some pinochle," he murmured. "Morriboy always
won at pinochle."

The woman's face was wet through, but he shone the flashlight on
it to try to light up some sense in her goddamn brain. He couldn't understand what she was gabbling; even a native would've found it
hard, he reckoned, under the sighs and the gasps and the sobs.

But he'd got the painting. And that was the main thing. I have got
the painting, he thought. And that is about all of it, I guess.

It was just next to him, the map pack still hooked around his shoulder. The woman sat up a bit. She told him her name yet again, *Frau Hoffer,* putting her hand on her chest and then crumpling again into sobs.

He told her his name was Parry, Corporal Parry, but she wasn't listening.

Why had he told her his rank? Neither had told the other their Christian names. Neither could say anything much more that would be understood; he didn't want to say *schlafen, schlafen?* to a fresh and grieving widow, and he wasn't about to fish for his German phrase book in the map pack and ask her where the nearest pillbox was or tell her to drop her weapon or reassure her that he came in peace.

All he could remember was *Ich verstehe Sie,* "I understand you," because that was on the cover of the phrase book, and *Berlin ist eine Reise wert* because that was on the side of a toy bus he'd been given as a kid by his world-traveling Uncle Robert.

"Berlin is worth a visit, OK?" he murmured. *"Berlin ist eine Reise wert."*

She looked at him in a different way, then. Hell, she started gabbling in German with her hand over his breast pocket, where veterans told you to put your eating irons and cigarette case and spare ammo clips in case a bullet needed stopping. His pocket only had a couple of fucking picture labels in it. Maybe he wanted to get dead.

He shook his head and shrugged. He couldn't even say how sorry he was, but then her husband in the round spectacles might have been a very bad Nazi you'd want to kick the living shit out of all day.

"If you think I speak German then take it easy, that's it," he said.

She gave up the German. Her face was dirty and dust-streaked in the flashlight's beam, and her hair was a mess. He ran the light over her as she lay against him. She was done up in a dress patterned with hundreds of yellow and orange flowers like a meadow—the effect was almost three-dimensional; over that there was a kind of thin blue open cotton blouse or sweater—Parry wasn't too strong on women's clothing. There were bits of masonry stuck in the cotton of the blouse, and the elbows were white with dust. The dress was torn a little, and her bare calves were scratched; he could see dark streaks of blood. Her shoes were in bad shape. The dress was unbuttoned at the neck and he could see the tops of her round breasts. Her mouth was too thin and her face was mussed up like she had just risen but that was not her fault. He was soothing her now. Stroking her hair and no longer feeling so embarrassed. Her body was soft and warm against his. She could be thirty-five, maybe forty. There was a woman in her forties in the apartment below his in downtown Clarksburg, and she bathed daily and the smell of her strawberry bath crystals would waft up through the trapped air of the backyard and he would stand at his open window and be sexually aroused, breathing in the thick strawberry air.

I am now getting out of breath, he realized. I have killed men and I got out of breath too.

They could just stay here all night; it was comforting even though his back was getting chilled. He needed a cigarette but his throat was sore and the tin was in his thigh pocket on her side, along with the lighter. He didn't want to disturb her. The darkness of the ruins was shifting into many tones of gray; his eyes were adjusting like they'd adjust to see the stars out at Uncle Robert's place, when they'd step out of the porch light and the stars would grow until they were crowded and Uncle Robert would say, "Hell, you can tell this was Indian country."

Here it was like being in a wild place full of towering crags and mesas. The desert in New Mexico, maybe. Alamogordo. Truth or Consequences.

She was breathing against him.

I have fought my way into this town. I have occupied the consequences.

He liked these darknesses where there was no electricity. Now and again there were lights from a vehicle that did empty things with the shadowy crags and then darkness fell again. A glow kept pulsing farther off, between two of the crags, from what he reckoned was a cooking fire, and he thought of the boys sitting around it and chewing on their chicken and felt hungry for the first time in days. He was not well, but he felt hungry.

You know, this could be not too bad.

Holding the grieving woman made him steadier; he'd gotten shaky down there in the blackness of the vaults and another human being had come like a saving angel, and now he realized the importance of just holding someone. It helped she was a woman. And not in any way as dead as a log or waterlogged or rotten like a log could be. He'd admit that. She was full of grief and she needed comforting. The enemy was one side of the line and then you crossed the line and they were no longer your enemy. There should not be lines.

Hell, they'd been warned about this, back in England. There would certainly be a million sex-starved widows and you'd better watch out; syphilis is endemic, out there in the barbarian lands. Wotcher, cock. Cor blimey! I'll say!

They must have been told that too many times.

It hadn't been exactly like that, so far. They were buried under girls and fruit and flowers. Then the real action had hit them with sharp bullet teeth and the girls had gotten thinner and more serious. They weren't even widows. They were doing it mostly for food or cigarettes or soda.

This was his first widow, the first real widow—she couldn't have been a widow for more than two days at the most. She was a fresh widow, newly plucked. She'd stopped shaking and sobbing now and turned real still against his chest.

There is only her breathing, the firm rise and slow fall of her breasts.

I wish I had a mirror all the time, like Emma Bovary. Like Emma Bovary, I do not exist. I have never existed. Therefore there are no traces of my existence. I must keep it that way. If I think myself into invisibility, I will become invisible. It is all a matter of will.

31

It would take one shell through that fancy plasterwork ceiling above the Kaiser Wilhelm *Dawn,* and he would be finished.

He felt so tired, and now Werner had upset him, humiliated him. If it wasn't for Sabine and the girls, he wouldn't care too much if a shell did come through that fancy ceiling. He couldn't move a limb.

And Werner had broken that marvelous Mendelssohn. What a sad, irritating fellow he was. To think he'd only joined the staff in 1934! To think he was once a new boy, wet behind the ears!

I am senior to him, Herr Hoffer considered, in terms of length of service, by three years. One forgets that.

No, he *would* care. He would definitely rather live and try to do good in the world. When his grandmother had died after sixty-one years of marriage, his grandfather had said, "Well, it was good while it lasted." That's the spirit, thought Herr Hoffer—sitting aboveground as he was.

The unbefitting place of darkness.

This was precisely where he had spotted Bendel nibbling Sabine's ear. Or maybe just whispering into it.

It was at that wretched donors' reception they'd had to throw, just before the war, for the Friends of the Reichsführer SS. At the instigation—no, the insistence—of Herr Lohse, manager of the thermometer factory and local chairman of the Friends.

Oh, how I hate receptions and parties! thought Herr Hoffer. But they'd had to thank them somehow. However much he loathed these people, they were the business and social elite of Lohenfelde. They would do very well out of a war, and there was an excitement in the air. Without them, the museum would not have been able to, et cetera. And there was Bendel, in full uniform, looking upon the whole thing with a faintly superior air.

Yes, it was just here that he'd seen Bendel and Sabine together, by the cold marble *Dawn*. That was when he first suspected something was up. A killer whale nibbling at a supple porpoise. That was how he'd pictured it, afterwards, tossing in his bed next to her.

"What's up, Heinrich?"

"I can't sleep."

"Why?"

"Worrying."

"Stop worrying."

"I can't."

"Whatever it is, you can't do anything about it now. Please let me sleep. I've drunk too much. I've worn myself out, chatting to all your guests."

"Yes, my sweet. That's what I thought."

He could see why she was drawn to Bendel. He was different. He differed, for instance, from the very tall and bony senior SS officer whom Bendel had dragged along to the reception.

"Herr Hoffer, may I introduce our guest of honor, SS Brigade-führer Eichler from Berlin. A personal friend of Herr Minister Goebbels and a close acquaintance of Herr Minister Bormann. He is staying in Lohenfelde for a fortnight."

"Charmed, I'm sure, Herr Brigadeführer. Though everyone here is a guest of honor, of course."

"I would like a guided tour," Eichler said.

"Naturally."

Why had he obliged? Because there was no choice. Sabine and several others had joined them. Sabine had never once heard her husband's lectures. Herr Hoffer waxed lyrical through the galleries in strictly chronological order. The nearer the denuded twentieth-century collection approached, still housed in the spacious Long Gallery with its glassed roof, the more his nervousness grew. The bare areas of wall had been kept as a subtle reproach; even Bendel had spotted that and had remarked on it some time before. Although it was now two years since the purge, it still smarted in Herr Hoffer's consciousness, especially since being forced by the city authorities to exhibit some examples of Munich kitsch by the likes of Gradl and Peiner. These dreadful works he had spaced out to look maximally uncomfortable between the four naked marble warriors from the Klimsch workshop.

Now his voice was starting to sound like a girl's as his throat constricted. He kept having to wipe his spectacles and clear his throat.

"Have you got a cold, Herr Hoffer?" Bendel asked.

"No, no, I'm quite all right, thank you."

The superior officer had said hardly a word but appeared to be appreciating Herr Hoffer's skeletal version of his Tuesday lectures. When the SS Brigadeführer did speak, he had an accent: Norwegian, perhaps. He certainly looked Norwegian. Or Danish. When they stopped before the Cranach drawing, the SS Brigadeführer had the strange notion that Lucas Cranach was Jewish. Both Bendel and Herr Hoffer denied it, although the others were not sure. In fact, Herr Hoffer went so far as to say almost automatically (out of nerves), "Do you think it would still be here, if he was Jewish?"

The others had laughed. He then had a suicidal urge to ask the SS Brigadeführer if he liked the perfectly Nordic painter Edvard Munch, and the effort of not asking brought out beads of sweat on the Acting Acting Director's brow.

In the eighteenth-century gallery, of course, it was the nudes that the Brigadeführer most appreciated. He said very little, and his expression did not change, but from the way his small pale eyes were running over the respective canvases, he was fully appreciative of the superb plastic qualities of the painted flesh. They entered the nineteenth-century gallery in silence, as if in church. The reception's murmuring below, the whistling in the SS Brigadeführer's nose . . . Sabine had suddenly giggled at the back and Bendel, next to her, had the air of one who had just told a joke. Neither had been listening. He felt like giving each of them a poor mark.

"This fellow," said the Brigadeführer, pointing to the Hans Richard von Volkmann, "died in 1927."

"His spirit belongs to the nineteenth century," Herr Hoffer explained.

"Why?"

"A question of sentiment and style."

"You mean he is a good painter?" exclaimed the Brigadeführer.

Everyone had laughed.

The little flotilla settled in front of the Lovis Corinth.

"Another good painter?"

"You can almost smell the orange peel," said Frau Lohse, who was wearing an enormous hat.

Herr Hoffer remembered this moment as one of those awkward ones in his life.

"Now, Corinth is very interesting," he said. "He is also in the twentieth-century gallery next door."

"Oh, did he suddenly become a bad painter?"

"He had a stroke, in 1911."

Everyone laughed, which was painful. Herr Hoffer much preferred the smudged and furious later work to the academic naturalism that preceded Corinth's stroke. The Degenerate Committee had removed the two later paintings for their exhibition, so that Germans could shriek and point their fingers at them.

"They have been temporarily removed from view," he added.

"I should think so."

SS Brigadeführer Eichler was quite a wag, it turned out. Or maybe the others were tipsy on the museum's account. Bendel was being very gentlemanly towards Sabine, proffering his arm. She took it. The SS Brigadeführer admired the Wilhelm Leibl and the exquisite Courbet, was intrigued by August Holmberg's large *Troubadour* (a theatrical showpiece set in a medieval dining hall with drunken, erotic fumblings around the table), and nodded at the Volkmann landscape, which made the rolling hills of the Eifel look like the American West.

"I feel I'm there," he said, "breathing the lovely Eifel air. That's real skill."

Everyone agreed. The numbers had grown, Herr Hoffer realized. At least five SS officers, apart from Bendel and Eichler. There was a sweet smell of booze and cigarettes. He felt a little tipsy himself.

Then they came to the van Gogh. SS Brigadeführer Eichler stood in front of the collection's jewel and said, tapping the frame, "Tell me about this, please."

His black-gloved fingers began to stroke the acorn-shaped silver tassel that hung from his sword hilt. A lot of the "blackjacks" did that. Even Herr Hoffer reckoned that he himself would look good in black, with a long sword and those tall black boots buckled at the front. No wonder young chaps joined the SS in droves. He glanced back at Bendel, who might want to wax lyrical himself, given his obsession with the painting. But Bendel was once more sharing some sort of private joke with Sabine, his black peaked cap bobbing about over her flaxen hair.

"Well?"

"It's by Vincent van Gogh."

"So?"

The group was not sure, now, whether to laugh or not. Herr Hoffer, with admirable presence of mind, told of Vincent van Gogh's lone struggle with his art, his saintly poverty, and the genius that drove him out into the hot fields to paint. He left out the artist's madness and suicide. The group stirred appreciatively. The Brigadeführer nodded perfunctorily and leaned forward.

"Where is the artist? It says here *The Artist near Auvers-sur-Oise*."

Bendel had come forward. He made faces at Herr Hoffer behind the officer's back.

"That is an interesting question," said Herr Hoffer.

"The title's a lie," broke in Bendel.

"A lie?"

There was a murmuring in the bunched audience.

"Let me explain," said Herr Hoffer. "Although these rough dabs of color in the swirling wheat seem to show a man in front of an easel, no one is sure of the provenance of the title. It was fixed to the frame by the time the museum bought it in 1923."

"Why did you not change the title?"

"Well, while the little fellow here has been interpreted by certain scholars as a peasant in a large sun hat, holding a rake, other specialists have disagreed. Our own researches discovered traces of wheat husks and seeds and even flies in the hard surface of the oil. This means that the painting was achieved 'in the field,' as was Vincent's habit. Thus it is very likely he painted what he saw directly in front of him."

"He can't be seeing himself directly in front of him."

"No, exactly."

"And what's he doing with a rake, this fellow, if the corn's not cut?"

"I don't think we should—"

"Unless the fellow was added afterwards," said Eichler, jabbing a finger at Herr Hoffer, as if trying to catch him out. "Back in his house. Before he shot himself!"

Everyone in the group had their eyes on the Acting Acting Director, who was feeling hot and a little faint.

"Impossible, Herr Brigadeführer," said Bendel, stepping to the front. The eyes swiveled. "Apart from the fact that the artist followed Leonardo rather than Rubens and painted from dark to light, a study of the brushwork shows that these strokes here are slightly below the much paler dabs of corn. The ultramarine of the peasant's shirt being actually carried into this cream sweep of paint—"

"How clumsy," Eichler interrupted. "He should have let it dry. Excellence cannot be hurried."

Everyone nodded in approval except for Bendel, who looked pained.

"What a pity it is not as the title says," Eichler went on. "Though less egotistical, *A Peasant near Auvers-sur-Oise* has not quite the same—ah, attraction. That is no doubt why you have not changed it."

Herr Hoffer swallowed as the others laughed.

"Probably," he said.

"It wasn't clumsiness," Bendel said sharply.

Eichler looked at him.

"What was it, then?"

"Life," said Bendel, staring at the work with bloodshot eyes. "The pure force and energy of natural life."

"Of course, Herr Sturmführer," Eichler snapped. "Everyone knows that. But you don't find these colors in natural life, do you?"

"Well," said Herr Hoffer hurriedly, "we have to remember that there are two words for color in Dutch, *verf* and *kleur*. . . ."

His voice sounded strangulated, very tense, but he soldiered on. Bendel made his way back to Sabine, as if she needed him—or vice versa. Eichler stroked that nutlike silver tassel with his black-gloved finger and thumb as a child might rub the paw of a cuddly toy. The other SS officers yawned, quite openly. Frau Lohse adjusted her enormous hat. Sabine swallowed some of her wine and coughed and Bendel seemed to be rubbing her back. But at least he was safe there.

There was a silence. Herr Hoffer had run out of information. If nothing else, he had bored everyone silly about van Gogh.

SS Brigadeführer Eichler nodded, smiled slightly, and said, "He was pea-brained, wasn't he?"

"Pea-brained?"

"Everyone knows he was pea-brained. He painted like a child because he was pea-brained. He wanted to paint like an adult, but he could not. So he was driven round the bend."

Then he touched the painting, stroking its uneven surface with the same finger that had rubbed the tassel. Herr Hoffer gulped. The gallery was silent except for the creaks of all those tall black boots against their spurs—the pseudocavalry ranged behind and ready to charge. SS Brigadeführer Eichler was leaning forward and stroking the frozen clots and stipples of paint—the chrome yellows of the corn, the Prussian blue of the sky. Bendel's mouth was open in horror; Herr Hoffer was very afraid he might try to strike down his superior officer. Light poured in from the windows in sloping columns of dust motes, burnishing the parquet, glittering off tiny woven eagles and death's-heads. The finger was now following the depression of a tree's long shadow—the same inky black, as it happened, as the glove that touched it.

Watching the finger touching the paint was like watching some-one scrape at a fresh burn.

"He put the paint on very thickly," said the officer at last, retiring his finger as if he had inspected it for dust and was now satisfied. "Just like a child. If he was not so famous, he would be nothing. And he was famous only because he was driven round the bend—by the knowledge that he was pea-brained."

He gave a little grunt, as if amazed at his own cleverness. The oth-ers smiled and started to move on into the Long Gallery. Sabine squeezed Bendel's arm and his expression softened. Really, there might have been the most awful incident, if Sabine hadn't taken Bendel in hand.

It was difficult. Apart from a beautiful Erbsloh nude, Paul Burck's birch forest, and the chilly marble of Klimsch's naked war-riors, the contemporary collection now consisted of nothing but a couple of impressionistic seaside scenes by Ludwig von Hofmann, a chocolate-box landscape by Diebitsch, and Führer favorites like Gradl or the watery Kriegel—along with a local artist, Klaus Ner-dinger, who specialized in dogs.

The white unfilled stretches of wall were witness to Herr Hoffer's fury and grief. He pulled out his handkerchief and dabbed his per-spiring forehead. He must not faint. He must not look at the white-ness, which was shifting and swelling horribly around him, as if he were stumbling through drifts.

The SS Brigadeführer nodded at the snowy stretches as if in ap-proval, however. He then wondered why the museum had not seen fit to fill them up with, for example, the excellent portraits of ordinary Party members painted by Wolfgang Willrich.

"Do you know his work? You could have filled up these spaces with Wolfgang Willrich."

He was striking the bare wall sharply with his black leather gloves.

Yes, with the artist's intestines, thought Herr Hoffer, who had re-covered his nerve with the mention of Willrich.

"I do know him, yes, Brigadeführer."

Herr Hoffer did not say that he thought Willrich's portraits to be talentless daubs of pig swill incapable of holding their own in a village show of crippled weekend painters, but murmured something instead about funds. The SS Brigadeführer pulled a long face and looked at his watch and clicked his heels together and said to the others that he was sorry to announce that he must be leaving, and asked Herr Hoffer for the whereabouts of the toilet. He paused only to glance up at Wamper's bronze *Conquest* on the landing, with the hand outstretched like a Roman emperor. The dreadful thing had been especially polished for the occasion by Frau Blumen, and Herr Hoffer could see his face in a massive thigh.

"Looks like he's testing for rain," said the SS officer, who was allowed to say things like that—without smiling.

Herr Hoffer did not rise to the bait. It might have been bait, after all. It asked to be capped with the story of the Jewish comic he'd seen all those years ago in Berlin, holding out his arm in a Hitler salute and saying, "That's how deep we are in the shit." But Herr Hoffer merely smiled and let the officer go first down the stairs.

While SS Brigadeführer Eichler was relieving himself, SS Sturmführer Bendel congratulated Herr Hoffer on a superb performance. They were in the office, on their own; the reception in the entrance hall was horribly noisy, with business types guffawing and their wives shrieking and the echoes bouncing everywhere. Bendel seemed to be drunk.

"You have no idea of the extent of that man's influence, Herr Hoffer. He has the ear of the Chief himself. He's an old mate of Bormann's too, of course. Peasants both. They probably shit in the handbasin, if you're lucky."

"As long as he doesn't go telling everybody how wonderful it is here," said Herr Hoffer.

"He certainly enjoyed *Dawn*."

"Oh, he can take her with him, if he wants."

"I hope you appreciated the brilliance of my reference."

"To Hiram Powers?"

"I've seen the pussy myself, in Washington. She is every boy's wet dream."

"The link is not proven," said Herr Hoffer, disliking Bendel's coarseness. "Rotmann's is much more a feeble borrowing of Michelangelo's *Dawn* in San Lorenzo. Except that Michelangelo's *Dawn* is waking up with a sorrowful face, as if daytime reality is worse than sleep. I can't blame her."

He was a little tipsy. Bendel's face darkened.

"She might be waking from a nightmare," he said.

"Maybe we will too, one day," said Herr Hoffer.

Bendel snorted. "I refuse to be beaten," he said, waving his gloves about. "Both Powers's and Rotmann's nudes are in white marble, have the same hairstyle, and there's a chain around *Dawn*'s wrist. Rotmann's, I mean. That's a reference."

"That's a bracelet."

"You don't even know Powers's work."

"I don't suppose it's worth knowing," Herr Hoffer said feebly.

One of his lenses had misted up, but he couldn't be bothered to clear it. He was exhausted by the strain of his effort, and now by Bendel's usual eagerness to engage in a fencing match where the scars were cultural. The flex for the telephone, which came straight down from the middle of the ceiling onto the desk, appeared to cut Bendel's face in two.

"Anyway, what's wrong with saying how bloody wonderful the collection is?" Bendel pursued.

"I just hope," said Herr Hoffer, choosing his words carefully, "that I haven't brought too much attention to certain wonderful elements in our collection. I seem to remember that was your advice. You called it the *secret*, if you recall."

Bendel laughed one of his loud high-pitched laughs. He wasn't even bothering to keep his voice down, not with the racket through the wall. His eyes were bloodshot.

"That man's a complete ignoramus," he said, his words increasingly slurred. "A Ukrainian, I believe, with a German grandfather. His grandmother was probably a whore, screwed by a German. Do you know the Ukrainians? It's surprising, but they're basically savages. Like all Slavs. They're almost as bad as the Russians, in that they've never evolved. Ninety-nine percent of them are backward peasants. For him, van Gogh is a complete puzzle. He only knows everybody because he's rich. But he's an absolute bloody knucklehead. And a show-off. He made a whole load of Jews get on their knees and mow an entire lawn with their teeth, which is supremely vulgar. Vulgarity is disgusting."

"That's horrible," said Herr Hoffer. "If I'd known—"

"And did you hear what he had to say about Vincent? Our marvelous Vincent? *He's pea-brained, isn't he? Not like me!*"

He was a good mimic. They heard the door opening and turned. It was Frau Schenkel, swaying slightly, her hair loosening at the ears.

"The SS Brigadeführer is waiting for you in the hall, gentlemen," she said. She all but curtsied. She too had drunk too much. "I think this is a great success," she said, finding the door again. "My husband says you ought to have one every week on his day off."

"So don't fret," said Bendel, giving Herr Hoffer a wink and a slap on the shoulder. "You did bloody well, old man. You were wonderfully, brilliantly tedious. Our sacred relic will not be leaving its cathedral. At least, only over my dead body."

"I thought you liked unevolved cultures," said Herr Hoffer, a little upset. "Purity and all that. Like that doctor in *Uncle Vanya*."

"Unevolved peasants are not pure," said Bendel, almost snappily. "How can they be? I mean, agriculture *itself* was the start of the disease, for God's sake! And Chekhov is Russian. We don't like the Russians."

"Jean-Jacques Rousseau, then."

"That bastard's French. Even worse. We *hate* the French."

A little later in the evening, when Herr Hoffer had stumbled on Bendel and Sabine right at this spot, in front of *Dawn*, looking suspiciously intimate, he had been incapable of a single word. It was such a shock.

"I am just telling your lovely wife about Hiram Powers," said Bendel, swaying slightly in his sleek black plumage, his death's-head cap slightly askew. "*Greek Slave*. It makes this little hussy look frigid."

"You don't mean me, I hope," Sabine giggled.

"I do not think I do," said Bendel, staring at her. "When the heir to the Austrian throne was shot," he added, with his hand resting on her bare shoulder, "my father was with my mother in Mürzsteg. It was their honeymoon. They were making love."

"During the day?"

"Oh, I don't know the details. It was their first time together. I don't know any more details."

"Just as well." Sabine giggled, her cheeks red as cherries.

"My mother became pregnant, of course. And little Klaus was born."

"How romantic." Sabine sighed.

"That very day," Bendel added, his gloved thumb stroking her neck.

There was no hair visible under his cap, even though it was askew. Only the nicks of his razor high above the ears. Herr Hoffer felt like throttling the smooth neck. But everyone was drunk. Nobody knows what they are doing when they are drunk.

And then, anyway, it was war.

The lake is very deep. Someone is pulling on the rope. My head is growing again like a bud. But then I know you are all still alive, thank goodness. I read the signs: If the spider crosses my hand onto the beam, you are alive, every one of you. One day I will be standing in a field of flowers and you will join me, running into my arms. You will have to take turns to be hugged, though. "Ah, for your moist wings, O West, how sorely do I envy you!" If only I knew the whole of Goethe!

32

It would be so hard to paint their surroundings, he thought; you could do it as an abstract, all in tones of gray with red showing through. You could make pigment out of ashes and paint this and make quite a shout about it, keeping sullen in the way you had to look for the magazines. You could make a lot of pictures with these ashes.

"How'd you like your face in *Picture Post?*" he murmured to the dame.

How many paintings would the ashes of a man or a woman make? A child would make less. Maybe not even a small painting. Maybe they liquefied to a smear.

He wished his ass didn't gall so much and that the blanket was not so full of fleas. He swiveled his eyes downward and held her tight, now, his chin in her hair. The whole length of her was so heavy and warm. This was what you forgot in your isolation and terror: the beauty of the human weight. Fireman's lift. You didn't know it until.

In how many life classes back in Clarksburg—Tuesday evenings in the Old School Hall—had he tried to get down on paper that weight, that humanness, and ended up with nothing but a charcoal smudge.

Enclose space, the tutor had said.

Yeah, the guy was nuts on Kandinsky, on reducing everything to dynamics and lines of force like you were drawing a ladder and a basket instead of a naked human being. What about the weight, mister? What about the smell of her smoky hair? Who the fuck needs Kandinsky?

It was good not knowing her language. Sometimes talk got like a dime novel; it took you someplace you didn't want to be, very shallow and far away.

Berlin ist eine Reise wert.

Right at this moment, in the ruins, he was happy holding in comforting intimacy a human being he did not know and could not talk to. There was something prehistoric about it. Something intense and fiery and prehistoric, as if he were rocking her deep in the cave with the sabertooths prowling in the snow outside.

And he'd eaten her hair. Chewed it a little. Now she was his, not Heinrich's.

Not poor old dead Heinrich's at all.

There is always something to live for, if you choose to. That does not mean one always has the choice. Why do we live? To remember. Is that all? And what if we die? What happens to our memories then? I asked the thin one about this when he came up, but he had no answer [behind] his spectacles.

33

Even this awful nude, with its polished nipples, had become so familiar to him that he felt some warmth for it.

The familiarity of the museum was something he treasured; he would walk around it before going home, in the good old days, after everyone else had left. It was like a country, the museum, with its obscure regions and wild parts, the light falling differently, the great distances covered. Now and again he would pause before a picture as if seeing it for the first time.

Now there was nothing!

Except Party rubbish like *Dawn*, with its stupid, sex-satisfied smile—everything reduced to this hard, pure nub. He felt like hurling it down the stairs, turning into a muscle-bound superman and hurling it all the way down so that it shattered.

Instead, he ran his hand along the line of its marble shoulder, thinking of Hilde Winkel's shoulder touching his, of his hand on her thin and living back. How cold and lifeless was the sculpture's naked back, in comparison! Supposing this rubbish was all that survived of modern art, for the millennia to come?

Where are the paintings of classical Greece? Smashed, worn away. And all her bronzes? Melted down—to pay damned armies!

A dull thud outside made no impression on the reclining nude, even though bits fell from the ceiling. One piece rested in her navel, another lay on her open lips like a finger. He looked up: The fancy plasterwork of shells and grapes was badly cracked. The building was suffering from the pounding of the ground. His anxiety increased, but a great inertia filled him. He couldn't be bothered to move, despite the danger. Was this despair? The shiny marble breasts were stimulating him. The Führer felt that only Botticelli understood breasts, apparently, so Rotmann had miscalculated. All Herr Hoffer desired was a woman's comforting arms, to lie between a woman's firm warm legs and lose himself there. Sabine had lost the taste for that, since the air raids had started. She used to want it so much, but now she was too anxious and too tired. Her nervous fits took it out of her. She was so fearful for the children. And so was he! But he couldn't move from the bench. Maybe he was having a breakdown. Or the beginnings of a migraine. Please, dear God, not now.

He laughed, suddenly, as if he were going insane.

It certainly isn't Bendel's fault! Bendel is probably dead!

The very last time he'd seen Bendel properly was in the winter of '42, well over two years ago. He had been posted elsewhere, he said. Where? A secret.

Herr Hoffer didn't like thinking of that very last time. He had come back from work early with a light migraine one day and there he was: Herr Bendel himself, sipping tea with Sabine, like an English gentleman.

Sabine's hair was unpinned, loose. Bendel's jet-black tie had been hastily knotted. One spur was unbuckled, the strap dangling off the ankle. The tea was cold—Herr Hoffer had accepted a cup and it was stone-cold.

"Oh, is it? We must have been so busy chatting, Heinrich my darling. Poor Klaus—Herr Bendel, I mean—is leaving us. He won't say where. He's back just for today, to clear up his desk at the office."

It was, to a migrainous mind, unbearably suspicious. Bendel rose and had to hunt for his cap, which was behind the sofa, and its little death's-head badge snarled at Herr Hoffer as they shook hands and said the polite necessities, and then Herr Hoffer had gone off straight to bed, lying there with a black sock over each eye and a bowl between his hands. What else could he have done, challenged the fellow to a duel?

A killer whale in an aquarium tank. He had seen only a few fuzzy pictures of killer whales in some book, but they were white and black and sleek, he knew, with giant mouths full of razor teeth.

And the world was full of porpoises.

But really, Bendel was a stimulating young man. Killer whales were intelligent. And attractive. Give Bendel a room full of paintings and, really, he was the most stimulating company possible.

And Sabine is my darling, Herr Hoffer thought. She is my sun and my moon. He had absolutely no proof of anything but a forty-year-old's girlish sentimental fling. It was probably nothing. It had cheered her up. One had to forgive. One must always try to be Christian, even if one fell short of four-square belief.

He himself had been awful company for her, of course, with all his gloom and worries. He should have worn spurs on his boots. But he only had shoes, to start with.

Bendel had not been back. Yes, he might very well be dead. The Vincent had passed into the windowless Luftschutzbunker with its odor of toilets and then, in Bendel's absence, had slipped down into the vaults. The Kaiser Wilhelm's van Gogh was safe at last! Ssssh. Secret. Deep. Very deep.

Thank God the fellow hadn't been around for the wholesale evacuation in March '44! When the Party dross remaining in the galleries was finally carted off to the salt mine, along with the works stored in the Luftschutzbunker, Bendel would have certainly smelled a rat or two, if he'd been around.

The inventory on the pinkish octavo paper did its job perfectly. Oh, yes, that had to be admitted by all and sundry, even by miserable old Werner Oberst. All Herr Hoffer received was a minor ticking-off from the middle-aged Hauptstellenleiter in charge of the evacuation (wearing a dented Russian helmet), for the museum staff's "carelessness and disorganization," but otherwise the paintings and smaller sculptures were removed by weary men of the Self-Protection Service who couldn't care two hoots about art. Most had been up the previous night dragging bodies out of buildings near the industrial sector. It was a good time to be agile, because there were so many distractions! Even *Mademoiselle de Guilleroy au Bain* was not noticed as missing, let alone the van Gogh. This also meant, however, that the paintings and sculptures were not treated with complete respect. Herr Hoffer had trotted about, getting very puffed, trying to ensure at least a modicum of care in the handling. An Adam Toepffer landscape was slightly scratched by the truck's mudguard, a Kaulbach *Mädchen* had her pretty eyes splashed by mud, and a brush drawing of an angel playing a lute by Gaudenzio Ferrari, set in a period frame, was deposited for a moment on the hood and dripped on by fog condensation running off the vehicle's roof.

Herr Hoffer half anticipated an angry letter from the Propagandaministerium, demanding the whereabouts of the van Gogh, but nothing of that sort came.

SS Sturmführer Bendel was no longer even in the shadows, was he?

The shelling and bombing were far off, it seemed, but at any moment that could change. *Dawn* had a death grin on her, not a sex-satisfied smile.

After what seemed like hours asleep but was in fact an involuntary nap of a few profound and delicious minutes, he forced himself off the bench and moved on into the Long Gallery's whitenesses, shaking plaster from his hair, still a little giddy.

He advanced into the vast room and stood in the middle. There was somebody waiting for him at the far end. He couldn't see anyone, but he felt it. It was Death. Death slithering about waiting for him, as if he were Schubert's poor ailing maiden. He looked up, heart hammering, and was amazed to see the long sloping skylights above him still intact, cross-hatching the skeins of smoke like a draftsman's enlargement grid. Birds would fly slap-bang into it, this roof of glass.

At any moment it might shatter and rain down on his eyes. He was quite scared. He had managed to scare himself. Now stop it.

Really, Bendel was quite a decent chap. A little unstable, that's all. He had come to several of the Tuesday "Hoffer" lectures, particularly "German Romantic Landscape: A Yearning for the Infinite." Herr Hoffer had toyed with the idea of giving his course of talks on modernist painting (from Post-Impressionism through Expressionism and Abstraction to Dada) against the bare stretches of the walls, once the works had been appropriated, but Herr Streicher thought this suicidal.

"The Dark Dwarf has just forbidden all independent art criticism," he had said. "We'll have to cancel your Tuesday lectures, Herr Hoffer."

"Not at all, Herr Acting Director. I have thought of a way round it. 'Modern Art from Vincent van Gogh to Kurt Schwitters' is to become 'The Story of German Art.'"

"And the content?"

"A little suppleness is required, that's all."

Herr Streicher smiled behind his pipe.

"I like the idea of you being supple, my dear fellow."

Herr Hoffer's gathering plumpness was a joke between them: Herr Streicher was tall and thin.

"For instance," Herr Hoffer went on gamely, "I have prepared a whole new section on the influence of early German draftsmen on the standard use of the curved line as a shading technique."

"That," said Herr Streicher, "was poor Gustav Glatz's thesis."

"To be put to very good use," said Herr Hoffer, blushing profoundly.

Bendel had congratulated him after the lectures. A sharp fellow. Always putting pertinent questions.

Yes, he was very glad that Bendel wasn't present when the collection was carted off to the salt mine. He would certainly have noticed that the Vincent was missing from the inventory, let alone all the others.

Ah, one has really done rather well. One really has, all things considered. Death is not here. One is not an ailing maiden.

He left the Long Gallery, passing the Wamper sculpture on the landing and descending by the back stairs to the Fossil Room. Its glass cases were empty. They had once been full of trilobites and brachiopods and delicate stone ferns from the shale deposits near

Kreiburg Hill. It may have been his nerves again, but he thought he heard someone scuttling off, for real this time. There were mice, of course, scuttling about in the Fossil Room; hunger was forcing them out of the wainscots and into this frightening bareness of floor and wall. Perhaps they were the souls of the German people—those who had lost their souls and gone into a kind of Party trance, millions of them. Was that not what the northern folk had once believed, in heathen times? That the soul escaped from the body in the shape of a mouse?

Thank God he was not a mouse.

He paused before knocking on the janitor's door, noting how the bombardment had become even quieter. Perhaps the cretins had surrendered. What would the American soldiers be like? He pictured them sitting atop tanks, with black negroid faces, chewing gum. Many were white, of course, no different from those visiting Berlin before the war, but he had difficulty in picturing that type of American atop a tank. He did not for one moment believe the lurid stories of the press, but nevertheless he was frightened. There would be Jews among them, for a start, wondering where all their fellows had gone. Perhaps the German men would be sent to concentration camps while the women fell into the American soldiers' arms. He could see Sabine doing that, horribly easily; she was fun-loving, and he did not bring her enough fun. No German did. The war was a personal affront to her, because it stopped her having fun. When a friend organized a folk dance for the Lohenfelde Shopgirls' Club last year, it was all Herr Hoffer could do to dissuade Sabine from taking along some jazz records he'd bought years before in Berlin. Only by making her think of the danger to their children did he succeed in dissuading her. This is why she had her fits, when she would scream and beat her fists on his chest. She had one of them right then, breaking the jazz records over his head. He'd had to carry her to bed, which was an effort; thank God she was so thin!

He realized, gathering his strength by Herr Wolmer's door and feeling the cool April draft through the shattered Kluge window, that he had forgotten what it was not to be permanently anxious. It was as if, every day, he had to face an appointment with a doctor concerning a verdict on some possibly life-threatening ailment. Each day he experienced the same shortness of breath, the same looseness of the bowels, the same irritable anxiety—pacing up and down for hours and hours, as it were, in that imaginary doctor's corridor before the dreaded door, which was possibly Death itself, or which would yield either life or death on a simple word. Yet he could not get used to this state of anxiety and exhaustion; it was not natural to him. He dreamed of lampposts, when he slept at all, never of a hooded Death. Mostly he lay awake, and so in the morning he would rise from the bed with hollowed-out eyes, with circles like a film actor's mascara—just as if he had lain down only ten minutes earlier.

Now it all promised to be over, and it was a shock to realize this!

He stood before the janitor's door, with its office times in faded ink, feeling faintly embarrassed about disturbing Herr Wolmer again, so soon after fetching the candles. Not even an hour ago! Ridiculous, that he felt embarrassed. They were under bombardment and about to be conquered, like something out of Herodotus or Livy. It was only natural that he should check on things.

Laying his hand on the door's handle, he felt as if everything in life might be repeated in an endless circle of actions, which he was sure was a Far Eastern belief, just as it was a Far Eastern practice to return to the same painting over months or even years, applying a single stroke until the work was complete.

Ah, it was good to be alone with one's thoughts. It made one feel more solid and true, did a few moments of solitude.

*If only you would return. I am waiting and waiting. Yesterday
was my eighteenth birthday, but nobody knew. I have passed
three birthdays on my own. Nobody remembered, because nobody knew.*

34

Parry thought of human history as a nickel-in-the-slot phonograph
with just two records: *War* and *Peace.* The *Peace* record was clean
and fresh, and the *War* record was dusty and scratched because it
was so goddamn popular. He needed a beer.

"You lose a war you lose a war," he said to the dame, who was
shuddering a little against him. It was between a hiccup and a shudder. It meant she was still grieving. He reckoned it was Germany she
was grieving for. If it had been America in this fine state, he might
have been grieving too. Like the Brits grieved over their cuppas for
London, Coventry, Portsmouth, you name it. Exeter Cathedral. With
millions of dollars of colored glass on the sidewalks and the lawns.
Maybe hundreds of thousands of dollars. Anyway, people were crying
because the goddamn glass was a thousand years old, almost. Five
times at least as old as the United States of America. Not as old as
Indian America, which they did not call America. Maybe the goddamn Indians like his grandmother's father grieved like this woman,
and some had their innards cut out and stretched over the saddle of
at least one Methodist minister's horse, and that was not even war
but sheer conquest. He was a divided man. Some said they were
stretched vaginas but this sounded unlikely from a medical point of
view. Maybe not. Maybe they were like stretched mouths. Screams
on a pommel.

It might just be a story. As the wholesale massacre of the Jews of
Europe might just be a story. They had been told to watch out for
that particular shadow. To case suspicious factory joints, to not think
of a beautiful meadow as a beautiful meadow when it might just be a

mass burial ground. And the political niggers among them had said, "Nobody watched out for us while we was being lynched."

He still thought he might open a hatch in the ground and out would flood some millions of living Jews, blinking in the light. Clarksburg had a dozen or so Jew shops, and they were damn good. He would be a hero, then. They told some good jokes and you could run on credit.

He did not wonder even for one moment why the woman—Frau Hoffer, as she called herself—was clinging to him so because he could understand it as he lay there, cradling her. He could understand it very well. However, she was beginning to disturb him like an ache. Most of them, although they were starving or had nothing, did not cling to you like this. Maybe it was simply and truly because he'd taken her goddamn hair in his mouth!

The warmth was very nice, though.

The old thin one came up today and comforted me. He gave me an apple. When he went, I felt I had no meaning [Sinn].

35

Herr Wolmer was reading the newspaper!

He was sitting at his desk, in his burnished spiked helmet and trench greatcoat, reading the newspaper as if nothing had happened—an old newspaper, months old, as no proper newspapers had been produced in Lohenfelde this year since the January air raids.

He hardly looked up as the door opened. Herr Wolmer was still the janitor, rather slow and dour and difficult, but without whom everyone would be lost. Effectively, while the world had changed, Herr Wolmer had not. The sampler above the door—*Ein' feste Burg ist unser Gott*—had apparently been embroidered by his great-

grandmother and was dated *1831*, while a very flowery sign on
the wall near the sink declared *Mein Feld ist die Welt,* as if the janitor
were a world traveler; in a funny sort of way, it was true, because all
the world might be concentrated here in this stuffy box of a room.
Herr Wolmer's table only just fitted between the sink, the broom cupboard, and the crooked stove with its copper pot; the spare wooden
chair, with its cushion covered in Caspar Friedrich's hairs, meant
that one had either to step aside on entering or sit down straightaway,
awkwardly. But Herr Hoffer liked this room almost more than any
other in the museum.

It was, in Herr Kirschenbaum's long-ago humorous description, "a
still life of the naturalistic school."

By that he meant that it was solid and substantial and never altered. Even the rich smell—of coffee, tobacco, and scrubbed draining boards—was unique. There was no longer any real coffee, only a
watery substitute, but the smell lingered. Herr Wolmer himself may
have been dour, but he was rarely disagreeable. One had to make no
effort: The janitor was always the same. The view through the yellowed lace curtains, with their embroidered scenes of peasant country life, was of the open area in front of the museum and the
beginning of Fritz Todt Strasse, the tree-lined avenue on the other
side of the modest museum garden with its iron benches. So very familiar—but familiarity turned into somewhere else and of a different
time. Herr Hoffer sometimes imagined that this was how Lohenfelde
must appear to a worker or a peasant. He liked to sit there every now
and again, sipping from one of Herr Wolmer's chipped cups, talking
about guttering or hot-water pipes or the electricals. The little room
had never been any other way, obviously. The museum had been
built around it, as Herr Kirschenbaum would joke, long ago; it was
everyone's homeland. All one needed was a clay pipe.

Ein' feste Burg ist unser Gott.

"You back again, Herr Hoffer?"

"My dear Herr Wolmer," he said, settling himself in the chair, "I
admire your courage."

"What courage?"

"That's exactly it. I have done the rounds, by the way. I came up to see if you are all right."

"Have you done the attics?"

"Ah, no. Would that be a good idea?"

"Incendiaries. They're using incendiaries and phosphorus, the bastards. One exploded in the street. I saw it bounce. You never know, one might have lodged itself in the attics."

"Yes, I suppose it might."

Herr Wolmer folded the newspaper and placed it on the table before him like a precious relic.

"Don't worry, Herr Hoffer, I'll check the attics myself, in a little bit. It's a long way up, and you can't be in two places at once." He adjusted his spiked helmet, which was a little big for him. "No need for you to go."

"Your place is here, Herr Wolmer."

"Don't worry, Herr Hoffer, *I'll* do the attics."

Herr Hoffer's heart sank. He would have to check the attics himself; he couldn't let Herr Wolmer limp all that way up and abandon his post. The museum had three distinct portions, in its architectural clutter, where the roof sloped steeply and encased a veritable kingdom of attics—lofty beamed attics in the tradition of the Swabian farmhouse (the architect hailed from Swabia)—as if hay might one day be stored in them. The glass-roofed Long Gallery was a converted attic, in fact; the others, higher by a floor, were dark and dusty and full of mice and spiders. No paintings had ever been stored in them. The thought of an incendiary bursting into flame near all that dry tinder gave Herr Hoffer the shivers.

"Would we have heard a shell coming in through the roof?"

"Of course not. Would've gone through the tiles like a knife through butter."

"Don't mention butter, Herr Wolmer. I give our weekly thimbleful to the girls."

"That's good of you, Herr Hoffer."

"Do you think they've stopped shelling us, Herr Wolmer? It seems to be quieter. It seems to be farther off. Maybe it was a false alarm and they're not—"

"That's where the SS boys are, I reckon," Herr Wolmer interrupted, cocking an ear. "They wouldn't waste their shells on civilians. What they don't know," he added with a chuckle, "is that here's the Wehrmacht, ready to die for the Fatherland."

Herr Wolmer was jabbing a finger at Herr Hoffer, who nodded lamely.

"I don't think that'll be enough excuse to shell us, Herr Wolmer. You see, I don't want the museum to be hit."

"Of course not, Herr Hoffer."

"We need the museum for future generations. I know it's got very little left in it, but it's still the museum, and it's a marvelous place."

"That goes without saying, Herr Hoffer."

"A really marvelous place. So if the worst comes to the worst, it might be sensible to put out a white flag and surrender, for the sake of the museum, Herr Wolmer."

Herr Wolmer stared at the Acting Acting Director from behind the large old-fashioned Kaiser mustache. It was not a friendly stare. Then he rose stiffly and opened the door of the broom cupboard and took out a rifle. He placed it on the table next to the folded newspaper, almost knocking Herr Hoffer's nose with the muzzle. It was an old rifle, Herr Hoffer saw that straightaway, but it was still a rifle. Even an old rifle could kill. Even an old rifle in the hands of an elderly man could kill. The Americans wouldn't think twice. Everyone knew the rules: Anything put to defensive uses becomes a legitimate target. Churches, schools, museums. Even hospitals, in certain cases. Orphanages. He wasn't sure where the likes of Dresden fitted into all this, but no doubt there was some brutal military justification.

The metal gleamed with grease and the wooden stock shone with oil.

"That's very impressive, Herr Wolmer. But as the person in charge of the museum, with responsibility for the building, I must forbid you to show any armed resistance to the invader. The gesture would be futile and possibly disastrous for the establishment in my charge. Think of Strasbourg Cathedral in 1870. We only bombed it because the French erected an observatory for artillery officers on the tower—"

"What rank are you, Herr Hoffer?"

"What rank?"

The janitor tapped his own Volkssturm armband. It was a fetching yellow and orange, the eagle and the letters stitched very neatly by Frau Wolmer, a professional seamstress. In terms of quality of arm- band, Herr Wolmer ranked higher.

Herr Hoffer sighed.

"I am a private," he said, "not even first-class. But I can't take that seriously. I'm not a member of the Wehrmacht, I'm a private citizen wearing a silly armband. That's the truth, Herr Wolmer. Do with it what you will."

Herr Hoffer pulled off the armband, wincing when it passed over his injured hand, and tossed it onto the table.

"It's meaningless," he said. "Here all that counts is my position within the museum, and in that position I am asking you, Herr Wolmer, not to commit suicide."

Herr Wolmer, a large man when standing up, seemed to expand even farther, filling one side of his room. His face was turning red.

"I've had enough of bloody armbands," Herr Hoffer went on, warm- ing to his theme over the pounding of his heart. "I've had enough of armbands and uniforms and badges. Look where they've got us. With- out these ridiculous bits of cloth, National Socialism would have gone nowhere. That's what's led to this catastrophe, Herr Wolmer: bloody bits of ornamental cloth! The dressing-up box!"

He actually thumped the table. He didn't know why he was talk- ing like this. It was Herr Wolmer's room; this little, cozy room made him inspired. He couldn't bear to see Herr Wolmer ruining it all out of stupidity and pride and misplaced patriotism. The rifle lay be- tween them, neither on one side nor on the other. It looked light, but Herr Hoffer knew it was heavy. It smelled of oil, naturally. It could kill a man. Such things couldn't be wished away. He dared to look the janitor in the eye. The janitor was crying. At least, his face was crumpled up behind the big mustache and the eyes were shiny with moisture. This astonished Herr Hoffer. He didn't know what to say now but felt pleased that his speech had moved Herr Wolmer to that extent.

Then Herr Wolmer said, "Herr Hoffer, you're a traitor. A traitor to your country. You do not wish to defend the Fatherland against the foreigners. I don't care a fuck for those tin-assed jumped-up pricks as went and emptied this place of its valuables, but I do care for my country. I never thought to hear a man say what you've just said, Herr Hoffer. Even in the trenches, in the muck and filth and cold, never did I hear such a terrible thing as what you've just said to me, Herr Hoffer."

Herr Hoffer felt his whole body go cold and then hot. His face was on fire. It was a flush of shame, beyond the control of his mind. This was dreadful. He got up to leave, incapable of any coherent reply, but Herr Wolmer snatched up the rifle.

"Herr Wolmer," came a faint voice that Herr Hoffer recognized was his own, "what are you doing?"

"Running you in."

"Please, stop pointing that gun at me."

"You're a deserter," said Herr Wolmer, nodding at the crumpled armband on the table. "Untrue to the colors. A capital offense. I'm only doing my duty."

"The Americans have thrashed us all the way from France to Lohenfelde, Herr Wolmer. I am not armed. I don't have a uniform. They have tanks, machine guns, grenades, bazookas, shells. My commanding officer was last seen pedaling off on his bicycle. I do not wish to commit suicide. Now I am going to do my duty and inspect the attics."

The gun wavered. It could so easily go off, thought Herr Hoffer. It was pointing at his stomach. In the silence, his stomach made a squealing digestive noise. If the gun were to go off, his entrails would splash the whole room with red and brown and perhaps pink. Herr

Wolmer's hands were not steady. His gnarled finger was on the trigger. This would be a truly terrible way to go. There was a sudden gunshot, and Herr Hoffer hit his head on the table as he fell.

I am reading Rilke. The one who shows his tongue brought it to me. "If I shrieked out in pain, who would hear me from amongst the angels?"

36

He had to find someone in the unit like Harry Scholl, who could speak Heinie, or maybe a German who could translate into English—but he didn't want another person around just now.

Cut it out, he thought. Every fucking honest Joe looted stuff like beer and cognac and eggs or enemy equipment for souvenirs, but only the Muscovites were criminal and stole antique paintings or whatever because they were no better than the Fascists. That was punishable, stealing works of art. It was not what a modern infantryman did. Hyena of the battlefield. He could see the court-martial, the ranked officers of the tribunal, as if it had already been decided. There were art experts with the advance units, apparently, who would testify that he, Corporal Parry, had not consulted them over his find. He didn't give a shit for those art experts, who had not exactly made their presence known but were probably, as a Brit would say, cozy base wallahs. They did not deserve to be cradling any woman or climbing out of any vaults with what seven months of fighting had brought him as a slim reward. They had no doubt kept their smooth thoughts smooth and spoke like schoolgirls with a lisp, but he had not. He had been roughened to the point where—

She was looking at him. Then she hid her face in his chest again.

Brother, I need to think. First, I need to get that nice salvage wrapped up and in my pack and out of sight. If I am hit and wounded or worse, maybe things will get complicated, but I guess I'll have other priorities in that kind of situation.

She was quieter now in his arms, and he felt like he was cheating on the dead husband with the spectacles only because the weight of her against his body was exciting him. Her hip was positioned on his crotch and it was getting agreeable. If only the air everywhere didn't smell of sewage.

She was melting into him and she was relaxing. Her breasts were company, they were crushed against his upper ribs, he could see even in the darkness how the buttons on the front of her dress were undone far enough that her low undergarment was showing. He only had to place a hand there and feel the firmness, the nub of the nipple through the thin white cotton. He had wasted so much time, before Maureen had come along. He had been in this position of intent so many times and then Sophie McConnell would appear with her messed-up face and glowing eyes and he had felt dry hair deep in his throat and turned numb and retreated. So much time had he wasted and he was never sure how much time was even left and he had his mouth open now.

She must be able to feel his surprise right now, he thought. That's what Maureen called it. They had borrowed her friend's Studebaker one evening and driven out beyond Water Street to the first clean woods, and because it was cold they had stayed in the car and there were dog hairs on the rear seat and she lay face downwards out of modesty and she said, when she felt it under her skirts, that it was a helluva surprise. That was afterwards she had said that, when she was refashioning her lipstick mouth.

Now his surprise was pressing against another woman's hip bone, but she didn't move. She was breathing deeply, but he saw with a kind of shock that her eyes were open—the glow from the far-off fire was enough to see her eyes and they were gleaming with wetness. Her fingers were over her mouth, like an infant sucking on its knuckles.

He felt bad, now, about his sexual excitement.

The animal in him was struggling against the sympathetic human being. He'd read a book about it recently: the way our brains are

divided between the old ape or caveman part and the more sophisticated section on top. There was this perpetual struggle going on
since the dawn of humankind. He guessed Hitler and the Nazis had
brains that were mainly given over to the ape or caveman part. Maybe
it was because Europe had the cavemen way before America, who
only had the Indians. Even his own Apache forebears were way more
recent than the first Europeans.

He stroked her hair and felt embarrassed thinking about his
Apache forebears, how primitive and wild they were with their
bloodcurdling whoops and half-naked bodies. It was a shame he had
picked up so much of it in his face, in his eyes and skin color. People
kept taking him for a full-blood. A few years back, there was a pretty
girl in tennis whites who said he looked like a photo she had of Jim
Thorpe hitting a home run for Boston in 1919, which was nice. He
should have taken her to the nearest good fun. Yet he felt almost bad
when he considered what his compatriots had done to those people,
among whom were his own forebears.

He was stroking her hair, and her hip bone was pressing on his
surprise. She was very still, now, and he let himself stay there, brooding, drawing his own comfort from her human warmth.

His grandmother's father had died at the hands of white men, for
instance. Blown clean dead off his horse during a raid by horse
thieves when his grandmama was only three years old. This great-
grandfather of his was in the Indian wars and had fought with Geron-
imo and then was shot dead by a goddamn teenage horse thief in
1863. Gee, the same year as the battle of Gettysburg. His great-
grandmama having died of cholera the year before, his grandmama
was adopted by a missionary family so fresh from Scotland she could
not understand what they were saying, and she was a Primitive
Methodist and did the chores. There was something shameful in it
all, and he didn't know what had been left out or how much of it was
even true. For how come she couldn't understand what they were
saying when she was with them from so young? There was stuff that
didn't shake down. There always was, except in a dime novel.

He hardly remembered his old Indian grandmama, except that her hands were bony and strong and she smelled of stale milk when her chins unfolded. In school once, when the teacher told them to write about their forebears, he'd written how his great-grandfather had died at the battle of Gettysburg in 1863 and he'd received a better grade than most times.

The woman shifted slightly in his arms, and Parry laid his cheek against her temple and closed his eyes. He would comfort her. He would not do anything else. Then he would leave her in order to deal with the painting; she was not his responsibility. He wished he were in a feather bed without this goddamn uniform galling his ass and the torn blanket making him scratch and the remains of the town museum rolling his vertebrae. He wished he were naked next to this woman, in a deep feather bed.

Not even his trousers were his own. The edges of the pockets were frayed, and in one of them he had found a mess of dried-up lint. When a man was wounded, the medics ripped the cloth like they were opening a present.

He wondered why anyone bothered to play the *War* record on the nickel-in-the-slot machine over and over. He started to kiss the woman on the face until they found each other's mouths very well and warm and whole.

Happiness is a mountain range, snowy and in the distance. It is behind me, but all I have to do is turn in the deep valley and it will appear in front of me. But I can't turn. Something pushes me on and I can't turn.

37

He came to on the floor, squeezed between the chair and the door, Caspar Friedrich's cushion on his legs.

He didn't know where he was for a moment. He felt his stomach.

It was intact. He was entirely intact, in fact. He wasn't sure whether he had blacked out or simply dived. His forehead hurt, but it was not cut. He peered over the chair. Herr Wolmer was looking through the window, rifle in one hand.

"They're out there," he said.

Herr Hoffer felt elation more than fear. He sprang to the window, ignoring his nausea. There were soldiers pushing a big manure cart towards the stone base of the smashed burgher's statue. They were not Americans. They were his own countrymen, in field-gray uniforms. Artillery.

On the manure cart was a gun with a very long barrel, sitting crookedly. He screwed up his eyes behind his dirty spectacles, just making out a black patch on the collars of the jackets, a thin black line on the cuff: Waffen-SS, they must be. One of them had his arm in a sling; another was limping. Two of them had lost their helmets. Another was standing at a distance from the others but nearer to the museum, aiming his rifle down the street. It was this man who had fired, not Herr Wolmer. The fellow fired again, then looked. Perhaps the Americans were very close, close enough to be fired at. Or perhaps he was firing at nothing. The others were having difficulties guiding the manure cart, or perhaps the gun was too heavy for it. They needed a horse or a pony. The long barrel was facing the museum now.

"What are they doing, Herr Wolmer?"

"Setting up a position. Antitank, it looks like. They're an artillery crew, SS boys, but they've lost their chassis. Or maybe it broke down like they all do. Looks like a big twelve-eight off a King Tiger, don't you reckon, Herr Hoffer?"

Herr Hoffer admitted that antitank guns all looked the same to him.

"Very powerful, if it's a twelve-eight," Herr Wolmer went on. "I think it is a twelve-eight. They're defending their position, Herr Hoffer. It's a good strategic position. Covers a wide angle down both streets. That's solid stone, that base is. Perfect cover. We're not going to go down without a fight now."

There were no more than ten or twelve of them. After some shouting and struggling, they got the gun to face away from the museum,
to Herr Hoffer's relief. It surprised him that they weren't using the
museum for cover. The tower, for instance, would make a perfect
sniper's nest. But then it might fall down and that would be the end.
The cart abruptly gave way at the front and the end of the barrel hit
the ground with a clang that Herr Hoffer felt through his feet. The
cart's front wheels were splayed flat. One of the men seemed to be
knocked over and lay unmoving while the others shouted and
screamed at one another, ignoring him.

He remained flat out while his comrades, by lifting together,
pulled the gun off the broken cart and rested the barrel on the flat lip
of the base where the white marble changed to some gray stone, perhaps granite. The lip was just the right height—in normal times,
people would sit there for a breather. It had been a favorite place for
drunks, years before, lifting their faces to the sun or singing.

It all looked very desperate. Bodies still lay about from the shell
that had blown the statue to bits and broken the Kluge window, their
elbows raised as if warding something off, their faces puffy and dark,
with peculiar patches on them that Herr Hoffer avoided looking at,
as he avoided the nearby lumps of what might have been butcher's
tripe. The gun pointed over the crater, up the long street towards the
center of town.

Herr Wolmer was excited. His nose was wet, glistening into his
mustache. He gave a big sniff and let the lace curtain fall.

"Still thinking of putting a white flag out, then?"

Herr Hoffer shook his head.

The janitor adjusted his spiked helmet, its leather scarred but
shining with boot polish.

"I could go and ask them what the latest combat news is, Herr
Hoffer."

"Be careful."

"They're not shelling us here, not for the moment."

"I was thinking of the SS boys, not the shells."

"They wouldn't hurt me, Herr Hoffer. I'm a fellow soldier."

Herr Hoffer kept watch over the main door, locking it after the janitor had left. Through the hallway's large barred window he watched as Herr Wolmer, in his wobbly helmet and with his trench-coat flapping, cradling his rifle, limped towards the SS boys, now settled around the antitank gun. Herr Hoffer half expected them to shoot Herr Wolmer, but instead they seemed to laugh. The janitor clapped his heels together and gave them the Hitler salute, but this made things worse; they returned it rather wildly, still laughing. Perhaps they were drunk, like those drunks of another time who would lift their faces to the sun and sing.

After a few minutes Herr Wolmer came back.

"Well?"

"Young tykes. No respect."

"They know they're going to die."

"So did we, in the trenches. But we never lost respect for our elders. It's a bad sign."

They were back in the little room. Herr Wolmer stood by the window.

"A bad sign," he said again. "It means the Führer's lost his grip. No decency or respect now. For twelve years we've had decency and respect. Now it's all gone."

"My father would say that family life had already disintegrated by 1918. Which was why the Party had to sort things out. I will inspect the attics."

"Anyway, one of the young tykes did have the politeness to tell me as how five or six units from their division are consolidating their positions in town and how the enemy are pinned down on Kreiburg Hill."

"And the American advance down the motorway?"

"Held up by ambushes. Huge enemy casualties from the ambushes. Ordinary SS and Luftwaffe personnel, mostly, but well armed. Waiting in camouflaged foxholes until the convoy's mostly passed and then hitting them in the backsides. That's where we should be, you and me, hitting them in the backsides with everything what we've got."

Herr Hoffer nodded, torn between dismay and patriotic pride.

"Herr Hoffer?"

"Yes, Herr Wolmer?"

"Do you think I look like a constipated lunatic with lop ears?"

Herr Hoffer left the janitor looking at himself in a tiny mirror embedded in an Alpine photograph of Königssee. Did the attics really have to be inspected? He supposed so. Duty! He wasn't sure what he would do if he found something smoldering up there, or an unexploded shell lodged between the beams. The water was cut off, and there were no buckets of sand in readiness because all their buckets had been taken to be turned into tanks. He could hardly phone the SHD firefighting fellows. Anyway, even the SHD lot were probably on Kreiburg Hill—or running off with the others. Herr Wolmer had insisted on going himself, but Herr Hoffer wouldn't hear of it. The Acting Acting Director still had his pride.

"All you need to do about them rats," Herr Wolmer had advised, "is thump up that ladder like an army. Then they'll hide, right enough."

Herr Hoffer ascended the main stairs, not quite able to believe in the whole situation. The things one did. He tried not to think about the rats. He'd go back via the cognac, anyway.

The antitank position was a catastrophe. The Americans would shell it or fire mortars and the museum was only thirty yards or so behind. The SS boys were bound to retreat to the museum. He had feared this as much as anything: the museum as one huge pillbox, never mind Herr Wolmer and his rifle. The end of the war struck him as being like a large cloth pulled through a tiny slit in a hoop made from taut rice paper; only a magician could do it without tearing the world in two.

He took the back stairs from the first to the third floor, climbing slowly step by step, feeling very dejected. Much more dejected than fearful. He ought to be happy that the Americans were pinned down, but he wasn't. It would only make the agony more drawn out.

He wished he had a helmet. His head felt very exposed. He was entitled to a helmet, but there were no helmets. He had seen one man with a colander on his head, during a raid last week! It was like a village performance of a mystery play. Or that agit-prop cabaret about war in a Berlin street, all those years ago, with kitchen utensils instead of armor. He had watched it with pleasure and amazement; he recalled a sign saying KATAKOMBE and a girl playing the saxophone and a long poem read by Fritz Sternberg himself.

The upper corridors were dank and neglected. A railed loft ladder led to the first attic. He remembered Herr Wolmer's advice to thump up it. As he stood at the bottom, recovering his breath from the stairs, he heard someone moving about overhead.

He wondered if it might be Gustav Glatz. It couldn't possibly be a rat. Those were feet, not paws.

It was bound to be Gustav, wasn't it? Many times over the last twelve years he had discovered poor Gustav wandering about, particularly after closing time. It was hardly surprising. Poor old Gustav— he had been such a brilliant scholar, with a shining career ahead of him. His thesis on bracelet shading was a model of its kind. Even Bendel thought so.

What the hell do I care what Bendel thought or didn't think?

Herr Hoffer felt giddy and nauseated again. The glorified loft ladder stretched up like the flank of Everest. If only Gustav had not gone out and torn that election poster down. No. If only the two SA men had not spotted him. The poster was a huge one; Hitler glared down from it like a demon. Gustav tore the poster down the middle— it was only pinned to the museum's delivery door and was easily done. The huge face of Hitler torn in two, as if peering out from behind a wall. It might have been a work by Kurt Schwitters, entitled *Doppelgänger*. But it wasn't, it was a poster for the election that would legitimize the seedy barber's appointment as chancellor. That's how Gustav put it, wasn't it? The seedy barber's appointment as chancellor. He wasn't ever a barber, but he looked like one. In fact, he had started life as a painter, a postcard painter. That was hard to imagine. The artist hero was a very minor watercolorist. A Viennese bohemian who slept in flophouses and sold his pictures as street vendors sell rubber collars or badly stitched handbags or sour cigarettes.

There had been shouts and these two figures running up. He hadn't quite understood in time.

If only they had not thrashed poor Gustav quite so badly! Herr Hoffer caught the end of it through the open window of his office, hearing a sound like a dog settling into a bone and noting how one of the SA men wore peasant clogs instead of leather boots. He had a large hole at the back of each sock, exposing dirty ankle bones. Then the thugs had bolted. No, strolled away, laughing. Thirty seconds, and it was done. Certainly not more than a minute.

Poor Gustav. He was quite unrecognizable. His teeth seemed to be protruding through his lip.

Bound to be him, thought Herr Hoffer, mounting the attic steps, which creaked horribly. He'll show me his tongue and say slurred incomprehensible things with great eagerness. It was all rather tiring, being nice to poor Gustav. He hardly remembered to thump, convinced it wasn't a giant rat.

Almost as tiring as being nice to members of the Party.

Life, when you come down to it, he thought, is an uproar in which you seek your solitary bed.

I have been asked not to move in the day. I can come out from my hole, but I must not move about. I feel I am an ox wagon, carrying my own dung. All the signs tell me that you are waiting for me, somewhere near.

38

Parry did not think anymore. For a short while, anyway, he just gave up. He let himself be washed through by sex. Whatever logic there had been to the straight line of his actions, sex chewed into it, sure as hell. The straight line became a wave, then blurred into something without craft or suspicion, and he lifted up her dress. She was laughing.

Laughing! Why the fuck was she laughing? She was crazy. He was without suspicion, though. They had even been warned. This made him open all the doors even wider. He banished those medical jerks from his sight. There was firelight on the creek and he was floating in the hired canoe. The Studebaker was rocking with its goddamn dog hairs. No Sophie McConnell in his throat, either.

The front of her dress tore down to the hem as he pulled her breasts out from the loose neckline of the undergarment. He did not mind the faint dishcloth smell of his own saliva as he returned to each nipple and held it in his mouth like an infant. Because that's what he was: an infant of great thirst and moment. She held his head tight against the breasts, against their great strength and smoothness, and kept on laughing.

In the back of his mind, right up in the corner, there was a wicked little face with a bubble that was saying, *That guy with the spectacles can't have fucked her too well.*

He, Parry, was doing it so well they were almost exploding.

They had slipped off the beam and the rubble could hardly take it. You sack a city you sack a city and you get the girls. The town was digging into his ass and his spine through the blanket but he wasn't complaining; she was riding him like she wanted to crush the rubble to powder under them both. Panting and exerting like animals. Crying out and laughing. Pushing him deep into the rubble and crying out as if they were dying and laughing at the same time. Which they were.

And who cares about the noise?

He knew he was loving her just for this time, not for any other. She was not beautiful until he started the loving. Like he had not loved Morrison until he was dead and the blood had flowed past and over those goddamn steps and down the path where the paving was jointed. They used to say that Germans could not keep the thread or join up good—he had read that somewhere—but now they were changed and it suited everybody to call them inhumanly efficient and good at keeping the thread that was steel or iron. And he was proving that the enemy was not of steel or iron or something you just dropped

phosphorus on like it was Monday and the day for phosphorus dropping and doing the wash. He hadn't even eaten Morrison's hair, but
the stupid guy was splashing him all over with that goddamn blood as
the woman groaned and squeezed him up deep inside her belly. Her
hair falling like a net curtain over her face and his.

Hell, he was getting sore. As she was riding him. He was pinioned
by her. This is what happens, he thought, when you take some nice
girl out in the Studebaker beyond Water Street. They might have
brushed off the goddamn dog hairs. And he knew what kind of a dog
it was. So large and fat it dented the smooth front lawn just lying
there yards from the sidewalk.

It wasn't Morrison. It was this goddamn infection, this burning at
the tip whenever he pissed. It was never changing his underwear and
having the GI common condition. Of the runs. It was museum masonry digging into his back, and it was all the fucking war. He came
out of her. But she had had a good time.

She used her hand, then. She tried to pull him off against her
belly, using her left hand, her eyes shining with tears as she watched.
Hell, he had to stop her. It hurt. He buttoned himself back into his
pants and she tugged herself back into order in the way women do.
And the blur hardened back to the straight line.

She lay next to him on the blanket, her arm across his chest. She
was staring upwards and jerking a little as if she'd been sobbing instead of laughing. They couldn't speak because she was a Heinie and
he was an American, yet there were no secrets between them now.
He knew the secret of her, the hidden heat behind the cool skin of
her forearms. He turned to look at her in the sudden orange glow
that was a fire somewhere nearby, taking up the slack from a shelled
block, lighting the night sky as brightly as the refinery chimneys did
back home.

She was not so ugly, though. She had a nice nose and a firm, almost lipless mouth. Her eyes were shining orange beneath the lit-up
sky. Then the flame must have died because the sky went cold and
dark again, and with it her thinking face all but disappeared. She'd

looked like she was thinking out some things that maybe he would rather not know.

The cliff of the ruined gable end way beyond her face was pale, almost white, and against it her profile was a dark cutout. You would start with the profile and then the sky and last of all the gable end. Unless it was watercolor, whose radiance was the paper and not the paint. If it was watercolor, you would paint the profile last. He wanted the smell of linseed oil and turpentine and a piece of cheese near the palette. He'd applied to be a war artist but they did not want a commercial artist who did dishes of macaroni and a girl smoking Kensitas in front of a waterfall. Her face was very dark against the gable end, but really the gable end was not that pale; it was only the contrast that made it so. He knew like a secret that your shadows had to be very deep or the light would not look light and the half-tints in between would not be singing and people would not say how fine and real it looked because you could see the wet on her lip and in her eye there is this tiny window. Hell, he had to make lips kissable for some of those magazines and the bosoms still had to be reasonable and warm with their soft highlights; he was not painting freaks. This is what he told them, when he got angry. He had an idea, now.

He got up and made her stand, and together they picked their way carefully over some big lumps of marble to the pale wall of the gable end. He took a piece of burnt wood and scraped black figures on the wall. The moon was up, it was a clear April night and their eyes were adjusting; he didn't need Morrison's goddamned flashlight.

He scraped a man, a stick figure, with big round glasses. Then a woman in a dress and loose hair. Then a question mark. It all came easily to his hand, which was black now with the burnt wood.

He knew he should sketch each day living scenes of war but, hell, he had not yet filled one lousy pad. Sketch his comrades filling up a jerry can and civilians with Saratoga trunks and the puffed-up deads and the burnt ribs of TCs and then look sullen for the magazines.

She nodded and took the burnt wood and wrote *Heinrich, mein Mann,* and *Sabine* under the woman. Then, as an afterthought, *Herr und Frau Hoffer.*

She was doing swell, he told her. He would like to bet on it that they could hold a conversation about the weather and clothes and the history of philosophy with this goddamn piece of burnt wood. She didn't understand.

Then she crossed out the *Herr und* and really cried, and he held her. She was a widow. It was confirmed, it was official. The papers were stamped and the doors were open.

They were on their own in the rubble of the museum and no one could see them. She had never wanted to hurt anyone and he had never wanted to hurt anyone. He cradled her a little against his mackinaw.

Then he drew much smaller figures in childish style and followed that with a couple of question marks. She took the burnt wood and drew two stick girls with a trembling hand. Then she rested her forehead against the wall with her fingers in her mouth and her eyes closed. It was as if she were praying.

She stayed like that and Parry didn't know what to do.

Dear sweet Jesus, he thought, she had better not have lost her kids, on top of being a widow. There is no official name for a woman who has lost her kids. It is beyond any names. Hell it is, and more.

It made him feel seasick, this possibility. But looking at the ruins around them, it was pretty possible and even likely and now he would have to deal with this.

And then he saw this mad clown grinning at them through a hole blasted in the gable end. Hell. It gave him a shock like a bullet.

It was sticking out its tongue and grinning, and it was all white.

The big man with the Kaiser mustache came up again tonight with the mirror and gave me some bread and water and took away my pan. For the first time he talked to me. He was saved by a Jewish comrade in the trenches. I am to be his deranged niece. I am not to write down any names in this book or they will all die. My own name is gone.

39

He stepped into the attic with great caution, remembering the time he had knocked his head on a beam. He tried not to think about rats. The thought of poor Gustav was almost comforting.

He called Gustav's name, softly.

Silence. The muttering and sighing was the war. Amazing, how you got used to things.

His eyes adjusted to the gloom of the first great attic as he caught his breath. The architect had used whole trees for beams, still scabbed with bark. It smelled of mice up here; he didn't mind mice. Rats did not smell like mice. Light filtered in through the odd glass tile in thin beams made almost solid by the dust he stirred as he moved. Dim and ancient cathedrals, these attics were.

He moved through them like a demure monk. They had reduced the bombardment to strange mutterings and murmurs—like prayer, he thought, or the grief of the Nibelungs as they recounted their bitterest sorrows to Gudrun in the green depths between the boughs.

Life, he thought, is too broad a river. He would love to visit Iceland and Peru and Egypt.

There was nothing untoward in the first attic. He was startled by a mouse scurrying away, but mice were welcome. Mice (or rats) only leave a sinking ship, and the attics with their trusses reminded him of the inverted holds of ships, of great galleons. Mice were like their greatest enemy, Caspar Friedrich. They would have sensed the earthquake coming and poured out of the building.

The Americans were no doubt already pouring into Lohenfelde. They would not be pinned down for long.

He should be at home, with his family. And their three suitcases, in case.

But the Americans were reasonable. It was the Bolsheviks who were savages. The Asian hordes.

What on earth was he doing up here, so close to the sky? His duty, that's what. He felt warmer, thinking that.

He should remove all Party signs from the building. The banner would provoke the Americans. He'd heard (from a refugee who'd seen it) that they shot at doors to dispossess people of their homes. He'd also heard, from the radio and from Party sympathizers, that they stole and raped and slaughtered and bombed and burned whole villages and towns. But that was Party rubbish.

He had to remove the swastika banner, at least. It was out of sight of the SS men and only faced Count von Moltke Strasse, that empty street at the back. It was the result of a semiliterate letter from the local Ortsgruppenleiter (a retired baker, and a drunk), but Herr Hoffer had draped the banner on the quietest side. The flag had not quite found its way to the top of the tower. The Ortsgruppenleiter had been dismissed for embezzlement soon after.

You see, Captain Clark Gable, we have had to use our wits to avoid committing suicide. You would not believe the mediocrity of the Party leaders, but they held the whip hand. For twelve years, they held it: a mere squeak in the long symphony of our people, but a very long time when you are in it. It was a risk even to take my children to the doctor's. Why, Captain Gable? Because a great number of doctors were Party men, I'm ashamed to say. You can't control everything your children say. Yes, I removed that dreadful banner at great personal risk. And my family's risk. We must not forget that they liked to punish one's family too. Thank you. I would like to try some chewing gum. That is very kind.

He left the first attic and entered the next. The attics, although huge and dry, had nothing stored in them apart from odds and ends:

dismantled frames, a broken deck chair, someone's paint-splashed overalls hung long ago from a nail, a pair of old clogs, a rusty cross from the bombed cemetery, some big empty barrels lying on their side, a chipped soup tureen. Kurt Schwitters would make a sculpture out of all that. Another version of *Merz*!

No, it was pointless junk. Or emergency firewood. Even most of the third-floor rooms had nothing stored in them. The museum had been conceived for a much larger city, or perhaps in those days they had lavish hopes that the passage of time would fill it—that an expanding imperial glory would accumulate riches like a barn accumulates the harvest. The passage of time had, in fact, emptied the building.

He felt the emptiness, underneath the rough planking of the attics, as something solid, like solid blocks of ice. The actual contents, buried now in the salt mine or the vaults, felt vaporous.

He opened a tiny low skylight set into the roof—what thought and care that architect showed back in 1904!—and looked out cautiously upon this quarter of Lohenfelde: a jumble of roofs, steeples, and gable ends in which smoke was set every so often in a kind of fat black column rising to a brownish haze; nothing more dramatic. There was something of a burnt smell on the cool air, but that was all. A perfect sniper's nest. A perfect lookout for the artillery.

The bombardment was clearly concentrated elsewhere, in another quarter. He tried not to entertain the idea that it might be his home quarter, where Sabine and Erika and Elisabeth were crouched underground with their three suitcases, but the thought gnawed at him anyway. He shut the skylight as if that might help. The sloped attic ceiling ended in a low stone wall, a little farther on, which was where the tower cut up through the roof.

His foot kicked an apple core.

It was fresh. That was odd! Herr Wolmer must have done his own tour this morning, although as far as he knew the janitor never made it up to the attics, not with his limp.

Gustav, he thought.

Again, he called Gustav's name. Nothing. Gustav Glatz is not dangerous. Gustav is like a little child.

And if it wasn't Gustav Glatz?

For an awful moment he thought someone—a Jew, a Communist—might be hiding up here. Even now, at this late stage, that could get them into appalling trouble. The mere thought of it chilled him. That was the problem with refugees who hid themselves: They were selfish; they put everyone else in danger. Not that he could blame them. He had never minded Jews, personally. His finest overcoat had been made to measure by old Mordecai Grassgrün, for instance, in what was now Fritz Klingenberg Strasse, even as the Party was coming to power. That fact would stand him in good stead, as much as his support for Jewish artists in the old and golden days. Not that he'd ever thought of them as Jews. They were artists, first.

He hoped Mordecai would make it back here, to bear witness. Although his memory might have suffered. No doubt conditions were not the best, in the camps. It would not be Saint Moritz, in the camps.

It was something that had always worried him, in fact: that the Gestapo would find someone crouched in a museum cupboard and blame the staff. Then you could kiss goodbye to the paintings. And the staff also, probably.

On the other hand, a well-concealed Jew was useful insurance for when the Reich collapsed and the enemy came. Everyone knew that. The enemy was coming now, he reminded himself, although the real Party hundred-and-fifty-percenters would be at their most dangerous at this time, cornered and snarling.

Yes, it was said that quite a few of the big boys in the Party had their personal Jew hidden away, for after the end.

He wasn't big enough to get away with something like that. He would be carted straight off to Dachau or worse. And then the paintings would be lost for good.

Herr Hoffer shuddered, throwing the apple core over his shoulder. He was sick of apples, of spreading apple compote on his bread every morning instead of raspberry or honey or orange. Honey! Orange! Lemons!

A shell made a sound like someone hitting an egg with a spoon. Close, again. Annoying, he thought. Go and play elsewhere, please. You might break a window.

Captain Clark Gable, I was very worried at one moment and thought of you as a naughty boy playing with his ball. Thank you, I will indeed have a glass of your famous Coca-Cola. Yes, my girls would be delighted to. Erika and Elisabeth: I believe you find these names in America too. Hm, it is delicious. Quite out of the ordinary. Do try this excellent old cognac of mine.

These attics were beautiful spaces, they really were. One could create such things in them! He ran his hand along a hewn joist. Oh, how he loved the scent of wood. Wholly natural. The more he concentrated on the materiality of it all, the way the light touched each surface and yielded texture and complexity, the less likely it seemed that it could be effaced. Impossible, in fact.

He felt euphoric, suddenly, stroking the joist, as if some immortal flame had sprung up, blazing, behind his tired eyes. After the war he would open up these attics to artists—yes!—to young, fierce, idealistic, and penniless young artists who would germinate great movements here, just as *die Brücke* was germinated in Dresden all those years ago: Kirchner, Bleyl, Schmidt-Rottluff, Nolde . . . open-necked and quoting *Zarathustra* as they leaped up their attic stairs, full of hope, the trenches not even a rumor in their nightmares. These names were a kind of rosary for Herr Hoffer: He would run them through his mind and finger them mentally. He was sure one day they would be renowned in the world, unstained by what the National Socialists had done to Germanness.

This sudden surge of inspiration made his heart beat quicker, as if Heine's wings of song were beating within him on that lovely melody of Mendelssohn-Bartholdy: the inner sound of the spirit! The excitation and fear of the last few hours and the imminence of the arrival of the Americans—these made him almost dizzy with inspiration as he stood there in the great second attic by the tower and saw the space opened to the world, to all the healthful modernist currents in the world, its solid bark-encrusted beams from the deepest forests supporting the newest and most exciting ideas in art. . . . Ah, how he dreamed! He even saw where he would place the glass, the long skylights. Would it matter if they were facing east? Was that not a symbol of hope? The rising sun casting its dawn light on the youthful artists at work, inventing anew?

He pictured himself visiting the attics as a very old man, after they had become renowned, the proud benefactor applauded by the fiery youths spotted with paint or glue or varnish, smiling and cheering him in front of their extraordinary works. He placed both hands on the huge central beam and placed his head between them, his ear against the bark, and cried out in a kind of ecstasy, his anxiety fled or perhaps transformed into this strange, sudden inspiration.

The Lohenfelde ateliers!

He gave a great sigh, clapped the shoulder of the beam like an old friend, and moved on, muttering to himself as he would when alone and excited. The hoop of rice paper did not have to tear. This vision of the attics would see them through. How could it be otherwise, with his famous agility? Had they not survived so far, against all odds, thanks to his suppleness and agility?

Things might still be marvelous, he thought. They might even draw the vengeful sting of the Jews by soothing words and humility. They themselves—the ordinary German people—might even have to get down on their knees and eat grass as a sign of contrition, to avoid the returning Hebrews' biblical vengeance. Though it would be worse in Poland, where there were millions of them, teeming like disturbed ants. Yes, he would certainly be willing to crawl and eat grass as a symbolic gesture of contrition, to save his family from the Hebrew ire! At the very least, he would sport old Mordecai's bespoke coat.

Then he could get down to the real business of creating anew.

When a loud crash from the bombardment trembled the roof's very structure and filled the air with dislodged dust, he considered it only as a kind of affront to his own marvelous vision.

I didn't even say goodbye to you properly. I didn't even look back when I ran past the pear tree and out of the gate.

40

The face with the stuck-out tongue disappeared, but not before it had laughed. It had bobbed and looked like the moon bobbing in a break in the clouds when really it is not the moon that does that but the clouds. Here it was the face, because a face is alive and that is its sign of life: that it moves. A dead's face does not move. The difference between a dead's face and an alive's face is infinitesimal, but it makes all the running. A sleeping alive's face twitches after a minute or so of watching and that's how you can tell when a guy is lying sprawled without even a blanket because he is so tired, but it still can give you the willies, seeing him there.

But the white face with the tongue vanished and he kept his hand on his rifle, not knowing why he did not scream. Maybe because fear is repetitious. He thought the creature might have laughed.

And then it is really terrible, the vice versa: when you think an American kid is sleeping and he turns out to be deader than your great-great-great-grandmama whom you will never meet this side of the last goodbye. And you think: His folks don't know yet. I have got there before them. And I don't even know the guy. You don't expect to think the same about the Germans until you see one dead who has not tried to kill you and you think: His folks don't know yet. Crazy. You think even of his goddamn momma washing the dishes in the sink and not yet knowing. And then when you come across a real momma and the little kids sprawled who are not sleeping either, then your thoughts blow too hard even to stand up, so you close up and keep that goddamn wind out of your head and just step over and pass on.

So Parry was suddenly tired of this crazy widow, crying against the wall. He had closed up out of self-defense. He could not go through that particular door. The crazy white face and its stuck-out tongue had shocked him.

Somewhere outside Luxembourg he had spent a night in a building with the roof blown off and five men from another unit lying dead under canvas in the front hall. Snow blew in through the roof into the upper rooms and through the broken windows into the hall, but the back rooms on the ground floor were untouched. They lit a fire on the hearth that threw wild shadows in the darkness, improvised oil lamps out of shell cases, and boiled up some old rooty potatoes that went OK with the dehydrated stew. There was no liquor, because nobody had found any.

There was a piano, however, almost in tune. A couple of handsome German ladies in their middle thirties, well-dressed and firm in the chest, sang a lot of the standards in English and French and then went into the next-door room with some of the men. A fire had been lit there too. It was the dining room; it had a big oak table with fat legs.

Parry hadn't gone. He'd stayed with the remaining six or seven men who were too shy or tired or morally upright or militarily obedient or who maybe didn't like girls, and they'd stared into the fire, feeling a mixture of superiority and shame.

They heard noises coming through the wall and door, as if the heavy wallpaper was not enough to cover the truth. Nobody spoke.

All they did was smoke, smoke until their tongues were sore. Some of the men kept grinning and some of the men looked straight ahead into the fire. The kids with spotty faces and anxious eyes, eighteen or nineteen years old, who were very tired and whose time for such things was running on credit—they were restless but they did not move at first. Parry poked the fire and the bits of shattered house timbers spat, bubbling brown paint or lacquer or black creosote, but the noise wasn't enough to cover over the animal sounds of enjoyment next door.

Not one of them present could play the piano. Not even hymns. Not "Chocolate Soldier" or "Good-for-Nothin' Joe," even.

Parry had a novel in his pack, but he didn't fetch it; none of these guys read anything other than comic strips. And *Yank,* maybe.

"You don't make an omelet . . ." was all one of them said, suddenly and slowly.

Which every man there found so funny he was crying into himself, shaking with it. But even that did not generate a conversation. The noises held them, and maybe the warmth of the fire, which was end-lessly fascinating and better than a movie or a top baseball game. The air was very thick.

Gradually, one by one, the other guys crept away. They got up one by one without saying a word and slipped through the door into the dining room. Each time the door opened the sounds grew louder for a moment, fanning the lust of the men left behind. Maybe they went only to watch; Parry didn't know. And then he was the only one left. The last little Indian.

The fire burned on, giving out a good heat and a soft light. He sat in a comfortable easy chair with lacy stuff on its arms and watched the flames chew and grind away at the shattered timbers. There were thumps and muffled cries, but he was above all that. Part of him—about a third, he reckoned—was eager to get up and see what was happening next door in the dining room with the big oak table. Maybe that's where it was all happening, on the big oak table. He imagined it as being serious and concentrated. The two thirds re-maining in him sat it out, gaining amazing pleasure from the comfort-able chair and the heat from the fire and the flames themselves, tamely blazing on the fine marble hearth.

He went to sleep like that.

When he woke up it was morning. He was cold. There was no one else in the room. The door into the dining room was closed. He didn't want to open it, to have everyone stirring and staring at him.

He went into the hall instead. The five dead men were still under canvas, their boots poking up from one end. He looked out into the wide street. There was a smell of burning and explosives, but other-wise all was quiet. The ruined houses softened with light snow and the upright houses looking peaceful.

One of their trucks went by, empty; then another going the oppo-site way, slowly, this one full of men swaying under the canvas. He acknowledged them with a humorous salute, though he didn't know them and not just because they were Brits. They raised their hands and shouted things he mostly didn't catch but which were nice and friendly, in a British accent.

"Wotcher, cock!"

"Which way'd they go, mate?"

"Hard luck! Yer've missed it!"

"Stand back, mates! It's the Yanks!"

He felt good, not succumbing to the German ladies; he felt very clean in the crisp morning air.

He watched the truck go up the street, feeling a whole lot better after a night's sleep in the chair. Then the truck lifted up and something clapped, like a huge sail clapping in the wind next to his ear. The truck blossomed into fire, a ball of fire that turned tulip-shaped and dark and folded over into black smoke rolling up the street towards him.

He ran towards the burning truck, but the heat and smoke made him turn back. Some of the guys who had enjoyed themselves in the dining room appeared in front of the house, buttoning their pants or tunics, looking anxious.

Parry told them the truck had hit a mine; the bastard Heinies had mined the street before leaving. The smoke was moving quietly through the sky and the truck kept on burning, the canvas top shredding away in scraps like golden butterflies. No one had leaped or fallen out; they just burned like dolls.

Then he saw one man ablaze because he had leaped down, and he was walking for a few yards and Parry was sick of that kind of thing. The man knelt down, still burning at the neck.

The two German ladies appeared at the door, looking tired, holding their collars close to their throats. The men with Parry turned to them and grabbed them by the hair and threw them into the snow, where they floundered like dying fish. Apparently they'd said last night there were no mines set around here; the only mines were themselves, full of dynamite.

Perhaps they didn't know—why should they have known?—but the men were disgusted by them now and kicked them hard as the black smoke billowed down the street and then they shot high after them as they screamed, stumbling off through the snow.

Parry hadn't felt this disgust, and he'd known why.

But now he felt for the widow a little part of what the men had felt for the two German whores. She was just standing by the charcoal scribbles on the gable end and clawing her mouth with her fingers, turning even crazier. He might have crossed out the stick drawing of the kids, to see how she reacted, but he couldn't risk it. She was grieving for her kids, not her husband.

The face with the tongue had not come back.

In any case, he was not going to get involved. He was going to stay in the next-door room in front of the fire. He was not going to listen to her cries.

My heartbeat tells me I'm alive. It continues. It goes on and on, without reflection. What makes it go on and on? It does not stop when you order it to. How strange. The good news is that I think I am going to see you all very soon! I am safe. This is because I am living in a kind of death. It is easier to stay alive when you are not trying so hard; no one notices you. Now it doesn't matter if I am noticed. I am visible, but I have never felt so small and unnoticed. I am waiting for you. Then we [. . . ?]

41

Herr Hoffer coughed in the dust and decided his inspection of the attics was over. The third attic stretched beyond the darkness, but it was evident that it was not ablaze or even smoldering. What could he do if it were? Very little.

He did not even have a helmet.

He made his way back to the steps, feeling vulnerable. His legs and back ached and he yawned and felt tiredness surround him as if he had fallen into a huge suffocating flower. Tiredness would always do this to him and his thoughts would go jumbled as if he were falling asleep although he was still upright and busy. It was almost warm, up here, with the April sun on the roof tiles and all this wood and all he wanted to do was lie down and sleep long and dream of happier days, days spent in summer barns full of hay, the dust lit by bright golden shafts of sun as fine as sword blades; eggs hunted for in the nooks and crannies, eggs warm with life; summer days of barns and rivers and summer nights crowded with stars. He was crouching at the low door above the steps when there was a dull thud on his head, although he actually heard it as a wash of water or liquid glass and then the silence rang in blackness that was a falling sensation he was trying to get a grip on. This was, in fact, the moment of coming to after centuries of unconsciousness when his body was swaying on springs. He had a memory from childhood of falling and getting up again in long summery grass that rustled, too tall to see over. His mother was calling him. She couldn't see him. He had to call her, and he was trying to call her from within the grass but his voice wasn't very strong; it had something stuck in it. He tried harder. He was shouting for his mother as a grown man—he woke himself up with it. He stopped shouting for her, feeling sick and giddy. There was disorder around him, he knew that. He had no idea where he was. There was a lot of daylight filtering through whirls of smoke or dust. The noise had been too much for his head and he had fallen asleep and tumbled down and somehow flown up again to where he was before. There were diagonals, thick as trees, as if he were lying in an ancient forest where the trees had fallen upon one another. There was a warmth flowing over his face, which he touched. It was dark blood. This surprised him. His hair was full of it, making sticky clumps. He had been wounded in battle. A saber had descended upon his skull. Wielded by a Frenchman. Now an SA man's huge close-shaven head was butting him just above the forehead. He could not persuade the SA man to stop, because he could not see the face, only the shaven skull. He felt an oppressive weight over his eyes, like bone, like a primitive cave dweller in pictures. He shifted his legs, being careful not to squash the mushrooms of Moholy-Nagy. Didn't Moholy-Nagy end up as a Bauhaus professor? Probably. He cut his chair legs shorter for firewood; it was not art after all. Who visited him and thought it was art? Schwitters or Schlemmer? Wuppertal or Norway? Or neither. Norway is at least cold. Then he passed out again.

42

A seventeen-pound high-velocity shell from an American 76-mm field gun positioned behind an improvised V of corrugated-iron fencing in an apple orchard on the western edge of town had grazed the Kaiser Wilhelm Museum's tower on one side and exploded, the violence of the blast sending blocks of masonry from the upper tower onto the roof below, which gave way in places under the weight of the falling material but was not set alight. A bang and a quiver were felt by those in the vaults, and Herr Wolmer's tiny mirror embedded in a view of the famous Alpine lake of Königssee fell off its hook and shattered, scattering its silvery confetti over the janitor's legs.

About twenty minutes earlier, on the other side of town, a shell had struck the stone facing of the Hoffers' apartment building and fallen into the street, cracking the tarmac.

The shell did not immediately ignite but bounced and rolled wildly until it came to rest against the knee-high wall, topped by iron railings, that enclosed the thin strip of garden separating the Hoffers' apartment house from the street. Another high-explosive shell from a Waffen-SS field gun in Schulstrasse fell short a few seconds later and penetrated the roof of the building next door, exploding inside and starting a fire. The vibrations of this impact touched off the faulty shell lying on the street, disintegrating the wall, twisting the railings like licorice, and causing a percussive wave to proceed right through the apartments—experienced by the people in its air-raid cellar as both heat and pressure as well as noise. Apart from severely damaging the façade and blowing out windows, the blast caused ceilings and walls to collapse in the front half of the building. The considerable amount of rubble that even one inside wall creates, when no longer flat and smooth and upright but reduced to a chaos of its constituent parts, made its way down the stairs to the cellar in a fog of dust and rested against the door.

The people inside, who included Erika and Elisabeth Hoffer, were trapped.

What is more, the blast had shorted the apartment building's electrical circuitry and burst several pipes in the hot-water system. Steam joined the dust in the air as boiling water began to flood the rooms with a hiss and a noise like many fountains. The people down in the cellar were screaming in pitch-blackness. They continued screaming even when someone switched on a torch. Frau Hoffer's two small daughters were also screaming. They needed their mother, but their mother had gone upstairs to fetch a toy rabbit at the insistence of little Erika. Erika had left her cuddly toy tucked up in her bed, its floppy ears spread nicely out on the bolster, the sheet folded back just under the leather nose. She needed its smell and its woolly touch against her cheek and mouth. She could not suck her thumb without its floppy ear squeezed between her second and third fingers. In the darkness of the shelter, she could not breathe without her woolly rabbit, so Frau Hoffer had run up to their apartment to fetch it.

At the very moment Herr Hoffer was being threatened with Herr Wolmer's rifle in the janitor's room, his wife was being blown off her feet in the back bedroom and his daughters were screaming in fear.

The cellar had started to fill with steam and smoke and dust alarmingly quickly, probably by way of the air vents. The stronger people present flung themselves at the metal door (toughened with steel plate and rivets in 1942 by order of the city area's Zellenleiter), which had been dislodged slightly, but could not open it farther against the rubble piled up on the other side. The situation was made worse, if anything, by the fitful light from the rubber torch cast on terrified faces. People coughed and held handkerchiefs over their mouths. Some continued to push against the door or started scraping at the brick walls of the shelter with any instruments to hand—even, in one case, a nail file, which made surprising inroads on the damp-softened cement joints. A neighbor, a childless widow, held the Hoffer children tight against her, like the other mothers and grandmothers with their children, and told them to stop crying; everything would be all right. Erika and Elisabeth buried their faces in her dress, their plaits hanging down like tassels beneath her breasts, and wept and coughed and cried out for their mother. A Panzer tank passing in the street above (along which the two girls would normally have walked to school this morning) burst through the flames and, after continuing a little way with smoke twirling from its turret, summarily exploded. Lohenfelde was falling to the Allies.

43

He'd had no news of his brother or of his ninety-five-year-old grandmother in Eberbach, now in the hands of the Americans. Or of his sister, who persisted in staying in Berlin. Two cousins had been killed in action, plus a spinster aunt in the bombing of Dortmund; his sister-in-law, Lotte—five years younger than Sabine—had been evacuated to Bavaria from Stuttgart. But, unlike Sabine's small family, the Hoffers were a large tribe, well spread out, though their spiritual heart was in a lost village in the Sauerland. It might have been better had they stayed in clogs, turning the earth between the hills and forests. But they hadn't.

His grandfather, a bright fellow who had served under Prince Kraft of Hohenlohe-Ingelfingen as a liaison officer during the 1870 war, became the village schoolteacher and married the strapping postmistress. His father became a teacher in turn—in a Catholic grammar school in Eberbach, where he stayed until his retirement. His mother, who owned and ran a smart hat shop, was never very well after her youngest son's birth, and took to her bed for long periods, reading magazines and colored catalogs from large stores while Heinrich played around her. The hat shop closed and there were money worries. His father was stern and religious, with very conservative views, but not unloving. He had a lot to cope with, including three children separated each from the next by eight years, of whom Heinrich was the youngest. Heinrich was sickly as a child, with stomach problems arising, it was thought, from anxiety at his mother's poorly state.

Little Heinrich was frequently bullied at school, for being plump as well as being the son of the headmaster (who beat the boys vigorously, although he was never violent at home). His mother faded away in his twelfth year, and immediately after the funeral his stomach problems converted into a mental restlessness that surfaced either as migraine or a compulsion to go for long solitary hikes in the woods around Eberbach. His schoolwork deteriorated along with his eyesight, and he developed huge sties his schoolmates found both repellent and amusing. He was not cured by a Wandervogel summer camp of long marches and evening guitar-playing and extracts from the works of Professors Waitz, Maurer, and Treitschke on the early and uncorrupted German tribes and the awfulness of Sodom (France). In fact, rather ironically, he was sexually molested by two of the older boys (quite normal, they told him) and came back home feeling dirty and full of sin. He only discovered himself a year later when, at fourteen, he found—quite by chance in the school library—a book on the French Impressionists, with colored illustrations pasted in on gray cardboard. It was as though a window in a dim place had opened onto sunlight. Then followed a passion for Brueghel through a similar book. He would pore over it for hours, his eyes traveling so deeply into each peopled landscape that sometimes he would think himself back there in that time, a Flemish peasant of the sixteenth century, and wake up as if from a trance.

It was as one of those peasants, lying sprawled in a field during harvest with a flagon of beer beside him to quench his thirst, that Herr Hoffer imagined himself to be, before properly coming to after the attics had been struck by falling masonry. Everything was a cadmium yellow. His leather codpiece was warm in the sun. The old times before trains and cars and bombs lay generously around him. Horses snorted. Dogs barked. Flanders lay passive and replete under the August heat. Then he came to and saw a thick oaken beam with wooden pegs in it and the tiny boreholes of worm. He knew without a doubt, as if his thoughts were etched on glass, that he was in the attics of the Kaiser Wilhelm Museum, Lohenfelde, and that they had been damaged by a shell.

Herr Hoffer—

"Not now, Gustav."

He sat up stiffly and realized he was quite unhurt, apart from a gash on his head and the earlier cut on the hand. He was also alone.

Well, I am being protected, he thought. I am hidden and I am safe. The unbefitting place of darkness where no one can touch me.

He got to his feet carefully. He had a headache and felt a little sick, but the wound under the thin hair was no longer bleeding. Daylight came in through the interlocking curves and latticework of broken struts and joists, falling clearly on the piles of masonry from the gashed tower. He could see the tower through the hole in the roof, and the gash was considerable. Judging from his watch, he had been out cold for only a few minutes. Just a nap! The damage to the roof was impressive, though not extensive. It was like a piece of moth-eaten and frayed cloth, punctured clean through or showing the joists like thick threads. He could smell nothing like smoke, only the usual bitter trace of explosives and the felty tickle of dust.

He wiped his spectacles. One lens, he noted with surprise, had cracked. When he put them back on, the crack blurred his vision in the lower part; he had thought it was dirt. He was also surprised, looking down, to see that he had lost a shoe. He went back and, of course, could not find it anywhere in the mess of broken tiles, lumps of masonry, and scattered boards. He found another shoe, small and frayed and slipperlike, as if his own had shrunk. Odds and ends. The soup tureen was intact. The rusty cross was bent double. A barrel had become its hoops.

Turning, he kicked something with his foot. It was a book.

He picked it up: a notebook, filled with spidery scrawls in pencil. His glasses were fogged again with dust, it was dim, the hand was poor, so he could make out very little of it, but it was most likely Gustav's. He had always assumed Gustav was hardly capable of even writing his own name, but he might have been assuming wrong.

The notebook was the type that Werner used, with a red cardboard cover and a pencil tucked into its spiral binding. In fact, he saw as he peered that it had PROPERTY OF THE LIBRARY, KAISER WILHELM MUSEUM, LOHENFELDE stamped on the scuffed cover. Who else but Gustav? He might have dropped it years ago, on one of his wanderings. . . .

"Herr Hoffer—"

"Gustav, not—"

"Herr Hoffer, they have gracelessly used our wall without permission to place a very large and ugly image upon it."

"An image, Herr Glatz?"

His own voice, from far away.

"A full-face portrait of the little corporal with the eye bags, Herr Hoffer."

"How rude of them. If only we could tear it down."

"We can."

"Have they gone?"

"Yes, Herr Hoffer."

"*Soon hurry we soft through the door/Hurrah for our wonderful dance.*"

"Hölty."

"Yes, Herr Glatz. Yes."

And Gustav Glatz had hurried softly out. Herr Hoffer had not thought twice about it. He was busy at his desk at the time; he'd had no inkling of disaster. . . .

He pocketed the red notebook and squeezed his eyes. These voices always came upon one at the wrong time.

He left the attics, limping down the steps and wondering if it might not be better to go shoeless on both feet. For some reason, his lone shoe squeaked. He was sure it had not squeaked before. He felt so much more vulnerable without a shoe. Achilles with his heel. They got you in the end, every time. Even Baldur the beautiful, bringing light and joy to Asgard. But that was Loki, that was calculated evil. Craft and guile and venom. Loki was responsible. There is always someone to be blamed. Even the gods are vulnerable. Thor and Hrungnir and the death of Sigurd and the "Norns who bore the name of Vala" and the long and bloody journey of Tyr's sword fashioned by the dwarf sons of Ivald. Harshness and ruggedness. Fire and ice and the glitter of ice. The lonely marsh wastes of Nolde country. *The Myths of the Norsemen* in his father's study, with the naked Iduna draped by the pool, the page grubby with his thumbs. Iduna and her golden apples, conferring immortal youth and loveliness. Another one betrayed by Loki. Why did these things come back to you at the oddest times?

He had Gustav's notebook in his pocket. If it was Gustav's.

My God, supposing Gustav had been up there? He might be hurt! The notebook might have been blown from his hand!

Herr Hoffer stopped on the first-floor landing, looking back up the stairs as if Gustav might be there behind him. The ceiling here was painted with blue dwarfs and green trolls: Jacob Kluge again. The gods had fashioned them from the maggots in Ymir's flesh and they were cleverer than us. He felt sick and frightened; the lewd and rubbery faces grinned down at him, lipless mouths curling under hooked noses, ready to pluck him from life.

If he went back for Gustav, a shell or a bomb was bound to drop.

Look at those trolls. How thirsty for vengeance, dark, treacherous, and cunning! Were they not banished underground, these dwarfs, to the mines of silver and gold, where they banked their riches in secret crevices? He heard them blaring and cackling above him, just as in a Party film. He stood at the top of the stairs and felt as if he were on the edge of his own inner being. Staring into a chasm as the flame giant Surtur stares—his sword flashing sparks that spiral down to the iced blocks at the bottom of the abyss, hissing and melting the ice with their celestial heat!

He leaned back against the wall, his face shiny with sweat, clutching his shoe. He had taken off his shoe. A man in socks is vulnerable. Should he go back for Gustav, who might not even be there? One night in Berlin, returning alone from a weekend date with Sabine before they were married, a group of SA Brownshirts collared him, thinking he was a Jew. Maybe he looked like a Jew himself, maybe that would save him from the vengeance of the Hebrews and the anger of the Americans. The SA men had pulled his trousers down and seen that he wasn't a Jew. They laughed; with their hair shaven high above the ears, he could see the skin there wrinkle when they laughed. They were sure he was a fucking Bolshevik, and one of them had briefly touched his member. He was very scared but also indignant. He had drunk a little too much, and this encouraged his reckless indignation.

"And I'm not a homo either," he'd said, buttoning up his trousers. "You'll have to look elsewhere for that."

Herr Hoffer was gripped from behind and his shirt was torn open, buttons bouncing and clicking over the pavement. Herr Hoffer thought that he was about to have a screwdriver inserted into his chest or his member cut off. Instead, the SA man lifted up the undershirt and took Herr Hoffer's nipple between thumb and forefinger and squeezed it. He squeezed harder and harder, as if trying to extract some liquid. Herr Hoffer was prevented from wriggling by the others, who had their hard muscular arms around his neck, all but throttling him. The intense pain made him want to cry out, but he refused to let himself do so. He bit his lip instead. He watched the nipple being squeezed as if it had only something vaguely to do with him, trying to separate the pain into its constituent parts, while the beery breath of the Brownshirts made the night air clammy around him. It went on for a very long time (probably only a minute or two, in reality), and the torturer's expression was curiously serious and concentrated, as if engaged on a vital task, watching Herr Hoffer for a reaction. Herr Hoffer tried to avoid the man's eyes but kept being drawn back to them. They were surrounded by pale gleaming skin in which Herr Hoffer could see the open pores, and somewhere below was a rounded jaw set to one side with the effort, and blond hairs crowded into the corner of large nostrils. Then the SA man stopped squeezing and grunted. He was obviously drunk. He gobbed onto the pavement as if he'd run the length of the street and back, drew on a comrade's cigarette, blew the smoke into Herr Hoffer's face—and the others let the victim go, laughing.

He ran off clutching his trousers, with his undershirt up, letting the cold night air assuage his nipple—which swelled up and went a Veronese green.

The trolls would never hurt him, even if they were to swarm back over the border tomorrow. Why should they?

He had done nothing.

44

Parry followed the woman.

He wasn't sure why he was following her, except that she'd wanted him to, flapping her hands about, telling him to follow her. It wasn't that he owed her anything; he had not forced her into the act of sex. In fact, he had comforted her. He had done her a favor. Hadn't she laughed? He even felt some disgust at what they'd done together, as if she had been responsible. Maybe the world was so sad and broken that there was no other action he could have taken other than following the woman. That's how bad he'd got, how tired.

So he followed her through the broken streets, over heaps of rubble, loose brick and plaster, with flaky masonry everywhere underfoot so that at any moment you could screw your ankle or worse and it was like walking over deep sugar and you were a tiny goddamn bug.

Yet he followed her and it was not strange. While he was following her he was thinking. He thought well while he was hurrying along, it was always the same. About the typewriter he was thinking—the Remington that had been in the Dada postcard above his sophomore desk and was now on a windowsill in a ruined museum and although it wasn't the same one it made no difference, in the picture it was just thrown there into the corner next to this woman's shoe and this cut-away medical head and this cigar label and so forth and on the windowsill it was just thrown there by the goddamn blast. And chance. And photomontage is where stuff is cut out and stuck any which way. How now the whole world had got like that. A leg on its own, just there. Stairs stuck where they shouldn't be. How we'll all be seeing the world and it won't make any son-of-the-bitch sense. As if you're crazy drunk. Like the sight of the woman dangling upside-down by her feet in France and she'd been there five days and her face had been smashed up. A collaborator. Who says she was a collaborator? It was the French, not the Germans, who had done that— maybe the Communists, or maybe people who liked to cover their own dirt. And her arms were hanging down either side of her long hair and yet she'd tried to lift her nightdress up back over her thighs when they'd strung her up by her feet because she wasn't dead then, despite her face. That's what he had been told by a Brit who had seen the whole goddamn thing five days before. She had wanted her modesty back, mate. Maybe she had hurt a lot of fine people. Betrayal and revenge. Goddamn revenge. She had hit them and they had hit her back as hard. She wasn't the only collaborator he had seen, dead or just insulted or knocked about or with a shorn head. Then there were the ordinary rotted deads dug up out of that pit someplace in France with their high heels still on. That was the work of the Gestapo, in too much of a goddamn hurry. All that good detail stuck in his mind while the big picture and the names slipped away along with the maps. Those fucking high heels that were the only intact thing, with little ribbony bows on them.

Life can't hurt me, he thought. If you don't fool with life too much then it won't hurt you. He was following the woman down the ruined streets and his brain was firing like a new Ford engine and letting him make interesting connections. He had the snowy mountains and the golden valley in his map pack. He was going with the snowy mountains and the golden valley. The nice item of salvage. The tiny shepherd. Vollerdt. He was crazy drunk on all these things. He didn't know where the woman was taking him, only that she kept turning back to check that he was still there.

He was still there. The strangest thing is that your life is important and then, when you run along out into the garden of death goddamn none of it matters to anyone, least of all yourself. Not even in the white backwash of the whole thing.

She was twenty—maybe even thirty—yards in front, running and scrambling like a crazy person. He could hear her breath panting in and out, see her shadow lengthening wildly when they passed a fire.

He would follow her, he thought, into the jaws of hell. And the hell with her, when he thought about it. What did he care? But he kept on following her through the darkness as if he was in awe of not following her all the way to the end.

45

"Not very well," said a voice. "I was learning a Chopin étude, Opus ten, Number three. Do you know it? You have to stretch your fingers wide to play the melody and keep them like that all the way through."

Herr Hoffer surfaced from this memory. He had no idea to whom the voice belonged. He was going down the main stairs to the ground floor and the voice—a female's, very smart—murmured in his ear. Herr Hoffer wondered if he were going mad, because there was no one on the stairs. It was his tiredness: Through the fabric of the mind, the memories were breaking. For instance, his first outing with Sabine. They were walking in the park. His arm held her around the waist and he was enjoying the warmth of her, the movement of her form against his ribs, the muscles of her waist moving under his hand. As for rendering the waist in a life drawing . . . ! Absence of form, really, ensnaring one in pointless strokes. Minimum effort, maximum effect. Yes, to understand the waist, one had to hold one's hand against it and feel it move, supple and vigorous. *My darling?* It was no longer absence of form but presence. *I love your waist, my darling.* He loved all the waists of humanity but most particularly his wife's. His chest was inwardly enfolded with the love he had for his wife's waist and for all of humanity through it.

He kept his eyes on the stairs, still a little feeble and uncertain after the blow on his head. At the bottom of the stairs appeared a pair of scuffed black boots, the metal tips grinning at him like jutting lower teeth. He wondered who had left them there. He moved his head upwards and saw the boots had legs in camouflage trousers growing from them and then a tunic with arms and then a jaw with two SS runes on the collar patch, and he knew the face.

"I'm on duty" was all he could manage.

Bendel had a gun hanging off his shoulder. That nasty-looking type, all metal. One elbow rested on it.

"You're hurt, Herr Hoffer."

"Am I? I suppose so," he said, touching the blood on his scalp. "Goodness me, what a surprise, Herr Bendel."

The man stood on the edge of the flower mosaic by Hans Thoma. His epaulettes were edged with blue; one was hanging by its thread. He was still a Sturmführer. That was fine, then.

"You're not sheltering, Herr Hoffer."

"Tour of inspection. I was up in the attics."

"The attics?"

"They were hit."

"I thought I heard something," said Bendel vaguely.

He's in the Waffen-SS now, thought Herr Hoffer. He's a soldier. He looks worn out and filthy. He has a haversack for his bread and a leather satchel for his maps.

"It's a big building," Bendel added.

"It certainly is. Now it's not the same. Nothing stays the same. It's got a hole in the roof. I think the tower was hit."

"Fire?"

"Oh, no. Thank God!"

"They're using phosphorus."

"I checked," said Herr Hoffer.

"Good."

"Well, what a surprise, SS Sturmführer Bendel. Seeing you. I can't get over it. Look at my glasses. That's what happens."

He realized he was waving a shoe about. It was his own shoe.

"Actually," he went on, "I thought you were dead."

"Not quite. How annoying, having to go around in your socks."

Bendel smiled at him through a dark layer of filth. He had eye bags that aged him ten years.

"I need a seat," Herr Hoffer said. "You look as if you've been in the thick."

"You could say that, yes."

"I definitely need to sit down, if you don't mind."

Herr Hoffer, followed by Bendel, padded into the seventeenth-century gallery, where there was a comfortable double bench set like a green island in the middle of the room. Herr Hoffer sat down on its scuffed leather; the other man stayed standing next to it. The room was misty with smoke, shadowing the blank walls. It caught in Herr Hoffer's throat.

Three coats of size to stiffen the canvas. Why had he bothered? *If only we could tear it down.*

"Well, well," said SS Sturmführer Bendel, placing his feet wide.

"You could say that," said Herr Hoffer. "The smoke's from outside, by the way."

"I always thought you were unflappable, Herr Hoffer."

"Don't I seem it?"

"Not really."

"Oh," said Herr Hoffer, a little disappointed. "I thought I was doing rather well. Given everything. This is just the shock."

"I all but forgot your name, Herr Hoffer. Just for a moment. But that's normal. I haven't slept for weeks."

The submachine gun, slung casually off Bendel's shoulder, was as small and thin as a child's metal arm.

"Ingrid," Bendel went on, giving a short laugh. "Strange, the names that pop up."

Herr Hoffer closed his eyes for a moment. Shock, or whatever it was, was translating into nausea and giddiness.

"Heinrich," he said.

"A good easy name," said Bendel. "Like mine. Klaus."

"That's better," said Herr Hoffer. "I'll just lie here for a minute, if you don't mind."

"You should have been sheltering, Herr Hoffer. The town's getting well and truly plastered. In fact, you should be in the Luft-schutzbunker right now."

Herr Hoffer nodded, lying flat on the bench with his feet off the end. He had run out of words. His throat was so dry it hurt. Bendel does not know about the vaults, he thought, and he must not ever know about the vaults.

"Or even better," said Bendel, "you could use the vaults."

"The vaults?"

"Full of rats and very damp, apparently. That's what you told me, once. The old castle vaults. But better rats and damp than getting blown to bits, I'd say."

"I hate rats," said Herr Hoffer, opening his eyes.

The bombardment seemed to have paused, or perhaps they were trapped between two moments forever and ever. Bendel was standing very still in the middle of the gallery, his gun slung in front of him, across his chest. Its metal grip had frayed toweling wrapped around it, like a tennis racket, and the fat barrel nut was badly dented. There was no wood anywhere on the gun, not even on the stock. It had really been through things, from the look of it.

"Why are you here, Bendel?" asked Herr Hoffer, looking up at the ceiling. "There's not a lot to admire now."

He was smiling, but Bendel didn't smile back; he had his head lowered. Actually, he was a frightful sight. His trousers were torn in two places, his crumpled camouflage jacket was spotted with filth, and a stain darkened the SS runes on his collar patch. His eyes were rimmed in red and the dirty skin had folded into those bags beneath them, but he was not unshaven. In fact, it looked as if he had just shaved, from the nicks on his chin. Or perhaps he didn't need to shave! There were men who didn't need to, although otherwise quite normal: one-hundred-percent men, otherwise. His haversack and his satchel were frayed and soiled, like a tramp's bags.

Bendel said nothing, almost as if he hadn't heard. Perhaps he was partly deaf from the noise of fighting.

"Have you been fighting on Kreiburg Hill?" asked Herr Hoffer, in a louder voice.

Bendel shook, as if he had just woken up.

"All the way from the Meuse," he said.

"You look like it," said Herr Hoffer.

The bench appeared to be rocking slightly.

"These are wop trousers," said Bendel. "Autumn camouflage. Leopard spots."

"You can learn a lot from Mother Nature," murmured Herr Hoffer, who felt really sick now. He tried sitting up, his head lolling back. Better.

"Too tight," said Bendel. "Wops have small bones. A wop sergeant dragged himself to the first-aid tent until his guts plopped out, so I got his jacket. No time even to clean it. Hasn't been cleaned since December. Couldn't get his trousers, because he hadn't got any legs. All I did was sew on the epaulettes. I'm not so good at sewing."

He flicked the epaulette that was hanging by its threads, and it fell off. He laughed and kicked the epaulette away, which shocked Herr Hoffer. The jacket's ragged blacks and browns were overlaid with coppery patches, as were the pink and green and brown camouflage spots, like thumbprints, on his trousers. Herr Hoffer swallowed.

"Reversible," Bendel went on, pulling at the jacket. "White for winter on the inside. This is summer. He was wearing it winter out, so that side's not as stained."

"That's lucky," said Herr Hoffer, with a great effort.

"But I can't go prancing about in white when it's not snowing, can I? Anyway, nothing ever stayed white for more than a day, not in all that filth, so they could always spot you anyway. Sun filtering through the leaves, this. I'm a walking Impressionist painting, Herr Hoffer. Trousers by Seurat."

Herr Hoffer smiled, feeling too sick to speak.

"You won't believe this, but it was designed by Professor Schick. My old professor. Fancy that, eh, Herr Hoffer?"

Bendel had begun to pace up and down the empty gallery.

"Old Schick," he repeated. "Fancy that, eh?"

"Well, dear fellow," Herr Hoffer murmured, "it appears to be all over for us now."

"Eh, Ingrid?"

"I'm not Ingrid."

Bendel laughed his loud, sharp laugh. Herr Hoffer adjusted his glasses and felt really annoyed through his nausea. He focused on the dingy spiderweb where Jacob Marell's *Blumenstück in Vase* had hung for all those years. The crack in his lens was annoying. He kept thinking it was dirt, but he could see the painting's wonderful flowers quite clearly in his imagination—right down to the carmine red of the fallen tulip petal. The spider was no longer on its web. Maybe it had eaten enough.

What the hell was Bendel doing here anyway?

His sickness started to subside and he closed his eyes. Really, he thought, I ought to be with my darling wife and daughters, as Frau Schenkel had said. Sometimes she was right. Sabine had been so difficult. He had not told anyone how difficult she had been recently. He knew he wasn't perfect, but he had done his best. She had had fits and thrown china cups at him. They had broken against the wall. He felt a pang of worry in his chest, as if a cup had broken against it. His hand smelled dense, densely, of mice. Ingrid! What a thing to call me! The bloody cheek!

He felt the bench jolt violently.

"It doesn't matter," Bendel said, slumped now on the green leather next to him, his legs wide apart, his neck resting on the bench back. The gun straddled his lap. He was very smelly. "It's all over and that's that. You know what? It doesn't matter. Nobody really gives a shit. Either you're dead, or too hungry to think straight, or you're in the Waffen-SS and you're both. And they never even gave me another stripe." He laughed. The bench shook. The empty room echoed with his high-pitched laughter. That hadn't changed, at least.

"You went away," murmured Herr Hoffer. The reek of sweat and oil had revived his nausea.

He had realized that, whatever else might happen, Bendel must not go down to the vaults.

"I shifted jobs in '43, early '43. Bauer und Kompanie. Art restoration."

"Ah, yes. So you left the SS."

"Bauer is part of the SS, Herr Hoffer. I even went to Poland."

A lorry tipped out a load of rivets nearby. That's what it would have been in peacetime, at least.

"I think we should go to the Luftschutzbunker, Herr Sturm-führer."

"Part of Amstgruppe W, our Economics and Administration Department, run by SS Obergruppenführer Pohl. The tight bastard."

"I see," said Herr Hoffer. "Maybe we should be moving to the Luftschutzbunker."

He had the key to the shelter. They wouldn't even have to go to the janitor.

Neither man moved. The rumbling sounded complacent, as if it had all the time in the world.

"I went to France, mainly," Bendel went on. "Cataloging. A lot of private collections in France that Vichy had overlooked. Then Poland."

Herr Hoffer nodded. He remembered how Bendel had dreamed of visiting the places where van Gogh had painted, wondered if he should ask, decided against it, then asked anyway.

"Provence?"

"Yes, for a while. And Languedoc. The Pyrenees. Bordeaux."

"How very nice. As Max Friedländer once said, *The true artist loves nature, not art.*"

"Ah, Friedländer. Netherlandish Primitives. Have you read the great work?"

"Of course," Herr Hoffer lied.

"Overrated, I thought. He scarpered very early on, didn't he?"

"Not that early."

"Listen, I had the time of my life in France. Fancy old châteaux, a chair and table on the lawn, a secretary with a typewriter, a few burly types in flat caps, and the odd armed guard *pour encourager les autres.* To encourage the others."

"I do speak French," Herr Hoffer lied, again.

"Oh, and a furniture van backed up to the main doors. All I had to do was note down what came out through the main doors and into that van. You should have seen the size of some of those paintings, Herr Hoffer. Massive. Like theater sets. Poussin, Delacroix, David—. Rubens, even. You name it. Massive."

"I really think," said Herr Hoffer, feeling the bench tremble under his buttocks, "we should make for the Luftschutzbunker."

Bendel ignored him.

"They came out vertical and replaced real scenery for a moment and you thought, That's a lot better than the real view. Lots of nudes too. A fuck of a sight better than real nudes, you thought. Excuse my French, Ingrid. And lots of vintage champagne in the cellars. Jews' châteaux, most of them. You wouldn't think Jews had châteaux, would you? Luxurious villas, yes, but not bloody whole châteaux. Centuries of craft and guile, that is. Wisteria out, bees bumbling over the stonework. Cicadas singing. Pastis and champagne. Oh, God. I thought, What a lucky bastard I am. Then off to Poland for a few months, under SS Hauptsturmführer Mühlmann."

"Poland?"

"Cracow, the SS art restoration workshop in Cracow. Great reputation, Ingrid. God, the works we handled: Raphael, Rembrandt, Leonardo's *Lady with an Ermine*—"

"Good God."

"Antoine Watteau, you name it. The Lubomirski collection with all those Dürer drawings, the Lazienki palace, the Czartoryski family's stuff. And then I was sent back to Berlin, to type it all up."

"How nice," said Herr Hoffer, not really listening now, picturing the Leonardo.

"Pure bloody tedium: filing. Filing and documentation. Thousands and thousands of artworks. Even great names can get boring. All those Dürer drawings and bloody prints. Did you know Dürer was half Hungarian? I'll bet you didn't know that. And I didn't even get promoted. Enemies, you see. Göring was pissed off with Mühlmann for taking back the Leonardo. The Führer reckoned he hadn't had enough of the stuff either. So I stayed filing. Big names, small names. No van Goghs allowed, though. Oh, no. Vincent van Gogh was round the bend, wasn't he? Nazis are not round the bend. Are they?"

"No," said Herr Hoffer.

"My call-up papers came in the middle of it. So I got rid of all that desk shit and started to live. You see, life goes in stages. Each stage is complete in itself. That's my theory. You must never look back. No regrets. Life's too short to regret. Only sentimental idiots regret."

"I see."

The shelling sounded farther off again—someone making catarrhal throat noises. It might even have been the shale quarry at work on the other side of Kreiburg Hill.

"So." Herr Hoffer sighed. "It really is all over, in your opinion."

By breathing slowly, he had almost got rid of his nausea. He felt good about this, as one always does.

"Eh?"

"The war," said Herr Hoffer. "One can't know for sure, unless one's seen it."

"Seen what?"

"The battlefront."

Bendel chuckled. "What do you think I am, a reconnaissance plane?"

"No, but—"

"Were you in the last great balls-up, Herr Hoffer?"

"Not quite. I'm only forty-two."

"And now?"

"Member of the Volkssturm, but our officer has run away and we have no arms or uniforms. All we have is our dignity."

He wiggled his toes in his socks, then thought better of it.

"So you won't know," Bendel said, "that the average soldier does not know the first shit about anything bigger than what he can see in his gun sight. Despite the maps." He patted the scuffed satchel slung over his right shoulder.

"I see."

"Maybe we *are* winning on the Eastern Front, as the radio says. I don't know, see? Personally, I think we're fucked all round. But that's a subjective conclusion owing to my finding myself on the wrong side of the Rhine. However, the Americans are now pinned down on some fucking hillock out there."

"Kreiburg Hill."

"Probably. That's the only decent hillock round here, isn't it?"

"Not quite, dear fellow," said Herr Hoffer, who felt quite defensive about it. "By the way," he went on good-humoredly, "Dostoyevsky was specifically referring to Russian romanticism. He thought German romanticism was transcendental and stupid. *Letters from the Underworld*. I found the reference. I've been bursting to tell you, but you weren't around."

"I don't know what you're talking about."

"A discussion we had. Years ago, now. It doesn't matter."

Neither man said anything for a few moments. If only that noise *were* distant building work.

"Why are you here, in fact?"

The fellow had his eyes closed now.

"To find you."

"Me?" Herr Hoffer's heart turned turtle.

"I was happy here," Bendel said quietly.

"I'm glad."

"Are we the only ones?"

"The only ones?"

"In the building. Apart from that cretin of a janitor," Bendel added.

"Herr Wolmer. Yes, I believe we are. Apart from the admirable Herr Wolmer."

"And he's not exactly present anymore."

Bendel had fished a loose cigarette out of his tunic pocket and lit it. The man's nails were broken and filthy. Herr Hoffer found his voice at the bottom of his throat.

"What do you mean, Herr Sturmführer?"

"Who was the first girl you ever fancied, Herr Hoffer?"

"What?"

"The first girl you really fancied."

"That's strange. I was just thinking about her. She was in a book. A book of my father's on the Norse myths. A picture of Iduna. She was lying naked by a pool."

"I don't mean wank books, Herr Hoffer. I mean a real bird."

Herr Hoffer couldn't believe this was Klaus Bendel. He had been taken over by a Saxon prole.

"Then I can't remember."

Bendel gave a sharp laugh and pulled on his cigarette. "How's Sabine?"

"Frau Hoffer? She's very well," Herr Hoffer replied, too quickly. It shocked him to hear Bendel use her Christian name. It was quite out of order. His chest had well nigh exploded.

"You left her with the kiddies?"

"I saw them all safe and sound into the shelter this morning, with three suitcases full of the essentials. In case."

There was an awkward silence between them. Herr Hoffer's heart was slapping behind his nose, now, like someone dealing cards.

"One day I realized I was the only one," Bendel said suddenly. "All my comrades, they'd swapped their brains for shit. And I hadn't even been fucking promoted. We'd got back over the Rhine and there was no one left. I hitched a lift on a Tiger tank, all the way down the motorway, sitting on the front by the barrel and getting a bruised arse and mud on my face. Where else to go but Lohenfelde?"

"I can think of lots of other places."

Bendel gave an amused grunt and sucked hard on his cigarette, his cheeks going remarkably hollow. He blew the smoke out steadily and nodded his head. It was like a moving exhibit. Kinetic sculpture by Naum Gabo: *Construction for After the End*. It made Herr Hoffer want a cigarette. He was surprised he hadn't been offered one.

"Not me," Bendel said. "I'm from lovely Leipzig, if you recall. I can't go to Leipzig, can I, to see my folks? It's Bolshevik now, taken over by the barbarians. Too beautiful for barbarians, for savages. Don't even know if my folks are alive. Anyway, I was happy in Lohenfelde. I had some very good times here. Very good. *Extremely* good, in fact," he added, smiling distantly.

Herr Hoffer thought, I must not think what I am thinking. The air between them—just a few centimeters of empty space—seemed to thrill with suspicion and disaster.

"Leibniz was born in Leipzig," he said, involuntarily swallowing on the last syllable.

"And Richard Wagner."

"And Vollerdt," Herr Hoffer continued. "In 1708."

"Ah, yes. Where's your Vollerdt now, then?"

"In the salt mine," Herr Hoffer said briskly. "Actually, it was only a copy, if you remember. The original's in Magdeburg. Unfortunately."

It was almost like old times, he thought.

"You sure it's in the salt mine?"

"Oh, yes. Unless it was appropriated en route. By the way," said Herr Hoffer, "wouldn't it be a good idea to drop the—the uniform?"

"When I no longer need it."

Something about this statement gave Herr Hoffer a cold feeling in his spine.

"I suppose we should be moving to the shelter," he said, getting to his feet with an effort.

He stood there, waiting, in his socks. He didn't want to be next to Bendel's Waffen-SS uniform when the Americans burst in. If only he was in some obscure little village in the middle of the forest, with its church smelling of manure!

"Herr Sturmführer?"

Bendel said, not even looking up at him, "Where's the van Gogh?"

"The van Gogh? Oh, it's safe."

"Where is it?"

"With the rest of the collection."

"Come on, Ingrid, you know it isn't."

"Please stop calling me Ingrid."

"Sorry. Private joke. You know it isn't with the rest of the collection."

"What?"

"You know it isn't, Herr Acting Acting Director. It's here. It never left the building. You're a shifty bloke, underneath the charm."

Herr Hoffer flushed. "Sturmführer, please stop insulting me. It's not fair."

Bendel covered his face in his hands, the cigarette smoking between the knuckles. His eyes glimmered between his spread fingers. He was smiling.

"I meant to tell you, Herr Hoffer," he said, from behind the fingers, "I've been to the salt mine at Grimmenburg. The van Gogh is not even on the inventory. Neither is the fucking Vollerdt, I don't suppose. But I don't care about the Vollerdt, fake or no fake."

"Copy, not a fake," murmured Herr Hoffer. "Possibly by one of his pupils."

"What I care about is the Vincent van Gogh. It's right here, in this building. It never left the museum."

"You went to Grimmenburg, to the salt mine?"

"Yes."

"Why?"

"And the van Gogh's not in the Luftschutzbunker, because I checked."

Bendel's face reemerged and he sucked on his cigarette, still smiling. He reached into his top pocket and pulled out Herr Wolmer's set of keys on their brass ring. He shook them. Herr Hoffer had never seen anyone but the janitor shake them. "Empty heads have the most to say, Herr Acting Acting Director. There's nothing at all in the Luftschutzbunker. Just the usual smell of fucking toilets."

"The paintings were all evacuated," said Herr Hoffer. He felt weak and silly standing there in his socks, in front of this altered man, this demon. (What was a demon but someone from whom beauty had been removed by the gods?) "That's very bad news about the van Gogh, but I'm not surprised."

"I said it never left the building."

"I saw it leave the building myself, for goodness' sake."

"Herr Hoffer, you're just like all the others."

"What do you mean?"

"A liar."

"Thank you."

"Where is the van Gogh, Ingrid?"

"Stop calling me Ingrid!"

Bendel laughed. He was just a soldier, after all. Soldiers got like that. It stopped them from shooting themselves.

"Anyway," Herr Hoffer said, swallowing his annoyance, "why do you want to know?"

"Because I want to look at it, of course."

There was a pause. Herr Hoffer's mind had gone white, as if drained of blood. The gallery's bare walls were blinding him like sun-lit snow on the peaks. Sabine had always wanted to go to Saint Moritz, to wind up and up in the little train. Life was so expensive!

"Please," said Bendel, leaning back on the green leather and star-ing up. "Let me look at it."

"I'd like to sit down."

"Sit down, then. Your arse is on the top of your legs."

There was a chair on either side of the door, where the attendants had once sat in the good old days, dozing off while huge mustaches and horn lorgnettes and long lavish skirts wandered about, the skirts and the mustaches gradually getting thinner and shorter over time until there were none and there was no one at all. Herr Hoffer sat in the chair to the right of the door. The chair wobbled slightly. That was something he would have to see to, after the end. He noted the chair and its position in the gallery. God is in the details, his teacher used to say. You can't have a wobbly chair in a respectable museum. There would be so many jobs for carpenters and joiners, as after the Swedes. He gave a long sigh.

"I hope a shell doesn't fall on us while we're discussing all this," he said. "Poor old Herr Wolmer. I imagine he waved around that silly gun of his. I told him it would get him into trouble."

Bendel was staring at the parquet floor. The cigarette drooped in his mouth.

"You know," continued Herr Hoffer, "that there are, in fact, some of your Waffen-SS boys just outside? Artillery?"

Bendel looked up. "Listen, let's get this shit over with."

Another pause.

"The van Gogh might have been taken to Linz," suggested Herr Hoffer, too feebly. "For the Führer's culture center."

"It never left this building," Bendel repeated.

"You don't know that," said Herr Hoffer.

"Sabine told me."

Herr Hoffer snorted, but the snort turned into a gulp and he had to cough.

"Frau Hoffer? She doesn't know a thing."

"She knows lots of things," said Bendel, with a crooked smile.

"Please. . . ."

"What?"

"Look, she doesn't know that."

Bendel chortled in his throat. It was all quite deliberate. He's trying to bait me, thought Herr Hoffer. I would like to kill this man.

"About the van Gogh, I mean. She's not interested in my work."

"Herr Hoffer, I checked your inventory in Berlin. I looked it up in the files. On pink paper, it was. Some arsehole had ticked it off on the day of the evacuation. He didn't even notice that the van Gogh wasn't on it. That's why we've lost the war. Because no one fucking gives a damn."

Herr Hoffer closed his eyes. Bendel still had a pleasant voice in terms of its timbre, but it was turned to the wrong purpose, so it was ugly.

In the end, the main aim was to stay alive.

"Right, then. Just as I stated, in fact, it's with the other works. Not all the collection is in the salt mine. Some of it is here, in the vaults."

His heart was pounding in his ears, but he felt quite in control. Bendel was a lot younger, and he'd lied about seeing Sabine; he'd only seen the inventory. Thank God.

"The vaults?"

"Yes."

"But what about the rats?"

"We wiped them out," said Herr Hoffer.

"When?"

"Recently."

"And the damp?"

"It wasn't so damp down there, after all."

"Is this the truth?"

"Yes."

"When did you store the paintings in the vaults?"

"Just before the wholesale evacuation in late March," Herr Hoffer lied. "Last year. I forget the exact date. A year ago already! Very foggy. You weren't even here."

"I was in Berlin."

"I guessed that." Herr Hoffer nodded. "All those nightclubs, dances, concerts—"

"I don't like cities. I like trees, forests, wild woods. The Spreewald was full of tents and guns and barbed wire. We always fuck everything up. That's capitalism for you. And all our other political knickknacks: Bolshevism, Fascism, monarchic feudalism, you name it. None of them gets to the root."

He pulled hard on his cigarette and blew the smoke out through his nose.

"Fuck me, the vaults," he said. "I hope you did wipe out the rats. They breed very quickly, you know. They'll have a chew at anything."

"We used poison," said Herr Hoffer.

"Gas is better," said Bendel. "You could have pumped the vaults full of gas. Quicker. It's worked a treat with the Jews."

Herr Hoffer chuckled. "You'd better not make jokes like that when the Jews come back," he said.

Bendel looked at him, frowning. "What do you mean?"

"Jokes like that," Herr Hoffer repeated, out of a sudden burning flush of terror.

"What jokes?"

"Like that. About the gas."

Bendel stared at him with eyes as bloodshot as a drunk's. "It won't wash with the Americans, you know," he said.

"What won't?"

"Pretending not to know."

"Not to know?"

"Herr Hoffer, you're a fucking lousy liar."

Herr Hoffer shook his head, bewildered. Then he stood up, spreading his arms. Baldur was the god of peace. He threw his sunlight all about him.

"You know what, Herr Sturmführer? Or can I call you Klaus, after all these years? And you can call me Heinrich. Klaus, I've just had a vision of us two standing here in 1950, admiring the paintings. Chatting about them as we used to do. All this will be a bad dream by then, Klaus. I'll buy you a real coffee, with cream on top." (He used the informal *du*, without asking permission.) "And a cake. Promise. Now, if you don't mind, I must be continuing my tour of inspection."

The submachine gun came up and was pointing at him, suddenly. The gun's thinness was the worst thing about it, somehow. And the fact that it had no wooden parts. Bendel's eyes were very dark and bloodshot and hollow, behind the smoke from the cigarette in his mouth. He held the gun almost casually, still seated, with the leather strap sliding down by itself off his shoulder, very slowly.

"Sit down," said Bendel.

The gun remained pointing at Herr Hoffer, who sat down again with a bump.

"I was always reassuring Herr Acting Director Streicher, dear fellow, that your interest in the van Gogh was purely that of an art lover. Now I see how naïve I was. I'm disappointed."

He was breathless and his wretched spectacles had misted up again, rendering everything impressionistic. Bendel himself was merely a blurred shadow against white. Then the blurred shadow rose. Herr Hoffer moved his head slightly to find a clearer part of the lens on the edge of the frame—a narrow strip of clarity through which he could see Bendel holding the gun in a serious way by his lower chest, ready to fire.

"If you shoot me," said Herr Hoffer, in a voice like a little boy's, "you'll never find the van Gogh."

"It's in the vaults. You said."

"But it's hidden where you'll never find it."

"Really?"

"Yes."

He had the vivid sensation that his life was hanging by that single word: *Yes*. All other words stretched out far too lengthily in space and time.

"You've hidden it?"

"Yes," said Herr Hoffer.

"In the vaults?"

"Yes. But you won't find it without me. In fact, you won't even find the vaults. And even if you did, you'd be stuck."

"You mean," said Bendel, "they're locked and you've got the key?"

"No. I mean that I have concealed the painting in a place in the vaults that only I know of because I was the one who hid it. The painting."

"You're going to show me."

"As long as you put it back. Afterwards."

Herr Hoffer grinned like an idiot. He had got through. He knew he was unlikely to be shot now. Nevertheless, he was amazed at his own lack of fear. It was almost unnatural. He could even joke about things. If his voice refused to be a grown man's, that was not his fault. It was a physical reaction beyond his psychological control.

He could even imagine the bullets going clean through him without leaving a mark. Like the missiles flung at Baldur by the gods in Asgard: everyone laughing to see them bounce off the god of sunlight.

"I'm glad you didn't stay at home this morning, Herr Hoffer," said Bendel, "with your lovely children and your very agreeable wife."

"Thank you. Look, could—"

"What?"

"Never mind. What happens if I refuse to help you?"

Bendel ran a hand over his face, looking very white all of a sudden. "What's more," he said, ignoring the question, "we've not got very long."

"I thought we were friends. I thought there was something called trust."

"So did I," said Bendel. "That's why I'm so disappointed in you, Herr Hoffer. I only want to *look* at it, for Christ's sake," he added, after a pause.

46

The woman stopped in front of a big apartment building that had been seriously damaged, like almost everything else on the street. It looked like the whole street on both sides had shut its eyes and got wrapped up about a hundred years back, and the science of time had done the rest. There were a few civilians, mostly women and their kids and the kids' grandparents, going someplace down the street, slowly, as if they had a burning ambition that was so mysterious it failed to show in their eyes, though they had it and it was all they had. It was good and dark, except that fires were still burning here and there, out of windows and doors, casting a light on the faces that made everyone seem old and carved.

Parry had never seen anything sadder in his life—since yesterday, anyway. Sadness was something you experienced in the here and now, like pain. Each sadness seemed deeper than the one before. When it touched bottom, you were dead.

He guessed the kids were in there, Frau Hoffnung or Hoffmann's kids. He pushed back his helmet and scratched his sweat rash. She was holding his arm now, pointing and jabbering in Heinie.

Yeah, they are in there.

The trouble is, the place is wrecked.

A ton of bricks had poured out the main door. It had spilled down the hall stairs and right out the door, as if the building were vomiting its own insides. He knew enough German to know that *meine Kinder* meant *my kids*. He even knew that Mahler had written an anthem for dead kids, something called *Kindertod,* maybe.

Things were coming together.

He liked Mahler, just as he liked swing and jazz. He was a guy of broad tastes. He wanted to live a long time so he could weave all those tastes into something meaningful called a Life. He didn't want to scramble into a dangerous building to search for a crazy Heinie woman's dead kids. He had his fortune rolled up against his chest; the war was almost over; he'd make it through and go back and have a Life that might even be interesting and happy and prosperous, away from all this Old World sadness. He'd tell his grandchildren how he'd fought evil and helped good to rise again, shaking its old self a little and saying, "Hey, that was very close, but I'm in good shape, guys." He'd like to paint, paint properly. He'd like to be more than a dull commercial agent, a goddamn illustrator whose only thrill was a week's fishing in the timbered backcountry in August. Whose world was one of household appliances and goddamn Milk-Bone for the dog. And Maureen ironing his sweatshirts.

But the woman was tugging at his arm, imploring him, tears running off her cheeks and chin and nose as water does in a rainstorm.

"Hold it," he said. "Hold it, now. C'mon. Hold it."

He started humming "It's a Lovely Day Tomorrow" and dug out his flashlight and probed the beam through the door.

He didn't know why he was doing this, why he was climbing over the rubble spill and into the building with the woman close behind, actually holding on to his belt so he had to remove her hand. He didn't understand any of it, and part of him was saying no.

There is beauty in everything, he thought.

There is beauty in what I am doing, and his heart filled with delight, and even the danger seemed the very flower of beauty, even the darkness of the wrecked building that his light probed, the beam cutting through the hanging smoke like a searchlight through fog over a gray sea.

There is beauty in what I am doing, thought Parry.

47

If only, Herr Hoffer would often think, life could be as straightforward and as beautiful as a piece of fine music. As, for instance, Schumann's *Dichterliebe*, Opus 48. That too was a song cycle drawn from the poems of Heine. Sabine had given him the records for his birthday years ago, before she learned that Heine was Jewish. Then she wanted to throw them away, more out of fear than zeal. That had caused a great row, which he had won, putting them away in a deep drawer and locking it. Then she read that the Führer was attending a concert in Vienna with Schumann's song cycle on the program, and the records joined the others again in the living room.

Or Handel's oratorios; he had the whole of the *Messiah* on six records. After the war had begun, Sabine was nervous of his playing it, because the words were in English. She preferred old German dance music and folk songs. She liked jazz to dance to, but it was not approved of. She also liked Johann Strauss and collected many of his records. Herr Hoffer did not tell her that Strauss also had Jewish blood; he was not a man to indulge in spiteful matrimonial vendettas, even though he disliked Strauss's music and retired to their bedroom with a book whenever she put a Johann Strauss on the gramophone player. She did likewise when he put on Handel or Schumann. It was a battle of the records, he once said.

Not that Schumann was altogether straightforward. Especially not in his piano pieces. He would like to have discussed Schumann's piano pieces with Bendel, as in the old days. Like that time Alfred Cortot had played in Lohenfelde's concert hall, on his wartime German tour with Furtwängler, and Sabine had spotted Bendel in the Privileged Guests' box. They had talked in the interval.

"Schumann is the supreme romantic," Bendel declared, over a glass of champagne, "but saved from limpness by his internal struggle."

Sabine wished to know what this struggle was.

"He invented a double personality for himself, my dear Frau Hoffer. One was tender, one was savage. One was day, one was night. To hear Schumann is to hear a man confront his own demons."

Sabine's eyes had opened wide.

"Herr Sturmführer, you make everything so interesting."

"We are all divided, Frau Hoffer. But most of us are too obedient to our bourgeois selves to notice."

"What is your favorite Schumann, dear fellow?"

"The *Nachtstücke,* Herr Hoffer. I howl at the moon when I hear them."

They had laughed, and the other SS fellows had turned round to look. Herr Hoffer had felt quite on top of things that evening.

But that was the old Bendel. Now Bendel had become his own demon.

It was pitch-black in the cuddy. Herr Hoffer had been locked in the little storage room off the Luftschutzbunker while Bendel relieved himself in the toilets. Apparently, he had something approaching dysentery and had not used a toilet for weeks. The excitement had provoked an attack. It was faintly embarrassing. Bendel, with all Herr Wolmer's keys on their brass ring, was like a jailor. Herr Hoffer had plotted a roundabout route to the vaults, via various disused rooms. There was no point in trying to break down the door; the toilets were just on the other side of the partition. The darkness smelled of wax polish and of Frau Blumen's underarms. There was not much room among the invisible presences of boxes and tins, the bottles of bleach, the stifling hints of cleanliness. He felt dirty, in fact. The Romans were very clean. The rainwater collected in the center of the atrium. Echoing baths.

He hadn't been lying about the van Gogh. He was the only one in the world who knew where it was right now.

Bendel unlocked the door. He looked better.

"Come on," he said. "I half expected you'd hop it. Next stop: the vaults!"

He was almost cheery, was Bendel.

The vaults! The vaults! Back to the vaults!

When Herr Hoffer had first arrived, all those years ago, the vaults were already glorified junk rooms, with a single electric bulb casting weird shadows. One day, while bringing some order to the junk down there, he had happened to step on a loose slab. He tapped it; it sounded hollow. Within an hour he had prised it up and was gazing down on a hole like a small grave, carved squarely out of rock and completely empty. An oubliette, probably; somewhere a hunted man could vanish when the hounds of history were baying.

Herr Hoffer had returned home late.

"You smell funny," said Sabine. "Where have you been?"

She caught a whiff of cellars on his clothes and hair. His fingernails were dirty. She suspected him, in a strange leap of logic, of infidelity. She was very young and not long pregnant and grew easily jealous. The appointment of Herr Hitler as Reichskanzler that very day had brought her to a pitch of nervous excitement that was taken out on her husband. They had a superb row and actually broke their first china plate, but were interrupted by Reichskanzler Hitler's inaugural speech on the radio. It was rather good.

"This door?"

"Yes. Then along the corridor and first right."

"It feels a strangely roundabout route, Herr Hoffer."

"It's the correct route, dear fellow."

"That's what they say about democracies. The roundabout route that never gets there but is perfectly correct."

"We'll get there, all right, Herr Sturmführer. . . ."

Things undoubtedly failed to fulfill that inaugural speech's promise. The day in 1936 when the Party denounced lemons as un-German and exhorted everyone to grow and eat rhubarb, Herr Hoffer realized the nation was in the grip of the deranged—and not only because he hated rhubarb, which stuck in his teeth. The rhubarb announcement was the same day as the Degenerate Committee's purge.

The worst day of his life, in fact.

Oh, the purge.

He could not help it, he returned to that day over and over again, like a dog to its own vomit. Ziegler and Willrich had insulted the paintings. "Second-rate, pornographic, Jewish slime, pavement-artist rubbish"—why should he remember these words when so many lovely lines had slipped away into oblivion?

Silence, the next morning, in the Long Gallery. The clouds heedless through the hatched glass. Herr Streicher coming in and trying to light a pipe, but his hands failing him—Herr Hoffer lighting it for him. Herr Streicher standing with his head hung down, his white hair everywhere, not saying a word. Rather like God, Herr Hoffer thought, after Adam and Eve had let him down. But God might not be the God one imagined. He might be content, right now. He might be deeming them fools for even considering Schmidt-Rottluff, for instance, as a great artist, compared to the masters.

That yellow dribble.

Ziegler had shouted, on taking the Schmidt-Rottluff down, "Back to the kindergarten with you, my lad!" And everyone else had laughed.

One never knew about God. One did not even know about one-self.

"At least," he said at last, "they have not taken the jewel."

"The jewel?"

"The van Gogh, Herr Streicher."

"Ah, yes."

"Or the Cézanne," Herr Hoffer had added.

"The—the Poussin sketch?"

"Of course not. In fact, they took nothing from the other galleries."

"They have taken my soul," Herr Streicher murmured, blowing his nose.

"They cannot touch your soul," Herr Hoffer replied, with an awful lack of conviction.

"Yes, they can. I am a shell. I am a sucked egg."

Herr Hoffer's own soul had collapsed and recovered, but not Herr Streicher's. It had stayed collapsed. He suffered his first nervous attack a week or two later and was confined to his large house nearby, on Fritz Todt Strasse, for months of bed rest, with only his pretty young maid for company.

But it was not the thought of rhubarb everywhere or even Ziegler and Willrich's taunts that would keep Herr Hoffer awake at night during this period; it was the danger to the jewel. There were SS Sturmführer Bendel's visits and Herr Minister Goebbels's interest in the artist, as well as that dreadful directors' conference a year or two after the purge, in 1938, when Herr Hansen had officially declared Vincent van Gogh to be a mental degenerate.

He was living on his nerves.

When the Gestapo came in 1941, they sniffed about the canvases in the Luftschutzbunker without a murmur. They were looking for Jews and Communists. They examined the attics. The vaults were deep and secure and the way down to them secreted in a cupboard full of brooms. But Herr Hoffer was still alarmed, especially by the size of their dogs.

"*Straight along the corridor, last door on the left. Then through the cupboard and down the stairs.*"

"*Through a cupboard? Herr Hoffer, you are leading me to the Minotaur.*"

"*Nothing so exciting, dear fellow. . . .*"

Where to hide, when the hounds of history are baying?

He had entirely forgotten the oubliette!

As soon as Bendel was posted elsewhere, in '42, Herr Hoffer transferred the van Gogh and some fifty other paintings from the Luftschutzbunker to the vaults, making the total concealed just over a hundred. Werner helped him. It took them several evenings of hard anxious work—up and down, up and down, up and down. His shoulders ached, afterwards, and he had pains in his knees.

He told no one, not even Werner, about his plans for the van Gogh.

The staff regularly checked the paintings in the vaults. So how to transfer the jewel to the oubliette? That was the toughest knot.

One September day in 1943, while sketching (with a bamboo point and *encre de Chine*), Erika and Elisabeth asleep in their beds, the knot was cut.

He had turned to a new page in the sketchbook. Erika stirred and rubbed her face sleepily. How lovely she was! And Elisabeth, too, lying there in her innocent dreamland. . . . Lucky twice over! The blank page dared him to disturb its perfection, holding as it did the inward spirit of hills, mountains, trees, and his children's loveliness. Simply a matter of coaxing it out, in the ancient Chinese way.

"Papa, why are you drawing me? Let me see."

"Elisabeth, my suckling, I am drawing you because you make me so very happy. Don't move."

Though he was not much good, of course.

"I wish our Führer could come and kiss me good night."

"I don't think that would be a very good idea, my little poppet."

"Why not, Papa?"

"Because his mustache would make you sneeze."

"I wouldn't mind."

"*He* would mind, though. Because you sneezing would make him sneeze. And his sneeze is so big it would make our whole building fall down."

"I didn't know that."

"We're the only ones who know it. And you mustn't tell anyone else. Not even Erika or Mama. Are you good at keeping secrets?"

"Very."

"Then promise not to tell a soul about the Führer's sneeze. We don't know anything about it, do we?"

"I promise. Papa, let me see it."

"There."

"You haven't drawn anything."

"No. You kept moving."

"We can call it *Elisabeth Kept Moving*. Sign it, Papa!"

"We'll put it in a frame, my thumbkin. It'll be my best drawing ever."

"It'll make the Führer laugh, when he visits us. Papa?"

"Goodness me, I've had a very good idea."

"What idea?"

"Oh, just to do with work."

"Papa, will the Führer's laugh make the house fall down too?"

She was bouncing on the bed. Erika woke up. Sabine came in and was annoyed. But what did it matter? He had cut the knot.

A few days later, then, Frau Schenkel and Werner Oberst found themselves assisting the Acting Acting Director in the vaults by wrapping twenty of the paintings in brown paper and string, numbering the parcels on the front, and placing them back in their positions on the trestles. This, said Herr Hoffer, was for extra protection. Herr Hoffer had even got Frau Schenkel to bring some brown paper from the factory where her husband worked and had asked to borrow some string from Werner's library drawer. They had chosen the most precious works for this favor, with Frau Schenkel adding Paul Burck's birch forest and Werner choosing the lackluster Vollerdt copy because it reminded him of childhood holidays in Berchtesgaden. Herr Hoffer personally wrapped the van Gogh, and Werner numbered it: *19.*

"*This cupboard is a dead end, Herr Hoffer.*"

"*Move the brooms to one side. The handle's embedded in the wall, behind a flap.*"

"*How very cunning of you, Herr Hoffer.*"

"*Got it? Feel for the flap. Here, let me. Not far now, dear fellow. . . .*"

That night, alone in the vaults, Herr Hoffer carefully removed *The Artist near Auvers-sur-Oise* from its brown paper wrapping and swapped it for a blank framed canvas of the same dimensions. He had sawed the wood for the stretcher himself, nailed it softly together down in the vaults, and then sized the canvas with three coats, white upon white—as if it really was to be painted upon. He tapped it and it had resonance, like a drum. It had endless possibility—it wasn't extinction, after all! He had briefly considered whether he might copy the van Gogh, but not even Frau Schenkel would be fooled by a talentless daub. At any rate, there was no time. Now, wrapping the blank canvas in the brown paper marked *19,* he felt no nervousness at all. In fact, he felt exhilarated, as if the whole noble history of human culture was on his side—no, beneath him, like warm air, lifting him higher and higher on outspread pinions.

He took the van Gogh, protected by sackcloth, over to the oubliette and laid it in carefully, as one would lay a dead infant in the grave. As he dragged the slab into place, he was gliding in the empyrean without a single flap of his vast wings.

The jewel was hidden. Ah, the deep, comforting darkness!

The blank canvas was put back on the trestle, in the same place as the van Gogh, wrapped in the same brown paper marked *19.* Herr Hoffer alighted on earth with a sigh.

It had all gone so well that he gave a little skip of joy back in the office, placed "Auf Flügeln des Gesanges" on the gramophone, and drank a toast to himself as Heine's divine words and Mendelssohn's divine melody brought tears to his eyes in the darkness of the great building. He had served the gods, who were sipping cognac on their couches and nodding at him in approval.

At that moment a shadow had appeared in the door's frosted glass. It was Gustav, carrying half a loaf of gray bread and a book. He would let himself in by an obscure back door, to which he had the key. Herr Hoffer gave poor Gustav a shot of the brandy and vowed to change the lock. The fellow took out his teeth and showed Herr Hoffer his scarred tongue. The book, to Herr Hoffer's great surprise, turned out to be a banned volume—poems by Rilke. Rilke was a Jew. But poor Gustav got very agitated when Herr Hoffer tried to take it from him, and hid the book in his coat.

Herr Hoffer changed the lock the next day. He had had no idea that Gustav would break in at night, but the fellow was harmless. He looked even odder, these days, because he had gone bald.

Once a month Herr Hoffer would check the oubliette, heaving the slab back and parting the sackcloth and gazing upon its contents glistening in the candlelight: the signed *Vincent* daring the world, the tormented, inspired brushstrokes defying death itself (which, for the artist, was in fact only a few weeks away). Of course that rake was an easel, of course that little fellow was the artist himself! Caught up in the great wild flow of nature's bounty!

A triumph, this ruse. Yes, Herr Streicher, van Gogh and I are indeed close friends, in the empyrean.

"Straight down, Herr Sturmführer."

"After you, Herr Hoffer. I'm not that stupid."

"Thank you, dear fellow."

So far, in the two years since, no one had asked to see what was inside the brown-paper wrapping marked *19*: the "Chinese picture" had remained inviolate. Until now. Now it was going to be very awkward, he thought, the little metal prosthesis prodding his back as they began to descend the steps to the vaults, his feet feeling the cold stone like a man condemned.

48

There were others in there, beyond the sluice of bricks; Parry had clambered in with the woman behind and saw them now in the gray smoky beams made by his flashlight. They stood about like ghouls. The ceiling looked none too healthy above their heads, water was trickling down from a burst pipe, and there was a damp, sour smell generally. Maybe gas. He could taste it more than he could smell it. No one should be in this building, he thought. He wondered how many floors above him were not yet settled, just hanging on for a small vibration to shift them so they'd come down thoughtfully in a great white cloud of dust and kill them all.

What do you *think?* he said to himself, in his own head.

He whistled like a plumber you've called out for a small job who sees something he doesn't like, because he's a plumber who hears water slapping at the sides of every goddamn thing.

Even a whistle might cause vibrations.

It was smoky and sour and dark, but there was a glow from down below that settled on the faces turned towards him, and the looks of those faces were as if they hadn't been in the sun for twelve years. He made his way through those faces, sensing his power as a martial conqueror, as if he knew what the hell he was doing here.

In fact, the glow of light came from the bottom of a flight of stone stairs, cleared of its rubble down the middle. Apart from the bricks there were broken banisters, bits of cornice, metal springs, a suitcase, a pair of callipers, and some books with puppy dogs and kittens on the covers. It was all pushed aside like snow was cleared back home so that a narrow trail went down the stairs through to the three people working hard at the bottom. They were attempting to open a door covered in metal plate, bolted all over like the side of a tank. All they had to see by was an old kerosene lamp, the kind he'd seen everywhere in Germany.

The real problem was that the door was holding up the ceiling.

He could see that right away; the door must have budged outwards a few inches with the blast and was now holding up the ceiling.

The strange thing was, it was preventing the ceiling from falling farther with only a few inches of contact. That's what it looked like, anyway.

Parry was running his flashlight over the situation. The beam flickered over the situation as his mind was flickering over it.

The three people—two elderly men and a woman—were talking to someone on the other side of the door. Frau Hoffnung or whatever was just behind him, her hands up to her mouth, the fingers clawing at the lower lip so that it was curled down and gleaming. He was in a basement corridor. The ceiling was run with pipes and wires, and it had lowered itself at this end as if by magic and was touching the top edge of the steel door. He could hear crying. There were a lot of people behind the door. The whole building was sitting on top of them, and maybe moving the door would bring it down and bury them and also himself.

He was scared, but in a different way from when he was in combat. This was to do with forces that were not human. Even a shell was fired by a human being. But this was merely a matter of weights and balances, of pressure and force and gravity. It was mathematics or maybe physics. There was no mind involved. The only mind involved was their interference, and that interference might provide just the right element to bring down the whole structure, the entire world falling on their heads.

He looked up, his face bathed in sweat (it was hot down here, maybe from the fires), and saw how the plaster was coming down from cracks in puffs and sudden spurts, as if the building were considering its options. It seemed a very bad idea, what the three civilians were doing. They'd had no training; they were ordinary people, they were ignorant. He stepped between them and they looked at him and suddenly he was in charge. The American was in charge.

He said to them, holding his hands up, "Let's bust them out of there, but let's do it with intelligence."

They understood, though they were foreigners.

He shone the light into the crack in the door. In the slit between the black shadows there was a glistening eyeball. There was whimpering. Beyond the whimpering there was moaning. There were more than a few people in there. This must be playing out all over town, this kind of situation. It wasn't the first time over the last months he'd seen people caught in shelters under rubble. No, he'd not yet actually seen it, but he'd heard about it from first-aid guys white with dust. Most of the people he'd seen being pulled out of the rubble made by their shelling were in the dark for good; they were dead, or as good as dead, because of heat or gas or something. This was different. This begged for a professional hand.

He ran everything through his mind as the eyeball glistened.

He ought to go and get someone. But who? Some guy pulled from his drink, his nice warm fire, his girl? The clean blue waters were flooding in so quick that no one had time to sort out complex situations like this one—at least, it was not the armored divisions' job to mop up the mess, to save souls. That was left to the divisions behind, the ordinary goddamn infantry.

And he considered how he had failed Morrison, how he had never quite matched any situation with his full being.

Even fighting all the way from the coast, even slogging thigh-deep in snow and harrying pillboxes and not knowing whether this or that wall or tree or hedge was about to spit your darkness at you, he'd never felt he was matching the situation with his full being.

He carried out his orders and hoped he would live. His galled ass and the general discomfort from wetness and cold and the tinned prunes and the dehydrated bean soup got worse, that was all. You got dirt in your ears and there was no real choice. Here there was choice.

He felt responsibility welling up in him like something golden and good. He would save these people behind the door, he would take out from there Frau Hoffmann's kids, he would prove to them what courage and goodness were and he would not die because he knew he wasn't going to die; he was instinctively certain of it. The whole goddamn thing was on his side.

"I'm thinking," he said. Because the people there were staring at him, saying stuff in Heinie lingo he didn't understand. So he raised his hand and said, "Hey, I'm thinking."

And they went quiet, because they knew what he meant. And he made a deal with the higher powers or maybe just his own higher nature, there and then: If I rescue these people, I will merit the snowy mountains and the golden valley. Stored instead of liquor in my map pack. The nice item of salvage.

Because Parry was before anything a deeply moral man, reared by devout Baptists, and did not want to be troubled for the rest of his life by an unearned gain.

49

They stood halfway down the stone stairs leading to the vaults. Herr Hoffer felt he was about to dive into a pool of infinite depth.

"Well?"

"The vaults are there, through that metal door."

"Go on, then."

"My dear man, I can't allow myself to break my professional code—"

"Oh, shut up."

Bendel actually poked Herr Hoffer's back with the gun, so the tip of the barrel seemed to roll one of his vertebrae like a miniature billiard ball caught by a cue. It was very painful and somehow ugly. Herr Hoffer realized that Bendel had turned brutish. He had been so very elegant, almost debonair, as a young SS officer shoving papers about on a desk. Now he had turned into a thug.

This whole business is happening to someone else, thought Herr Hoffer. Even my stinging vertebra belongs to someone else's spine.

He wished Herr Wolmer's vengeful ghost would come back to life and finish the man with a single potshot, but that sort of thing only happened in films and books. The stairs were cold and damp through his socks, like the way to a castle dungeon. Those were certainly his socks down there on his feet. To his embarrassment, their gray toes were darned with black thread. Maybe the vaults had indeed been dungeons, where men were hung in chains or rotted on straw for decades, turning lunatic. He had never considered that to be likely, until now.

They reached the bottom. He rapped on the metal door. The door was opened.

"We have a visitor, Werner. SS Sturmführer Bendel. Remember?"

Werner nodded. Then they were inside and the door was closed behind them.

Herr Hoffer's eyes adjusted slowly to the candlelight. Werner had retreated into shadow, dry and suspicious, next to Hilde Winkel. That's my place, thought Herr Hoffer. Hilde, and Frau Schenkel opposite her, were frowning—Frau Schenkel with a cigarette hanging from her thin lips. It made her look common; she might have been a factory worker. The smoke was thick, in fact: Its floating layers in the dim yellow light swirled and twitched at their sudden arrival.

"Good morning," said Bendel, letting the gun point upwards. "So there are the paintings."

No one replied. Bendel stayed by the door, almost shyly. He hadn't expected people.

Herr Hoffer said, "I think you know SS Sturmführer Bendel, everybody. Fräulein Winkel, I'm sorry; you don't of course know SS Sturmführer Bendel. One of our most loyal customers. My joke, the term *customers*. He wants to look at the paintings. A private view!"

He was sounding silly, rubbing his hands.

"The tower was hit," he went on, folding his arms and looking directorial, "while I was inspecting the attics."

"Oh, dear," Frau Schenkel groaned.

"We thought we heard something," said Hilde Winkel, her upper lip discreetly hidden by her hand.

"The damage is not serious. Just the roof knocked about a bit. I was hit on the head."

"So it looks like," said Frau Schenkel, as if in reproval.

"The attics, Heinrich?"

"Yes. I am perfectly all right, Werner, thank you."

Werner actually stood up again. "Did you . . . ?"

"Yes, I did lose consciousness, but—"

"Did you—there wasn't anyone else up there, then?"

"I went up on my own. Herr Wolmer stayed on duty below. Funnily enough," he added, "I had a notion that poor Gustav might be skulking about. He's certainly been up there recently."

He produced the red notebook. He remembered with a shock that Herr Wolmer was dead.

"Is that poor old Gustav's?"

"I believe so, Frau Schenkel."

"Poor boy."

Werner leaned forward from his hips, like a mechanical toy.

"That's my department's property," he said—and grabbed the notebook from Herr Hoffer's hand.

Werner didn't look at it; he just slipped it under his coat.

"Rude to snatch, dear fellow." Herr Hoffer smiled, wagging a finger. The man was so odd. Still, after the end of all this everyone would be starting again from scratch, and no one would be odd anymore.

Oh, it smelled really unpleasant down here. Someone had let off, very badly. Probably Frau Schenkel.

"To what do we owe the pleasure of your visit, Herr Sturmführer?" Werner asked, in a slightly quavering voice. He had sat down again, and his question came out of the shadow made by Hilde's raised knees.

"Herr Hoffer will explain. I'm too knackered."

"Are you here to protect us?" asked Frau Schenkel.

"No," said Bendel, leaning back against the wall.

"I see," said Frau Schenkel, taking a deep pull on her cigarette.

"He would like to view a certain painting," said Herr Hoffer.

"Which one?" asked Werner, with a scowl.

"The van Gogh."

"The Vincent?"

"Yes, Werner."

"You mean," said Werner, "you want to put it in your pocket."

"A bit big for that." Frau Schenkel smiled. "It might fit in your haversack, though."

"I just want to look at it," said Bendel.

"That's what they all say," growled Werner.

He seemed upset by something.

"It's number nineteen, dear," said Frau Schenkel, waving her cig-arette towards the trestles. "One of the ones wrapped up in brown paper."

No it isn't, thought Herr Hoffer.

"I thought you told me it was hidden, Herr Hoffer," said Bendel.

Dear God, why can't the Americans just come right now?

He shrugged.

"We did hide it," said Frau Schenkel. "We hid it from the authori-ties, like all this lot. I do believe in coming straight out with it," she added, turning to the others.

"Quite right, Frau Schenkel," said Herr Hoffer.

"I mean, you're hardly going to do anything about it now, are you, Herr Sturmführer? You shouldn't even be down here, dear. You should be off up there defending the Fatherland."

"I've run out of cigarettes" was all Bendel said.

Frau Schenkel gave him one, but it was Hilde Winkel who lit it for him, still hiding her mouth.

"What's wrong with your mouth, sweetheart?"

"It got cut. It's not very pretty," she said.

"But the rest of you makes up for it," said Bendel, still stooping to her.

Hilde Winkel gave him a shy little smile, her eyes glittering. Of course, Bendel's a good-looker in the flattering candlelight, Herr Hoffer thought: clean-jawed, soiled by battle. The kind of thing that would excite Fräulein Winkel, drooling as she did over all that dread-ful marble kitsch for her thesis instead of bandaging real limbs.

Was that how the fellow had lured Sabine? He was on his way to a thump on the nose.

Herr Hoffer felt dizzy and sat down with a bump next to Frau Schenkel. The noise of the near miss continued to ring in his ears. Not so much the noise, more the thought of what a close shave it had been. Life was really very strange, yet one got used to anything so quickly. Even now he felt that he had, in one sense, been in this situation for his entire existence.

Bendel was looking down at them and smoking, as if he had all the time in the world. Because he had a gun and was in uniform, he was very much more powerful than anyone else present. If only war would keep to dewy fields with young men in uniform running around on them and cutting each other with swords, Herr Hoffer reflected. Instead, it was all about dropping bombs into private living rooms. There ought to be proper rules against it, as there were against the use of gas and chemicals.

No one spoke. Herr Hoffer very much hoped that Werner had not brought his pistol along; he was bound to fluff it. The bombardment grumbled and coughed. Maybe, in his battle exhaustion, Bendel had forgotten why he was here.

Then, as if reading Herr Hoffer's mind, the man looked over at the stacked paintings. They retreated into the gloom: at least a hundred of them. Bendel stepped past the various feet and stood between the paintings on their trestles. He smoked greedily, nervously, like a callow boy, as he ran his eyes over the paintings.

Herr Hoffer's heart sank; he had no plan, other than waiting for the next moment, which was no plan at all. Agility, Heinrich! It was much too embarrassing to admit that he had swapped the canvas for a blank. That he had cheated the others. Even with the best and most honest of intentions. No one had any honest intentions left, these days. After the end, honest intentions could flourish again.

What he most feared was that, on discovering he'd been cheated, Bendel would have a fit and shoot everybody, as he'd most probably shot Herr Wolmer. Right now the gun was dangling from his neck in front of his chest. It was a most horrible object to Herr Hoffer; he had never really noticed before just how ugly the standard-issue submachine gun was. Its grip was that of a pistol, but then the pistol had grown a monstrous tumor of metal. What one always forgot was the weight and sharpness of a single bullet. Which traveled so fast you heard the gun go off only after you were hit. No, you didn't hear anything whatsoever and ever again, amen, in all likelihood. Thus death came to you out of a silence. It was the bullet that finished you, not the gun. To be precise, like Werner would be. Pernickety.

Or it didn't quite finish you; that was the worst. To be hit in the stomach, for instance, and not die.

It was so quiet he could hear somebody's watch ticking. It was the quiet of all underground places, the muffled soundlessness of a cavern. It had been the same in the salt mine at Grimmenburg, when the SS man had stopped talking about knights and castles and switched off the light before moving out of the vast chiseled-out room of Shaft IV. It was a lightless silence, Herr Hoffer remembered: the dry nothingness of death. The blackness had seemed to press against his eyeballs. And his eardrums.

"Are these in any order, Herr Hoffer?"

"No. We stacked them in a hurry," he lied.

"Like for like," said Bendel.

He immediately began to hunt through the paintings, the cigarette smoking away between his lips. For a time there was no sound but the bump of frames, Caspar Friedrich's purring, and the odd tiny snarl from the Acting Acting Director's stomach. It looked as if Bendel was leafing through a giant gilded card index. He wasn't being very careful.

"All these old mates," he said. "Ah, the Poussin."

"I wouldn't mind looking at poor Gustav's journal," said Frau Schenkel.

"No," said Werner. "It's private. How much damage was there, up in the attics, Heinrich?"

"I would say," said Herr Hoffer, "that part of the roof was a bit moth-eaten, if you know what I mean."

"Shut up," said Bendel, his cigarette bouncing in his lips.

They were shocked, but they shut up. The bumping of the frames as Bendel hunted through was somehow horrible. Bits of gilt molding fell like crumbs. Every time he came across a work wrapped in brown paper, whatever the dimensions, he lifted it up brusquely to examine the number.

I will pretend to be totally bewildered, thought Herr Hoffer, but no one will believe me. There was a faint smell of sewage, rather than farts.

"Here it is," said Bendel. "Nineteen. Or is that One-nineteen? Too big, anyway."

"That's our Paul Burck. *The Rustling of the Woods.* Though personally I can't hear any—"

Bendel advanced towards the candle and started to tear the parcel open.

"You can't take that," said Frau Schenkel. "I wrapped it myself."

"He's not taking anything," Herr Hoffer reassured her. "He's only having a look. I can understand that—"

"Shut up," said Bendel.

He pulled the Paul Burck from its wrappings.

"Crap," he said, and thrust it into Herr Hoffer's arms.

"No, it's not," said Frau Schenkel.

She started to cry softly. Bendel ignored her. Herr Hoffer held the painting like a wall, behind which he could crouch.

"It's very nice seeing all these old friends," said Bendel, continuing to hunt through the paintings on the trestles. "A pity I can't linger over each one, as I used to."

He came across more brown paper and ripped it open, though it was much too small for the van Gogh.

"Look, the exquisite Corot, his lovely blue-gray alders. Or are they poplars? Reminds me of your excellent lecture on Corot and water and the dreams of Gérard de Nerval, Herr Hoffer. I hope the painting is here and you're not lying. I can't afford to waste time, you know. If I wasn't serious about this I'd walk out with the Corot and a few others and have done. But I'm not a thief. Never have been. So I'm putting it back."

"You did say you were only going to take a look," said Herr Hoffer plaintively.

He peered over the Paul Burck. His toes were curling in his socks. The black darn looked ridiculous.

"I said I'm serious. I'm not a thief, Ingrid."

"Ingrid?" exclaimed Frau Schenkel. Then she and Hilde and even Werner started to snort, as if they found it funny.

"How did you know that?" Frau Schenkel shouted.

It was awful. She was really shouting with hilarity and delight.

"You told me, once," said Bendel.

"I can't have."

"You did. You were annoyed with him, as usual. You told me. Years ago."

"Told him what?" asked Herr Hoffer, out of a sea of flames.

"This isn't fair," said Hilde.

"Your nickname, Heinrich" came from Werner in the shadows. "For as long as I can remember."

Herr Hoffer felt that this was the worst moment of his life, oddly enough. It was worse than Dresden. It was worse than the Degenerate purge. Ingrid. Yes, although he had no real idea *how* he was Ingrid, it seemed to fit him like a glove. That was the paradox. He didn't know how, yet he knew why.

And in that moment he knew as well, in his gut if not in his brain, that Sabine had slept with Bendel.

50

They were going to throw the biggest party in the history of the world. And the houses of the town would be set upright and everyone would say to everyone else, "You're looking good, boy," and that's how it would be. And they would pass out on beer, and Hershey's Tropical Chocolate would rain from the skies, incidentally. He had fished out his War Department Technical Manual TM30-606 because it was good for all the ills of the world, being a German phrase book, and without that and having to handle this whole thing by himself he would not be good for another day, let alone this one.

The words for *beam* and *saw* did not feature. *Are you hungry?* did, but *I have never heard that word before in my whole fucking life* did not, though it should have. *This shelter is authorized to receive only* (———) *people*. Now that was as much use as a bug in a hammock. You looked up the number. What goddamn use was that? Nobody was bombing their own side unless they were the truly lazy cocksuckers who had bombed them outside Saint-Quentin.

He tried something in Heinie but he had to show it to them on the page. He mimed beams with his hands. The book was no use and he jammed it back in his pocket and realized he still had the red notebook in there, taken from that dead with the ripped face in the museum vaults. Hell, he had so many goddamn pockets he didn't know what lay inside them unless they were going to save his life like a cigarette case might do one day or maybe even a field dressing or a clip of ammunition. What wasn't important was the question. Every goddamn thing was important, brother.

He used the red notebook and its pencil to show them what was needed. What they needed was beams. They couldn't open the door, or the ceiling and maybe the whole building might come down, so they had to replace the door with something else. They had to find something else to keep the ceiling up, like miners did. They had to construct a kind of miner's shaft or tunnel, a network of pit props. He was talking quietly and sketching, which was an international language. He was in charge now. There was a lot of writing in this notebook. The guy must have kept a journal and maybe there were intrigues in there and his courting days in peacetime. Or maybe it was all a soldier's philosophy, though he'd not been in uniform. A lot of the pages were stained purple-brown, one after the other the same, and then diminishing.

Yup, it was easy being in charge of people when they had nothing, when they were dazed and defeated and generally cut off from any sense of confidence in anything. It was not an achievement.

He had studied the ceiling a little and reckoned from the bulge in the plaster and the bent pipes that a main beam had in fact broken and slid down and been caught by the metal door; the door was the beam's only support on one end. Buildings touched by bombs could be like houses of cards: A shout or a jab of the thumb could bring them down. It did not take a genius.

Moving the door could be the jab of the thumb.

What he in fact communicated was something much simpler: *Do not touch door; door dangerous; need beams and saws.* Women in the streets, along with the elderly air-raid guys who'd stayed, were already clearing the rubble, they had saws and stuff and plenty of beams. The widow he'd had sex with, she kept squeezing her hands and calling out her kids' names by the shelter door. "Erika, Elisabeth!"

She was told to go up to the street; she was hysterical and in the way.

She went up, pretty well herded there, wailing like a demon. Parry wasn't sure whether Erika and the other one—Elisabeth—had responded. If they hadn't, it looked bad. He could hear groaning and moaning in there, like a whole lot of people making love or a first-aid station. Behind the scared voices at the crack in the door there was a lot of that groaning. So there was life, but maybe not one-hundred-percent life.

"Right away," he kept saying, when someone asked him something. It was never important, what they asked him in German, which was so far from English it was incredible. That they lived on the same planet was incredible. You could kiss and you could hug in all the languages of the planet.

Within fifteen minutes the beams and saws were coming down the stairs. Parry had sketched the plan properly in the red notebook because his service writing tablet had got wet a few days back and he'd used it for goddamn hygienic purposes and now they needed a clear drawing and so he had been right to take the red notebook. They were impressed by his drawing. He put some cartoon figures in and held the drawing up so that the trapped Heinies could see it through the crack in the door. The glistening single eyes were saying a whole lot of stuff that sounded panicked and bad. There was no light for these people, it must be very close and uncomfortable, they were like trapped miners. The crack was too slight even to pass a flashlight through, and no one had found any candles. He didn't even have a Hershey bar, but then that might provoke them into tearing each other apart.

Anyway, lighting a candle was a bad idea; he thought he could smell gas from all the broken gas pipes; it amazed him that these places still had gas and electricity right up to when they were blasted. Now they would not have anything like that for months. He could certainly smell the calls of nature because every goddamn intact building anywhere was a spaghetti of sewage pipes; it's just that you didn't think about it until they got broken. Every bombed and shelled town smelled like sewage. It was disagreeable and moistened your brain disagreeably, until you forgot about it under the bitterness and everything else.

Then, as they were measuring the beams, a guy came up who spoke English. He looked terrible, like he'd been fighting or hiding out for years. They all looked terrible, except the fat guys, the real big Nazis who had voices like bassoons and a goat's kind of cunning and would ship themselves off to Clarksburg, no doubt, and run the churches and the pawnshops very soon and then the whole goddamn country. If goats were cunning. This guy smelled of pigs.

"Hello."

"Yup."

"They are trapped?"

"Looks like it. You speak English?"

"Yes, I do. And French. I was studying the poems of Baudelaire and Verlaine before the war. My name is Anton Zucker."

He was youngish, maybe in his late twenties, early thirties. He looked smart through his dirt and exhaustion. Parry had been told to suspect guys like that, to ask them for their papers, but now wasn't the time.

"There are many trapped people here," said the young man.

"No, sir. It just looks that way."

"I am helping you?"

"Good of you to show up. Hold this, Anton."

"I must be helping. I hated the Nazis. They were shit."

"You'd better have hated them. But I guess you're all saying that. Pity you didn't hate them earlier."

"I was in a hiding hole for three years under a pigsty. I am a Communist with sensible information about the Nazis."

"I'm glad it's sensible, because nothing else is. Jesus. A pigsty. Now we're all done for. The world Red revolution had better not start here. Hold that beam and quit talking, Anton. Tell me what *Waldesraus* means, before you quit talking."

"You mean *Waldesrauschen?*"

"Could be, yup. Here."

He produced the wooden picture label from his breast pocket. Anton studied it.

"A whispering or a—a rustle of the woods," he said.

"Really? That's nice. I like that. A rustling of the woods."

They were calling out from behind the door: *"Amerikaner, Amerikaner!"*

"The Americans are here," he called back to them, "and, hey, there's a nice breeze through the trees."

51

He would not allow his gut knowledge to interfere and put them all in danger. A public cuckold is worse than a private cuckold.

"What about all those châteaux in France?"

"Sorry, Herr Hoffer?"

"You said you're not a thief, but what about all those French châteaux, all those palaces in Poland?"

"Irrelevant. Higher orders. Like the Americans and the British roasting Germans for breakfast with their bombs. Ah, the Cleopatra with the tits like apples. What a joke."

"It started with us bombing London," Werner pointed out.

"That was by mistake. They didn't know it was London. Anyway, no one cares who started it," said Bendel. "You might as well blame Cain."

"That's true enough," said Frau Schenkel, wiping her eyes.

Herr Hoffer wanted to find his self-esteem again, but the name *Ingrid* nailed him to his shame, and his socks were ridiculous. Bendel was an absolute bastard, he thought. He was exactly like a boy at school, all those years ago but very recent in the mind, Ludwig Rothenberger. Funnily enough, he was a Jew. Very short but very strong. He made little Heinrich's life a misery. He called little Heinrich "Beatrice," for some unknown reason. Almost as bad as Ingrid. He'd thought all that nasty stuff long past.

Bendel pulled out another flat brown paper parcel; Herr Hoffer knew immediately it was the right one. His stomach caved in. He might even have to be sick. He gripped the frame of the Paul Burck like a plank in a rough sea.

"That's it," he said weakly.

He needn't have said anything. He ought to have just clammed up. He hated the lot of them. He could so easily hate them anyway, if he were to put his mind to it.

Bendel was holding up the parcel so that the candlelight fell across it.

"Nineteen," he announced, like a teller in a draw.

He hesitated for a moment and then started to claw at the brown paper, not even bothering with the string.

52

Parry and the others worked as if they didn't want to hurt anyone ever again. Because if they made a bad move then everybody would get hurt, including the whole world outside. The great world Red revolution would not happen, however, because this guy Anton somebody was in fact the guy who was going to lead the Bolshevists after Stalin was shot and make one big Red Flag of the planet. That was one lonely advantage to this thing going wrong. Otherwise it was awful.

The clearing of the rubble upstairs had stopped. People were being kept away from the building. The kerosene lamp and Morrison's flashlight provided all the illumination there was. Outside it was night, it was cold and damp, and it was hungry and thirsty.

"Gentle up," Parry kept saying.

He was happy because he was totally responsible, he was fulfilled, he had a very clear objective. Fear was something he knew so well by now he could keep it in the corner, tamed like a girl with a cup of coffee. He never let go of his map pack, because the snowy mountains and the golden valley were in there. He would've liked to have had a look, he would've liked to have pressed on the buttons and released the flap to check on that picture, just to see the rolled-up thing that might have been one big puttee like the Brits had, only rougher, but it was not; it was goddamn ancient poetry in varnished oils. Mr. Vollerdt. Nice item of salvage. Also, he liked pressing on the metal buttons of his uniform, he liked the way the two hairsprings in the hole let go of the button when you pressed it out. It was well made and it was made with care. Those buttons had gotten so familiar to him he even loved them; they were on his ammo belt and his map pack and his breast pocket and just about everywhere else on his body. It was one of those feelings that if he died no one would recall, because it was his own boat he was holding and no one else's. Although the whole of the U.S. Army was covered in these buttons. Walking or hunched or asleep, it was covered. The war was won on account of the fact that nothing dropped out of your pockets unless you were the victim of something very bad or at the least serious, which gave you the willies thinking of, so you felt your buttons like you once felt the nose of your teddy bear long ago for comfort in the pitch-darkness, and you eased them in and out of their holes when you were waiting.

He shifted the map pack onto his back, though it impeded him when he bent down to help with the sawing. He was doing this for the snowy mountains and the golden valley; that was the heavenly deal.

"*Amerikaner! Amerikaner!*"

"Right away, folks."

But you made goddamn sure they were all clipped tight before moving on.

53

Of course, Bendel was angry and disappointed when he saw the canvas, as blank as fresh snow. His anger was the quiet and icy kind, however: like a surgeon's point of metal hovering over a vital part.

"Herr Hoffer, what are you playing at?"

"Ah, my Chinese picture."

"Heinrich," cried Werner. "What have you done?"

Herr Hoffer pulled a face. He really didn't care. Ingrid! All he wanted was to live on a remote island with his books and his paints, like Gauguin. Humanity was awful. He held the Paul Burck painting against his chest and peered over it, like a boy at the window of a train.

"He's done a swap," said Frau Schenkel.

They were all looking at him. They were people at a station. He felt as if he were gliding into a station where they had all been expecting him for days.

"The Chinese made blank spaces speak," he murmured. "In that is the mystery."

Werner was now on his knees, examining the torn sheets of brown paper.

"Impossible," said Werner Oberst. "That's definitely a nineteen. We wrapped it ourselves. Heinrich? What have you been up to?"

Bendel was holding out the blank canvas like a domestic with a tray. He looked more alarmed than angry.

Herr Hoffer, with the eerie calm of despair, pulled out the pinkish octavo paper.

"Let me check," he said.

For once, he had caught everyone on the wrong foot.

"I can't understand this," he said. "It *is* number nineteen, isn't it?"

He held the sheet of paper up, so they could all see. Against the number 19, the characters sitting rather unevenly on account of the age of Frau Schenkel's Remington, was typed *Van Gogh, Vincent; Der Maler in der Nähe von Auvers-sur-Oise (1890), 28 x 21*. It looked extremely convincing. Had he really set all this up himself? It was quite an achievement. They would frame this humble pinkish page, after the end.

The kneeling Werner whipped the paper from Herr Hoffer's hand and screwed it into a ball. When it's smoothed out and framed, thought Herr Hoffer, it will look even more authentic with the creases.

"You really are a curious fellow, Heinrich," said Werner Oberst, between set teeth. He had stood up now. He towered, only because Herr Hoffer was still sitting.

"I don't think Herr Hoffer would have swapped it," said Hilde.

"Thank you, Fräulein Winkel."

Bendel really had no idea what was going on. His hollow eyes glanced from one to the other. His mouth was open. The blank canvas stayed in his hands like an ivory tray waiting for a tea set.

The ball of pinkish paper, which was the inventory, bounced off Herr Hoffer's socks.

"No great loss," said Frau Schenkel, with a sniff. "I don't mind saying it now. He's messy, and I don't think he does people very well. But that's just my opinion, take it or leave it. He's a Dutchman, isn't he? Surprising. Very neat, usually, the Dutch."

"He was a mental defective, Frau Schenkel," said Hilde, as if it were embarrassing. "That's why he was messy. It was a certain view of art that we now see as being—as having much to do with the age of emperors."

Someone was crying. It was Bendel. The fine porcelain tea set had slipped off the tray and smashed.

"I just wanted to look at it," he whined, tears rolling down through the dirt on his cheeks and leaving white stripes. "Then I don't care."

The man was disintegrating. How could he ever have been feared?

"Have you taken it for yourself, Heinrich?"

"No, Werner. I object to that. I may be laughable, but I am not a thief. I may be a laughable fool, but I am not a vulgar thief like the Führer and his demimonde of crooked cronies."

Hilde Winkel and Frau Schenkel gasped. Hilde's fat lip started to bleed again, the drops squeezing out from under the loose lint and plopping onto her lap.

"You'll be dragged off to the camps for saying that, Herr Hoffer," she whispered.

"Or shot in his bathroom," Werner said, folding his arms and gazing down like a withered god.

"They only shoot you in the bathroom, the Gestapo boys, if you're of a certain rank and importance, Herr Oberst. That's what my husband would say."

"True, Frau Schenkel," said Werner Oberst, nodding so that his glasses flashed. "For Herr Hoffer, it would be the camps."

"Beg to correct you, Werner," said Herr Hoffer, raising a finger over the frame. "Herr Pischek's brother and sister-in-law were shot in their bathroom—actually in the bath—in Stuttgart."

"So?"

"I don't regard a grammar-school teacher of mathematics as of a higher rank or importance than a director of a city museum and picture gallery."

"Were they in the bath together?" asked Hilde, wide-eyed.

"I'm sorry, but I still think it would be the camps for you, Heinrich," said Werner, tugging at the knees of his trousers as he sat down with a little grunt and became mortal again. "It's a matter of an indefinable certain something."

"Don't worry, Herr Hoffer," said Hilde Winkel, looking at him below the eyes, "I think you would definitely be shot in the bathroom. Our neighbor Dr. Echterling was, and he had not nearly so much of that indefinable something as you. I call it dignity."

"Fräulein Winkel, I thank you."

"What the hell are you all going on about?" cried Bendel.

Herr Hoffer now felt marvelous. Yes, dignity was the thing, and so underrated these days! All someone had to do now was grab Bendel's horrible gun without losing their dignity. Because in a moment he would point it at someone's head, Herr Hoffer was sure about that.

"I know what you mean now," said Bendel, pointing a finger at him instead of a gun.

"Do you?"

"You didn't mean that it was wrapped up in brown paper, when you said it was hidden. You meant that it was put away where no one could find it."

"Really?" said Werner. "How interesting."

The child's metal arm swung in front of Bendel's stomach as he spoke, the barrel resting against the scuffed leather of the map satchel. All someone had to do was grab the gun. But it was still slung around Bendel's neck. It might go off. He might keep hold of it and shoot them all as he had already shot poor old Herr Wolmer. Herr Hoffer couldn't bear not telling the others about Herr Wolmer. It seemed like a surreal detail. The yellow and cream and blue swirls of *The Artist near Auvers-sur-Oise* danced in his head. Vincent was painting just for him. Vincent was a saint. He died in poverty. The greatest wealth is that which you give to others, as Martial said in the toilets. The hard stone floor bit into his buttocks through the thin cushion.

"Well, Heinrich?"

"He's right. I swapped the canvas, Werner. I wanted to save it from Party thieves and plunderers."

The shelling had started again, unfortunately. The walls quivered very slightly. Mortar pattered on the stiff white canvas at Bendel's feet like fingers on a drum.

"I'm not a thief," said Bendel. "All I want to do is look at it. If you don't tell me, I'll have to do something you won't like."

He tapped the gun's stock. The barrel was pointing, perhaps by accident, at Hilde Winkel.

Herr Hoffer thought about Sabine and his two little girls. How fast they grew up! How fast everything changed! What was it about life that was so determined to move everything on, like a Party official at a mass rally?

"Herr Hoffer," said Bendel. "Don't be so bloody mean."

Now was the time, thought Herr Hoffer, not for silly tricks but for miracles. He was not brave enough. This place was a ward in a madhouse. He was an inmate, too mad to know it, and there was no war going on at all. The nurses would be rattling the bedpans soon, and he would prattle on to them about Vincent van Gogh and Hilde Winkel's lip and SS Sturmführer Bendel, and they would nod and smile and give him his sleeping pill. Was it Baudelaire who said that life was a hospital?

"For fuck's sake—"

"Let me think, dear fellow," said Herr Hoffer. "I'm thinking. Give me a minute or two to think."

He looked at his own watch, as if timing himself. Just after ten o'clock. Where had the last hour flown? Then he stared, for some reason, at Bendel's boots. The folds and tiny creases on the officer's leather boots were real; he could see how they were charged with dirt and dust, and how painful it was to see the leather scraped raw in places or cut as if with a knife. This is life. Life is only this: a soldier's tired boots. It wasn't all the rest, the mental and emotional complications.

"I said I'd protect you from the Americans, Fräulein Winkel," said Herr Hoffer, "but I didn't count on the Germans."

Werner snorted and shook his head.

"I'll give you one minute precisely," said Bendel, and sniffed. The snout of the gun was a few centimeters from Hilde's forehead. She frowned, as if she didn't quite understand.

"Well, I don't know," Frau Schenkel sighed.

Werner said, no longer shaking his head, "Heinrich, don't be an idiot."

Hilde's eyes stared out, as if unseeing. The cat slept on her lap, its ears flicking in dream. Were animals wise or just plain stupid?

Bendel's boots shifted slightly as he studied his watch. The candlelight gave a rather lovely luster to them, defying their battered nature. They were so real. But Herr Hoffer saw such things in dreams too, in loving detail, and believed those to be real. He did so want to live, to appreciate such things himself. Maybe even to paint them. A pair of Waffen-SS boots. Even they could be beautiful, once battered and soiled! He raised his eyes and gazed upon the girl with the swollen lip and its patch of bloodied lint. She was the loveliest creature in the world, granted such loveliness by the moment. She had passed beyond the real. She had become other, inexpressible. Herr Hoffer was amazed.

"And all I want to do," this inexpressible girl murmured, "is get back to Erfurt and bury my dog."

Bendel looked up from his watch. "Your dog?"

"Our little terrier, Foxtrott. He was killed when the bomb destroyed our house. We had left him there when we went out to my cousin's farm to get away from the bombing. Then we were told we couldn't go back, I don't know why. We never went back. He was nearly eight."

"That's quite old for a terrier, Hilde," Herr Hoffer pointed out.

"Doesn't make any difference."

He asked when it was.

"Three years ago," Hilde replied.

"Blame the Americans and the British," said Bendel.

"Foxtrott," muttered Frau Schenkel. "Takes all sorts, I suppose."

Hilde closed her eyes and rested her head against the wall, her fingers in Caspar Friedrich's fur. Bendel's finger was tightening against the trigger. He glanced at Herr Hoffer, like a boy seeking permission. The eyes were dull and red-veined, like an alcoholic's. He had probably killed quite a few people in his brief military career, thought Herr Hoffer. Civilians, even. It would have become natural to him. Herr Hoffer could almost feel the trigger spring condensing inside his head.

"Bendel," said Herr Hoffer, "at least count aloud. It helps me concentrate."

"All right. Thirty, twenty-nine, twenty-eight . . ."

Herr Hoffer was pleasantly surprised that the numbers were still so high. He had to concentrate. A submachine gun was pointing at Hilde Winkel's head, wielded by someone desperate, unstable, and in the Waffen-SS. Bendel was counting down to zero, presumably. Zero was the bottomless shaft in the deadly mine. Hilde had her hands over her ears, Frau Schenkel had hers over her eyes, while Werner's were clasped as if in prayer in front of his chin. The three wise monkeys, thought Herr Hoffer, clutching the Paul Burck as if he could wander off into the silver birch woods by sheer effort of will. *Waldesrauschen*. But it was a very still painting, very still. Not a breath of wind. He could write to Burck and ask him why he had given it that title, back in 1913. He decided he would tell Bendel where the van Gogh was to be found when the count got down to fifteen. He was quite certain that Bendel would steal it, and he didn't want him to steal it. Maybe something would happen before they got to fifteen. Hilde was staring at him. She was clasping her knees now and staring at him, not below the eyes but straight in them. The gun was at her head, almost touching her hair, like a finger pushing away a curl. Nobody was saying anything. He couldn't bear the thought of the Vincent disappearing forever over the horizon. So many treasures had floated away over the horizon and disappeared. He heard the number thirteen, which surprised him. Twelve. Eleven. It was a contest between the sharpness of a bullet and fear, that awful solid bluntness of fear. He felt as poor Gustav must feel, overcome by somnolence, tottering upright. Bendel got down to eight—he was counting very deliberately and slowly—before Herr Hoffer spoke up. He was trying to keep his head fixed, to give himself more authority, but he had uncontrollable little spasms in his neck muscles.

"Look, if I don't tell you, you'll shoot Fräulein Winkel and then what?"

"I'll shoot someone else. Not you. If I shoot you, I won't know where the painting has been hidden. And I think you might well want to die rather than tell me."

"Thank you for the compliment."

"Whatever," said Bendel, "no man could watch a lovely German girl being shot if there was a way to prevent it. Seven. Six. I'll also shoot up the paintings, just for you."

"No normal man could shoot a German girl in the first place," said Herr Hoffer, his heart leaping as if horrified by his tongue.

Bendel laughed. "My dear Herr Hoffer, as Spinoza once put it, *God acts merely according to his own laws and is compelled by no one.*"

"You are not God," said Herr Hoffer, without enough conviction.

"Fancy an SS Sturmführer quoting a Jew," murmured Werner.

Hilde was trembling and staring straight at Herr Hoffer; the lint had dropped off her lip. Its swelling made her look like a village simpleton.

"Read Descartes on deception," said Bendel playfully. His dirty-nailed finger was genuinely pressing the trigger. "Six. Five. Four—"

"All right, old fellow, I haven't time to read Descartes. It's actually not even in the building."

"Where is it, then? Three. Two—"

"Ask Herr Streicher," said Herr Hoffer, sweat beading on his nose. All he wanted was to see his darling little girls—

"Herr Streicher?"

"He dealt with it. He's still at home, I believe. Fritz Todt Strasse. He says that if the Americans destroy his museum, he will kill them with his bare hands."

"I thought he was ill," whispered Frau Schenkel unhelpfully.

"He is," said Herr Hoffer.

"I did see Herr Streicher," said Bendel, to everyone's surprise. "I went to his house first of all. I thought he might tell me, being ill. I lied to him. I said I was ordered to protect the painting by the Reichsführer-SS himself, as it was not in the salt-mine depot. He was very cool. He just puffed on his pipe and told me to see you, as the man officially in charge."

"That's Herr Streicher all over," murmured Herr Hoffer.

"He didn't look very ill, just tired. He was being tended by a very pretty maid called Gretchen. He had a bed set up in his sitting room, and he was lying there in his nightshirt with an MG-34 on a bipod between his legs. It frightened the life out of me when I was shown in. An MG-34 is a fuck sight better than bare hands. The maid called Gretchen watches the museum through powerful binoculars. For the sake of the Third Army, I hope it is not hit."

"It has been hit," said Herr Hoffer.

"Winged but not downed," said Bendel. "You're lying to me, Herr Hoffer."

THE RULES OF PERSPECTIVE ▪ 309

"Hilde Winkel is innocent," he declared. "You can't go killing an innocent."

Bendel laughed in that old high-pitched way of his.

"Deception, Herr Hoffer. Just because you're not pulling the trigger, you think you're not responsible. You are wholly responsible. You have the choice. Anyway, none of us is innocent. That's the biggest fucking deception of all."

"I appeal to your common humanity, dear fellow."

"Bad luck. I've been to Poland," said Bendel.

Nobody said anything.

"Yes, I was in Poland," he continued. "Upper Silesia, to be precise. You take the train out of Cracow, and in about forty minutes you're somewhere nobody ought to go *ever* in their whole fucking lives, even if they're specifically invited—"

Bendel seemed to be trembling. That was not good, given his finger was on the trigger.

"We are not in Poland," said Herr Hoffer.

"Everywhere's Poland."

"Look, dear fellow—"

There was a sudden brief burst of machine-gun fire. It was incredibly loud. Herr Hoffer had squeezed his eyes shut—no, the noise had squeezed them shut for him—and he opened them again in the ringing quiet. Bendel had swung his gun around and shot at the paintings on the trestles. He had given them a licking. But they could be mended. It wasn't Hilde. The holes and rips could be mended. Herr Hoffer didn't know how many bullets had been expended on them but they would only have made holes, small tears. Everything could be mended, restored, varnished, saved. He wanted to cry and bit his lip instead. Hilde was whimpering, but she was intact. Caspar Friedrich had vanished. Herr Hoffer's mouth was wide open. All he could see beyond the candle was a splintered frame. His ears felt like broken teeth.

"Fuck all that humanity shit!" Bendel shouted into the singing echo, sounding like a Bavarian worker, or even a Communist, except that he was almost crying. "It's a bourgeois fraud, Herr Hoffer, a pathetic little capitalist costume. A party frock. I was in Poland for three months. The former Polish territories. I didn't *say* anything, of course, but I felt physically ill every day, especially because I have a soft spot for toddlers. I love the way they toddle about; even in that place no one ought to go in their whole fucking lives that I can't fucking describe, they toddled about on their little legs. Then I had my revelation. All this, I thought, is the beginning of the—the nature cure, I called it. A cleaning out of the Augean stables. Bound to stink, at first. The mucking out. The nature cure. My model is the shark; that's my fucking model. I've read somewhere that the shark, in its present form, is an extremely ancient animal. Pity is always for the self, in the end. If only we realized that everything is ultimately for the self, we might begin to grow into something as clean and beautiful as the shark."

He was really close to breaking down; his voice was strident, pitched too high, and almost all on one note.

"What utter pig swill you SS shits talk," Werner growled.

Bendel stepped over to him and Werner raised his arms.

Herr Hoffer shut his eyes.

He opened them again. The barrel of the gun was raised, hovering above Werner's face. All metal. The cracking noise would be dreadful, like a dog settling into a bone. Herr Hoffer had heard it when poor Gustav was being beaten up and on several other occasions. He felt that his heart was about to explode, it was beating so fast and fiercely, and his buttocks were tingling as if electrical pads had been applied. He would very much like to avoid Werner's imminent fate. Then, incredibly, Bendel swiveled and was facing *him,* Herr Hoffer—the gun barrel raised ready to come down on his nose.

"You're really fucking annoying me, Herr Hoffer!" shouted Bendel. "You know that? You're really getting me upset. In no way have you understood my point of view. That's because most of the human race are petty-minded blind cretins, starting with you, you jumped-up little fucker."

Frau Schenkel gave a tiny scream.

"All right," Herr Hoffer said, his hands up in front of him, both trembling like an old man's with palsy. "I'll tell you."

"So you don't mind me being shot, but you do mind being beaten up?" said Hilde Winkel in a hoarse voice, wiping away tears.

"I want to avoid further pain," said Herr Hoffer.

The truth was, he had already wet his trousers. He'd let himself go, down under, and it had simply poured out, warmly. He had almost soiled his trousers, in fact. He wasn't quite sure which part of him was capable of speech, but it was a noble and lonely part. The rest of him was cowering in a corner, petrified with terror. The gun was lowered. He couldn't stand up, because his trousers were wet.

"It's hidden under a loose slab, around the corner."

"Get it," said Bendel.

"I'm sorry, Bendel, I can't. If I stand up," he lied, "I'll fall over and pass out."

"Crawl there, then," said Bendel, grabbing the Burck painting from him and giving him a shove on the hip with his foot, stepping on Frau Schenkel's leg in the process.

Herr Hoffer crawled. He crawled off on his hands and knees around the corner to the back of the vaults. The others followed, herded by Bendel, carrying a candle that threw dreadful shadows in front of Herr Hoffer, as if he were being pursued by a legion of the dead. His thighs were wet and uncomfortable and his arms trembled and his injured hand hurt, but he continued to crawl. He wondered if he smelled of piss, like a tramp—but then everyone smelled, these days.

He felt around for the loose slab and found it and then, with Werner's help, he lifted it. The ancient cedarwood Mary Magdalene watched them from the shadows, her lovely arms raised, in blessing or in horror. Bendel watched too, with the gun trained on Hilde. He had a broken match set between his teeth.

Everyone (even Herr Hoffer, in the circumstances) was astonished to see the sackcloth parcel lying like a shrouded infant inside the oubliette. He took it out reverently: surprising, the lightness of paintings. His hands were literally shaking as he handed it over to

Bendel. Van Gogh was a saint and this man was a devil. Both were mad.

"My God," said Werner Oberst, brushing his hands. "First David Teniers the Younger, now Vincent van Gogh. What price trust?"

"I didn't do it for myself, Werner!"

"Shut up," said Bendel.

He tugged hard at the sackcloth, unwinding it impatiently and tossing it onto the floor. Frau Schenkel held the candle up and Bendel looked at the painting, his face gleaming in the candlelight. His expression hardly changed, but a ripple of emotion seemed to pass over it, as it does over someone who finds a photograph of a lost loved one. Nobody jumped him. Herr Hoffer wanted to jump him but nothing happened when he ordered his body to leap.

The Artist near Auvers-sur-Oise.

Then Bendel wrapped the painting up again in the sackcloth and herded them back, Werner leading and Herr Hoffer forming the rear, still crawling. He kept expecting a metal-tipped boot in the behind, but nothing happened. He slipped into his old place next to Hilde and her lovely smell of sweat; Werner was too slow and had to make do once more with Frau Schenkel. Herr Hoffer's palms and knees were filthy, and the linen of his trousers stuck wetly to his thighs.

Bendel ordered them to sit with their hands behind their heads, like prisoners of war. All except Frau Schenkel, who had to wrap the painting further in the covers off the cushions. She had to rip the old cloth up with her teeth.

Then Bendel unbuttoned his bread haversack and took out a shirt and a pale blue cardigan and a pair of fieldworker's trousers, all rolled up like a tent. He removed his camouflage uniform and donned the baggy trousers and woolen shirt and cardigan, keeping a beady eye on the others in case anyone tried to make so much as a single false move. Herr Hoffer did his best to make sure that he looked as if he were harboring nothing but the most honest intentions.

Which he was, of course.

54

Within the hour they had set up the basic framework of the props. It was a kind of thick scaffolding, a tunnel of beam and crossbeam. It was amazing how well people could work together, how ingenious were the works of man. There'll be no more bombing, Parry thought. No more destruction. The guy who spoke English was good to have around, he was young and efficient, his name was Anton—maybe he really had hated the Nazis and somehow escaped the draft. Maybe he really was a Commie or a Yid.

He needed a slug of whiskey. Too bad he'd broken the cognac. He needed a cigar store and a bar and plenty of time. And on the stoop is sunlight and it is Maytime, not too hot, so the sunlight is just bold enough to warm you and over there are the meadows and the woods and the woods are rustling like skirts and the air is very fresh and there are no lies in anyone.

Very soon the framework was in place. There were no hammers and no nails so they had to go back to carpentry joints, crude tongue-and-groove, as in very old pioneer times, though even the pioneers probably had nails unless they had dropped them someplace, say in a bug-filled marsh.

This was like a marsh. They were paddling about in water, warm water was trickling onto them from the joins in the strained pipes just above them, a few inches from their heads.

They had to work so gently and carefully, placing the props within an inch of the ceiling.

The older men, maybe in their sixties, were wheezing a little. One of them was a carpenter with missing fingers on his big hands; he was very useful. These are the same people, thought Parry, that we were shelling and bombing just over twenty-four hours ago. These were mine enemy. Now we're working together gently and carefully to undo the destruction. This is how the world's going to go, from now on. We're all going to go gently and carefully, undoing the destruction. Delivering creation into the hands of the good and the wise, and so the lying will stop thereafter.

Though maybe you still won't know what's sprawled and waiting for you around the corner.

They had to hold their breath, almost, placing the beams and fitting them together around the door and then slowly, ever so slowly, raising the framework by shoehorning it up with wedges, tapping the wedges very softly until the crossbeams touched the bulge of the ceiling, loosening fragments of plaster, pressing against the hidden laths as gently as a peach against a wicker basket: Whereupon they stopped and breathed again, whispering to one another in German, in English—in all the tongues of the world, it might have been, gazing upon their great and simple work with pride.

"It is excellent," said the young man named Anton.

"It's goddamn biblical," murmured Parry. "That's the strange thing. Now comes the Flood, you guys."

55

When Bendel had dressed and was holding his gun again, he told them they could lower their hands.

"Thank you for small mercies," said Werner.

The Paul Burck painting was lying next to Herr Hoffer. He picked it up and rested it on his chest again, covering his shame below.

"So you just wanted to look at it, did you, Bendel?"

"Shut up," said Bendel. "I'm too worn out to argue."

Herr Hoffer thought of Bendel emptying the châteaux of France and the palaces of Poland, huge painted canvases emerging on pallets and disappearing into trucks like—what was it he had said?—like whole pieces of the landscape, like life itself, disappearing into a furniture van. That is what will happen to genius, thought Herr Hoffer; it will all disappear into a furniture van and be driven off by louts and crooks. The van Gogh had disappeared farther into the cloth off the cushions; Frau Schenkel had knotted the string and Bendel had knotted the thin rope that held up the peasant trousers, now his trousers, soon perhaps to be someone else's. The human genius was to have invented knots, knots were very ancient, they permitted all sorts of things. Herr Hoffer was reasonably sure that even the most intelligent of the apes in the jungles of Africa had not yet come round to using knots. Nor had he come round to using guns and bombs. Frau Schenkel had handed Bendel the painting, neatly wrapped in the patterned cloth. Everything Frau Schenkel did was neat. It was enviable. Herr Hoffer could not wrap without making a mess of it. It was always Sabine who did the girls' presents at Christmas or on birthdays, until the paper shortages. His lovely girls! An unceasing succession of noises, like vehicles backfiring, announced some sort of renewed assault. Bendel could, at any minute, decide to shoot them all. It was his, Herr Hoffer's, job to make sure he did not. It was all that was left of his dignity, this job. He wondered what Bendel had meant by somewhere near Cracow that no one should ever visit in their whole lives. A mass grave, probably. It was said that all the Polish officers had been shot. That was war, martial law, Clausewitz, the indispensable severities whose ruthless application is the only true humanity (the *Wandervogel* camp, the cooking fire, the readings from those dreadful professors, the awful bigger boys against whom he was helpless). He, Herr Hoffer, would visit this place.

Bendel was using the equipment straps from his uniform to hang the painting off his shoulder. A peasant with all his worldly goods.

"You have no idea," said Bendel, like someone at an award-giving ceremony, "how happy I am to be in possession again of at least one of my works. The only work, I might add, that shows me at my easel."

There was a puzzled little silence.

"What are you on about, dear?" said Frau Schenkel.

"As soon as it's a little quieter out there," Bendel went on, "I'll take my leave. I can't risk a shell dropping on me now, can I?"

"I believe he thinks he was van Gogh in a previous life," said Werner, with his head in his hands.

"So it's true," said Herr Hoffer, to prevent Bendel from getting annoyed with Werner.

"What is true?"

"The title of the painting. Poor Gustav Glatz came to no definite conclusion. He said it might be a peasant in the field, not the artist. Then he was beaten up by the SA and could never come to any definite conclusion about anything."

He grunted as if he had made a joke.

"Well, you can tell him from me that I painted myself, from a distance."

"As if you were two people. Like Schumann."

"In a total life span," said Bendel, "we're hundreds of thousands of people. Not just people, of course. Animals and birds. Worms."

"What a horrible thought," said Frau Schenkel. "One's quite enough."

There was another slightly embarrassed silence.

"Odd that one always seems to be someone famous in a past life," said Werner, after clearing his throat. "If one isn't against the idea from the start. King Heinrich the Fowler. Vincent van Gogh. Never some anonymous little clerk, let alone a worm, as you say."

"So?" said Bendel. "Why's that odd? Some people are too great to be contained in one life, Herr Oberst."

"You, for instance."

Bendel smiled ambiguously. He looked odd in civilian clothes, like an actor playing a peasant; the tatty blue cardigan was too small.

The man is a complete nutcase, thought Herr Hoffer. Perhaps he always was. He has to be treated like fine porcelain.

"Like a certain little trench corporal with the head of a deranged barber," Bendel added.

"Who?" asked Frau Schenkel.

There was a deathly silence. Herr Hoffer might have believed in a visitation, if he'd been slightly that way inclined, for the air seemed to cool and darken.

"He has been traveling for a very long time through very many dark lives," Bendel continued, "and is now virtually hollowed out, with a very thin cellular body, and has no need of that body to operate. He will be operating without a body, like a dark angel. I feel the feeble barber's body is dead—"

Hilde Winkel gave a little gasp.

"But even now," said Bendel, "as the Americans pour towards us, the dark angel is slipping into their blood."

A long silence followed in which there were not even any rumblings of shells. The candle flame quivered, flattened, and then burned thinner and taller. The walls shook without any discernible concussion to be heard, and powder descended in puffs. Hilde started coughing.

They all looked up, as if there was a clue there.

Werner stirred in the shadows.

"The Führer is cunning and lies even more than the others, that's all," he said. "Don't make him into Lucifer, for God's sake."

"He doesn't lie," retorted Frau Schenkel. "That's one thing he doesn't do."

Werner snorted.

"Anyway," said Frau Schenkel, "you'll be grateful to him when the Asiatic hordes arrive. Then our boys will hurl themselves back into the fight and save Europe with their last ounce of strength."

"Frau Schenkel," said Herr Hoffer, feeling hopeless, "you sound like the wireless."

"I know what I sound like and what I don't sound like," she snapped, turning towards him and glaring. "My dear husband would be alive today, driving his train, if they'd had the right socks! And my only son, too! My dearest Siggi!"

"What's that got to do with it?" Herr Hoffer sighed.

"The trouble is," said Bendel, "Jews' hair is too thin."

"I'm not talking about Jews, if you don't mind," said Frau Schenkel. She had got into one of her moods. It replaced grief.

"You're talking about socks."

"Yes, not Jews."

"They're the same thing," said Bendel. "Jews and socks."

"What on earth do you mean?"

He looked at them in turn, with an almost shy smile.

"Socks for certain personnel. Such as train drivers. Only."

"Only what?" snapped Frau Schenkel.

"Made from the hair of Jews."

"What rubbish. My dear husband wouldn't have been seen dead wearing that. It's disgusting. They'd be all greasy."

Bendel laughed. Herr Hoffer laughed too, though he didn't really appreciate this joke about the socks. It wasn't the right moment for silly jokes.

"No waste, you see," said Bendel. "The ashes come back to enrich the German fields, and the hair to keep our boys' toesies warm. Certain personnel only."

There was another silence. Herr Hoffer felt wrong-footed.

Werner said, in a deep trembling voice, "What have you seen, Herr Sturmführer Bendel?"

Nobody dared to say anything more, because Bendel's eyes were like windowpanes looking onto death.

"I'm not crazy," he murmured eventually. "That's the whole problem. If I were crazy, it would be easier."

He cocked an ear, like a dog.

"I think it's quiet out there," he said, gripping the wrapped-up painting. "I think I'll take my chance."

There was a sudden crash as of many pots and pans falling off a heavenly shelf. Powder puffed again from the ceiling.

"Perhaps not just yet," he said. "There'll be a lull soon. There always is."

There was an awkward moment, eased only by a continual stammer of machine guns that was different from the backfiring vehicles. Herr Hoffer felt terrible. It was a little like waiting for a bore to leave a party. Only this bore was more than a bore. He was taking the museum's jewel. He had been in Poland.

"You don't believe me, do you?" said Bendel.

"About what?"

"About me being Vincent."

"My dear fellow," murmured Herr Hoffer, "if you believe it, that's all that matters."

"Give me a pencil."

"I haven't got one."

"Then find one," said Bendel, suddenly agitated. "And some paper!"

"Werner?"

"What?"

"You've got a notebook and pencil in your jacket," said Herr Hoffer.

Werner stayed absolutely still, staring at Herr Hoffer with what looked like sheer hatred. Herr Hoffer couldn't understand it. Surely Werner appreciated the situation! The man was liable to shoot them all in a few seconds. He was deranged. Nothing was more important than staying alive.

"Give it to me, please," said Bendel.

"I would like it back, afterwards," said Werner. "It's my private journal."

Private journal? That was surely a lie, thought Herr Hoffer. He had found it in the attic.

"Of course," said Bendel.

Very slowly, Werner reached into his pocket and held up the red notebook. Bendel snatched it from him and took the pencil out of the binding's spirals.

"Look," he said.

He flicked through the scrawled-on pages until he found a blank page. He rested the notebook on the gun's stock and licked the end of the pencil.

"Olive trees," he said, staring straight out.

He breathed in slowly several times, like an Indian yogi. His eyes widened and seemed to be looking inwards. His hand with the pencil in it, resting on the page, twitched and started moving. He wasn't looking at what he was doing, but staring straight out in front of him. Herr Hoffer thought, through his fear, The man has a personality disorder and ought to be in an asylum, with plenty of air, light, and sun. The eyes were like a cocaine addict's, but Herr Hoffer didn't think there was much cocaine about, these days. There weren't many asylums, either, offering air, light, and sun. The pencil moved over the page as if fired by electrical pulses. Herr Hoffer considered jumping him. But the twitching, spasmodic hand held him in thrall. It was genuinely as if Bendel were two people, his right hand belonging to another.

Herr Hoffer glanced at Werner, who was also fixated. His hand was hidden in his jacket.

Bendel gave a sudden little shudder, which made Werner jump.

"There," said Bendel.

He showed them the page, smiling.

"Look," he said. "I always drew olive trees like that. They spiral. Olive trees do spiral. I mean, it's the way they grow. You just look at the branches. The wood's corkscrewed. Maybe it's the wind: the mistral. I loved the mistral. Sharp and cold and clean, straight off the Alps. I loved it, just as I loved the fierce midday sun. I had my straw hat, of course. Otherwise I'd have burnt to a crisp."

The drawing showed some trees on a hill. It might have been an indifferent amateur's drawing of a well-known beauty spot. The only impressive thing was that Bendel had drawn it without looking.

"I see," said Herr Hoffer. "That's remarkable."

"Thank you," said Bendel, as if he'd just performed a turn. His voice had sounded different, almost girlish, up in the nose. Now it was back to Bendel's.

He flicked back to the scrawled-on pages.

"So," he said. "These are the private thoughts of the Chief Librarian."

"Chief Archivist and Keeper of Books," corrected Werner. "Now give it back, please—"

"I never thought you had it in you, Herr Oberst. Very philosophical. *I am at the bottom of a deep lake, without a head. My headless body floats among weed, attached to the surface by a rope. One day someone will come and pull on the rope. There is always something to live for, if you choose to.* I say, I do agree with that—"

"Give it back," said Werner, holding out his hand.

"Hang on," said Bendel, turning the pages, "this is much too interesting. Listen to this, everybody. *I am not at all certain I am alive.*

What is being alive? Occasionally I see birds. Birds, eh? I definitely think you are alive, Herr Oberst. On good days."

He burst out laughing again. Herr Hoffer felt a bubble of mirth rising in him too. It really was extraordinary, the idea of Werner writing such stuff up in the attics.

"Harken to this, class. This is a peach. *One day I will be standing in a field of flowers and you will join me, running into my arms.* . . . *'Ah, for your moist wings, O West, how sorely do I envy you!' If only I knew the whole of Goethe!*"

"Give it to me, Bendel."

"The Chief Librarian in love? Well, I never! Did you know that, Herr Hoffer? That's quite a revelation, isn't it?"

Herr Hoffer nodded. He couldn't help smiling at the thought. Werner was looking very uncomfortable. Bendel turned a page, enjoying himself immensely. It did Herr Hoffer good, seeing Werner so uncomfortable. Ingrid! In the end, everyone could be laughable—even Werner Oberst.

"By the way." Bendel smiled. "I'm frankly surprised you *don't* know the whole of Goethe, Herr Oberst. Every good German—oh, listen to this. This is most romantic. *If only you would return,*" he read, in an actorish, mocking voice, his gun bouncing on his chest. *"I am waiting and waiting—"*

He looked suddenly surprised. He had spotted something extraordinary at the door and Herr Hoffer whipped his head round to look. There was a terrible noise that bounced off every wall.

For a moment nothing more happened. Herr Hoffer's ears rang over a pounding that turned out to be his heart. Bendel looked as if he were about to tell them something, his eyes moving about uncertainly, quizzically. They alighted on Herr Hoffer, who pulled a face as if to say, No idea, I'm afraid.

There were two dark spots on Bendel's cardigan, just below the neckline. The red notebook slid from his hands and fell on the floor and his hands clutched at the spots. He looked at them, bewildered.

Werner shot again as they all ducked, but he missed—Bendel was already going down onto his knees. Then he toppled over onto Hilde's legs.

"My God," said Werner, still clutching his pistol in both hands. "It worked."

Herr Hoffer was crouched behind Paul Burck's birch forest, trembling from head to foot. The spots were holes, he realized. Hilde had pushed Bendel off her, shuddering, and his head had rocked on his neck as if the neck were rubber. He looked very peaceful, if a little taken aback, his eyes open a fraction. He was clearly only dead for now, thought Herr Hoffer; he'll be alive again soon. He had collapsed, like the German Reich, but he would be on his feet again soon. Herr Hoffer kept hold of the Paul Burck like the wheel of a car. His mouth was full of acid and his throat burned and his trousers were still wet. He could not let go of the painting.

SS Sturmführer Bendel was permanently dead, in fact; he sported a red toothbrush mustache that was starting to unravel over his cheek. His mouth was open slightly, as if he was about to say *Ouch*. The blood ran over his cheekbone and ear and trickled onto the flowery cloth containing the collection's jewel, making a circle the size of a billiard ball.

Werner pocketed the red notebook and, with the help of Frau Schenkel, dragged the body off to the far end of the vaults, the steel boot plates bumping on the stones. Herr Hoffer watched as the body left a trail of blood on the stones. He could not move a muscle. Hilde Winkel continued to shudder with her face in her hands, making little whimpering noises.

There was a black bullet hole in the bloodstained cloth wrapped around *The Artist near Auvers-sur-Oise*. Herr Hoffer managed to lean forward from behind the birch forest and drag the parcel towards him. Frau Schenkel had done it up very tightly and neatly, and his fingers were numb. He couldn't let go of the birch forest with his other hand, for a reason he would not investigate now. It was up to Werner, on his return, to check for damage.

Werner did so, unwrapping the painting without a word. The

blood did not matter, though it had soaked through and turned the sky violet. But the other damage was unfortunate.

There would be no more arguments about the artist or the peasant, the peasant or the artist. The bullet had replaced that contentious little figure with a black hole.

"Vicarious substance" was all Werner said, with a grim smile.

It was as if he didn't care.

He wrapped the painting up in its original brown paper and Frau Schenkel placed her finger for the knot. Her nail was very sharp. They took the parcel back around the corner. Herr Hoffer could hear the grating sound of the slab: it made him think of Christ's tomb and his own death—the unbefitting place of darkness, the possible light of another realm. He felt that he was already mostly invisible, in fact, like a cartoon character rubbing itself out. He was not really frightened of death so much as what he hadn't yet tasted of the world. He had always wanted to go to Egypt, for instance. Maybe Bendel had always wanted to go somewhere too: Greenland, perhaps. The snowy mountains of Persia. Herr Hoffer felt pathetic, but he was frozen stiff and mostly invisible. He could not quite believe that Werner was such a good shot. But, of course, Werner was the Chief Archivist and Keeper of Books. He was a hero and a soldier, and he was passionately in love and wished he knew the whole of Goethe. Did anyone know the whole of Goethe? That was a lot to know. It was like a country, with obscure corners that were almost untrodden. After all this was over, they would call on the greatest Dutch experts to restore *The Artist near Auvers-sur-Oise.* The question being, would they stitch on a blank patch or attempt to resurrect the figure? He, for one, could remember the way the brushstrokes went, the colors. And then there were one or two photographs, if of poor quality. He was sure they could do it. It would all be under his personal direction. There would be explanatory articles in the journals, of course—even in the popular magazines, with step-by-step illustrations. Everything could be mended, in the end. Such was human ingenuity.

Werner and Frau Schenkel came back and took their places again.

Hilde blew her nose and hiccuped. Werner put his head in his hands, his fingers pressing his forehead.

"Well," said Frau Schenkel, "that was a fine to-do."

Herr Hoffer couldn't say a thing. He tried, but his throat gurgled. He had considered congratulating Werner, but he didn't really feel like congratulating him. He felt mean and small-minded and pathetic. His stiff white canvas, face up by Hilde's legs, was spotted with blood. Ah, he thought: a cherry branch in snow, my Chinese masterwork! He almost wanted to laugh. To laugh and laugh until his head dropped off!

Werner looked even paler than usual. "I've killed a man before," he added, as if someone had denied it. "In a British trench. I saw his eyes."

"Well, anyone can see you've had practice," said Frau Schenkel.

She lit a cigarette and offered some around. Herr Hoffer opened his mouth, and she put one in and lit it for him. The bombardment seemed to have stopped. Perhaps it was all over. Frau Schenkel's upper right cheek was quivering. Even in the poor light, it was visible.

"Well, I don't know," she said. "I hope I never see that again."

The hand holding her cigarette had to be held by the other hand to stop it shaking.

"Heinrich, are you *compos mentis*?"

He was in a mold, like one of those bodies in Pompeii.

"Yes, Werner."

"Sorry?"

"Yes, Werner."

"You don't look it."

"Sorry. Can't get up. Fall down."

"You're holding that painting all the time."

"Psychological."

"Listen, Heinrich. Are you sure you saw nobody up in the attics?"

Herr Hoffer nodded. He breathed in slowly, making a huge effort. The mold cracked, and he rose from the dead. "If Gustav—was—sure he's—unhurt. No cries."

"He might have been killed," said Frau Schenkel.

Herr Hoffer coughed on the sour cigarette that hung from his mouth.

"That was not my writing in the notebook," said Werner, into his hands.

"I didn't think it was," said Frau Schenkel.

"I don't know whose it is," Werner added, rather too quickly.

He said nothing more. He still had his head in his hands. It was quite a relief, knowing that Werner was only himself, after all.

"Gustav's, Herr Oberst? Perhaps the poor soul can write after all. Let me have a look."

Frau Schenkel stretched out a trembling hand.

Werner shook his head. "I don't have it on me," he murmured. "Not now. Maybe it's incriminating. Hm? I'll go and check up in the attics. Just as soon as my head stops spinning."

"Werner," said Herr Hoffer, his voice flooding back again, "I would not have left the scene if I thought anyone was hurt."

"No?"

"Of course not. Are you all right, Fräulein Winkel?" he asked, as if to prove his point.

She nodded, the blood on her swollen lip glinting, a stippled highlight. Herr Hoffer stared at her over the Burck's frame. He was coming into the station and she was waiting for him there, desperate, in need of comfort.

"Apologies to you, Heinrich."

"That's all right, Werner. I'm sure it can be restored. It's only a hole."

"I mean, for killing your friend."

"My friend? Bendel? He wasn't my friend!"

"Ah," said Werner, raising his finger, "I hear the cock crow thrice."

"I must object to that. He was never my friend. I humored him, that is all. Herr Streicher perceived him as a threat. Clearly, he was."

"And all this time," said Werner, "I thought he was your friend, Heinrich."

Herr Hoffer blinked at his colleague. He was staggered at the lengths to which Werner would go, just to torment him. Perhaps it was a sublimated sexual problem. There used to be sexology clinics for such problems. Air, light, and sun. And seawater, possibly. Ah, the sea. Helgoland. Werner had put the pistol back in his coat, at least. He seemed almost unperturbed at having done away with someone. Or perhaps he was still in shock. After the war, Werner Oberst would have to be forced into early retirement. It would be seen to. He, Herr Director Hoffer, would see to it. And he would take his daughters to Helgoland and build them the biggest sand castle they had ever seen, with a moat full of seawater.

"Funny—one minute alive, the next dead," Frau Schenkel remarked. "It's always like that. Here today, gone tomorrow."

At that moment Caspar Friedrich reappeared and mewed at the door. Werner let him out.

"Take care," he said. "Folk have abnormal cravings out there."

"At least he didn't relieve himself in here," said Frau Schenkel. "I couldn't have stood that smell."

A sudden loud bang made Frau Schenkel's cigarette fall from her lips. It was as if somebody had dropped a huge cupboard. A trickle of mortar dust started above them, forming a cone on the floor and clouding the air, prickling their eyes with lime.

The cone of mortar dust was growing, like the sand in an hourglass.

"I'm sorry to tell you that Herr Wolmer has almost certainly passed on," said Herr Hoffer. "Fallen in the line of duty. He got in the way of Bendel."

There was a general murmur of astonishment.

"Oh, dear," said Frau Schenkel. "Poor old Herr Wolmer. He did have his good points."

"I wish to apologize," Herr Hoffer stated, "for failing in *my* line of duty."

He was still holding the Paul Burck painting upright in front of him, resting the bottom edge on his knees, hiding his shame. He gazed into the painting's airless sylvan depths where the muddy track climbed and vanished. What a discovery that was, the rules of perspective! Or were they laws? No, Alberti took the laws and made rules out of them. The rule comes after the law. Three dimensions out of two dimensions, all because of rules that came out of laws that came out of where? The eye? Nature? God?

They were all looking at him.

"But at least," he went on, "we did not lose our one van Gogh, for which I must thank Herr Oberst. There's nothing that can't be mended. And we are all still alive. Except for poor Herr Wolmer."

"Do you have to hold that damn thing in front of you?"

"Yes, Werner."

The vaults shook again, slightly. Oddly, the mortar dust stopped falling. The silver birches were preferable to Werner's triumphant look. It was hard to believe that at one point Werner had been a new boy, wet behind the ears. One had to keep reminding oneself of this, but to no avail. Werner had been around since the Creation. Herr Hoffer was gazing upon the silver birches with their dabs of titanium white where the sun fell upon their trunks, but neither silver birches nor titanium white were uppermost in his mind. He was back in the entrance hall in 1934, at the welcoming party for the new librarian. There was a loud woman in a strange hat who believed that the salvation of the world would be in leaving infants with pots of finger-paints, to make handprints all over the walls and splash each other with color! Werner was nodding with that dry little smile on his face, then he had turned to Herr Hoffer and said, quietly, "I know all about you now, Herr Hoffer."

"Do you?"

"You told someone to go out and tear down a poster of our great Führer."

Herr Hoffer blushed, but the loud woman had wandered off.

"I did what?"

"Well done," Werner said quietly. "Between these four walls."

"Yes, I suggested it. Just before the election last year. I'm not ex-actly a Party man—"

"And he got beaten up for it."

"Who?"

"The one you told to go out and tear down the poster of our great Führer."

"I didn't tell him. I suggested it, almost as a joke. Hardly that. It was, in fact, a bit of a misunderstanding—"

"I see," Werner had said, looking at him strangely. "I see, now. The whole thing has been simply a bit of a misunderstanding. But of course."

Within the first few minutes of their acquaintance, the man was tormenting him! The forest path wound up through the silver birches, unattainable, into the gloom and the verdant darkness. That too was a torment.

Frau Schenkel turned to Werner. "What was all that rubbish he was speaking about Jews and hair and socks?"

Werner shrugged. "Why, Frau Schenkel, are you worried?"

"I am a bit," she said, eyes shining with tears. "I don't like to think of my poor Dieter and my dearest little Siggi with socks like that on their feet."

56

When they tried to open the goddamn door, it jammed on the ceiling.

So they'd have to chip away at that part of the ceiling and then raise the broken main beam before they could even open the door.

"Gentle up," Parry kept saying.

In fact, the beam turned out to be a steel joist. The block of flats was built fairly recently, and its inner structure was metal. The joist hadn't broken, it had been dislodged from its support on the shelter side. Great cracks in the walls showed how the whole building had jerked and resettled, the joist slipping from its position despite the cement packed around it and then getting arrested in its descent only by the door.

"You can't ever tell," said Parry.

And the guy Anton, who was shiny with sweat and very tired because he was out of shape, did not understand what that meant.

The door had moved too. No one had tried to open it. It had been forced a few inches out by the vacuum created by the blast; otherwise the joist would've fallen all the way and maybe five or six floors of the building would have plunged down with it. Who was to know?

"Will you take hold of that," said Parry, looking at it and shaking his head.

And Anton did not understand this either.

The joist was resting right on the edge of the door, a quarter of an inch from the edge, a quarter of an inch from falling. It was like a crazy circus act. Like a long full shelf held up only by a book you wanted to read.

All these theories of pressure and force were going around in Parry's head as he wondered at the size of the exposed steel joist. Then he realized that the door was making noises. It was groaning. Maybe it was straining at the hinges, ready to buckle and fall under the weight of the great joist and whatever tonnage was above it. The laths in the cracked concrete above the plaster were of metal, one of those metal grids that he'd seen back home on building sites, leaning against fences, and that now you saw everywhere poking out of the rubble or draped over walls like shredded rags or even cobwebs. He hadn't been an expert in demolition before the war. Now he was an expert.

For the rest of his life he'd be able to paint ruins, he thought, un-romantic ruins with garbage and metal and bricks and lumps of ma-sonry in just any old position and any old country: ruins of every nation. Import and export. Chaos.

Now he was fumbling with the chaos, right at the heart of it, try-ing to turn the dial ever so carefully towards order and salvation. And the goddamn door kept making these noises over the desperate sounds beyond it. This was the Flood trickling around their boots. This was the quarter inch between life and death, order and chaos, salvation and the end that is maybe despair. And he didn't know what to do. He didn't know what the fuck else to do, because whatever he did would be wrong.

"You bitch," he said, just as Frau Hoffmann or Hoffnung appeared with a toy rabbit, but he didn't mean her.

It was a very filthy toy rabbit, and it flopped in her hand like it had given up. The others were standing around the pit props looking lost, waiting for Parry to have a good idea, listening to the groaning that was both the metal of the door and the people beyond it. Even young Anton, who did seem to have a real smartness about him and would lead the world Red revolution, was just listening to the groaning.

Then she went up to the shelter door and no one stopped her. She held the toy rabbit in all its floppiness up to the crack and called for Erika. She was calling her and saying something, maybe that she had the kid's toy rabbit, Parry didn't know. The U.S. Army's German phrase book did not cover all eventualities.

But he reckoned that's what she was calling out. This certainly wasn't the Big Picture, he thought. What I need is a chance to look and think, and she is distracting me with this toy thing.

And then the door moved in a strange way.

It moved soundlessly at first, just leaning back a little, maybe a quarter of an inch. And then this shrieking sound that was metal on metal engulfed Parry as he was turning his body away and trying to hide his head.

57

Herr Hoffer held the Paul Burck against his chest and realized that he should never have left his wife and children that morning.

His first duty was to his loved ones. As it was, he had been of no use to anybody in the museum. Frau Schenkel had been right all along. He hadn't even been of much use to Hilde Winkel, who was still shivering. He wished he had the courage to put his arm around Fräulein Winkel and comfort her. It would comfort him too, to do this. He was sure she wouldn't mind his wet trousers. Who could mind such trivial failures now? One's first duty was to others.

He decided that, after the war—in other words, in the weeks to follow—he would take much better care of such things. Other people, starting with one's loved ones. He imagined life would be very hard, in the months and possibly years to follow. Forget Helgoland. One had to be realistic. There might not even be any white beer or lemons, only rhubarb. But he would take his daughters to the park. It was unlikely the park would have been destroyed, and new trees would be planted to replace those smashed in the last bombing raid. He took his daughters to the park most Sundays, and they would run about and play on the grass. Especially Erika, who never stopped running. (This, Sabine joked, was because they had gone to the Berlin Olympics in the same week as her conception.) He had taken them last Sunday, for instance. Oddly, they always followed the same route through the park, skirting the big ornamental pond with its sluggish goldfish and weaving between the large glossy bushes in the shrubbery, before stopping at the swings. He must take a new route from now on. He would even start at the other gate, so as not to fall back into the old rut. They could begin with the swings and end with the ornamental pond, sailing their little boats. He would make his two dear girls even finer boats, painted red and blue and yellow, with glossy black funnels. Sabine sometimes accompanied them to the park, but more often than not she used the time to sit by herself on their nice green sofa and read old magazines or darn socks while listening to the wireless. Sometimes she waxed and polished the furniture. Whenever a bombing raid made the pictures go crooked, she would always right them, giving them a wipe as she did so. That's what had got them through, he realized. When the dust fell like a mist, Sabine was always there to wipe it away.

He would forgive her, right off, even if she howled with grief for Bendel.

Most of his compatriots who were not so fortunate would no doubt be paddling about in damp cellars or under tarpaulins, haggling for food and such things as candles or kerosene or wood. The younger men would join forces with the Americans and the British and drive back the Bolshevik hordes. The bigger Nazis—not the famous ringleaders, who would be put on trial—would probably be flown out to America with their nefarious gains, their criminal fortunes, their priceless works of art, while the lesser Nazis would flourish at home with what they had thieved and put aside. It was always like that. It had been like that since time immemorial.

Money, Herr Hoffer had long realized, was the key to all doors— except, perhaps, happiness. Money would be the new God.

But he, Herr Hoffer, would not worship that new God. He would worship the small domestic gods and the stranger god of love. Yes, Captain Clark Gable, that is my ideal. Let us call it German. My old German ideal. He would try to be as selfless as he could, to be a decent father and husband, to shield his loved ones from the hardships to come, through sheer cheerfulness and inner warmth. He would read them poetry and play them Schumann. The thought of Lohenfelde Park slightly depressed him, he couldn't say why. He pictured himself walking with his lovely daughters in the proper countryside, through an unknown birch wood beside a meadow, in a summer breeze, hearing the rustling and sighing of the leaves. It did not matter if he had failed, or if he had been laughable in the eyes of others who had called him a stupid and puzzling name; the important thing was to pick oneself up again and carry on.

He glanced at his watch. It was very nearly eleven o'clock. Things were much quieter. Werner, Frau Schenkel, and Hilde Winkel all had their eyes closed. It was really very peaceful, after the storm.

Yes, he would definitely forgive Sabine for the business with Bendel. She would grieve for the fellow, of course, but he would soothe her with the sheer force of his Christian patience and his Christian love. He would no doubt be very busy with the recovery of the museum's collection from the salt mine, especially if he was appointed official Director, but somehow he would always put his loved ones first. He might even teach his little girls to like paintings, with enough patience and care. He would not tell jokes about Jews and socks, if only out of precaution. He would once again buy his tailor-made overcoats from old Mordecai Grassgrün, the minute the crafty devil returned from Poland, or perhaps Romania, and reopened his shop in Fritz Klingenberg Strasse (which would have to have been renamed, of course). That way he would avoid the Hebrews' ire.

He was most uncomfortable in his wet trousers, but he ignored it.

The main task in the immediate future was not to be shot by the Americans. They were trigger-happy. Sometimes, on clearing a town, they fired on anything that moved. He had heard this from the refugees. On the other hand, they were unlikely to shoot someone in socks who had wet himself. He had closed his eyes. He must have dropped off; on opening them again, he was surprised by the extraordinary smell of burnt things, bitter in his nose. There was a man in front of him, a soldier. A shadow in a helmet. A pale and wavering form that seemed to glow from within, pulsing with some unearthly force. The form was moving into the depths of the vaults, like a visitant angel. Sounds made their way to his ears as if traveling over a great distance, distorted and faint and strange. He was in pain, but the pain was not quite his own; it was emanating from his skin, but his skin had been sloughed off somehow. He would have cried out in terror, but all he could manage was a silent cry. The sighing of the wind through the leaves took every last syllable from him, growing into a great rustling and soughing in which the creak of branches sounded and the rush of clouds above the wood roared like blood as he was whisked up into them and dispersed among them like rain.

Copy after Johann Christian Vollerdt (1708–1769)
Landscape with Ruins c.1760
Oil on canvas, 24 x 32
Rosa Luxemburg Hall, Lohenfelde

This undistinguished painting is nevertheless the best-known work in our 1964 Peace exhibition, as its ripped and blistered state has long symbolized the horrors of the Fascist war to the thousands who come to our city in order to gaze upon the ravaged canvas, hung and dramatically spotlit in the huge vestibule of our new town hall.

Recovered from the rubble of an apartment building on former Hermann Göring Strasse (now Karl Marx Strasse) in 1945, this copy—probably by one of Vollerdt's pupils—is one of the few works from Lohenfelde's magnificent prewar collection, housed in the former Kaiser Wilhelm Museum, to have survived. (The accompanying monochrome photograph is the only record of the original painting, destroyed in the bombing of Magdeburg.)

An eyewitness of the time, 31-year-old teacher Elisabeth Hoffer, gives us this account: "Lohenfelde had fallen to the Americans after a severe bombardment. Our apartment block was badly damaged, and many of us were trapped in the cellar for nearly two days. Brave attempts were made to free us. The building finally collapsed and only about half of us (thirty-three in total) were pulled out alive. All those attempting to rescue us perished when the building came down. Among the victims were my sister and my mother. My father, Heinrich Hoffer, who was not present, went missing during the same bombardment. It is possible that, as Acting Director of the Kaiser Wilhelm Museum, he had brought certain of its works home to avoid their being appropriated by either the Fascists or the invading American forces, and the Vollerdt copy was among these."

Exhibited alongside the painting is a notebook retrieved from the same spot, containing the diary of an unknown Jewish girl in hiding. The badly scorched notebook is of the type used at the time by the library of the Kaiser Wilhelm Museum. It is not known whether she was concealed in the attics of the museum (on the site now occupied by the Werner Seelenbinder Hall) or in the apartment belonging to Director H. Hoffer. Nevertheless, this anonymous diary is a moving testament to courage in the face of the Fascist horror, just as the painting has become a celebrated witness, throughout the German Democratic Republic, to the tragedy of war.

ACKNOWLEDGMENTS

I am most grateful to Lieselotte Neu, my brother's mother-in-law, for her courage in sharing long-buried painful memories of the Allied arrival in her town in 1945, and to Jimmy and Lieselotte Thorpe for the simultaneous translation—as well as for being my guides in Germany over the years.

Willi Barth of the University of Mainz has shown exceptional generosity and care in checking over the manuscript and making numerous suggestions as well as answering my many queries; I am deeply in his debt. I thank Susan Bell for giving up her time to do likewise from an American perspective. Personal accounts by GI veterans on infantry division Web sites have provided invaluable information, while among the countless published sources I would like to single out: Heinz Höhne's *The Order of the Death's Head: The Story of Hitler's SS,* Jonathan Petropoulos's *The Faustian Bargain: The Art World in Nazi Germany,* Frederick Spotts's *Hitler and the Power of Aesthetics,* Michael Kater's *The Nazi Party: A Social Profile of Members and Leaders, 1919–1945,* and Robert S. Wistrich's *Hitler and the Holocaust.*

For digging up obscure books or pointing me in various right directions, I owe much to Charles Lock, Niek Miedema, Angus Wright, Virginia Pepper, Elizabeth Gadsby, Yves Ruault, Ray Ward, and Jan Salas. For precious advice concerning art and its practice, I thank my tutor, Véronique Fabre of the École des Beaux Arts in Nîmes. Thank you to the distinguished historian Philip Mansel for sharing, on several delightful occasions, a passionate interest in German history.

My late father-in-law George Wistreich's aperçus, memories, and unpublished memoirs of Polish Jewry have been everywhere absorbed by the book.

I am, as ever, grateful to my editor, Robin Robertson, for his pertinent and patient advice at the revision stage; to my agent, Bill Hamilton, for his enthusiasm and encouragement; and to my wife, Jo Wistreich, for her love and unwavering support.

Heartfelt thanks go also to my father, Barney Thorpe, for answering endless questions concerning the war from a serviceman's perspective; and to my late mother, Sheila Thorpe, for telling me what it was like to be bombed—and for everything else.

ABOUT THE AUTHOR

ADAM THORPE was born in Paris in 1956. His first novel, *Ulverton*, was published in 1992, and he has written four other novels—most recently *No Telling*—a collection of stories, and four books of poetry. He lives in France with his wife and three children.